Spring in the City

Spring in the City

EDITED BY

R.B. WOOD & ANNA KOON

RUADÁN
BOOKS

BOSTON, MA

Anthology edited by R.B. Wood & Anna Koon
Cover Art & Title Design by Kip Ayers
Interior Design / Formatting by Dullington Design Co.

First Edition

RUADÁN
BOOKS
www.ruadanbooks.com

For Jim

"With so many trees in the city, you could see the spring coming each day until a night of warm wind would bring it suddenly in one morning."

—Ernest Hemingway, *A Moveable Feast*

TABLE OF CONTENTS

THE BOOK OF DREAMS

Mercedes M. Yardley

Mmm, springtime! It is truly a time of flourishment and joy. We move out of the frosty, frigid snow and ice into a season of hope and renewal. We shake the bitter wind out of our hair, allow the marrow of our bones to thaw, and turn our faces toward the gentle sun.

Springtime reminds us of tulips and newborn lambs. It is childhood incarnate. Spring was when we gathered together with our friends to fly kites amid laughter. The season is made up of tall, swishing grasses, picnics under trees, and rooftop gardening. No matter how jaded you are, spring still comes with a feeling of hope. Are there new possibilities? Is there a new future? How can I make it thus? And yet, hope is never easy. Sometimes it comes with a price.

It is my pleasure to introduce you to *Spring in the City,* the new anthology of dark speculative fiction released by Ruadán Books. R.B. Wood and Anna Koon have done it again, putting together this worthy sophomore book in their series.

They made certain to choose stories that both excite and enchant. This beautiful tome contains sixteen unique stories, all taking place in different cities across the world during the lovely springtime.

Roam with turkeys across Brisbane. Flee for your life in Chicago. Explore the legend of Mr. Splitfoot in Detroit.

Oslo. Montreal. Chester. Each setting is perfectly captured and integral to the story. The authors describe their chosen place aptly, breathing life into their worlds. They are no longer words on a page, but a *feeling*. An experience. You'll be swept away to several destinations, each one fully formed and brimming with activity. Feel the heartbeat of the city and smell the blood on pavement. Their rich descriptions will make your breath catch while you immerse yourself in each and every tale. You'll find a varied tone in voice and subject matter, assuring there is something for everyone. It truly is a book of dreams.

You will discover practitioners in Manchester and stroll through purple flowers in New York. Prowl with Jack the Ripper in London Town and be haunted in Taipei. Meet the Witch in Los Angeles and turn away from the strangeness in Cape Town.

But oh, there really is so much strangeness everywhere, really. This book is rife with it. I hope it surprises and delights you.

This is an anthology full of goddess, drowned women, and so much glitter, dread, horror, and magic that your heart will nearly burst. Please settle yourself in, my darling, to enjoy some truly stunning paranormal stories that celebrate both the beauty and pain of life in the city.

Yours in bittersweet hope,
Mercedes M. Yardley
Las Vegas, June 2025

STOCKHOLM

Xan van Rooyen

Gói

Iðunn wakes to blood and fire. Veins split, feathers singed—offerings from the downtrodden and deceived.

Across the sacrificial stone, they write their stories. Careful fingers turn red, spill into sigil calligraphy. Runes beseeching, pleading—revenge a sweet rejuvenation.

Darkness thickens before the dawn as frost crackles a waning defiance, but—inexorably—the season shifts.

Iðunn lingers beneath the mantle of winter dreams, ensconced in the nightmare memories of her own mistreatment. She breathes in the ash and salt of sacrifice, rage roiling in her empty belly. How she hungers for the retribution she was denied.

Awake, Iðunn shakes out the humus-knotted tangles of her hair and rubs her wrists, then presses her fingers into the divots on her ribs, remembering…the trickster's treachery, the giant eagle who snatched her in his talons—gouging, marring, scarring. How she was taken and how no one came for her. No one even lamented *her disappearance until the gods began to wither in her absence. Then came the grudging, fear-fueled rescue, and how she resents it, that to be saved she was made small and insignificant, folded into an acorn, stolen once, twice, all for the benefit of others. No justice, no righteous vengeance, only a return to the husband who sighed in relief when his longevity was restored.*

The sky ruptures, light herniating through the cloud as Iðunn stretches, her delicate fingers curling into fists.

I'd hoped to abandon my inner demons, to shed them like old scabs, but my demons are needy co-dependents, snarled up in my double helix, an epigenetic stain.

Somewhere above the wadi-sculpted expanse of empty sand, I morph from emigrant to immigrant, trade autumn for spring, depression for hope, and still these varmints of the mind remain. I'd hoped they'd be shredded by the x-ray soaking at the airport, had hoped border control would revoke their visas, prayed Customs might recognize them as contraband, but the voices in my head remained as I passed from red to green.

Välkommen till Sverige, parasites and all.

Stockholm is a city divided, its parts sheared and scattered across an archipelago, its heart fractured, its runnels filled with the snow-rimed waters of the Baltic. I'd imagined picnics on emerging lawns dotted with precocious flowers. Instead, pavements are slushed with melt during too short days, turned slick and treacherous by freezing nights.

I slip and skid and fall, each tumble smearing bruises over scars like lumpy frosting on a lopsided cake, about to topple. *Coming here was a mistake,* my demons cackle a relentless tinnitus. *Did you think a change of address would undo the damage?*

My new home lies well north of the postcard—perfect center in a neighborhood hugging the edges of a preserve littered with history.

Kista—the name means box. Or coffin.

As I navigate the meandering roads too narrow for a firetruck, I inhale. Onions and garlic, tamarind and cumin, cinnamon and coriander. My neighbors are Jordanian and Iranian, Eritrean and Somali, Russian, Romanian, Japanese, Finnish—near or far from home, we are all outsiders here.

"Watch out for ghosts," my landlady tells me with a gap-toothed smile. "See that hill? It's a burial mound." She points into the forest hemming my winter-rotten garden.

Something twitches deep inside my alleles, a chemical jolt within my mitochondria. Perhaps my Viking ancestors are moldering in that dirt. I hope the ghosts here haunt me. Maybe then I'll feel like I belong.

"Tack," I say when my landlady leaves.

"Afwan," she responds. "It'll get easier." She squeezes my hand and my eyes burn when she lets go. The door closes, and I am alone with the voices in my head whispering admonishment.

My new home, a corpse cradle.

*I*ðunn hunts.

She sashays down narrow alleys, cobbled and quaint in Gamla Stan. She struts along broad avenues in Östermalm where trees stand sentinel in cultivated rows. In shadow form, she slips under cracked panes in crumbling apartments or through ornate keyholes on antique doors. Late at night on the tunnelbana platforms, she wafts past stumbling bodies sour with piss and cards her fingers through their hair, their souls, sampling their apathy or despair. In the morning, she stretches in the guise of timid sunbeams across brunch tables, lapping at the laughter spilling from the beautiful and bejewelled. Sometimes she dresses in breath and bone to mingle at a bar—smokey-eyed and demure—or flirt at the gym—perspiring but mindful—peering behind entitled smiles to see the darkness festering beneath the perfect veneers.

Quarry found, she stalks them home before pouncing with nails like scalpels to open their chests. Her prey, all so alike, thinking they can take without consideration for those they leave bereft, without consequence for their greed.

With deft fingers she excavates the cavity, chews on gristle, savors the gore, all the while imagining the trickster who betrayed her and the jötunn who confined her, used her, almost broke her.

The hearts, picked clean, she keeps. In their stead, she leaves cursed apples, golden flesh concealing a putrid core, before snapping ribs back in place with a gobbet of saliva to seal the wound.

Finally, she will have her vengeance.

The fruit will glow, gentle and repentant, before it withers. Her gift, not immortality, but a lifespan just long enough to make amends.

Einmánuður

With spike-studded boots, I brave the slick trails. Joggers, dog-walkers, and the elderly armed with ski poles all leave me penguin-hobbling in their wake. I smile even though the cold makes my teeth hurt. I manage a greeting but mangle syllables when I attempt small talk. The steely eyed locals regard me like the interloper I am.

"Learn our language," they rebuke.

I'm trying, but the words—although similar to my native tongue—clog in my throat and glom my teeth, as I butcher the ancient prosody. There is no invisible umbilical connecting me to this land of my forebears, and the homesickness inside me metastasizes with every botched pronunciation.

At least the sun teases with the promise of a thaw. If I close my eyes and lean closer to the light, I swear I feel a little warmth.

I will myself not to miss the sunshine of that other life, to remember all the reasons I left, to forget…but the voices in my head taunt me, leaving me as raw and tender as my carpet-burned knees, and my shame unfurls in a welwitschia spread.

The rotary thrum of a chopper slices through the cacophony in my head as it whizzes across the brown ribbon river separating the municipalities. Neighborhood to the east, ghetto to the west.

My colleagues warned me away from those areas. They see only the violence and protest, the resentment and fear, bemoaning radicalization while signing petitions to keep reception centers out of the *good* zip codes where they live. They spit out "refugee" as if the word might leave blisters on their tongue, like it might stick between their teeth and force them to taste the loss in it, the devastation, the fury, the hope.

Is there a form I can fill in to seek asylum from the voices in my head?

At night, I wander, ignoring warnings to avoid certain train stations after dark where gangs of surly teens flash knives at rival crews. I nod in solidarity as I pass the flotsam youths, our roots similarly twined and tethering us to the same "dark" continent. I don't join my colleagues for coffee at fika or shots after work. I don't trust their polite and perfect smiles that never touch ice blue eyes; I know I'll never belong in their cliques. Instead I drink alone, knocking back bränvinn and akvavit, muttering *skål* as I try to silence the demon-sung dirges inside my skull.

*I*ðunn *prowls the crowded and colorful old town, greeting the ghosts seeping from the history-soaked stones, eroded by transient tourist throngs.*

What has become an urban sprawl and motley collection of architecture was once a lonely logging settlement, a gateway between the Baltic sea and Mälaren lake. The city owes its origins to merchants, its foundations built on trade. In several hundred years, little has changed. Only now there is more falafel and kebab than meatballs and herring.

She inhales burnt sugar and fried meat, and the rich, buttery aroma of a hundred foreign stories. Fleetingly, her thoughts return to the skaldic husband she once had, who noticed her abduction only when Time laced grey through his hair and creased his pristine face. He loved poetry and music; he tolerated Iðunn only for her powers of rejuvenation.

With the bitterness tucked beneath her lip like a pouch of snus, she plucks at the mesh of threads, unpicking the tapestry of shame and anguish, elation and remorse, joy and corruption—so many tantalizing tales—but one unravels fresh and heady, a teasing suppuration.

As the sun battles against the ax-fall of night, Iðunn tracks the lure to a tea house tucked between buildings leaning conspiratorially close as if they might trade the secrets of their tenants in moldy speckles across grazing shingles.

With light and dark evenly matched now, Iðunn grows stronger, bolder, assuming human form as she steps into the steaming humidity of oolong and chai.

There, snug in a back corner, where the shadows congeal like fat left in a cooling pan, there is her quarry.

"Is this seat taken?" She stands limned in gold, her hair a wild halo, burnished and shimmering. I am dazzled, my heart slamming a fist against my ribs as I shake my head and sweep my feeble attempts at verb conjugation off the table. Class starts in thirty minutes, and the dread of my ineptitude knots across my shoulders. Assimilation—the word a sibilant hiss, the unspoken expectation.

I've been chatting with my neighbors, more confident among others in the acquisition phase. What I acquire is "dirty," my teacher says. My sentences peppered with immigrant slang. It is impure and brands me an interloper, a self-imposed othering for which I only have myself to blame.

But thoughts of integration incinerate in the incandescence of the woman still standing beside my table.

"What are you drinking?" she asks as she sits. She smells like apple blossoms and sunshine. I inhale and nearly gag at the rancid aftertaste catching in my throat. Coppery like old blood; like the scabs I used to pick from the lines carved into my arms and chew into dust, as if I could bite back at the pain gnawing on my insides, or silence the voices in my head.

You are not worthy, they growl.

"Rooibos," I say, despite the snarling insecurities, and she orders the same.

I don't know what to say, cannot fathom the protocol. I cradle my mug, leaning toward the heat radiating from her body. For the first time since I arrived, I feel truly warm again. Perhaps this place will one day feel like home. But the word is a blade, reminding me I'm unwanted everywhere. Although my pale skin provides comforting camouflage here, my heritage is still a mosaic of jagged pieces, never quite the right fit.

*I*ðunn *has never been in love. Her body has been given and stolen and bound, but never her heart. She'd thought it atrophied, yet*

it spasms now in revolt against desolation as she explores the city in the company of quarry-turned-companion, seeing the familiar through new eyes.

At first glance, Stockholm is beautiful. Candy-colored cladding and neat flowerbeds, sparkling waterways and buildings restored, even the utilitarian made decorative, but Iðunn sees the puckers in the paint, prods gently at the ripples marring the surface, and senses the simmering dis-ease twitching at her touch.

She glances at the human beside her, mortal eyes reflecting the sun setting over the Baltic in shades of violence and delight, and her heart convulses. She traces the spiral of the human's ear, the strong line of the jaw, the delicate hollow where the artery throbs, capillaries like poetry unspooling through flesh.

Together they watch the moon rise over Södermalm, the effulgence as bright as Iðunn's waxing joy as the fragile human quotes Södergran and Boye, analysing metaphor and analogy, words as mesmerising as the emergent stars.

Together they lie in brittle grass entranced by cavorting streamers of green, the norrsken *dancing across the night, and Iðunn's pulse frolics in response as the discussion turns to sources of light in life, in art, mimetic, a subsurface scattering setting them both aglow.*

Together, together, together they fend off the lingering touch of darkness and cold, believing the promise of brighter days.

Iðunn has never been in love, but she is falling…

*H*er collection is nearing completion, and she is almost ready. *Every year, Iðunn is welcomed to the gallery, a menacing*

square structure with a black façade perched precariously near the water. It smells of salt and decay, the foundations reverberating with every passing train.

The space within the juddering walls is hers to decorate or desecrate. Every spring, she regurgitates gristle and horror, staining canvases and floorboards with the stories of those who woke her, fashioning art from denigration and righteous fury in murals of peeled skin and fragmented bone. Her motif has always been birds. Some years she twists collected viscera into sculptures of the raptors she loathes, carrion scraps pinned in wing formation; eagles and falcons sketched in offal with cracked beaks and broken claws.

Sometimes she has given sway to sorrow and hatched painted eggs, feeding the chicks on the blood of tormentors before snapping fragile necks. Sometimes she is consumed by rage and sculpts with fire, remains turned to charcoal abstractions and plucked feathers arranged in burning bouquets; her own pain searing as she tries to forget the talons that tore her from her home, tries to forget the giant who caged her, who thought he could have her, claim her, break her. He is ash now, particle scatter long lost to wind and time.

This year, the goddess is in love and so she sets out the hearts, examining each in turn, pondering the transmogrification of trauma into beauty.

She shows me the city, and together we ride the snaking underground rails: a lattice of red, green, and blue traversing the city, each station a unique exhibit. We critique the art while we endure delays, as if the murals and installations might distract from the struggling infrastructure. It's impossible not to notice the stations that are neglected. The immigrant neighborhoods clearly don't deserve beauty. I ignore the beggars, immune to poverty after growing up in gated communities nestled next to squatter camps, but she smiles and hands them coins—no, tiny apples. I blink, and the gifts have already been secreted away.

At a rainbow bedecked cafe on Stortorget, she feeds me fresh semla. I savor the cardamom and almond, and the light in her eyes as she licks whipped cream from my lip. The Nobel Prize Museum looms across the square; its shadow stretching toward us, dousing the fire in her eyes.

In Kungsträdgården, we twirl beneath the cherry blossoms. The trees are foreigners, like me. If only it were that easy to dress in pretty raiments and be adored.

We pass children dressed as witches wielding willow fronds spangled with colorful feathers. She hands them apple candies in exchange for pretty Påskris branches. Her smile is razor sharp as she strips away the feathers. She tells me I can keep the blessings.

She takes me to Skogskyrkogården, where we meander among the pines, past the graves of poets and musicians, revolutionaries, and actors. No ancient ghosts here though, the bones beneath us too new. We picnic in sight of the crematorium, nestled among the trees, and she tells me a tale of eagles and acorns and burning wings.

On a cruise through the archipelago, the wind steals tears from my eyes as I study the blurred landscape of brown turning green. Sunlight throws glitter on the water, making me squint as her fingers lace through mine. I wait for the voices in my head to assault me but my demons are muted in her presence. I hear only the susurrus of the parting waves, the snap of gull wings on the breeze, the speeding patter of my heart as I lean into her heat.

Home, this is home, but this home feels like a pair of new shoes, rubbing blisters into my heel and pinching my toes. I miss the comfort of my old boots, torn and broken as they were. They knew the shape of me, hugged every corn and callus. Nostalgia rakes across my mind and old fears stir, the voices muttering familiar aspersions, berating me for never being enough. I can't shake the memories of the nights spent bent in submission, trying so desperately to be worthy of love.

She kisses my hair and I scrunch my toes, embrace the blisters, appreciate the pain.

Eventually, we tumble into bed and slowly unsheathe ourselves. With gentle fingers she pops open buttons, and I follow her lead until we're both bare, exposed, revealed.

She takes my hand, traces the ladder of cut stripes up my forearm. She kisses them, lips brushing the uneven edges of imperfect healing.

"Poetry," she says. "A saga etched in flesh."

"Yours too." I ghost a finger over the puncture wounds in her side. They're obscured by dark red ink and I follow the strange calligraphy, the jumble of symbols clotting between her breasts and trailing down her belly like wine spilling from a glass.

I want to ask her to decipher them for me, the tattoo illegible, but then perhaps she might ask the same of me. I want to tell her I've tried to bleed it all out, to excise the demons I couldn't exorcise—how every wound only seemed to cause the infestation to multiply, a compound interest I'll never be able to pay—how I'm too exhausted to keep fighting this emotional bankruptcy.

"I know," she says, as if she can hear my thoughts. She holds me, whispers into my hair, her breath rich with apples and blood. "I *know*," she says again, as if she can read the secrets written on my skin.

Tears escape my lashes when she kisses me again. She pulls me close, her body covering mine as I sink my fingers into her tender softness. Impossibly, the ink seems to move, to part at my touch, but she opens her mouth against mine and I close my eyes, wincing a little when she bites my lip.

I'm boiling inside, the memories thrashing as if caught in a riptide. She kisses me deeper and the memories are tugged away from the shore of me; claws scrabbling for purchase. The pull is too strong and they're wrenched away. Their fangs tear out chunks I don't think I'll miss: moments of violence, words sprayed like acid, corrosive and destructive, until all I was flaked to rust.

"I know," she says again. "It wasn't your fault."

Her tears salt my lips, or are they mine?

I lose myself in the pounding rhythm of our hearts, our bodies, then surrender to the primal undertow, no longer able to resist.

On Djurgården, the people have already gathered to set the night aflame. Valborg, they call it, an imported practice but one Iðunn has come to appreciate. Choirs sing, voices raised in celebration, songs of welcome to the season of sunshine and the death knell of winter.

In the center, the bonfire, and Iðunn approaches. She coughs up blood, every droplet a potent truth, a story distilled and flammable. She shakes the rubies over the kindling, letting each kernel spark in anger.

All across the city, fires burn, but she cares only for the bonfire before her. She exhales and tongues of orange reach higher, lambasting the air with scorching recriminations.

The day she was unmade, reduced to nothing but a seed, the promise of life and growth, carried in claws from one captor to another. The bonfire built on Asgard's battlements became a funeral pyre.

Iðunn gulps in a breath, her body tremorous as she relives the rush of flight, the certainty of demise, the perilous pursuit. How she was unceremoniously deposited once more at her ambivalent husband's side, forced to watch the eagle plummet into flames—her vengeance denied.

She still hears the roars of the dying giant and the laughter of the trickster god who thought it all a game, her life to be bartered and sold; she merely the fountain of eternity from which the gods could take their fill.

She screams, her voice the crackle snap of kindling.

Now smoke and ash joins with clouds of pollen, a turbulent mix blanketing the city, dispersed by the warm wind of *approaching summer. Iðunn feels her cousin's threat of humidity and thunderstorms, but tonight is still hers—her work incomplete.*

Iðunn's rage peters into resignation as ash and pollen fall on Stockholm. This, the detritus of spring scratches eyes, fuzzes lips, and penetrates skin to settle in hearts. Once cold and indifferent, they now bear the gritty fragments of others' tales, the seeds of compassion sown.

Soon Iðunn must return to slumber, but first there is one last heart in need of tending.

My demons are more subdued these days, the voices quiet mutters, so I can almost believe the words she whispered across my pillow before she left.

The gallery takes up all three floors of an old factory building repurposed through gentrification. Perhaps this is what I need in order to survive here, a complete renovation: gut the insides, scrub the outside. My bones the rebar, my flesh the cladding, my skin the façade to be repainted, hiding those blemishes of the past. Stripped, I can reinvent myself. Renewed, I can find fresh purpose.

Entrance is free but the exhibit, titled *Renascence,* isn't busy. I'm the only one here. The hallways are empty, lit only by the struggling dusk seeping through the windows. A dull thudding, like the beating of a heart, draws me forward.

The rhythmic thumping pulls me into a side room, past pale protrusions pleached together like ribs to a sternum. I step inside a chamber doused in burgundy light.

"You came," she says, resplendent in a dress sewn together

from flower petals and moss, her hair a wild tumble of leaves and feathers.

"What do you think?" She gestures to the artwork filling the cavernous space.

It's an orrery with a golden apple at its center in place of the sun. I step closer to study the objects in orbit in the crowded solar system. Some are black and wizened, some scabbed while others are spongy; some are marbled with fat, others are little more than dry husks, crumbling as they complete slow rotations on the skewers acting as axes.

Hearts. A few are still dripping, beading the concrete beneath them as the apparatus spins in time with the thudding pulse. There is one empty prong and I reach for it as it bobs past me. She catches my hand before I touch the thorn-sharp tip.

"It's yours," she says. "For the one who hurt you. He lies beyond my reach, but if I could, I would turn his heart to pulp." She raises her fist, her nails stained red.

"Why?" I choke out the word and she smiles, a solar flare engulfing me in a warmth conjuring one word, the one she left on my pillow, a single syllable, four letters, but it makes me tremble with terror. What will happen when she opens my chest and is disappointed by what she finds?

She looks me in the eye. "You are not alone," she says. "You never were." She touches the nearest heart as it swivels past us and I hear a voice, faint but clear.

Me too, it sighs. *Me too, me too, me too*—a dozen voices in a lilting melody, a sweet accompaniment to the retribution on display.

"May I have your heart?" she asks.

I nod and she kisses me.

Agony lances my ribs but this is a pain I choose, like the lines carved into my arms, a suffering I can control. I grit my teeth as she pares open my chest, pries apart my ribs, and removes my injured organ.

She cradles my heart in her hands, then, with elongated nails, she peels it like an apple and slices away the damage, licking away the purulence with a darting tongue. She impales the shriveling shard on the empty skewer before reaching toward the glowing apple. With bloody fingers she cleaves away a perfect slice, the flesh dripping liquid gold. She presses the wedge of fruit into the gaping hole—a perfect fit—before folding my heart back into my chest. She sutures my body with kisses as warmth permeates my core.

I have been refurbished.

"My love." She rests her hand, palm flat against my chest. "Always."

The orrery spins, and I watch the broken piece of me carried away, withering and crumbling into nothing. Something releases inside of me, talons unhooked from perches, and the final wisps of my inner demons flutter on shadow wings—barbed feathers cremated as she says again, *my love.*

I'm alone in the silence inside my skull, but whole.

Iðunn prepares for sleep, sated and eager to dream.

Next year there will be more hearts to harvest, more hurt to ease, more souls to mend.

Light chars and she flinches from the heat. The first thunder of the summer warns her not to overstay her welcome.

Iðunn melds once more with the towering oak beside the ancient burial mound in the neighborhood north of central Stockholm known as chest or box or coffin. She closes her eyes and smiles, remembering...

And there below the tree, sitting on the sacrificial stone, the human carrying the piece of the goddess's heart strokes the bark, whispering plans and promises for next spring.

The sky ruptures, lightning ripping through the clouds.

Iðunn yawns, stretches, and unclenches her fists.

END

—

Climber, tattoo collector, and peanut-butter connoisseur, **XAN VAN ROOYEN** is an autistic, non-binary storyteller from South Africa, currently living in Finland where the heavy metal is soothing and the cold, dark forests inspiring. Xan has a Master's degree in music, and—when not teaching—enjoys conjuring strange worlds and creating quirky characters. You can find Xan's stories in the likes of *Three-Lobed Burning Eye*, *Daily Science Fiction*, and *Galaxy's Edge* among others. They have also written several novels including adult aetherpunk novel *Silver Helix* (Android Press) and forthcoming YA Gothic cyberpunk novel *Second Soul* (Tiny Ghost Press). Xan is also part of the Sauútiverse, an African writer's collective, with stories in the multi award-nominated anthology *Mothersound* (Android Press) as well as the forthcoming *Sauúti Terrors* (Flame Tree Press). Xan has also had a number of non-fiction articles published which you can find in *Afro-Centered Futurisms in Our Speculative Fiction* (Bloomsbury, Australia) and *You're Not Alone in the Dark* (Cemetery Dance), among others. Feel free to say hi on socials @xan_writer.

MANCHESTER

Tim Lees

It's a different city these days. Catch it in the evening, with the sunset blazing on a brand-new skyscraper, and far below, a tiny, antique pub, sunk in the shadows, looking like a child's lost toy.

A different city, in a different world.

That's not how I remember it.

What I remember most, I think, is the darkness, and the cold—and the magic.

We gave it other names, of course. "Magic" sounded… silly. Childish, I suppose. But what else was it, after all? How else would you describe it?

"We're *practitioners*," said Gail, face hidden in a puff of cigarette smoke—and I smiled, all smug, and told her, "Thought you were," which made her best friend, Sari, look up in surprise.

"What? You could tell?" she said.

"Seemed like a possible."

Score points to me.

Of the pair, I'd say that Sari was the more straightforward. She wore Docs and a biker jacket and took care of all the practicalities; she always knew the times of buses home. Gail, by contrast, was slender, almost fey-looking, her wardrobe full of cheap, second-hand clothes that seldom suited her. "We're not a couple," she told me, though people often thought they were. They shared a flat in Whalley Range and had a clock on the wall where the hands ran backwards; I'd go there, sometimes, drink Polish vodka, listen to the Slits and the Jesus and Mary Chain, talk books, music, and what they called "the practice."

Their thing was killers.

The nastier, the better.

That was their trick, their twist—their *modus operandi*, if you like.

They'd been to Southern Cemetery, they said, to see the graves of the Moors Murderers' victims. "We took flowers so we'd look like friends or family," said Gail. They'd carried out some kind of ritual at the gravesides, though they wouldn't tell me what.

"I felt a bit odd after," Gail said. "Didn't you?"

"A bit," said Sari. "And I dreamed about her."

"Oh, you did! I'd forgotten that."

The Moors Murderers were child killers. Sari'd dreamed about a ten-year-old they'd tortured and killed, yet the dream itself had been peaceful, even reassuring.

"She was ordinary," said Sari. "Just a nice, normal kid, you know, playing in the park, with all the other kids. I don't think I even spoke to her. I just knew who she was, that's all."

"And…what?" I said. "You think it was, like, a spirit or something?"

"Hm. Maybe."

"I think so," said Gail, who was usually the more decisive, quicker to draw conclusions. With one hand, she rubbed her friend's back. "I think you saw her. I think she came to you."

"That's nice," I said.

Sari nodded, still a bit uncertain. "It was…good to see her. It gave me a good feeling. Yes."

The world did not belong to us. We knew that. We'd never become bankers, lawyers, corporate executives. We'd never be financiers or media tycoons. The chances were, we'd never even hold a decent job. But there were other ways to leave a mark on life. Some of us played in bands or started businesses or worked as activists for one cause or another; while for a few of us, a very few, there was a different course. Quiet, clandestine, and hugely powerful, as we believed it then. Although in retrospect, perhaps not powerful enough.

I thought of it as punk magic. Do it yourself. Make it up as you go along. Find out what works for you, specifically, and run with it. If you were a poser, you might call it "the Craft," though I wouldn't, personally. I wouldn't talk about "practitioners," either, come to that. It made it sound so cut-

and-dried, where to me, it was more like fumbling in the dark, hoping to get lucky, like a million cold calls on the off-chance there'd be one, just one, that changed your life.

All else failed: jobs fizzled or became unbearable; friends fell out, rents went up, and lovers left. But the magic stayed. The magic was the thing you fell back on, of necessity, of desperation, and sometimes—yes. Sometimes, it worked.

You could follow books or take the quick route. Pick a totem, pick an object, an event, a person—whatever got your blood flowing, to kick you into higher gear.

Something you loved, something you hated. Something that scared you half to death—that was better still. It all worked. And once you'd started using it, it tuned to you. You put your stamp on it, and made it *yours*.

The props were various, but ultimately, that's all they were: just props. The rituals, the drugs, the icons, the paraphernalia. What mattered was the *attitude*. Punk magic, like I said, same as the music: it wasn't what you played, or how many chords you knew, or anything like that. It was how you *felt*.

You built your psychic energy. You built it, channeled it, then gave the world a little, surreptitious nudge.

And hoped.

Simon Ellis lit a cigarette, his third in ten minutes.

"Now to us, see, we call it 'Western Esotericism.' Less stigmatized like that, eh?"

"You're saying that it's stigmatized?"

"It's looked down on, academically."

"I'm not an academic, Si."

"Still need the studying, though, don't you? Everyone needs that."

"I need results."

"Which is where the studying comes in! See?"

He wagged his latest cigarette and grinned a smug, enlightened grin.

I said, "You get results, Si?"

"There's always *results*. Question is, are they the ones you want?"

"That's what I'm asking. Do you get results?"

For Simon, it was the schoolboy route: books, lectures, seminars, and some bloke he dutifully referred to as "the Master." Si was my age, but he'd all the self-assurance of a true disciple, and he was keen to spread the word. Whether I could use what he was telling me, I wasn't sure.

"So there's your Golden Dawn, see? Start of the modern era. And your Crowley, that's an off-shoot. Ritual, like. Then there's your chaos magic, and—"

"But what d'you recommend, Si? You, personally?"

"Oh, I'm a ritual man. Every time. Ritual's dependable. And you're protected, too. You need that."

"But does it work? For you, I mean?"

He tipped his head back, blew smoke.

Pulled his fourth cig from the packet, ready.

"I'd say...most of the time. Yes. But, like, that's the Craft, isn't it? You never really know..."

"'The Craft.'"

"Like the Master says—it's not exact science. That's why you need the learning first, see?"

Not exact science.

But I *wanted* an exact science. I wanted something that would work, every time, with absolute, coin-in-the-slot reliability.

Where Simon, as it seemed to me, just wanted somebody to tell him what to do.

And there were always people willing to do that.

"I can change your life."

That was Pete Briggs, the night we met.

I laughed.

"Not mine, you can't," I said.

"Peter Magus," he called himself, a name I utterly refused to use. Third floor, Charles Barry Crescent. The council-flat Crowley. To see him, you had to give the "secret" knock, which, naturally, everybody knew: morse code, V for Victory, Beethoven's fifth. Most people went there for his drug connections, but he'd usually have a coven of the faithful with him, too, if only for his ego's sake. There was a lot of subtle bullying at Pete's—and the other kind, as well. "Can you hack it? Can you take the pace?" If he could shock you, throw you something that you couldn't handle, for Pete, that was a win. "Come on!" he'd sneer. "Catch up!"

I saw my first and only snuff film at Pete's place. A dozen

of us in his main room, sitting on the sofa and the floor. VCR counting the numbers, telly flickering, volume right up. Screaming. Whimpering. The sounds of real, honest fear. I hated it. I would have walked, but I was trying to score some speed, and sitting through the film show was an implicit portion of the deal. Plus, if I'd walked, then in Pete's eyes, he'd have beaten me, and I was just macho enough back then to stick it out.

So I sat, while he laughed and slapped his thigh and said, "Look at that!" and, "Fuck me, that finger came right off!" Even now, I don't know whether he was actually enjoying it or just trying to spook the rest of us and show how tough he was. If it's the first, then he was even sicker than I'd thought.

"You can't be an ascended fucking master if you let a bit of blood put you off," he said.

He kept his flat half-dark, the curtains drawn, and all these weird junk-sculptures, leering at you from the shadows. But Pete, as it turned out, wasn't the dangerous one.

He'd have been so pissed off if he'd known that.

We were underground, invisible, a subculture you'd never see on TV or in magazines. We weren't visual. We weren't about a fancy haircut and some trendy clothes. The things we did took work and risk.

How much risk, I don't think any of us really knew.

You could lose yourself. That was definitely true. You forgot, sometimes, the normal world continued in your absence, the same world you'd once lived in; it was all still out there, somewhere. You forgot the seasons changed, the winter passed, till one day you were shocked to see sunshine and blue skies, the buds on trees unfolding into great green clouds, the parks and gardens bright with daffodils.

And on an evening like that, I strolled over to Gail and Sari's place, and we drank Polish vodka—"Popov," it was called—and moaned about the things people our age always moaned about: that relationships never worked out, and jobs were shit, and to do them, you had to dress in ways you loathed ("Pencil skirts," groaned Gail), and we talked about music, and books, and "the practice," and their own, peculiar way of getting it to work.

"I thought you'd go for Sutcliffe," I told them.

Peter Sutcliffe, the Yorkshire Ripper. Killer of prostitutes, stalker of students, nurses, and any woman in the wrong place at the wrong time.

But Gail got prickly over that.

"Why?" she said. "'Cause we might've been *victims?*"

"No, but—" I backtracked hastily. "But I can see the Moors would be good. I get that. Brady and Hindley. Why not?"

My problem was, I fancied Gail. Sometimes, I *really* fancied her. Tonight, she wore her diamond-pattern sweater and the skin-tight gray jeans, and I watched the way she put her cigarette up to her mouth, the way her lips would fold around it... There was something to her, an air of being—I don't know. A little less adrift than most of us, perhaps, as if she'd got some secret locked inside her, and it drew me, like a door that I was desperate to open, though I didn't yet know how.

Plus, the killers. That was their power node, their shock tool, their cattle prod. Like Pete's snuff films, it got the adrenaline up, the mind sharp. Meditate on it, they said. Live it, think it, breathe it. *Feel* what it was like. Each death, each act of torture. It's a tool. A way to get the power flowing.

"You feel it from both sides," said Gail. "Both sides at once, if you can."

If you can…

"And with the Moors," said Sari, "there's a woman involved, too. That's special."

I agreed. "Women serial killers. Very rare."

Gail said, "It's sex."

And I looked up at that.

"Sex and death," she said. "The biggest things in anybody's life."

"That's true," I said.

Another complication: I was pretty sure that, once upon a time, Sari'd fancied me. But she wasn't the one I wanted.

Maybe that was one of *my* power nodes: a way to get my own emotions up, to make me feel I had the strength to tell the universe just what I needed from it.

"Brady and Hindley," said Gail. "They're extreme. And they're iconic. I mean, killing kids—"

"A *woman* killing kids!" said Sari. "That's really *transgressional*, you know?"

"Trans*gressive*," said Gail.

"It works for you?" I asked.

They looked at one another. "I think it works," said Sari. "Sometimes, anyway…"

"But, *every* time? Suppose—"

"You have to make a sacrifice," said Gail, "to get the real power."

Sari said, "That's right. You can't just think about it. You have to do it."

Gail nodded, and I'd a feeling this was something they'd discussed before.

"Someone you love," she said.

"Or some*thing*," said Sari.

Gail sucked her lower lip. "That might work, too," she said.

"And—you reckon that's what they were trying to do?" I said. "Brady and Hindley? Some kind of working?"

"Maybe. Though I don't suppose they thought of it like that."

"No," said Sari. "I'm sure they didn't."

"There's more to it, though, isn't there?" I said. "Like, we could all be killers, except the rest of us—we stop, right? We don't go there. So, why them, not us?"

"Sacrifice," said Gail again. "That's what I think. Taking away something everyone values. Like kids."

"Is that what *they* were thinking, though?" I said.

Silence. Then Sari said, "Well…we could ask them."

I thought she meant, write them a letter.

But she meant here and now.

So we held a séance—sort of. We were all a bit drunk by then. Or a lot drunk. And it seemed a reasonable thing to do.

Divination by serial killer.

The girls picked Brady, not Hindley, the woman, who'd always tried to weasel out of trouble, telling folks she'd been led on, or blackmailed, and it hadn't been her fault.

Brady, on the other hand, remained what he had always been: Nazi wannabe, self-declared superman, and general, all-round shit.

Unless you're English, or you're really into true crime, you probably don't know about the Moors Murderers. Think yourself lucky. Ian Brady, Myra Hindley. *Folie à deux.* They're the reason why, as kids, we were told never to get into a car with anyone, never accept sweets, never go to anyone's house… What we weren't told was what might happen if we did: that we'd be tied up, tortured, sexually abused, and buried on the moors.

Every childhood's got its bogeyman. But ours was real. Ours was local. Years later, I worked with a woman who remembered, as a child, being approached by a blond woman in a car, who'd asked her if she'd like to go for a ride.

Myra Hindley.

Who else could it have been?

We did our seance. Brady was still alive back then, so the girls and I held hands and fixed our minds on him. We took long, slow breaths, listened to hypnotic music, and for a while, it seemed that nothing happened. The backwards clock kept ticking. The music rose and fell. I felt my breath get deeper, faster, and I grew self-conscious, trying to stay calm. Then—

It wasn't exactly a manifestation. No visions, knocks, or bumping tables. But at some point, we all felt—wrong, somehow.

Sari caught it first, jerking back as if she'd suffered an electric shock.

"I think I've had enough," she said.

I was slower. But as soon as she'd said that, I felt a chill inside me, like the heat just drained out of my body, and I shuddered—literally shook with it.

"Oh, fuck," I said.

"You hear a buzzing sound?" said Gail.

Sari looked at me. "OK?" she said.

"I'm—" I took a couple of deep breaths. "Yeah, I'm fine."

To prove it, I stood up, went across and turned the lights on. "Yeah, I'm—yeah. I'm OK."

But I wasn't. I sat down again. "Someone want to switch the music off?" I said.

Sari stopped the tape, and I caught the way Gail looked at her, eyes narrow with concern. "All right?" she mouthed. She reached out, clasped her friend's hand.

Sari nodded.

"You?"

Gail chewed her lower lip. Then she, too, gave a nod.

It was a tender moment, and I should have found it heart-warming. Instead, it distanced me. Here was a friendship I would never share, an intimacy I could never be a part of, and to see it like this left me feeling empty and shut out.

To lighten things, I said, "Fancy the pub?"

"Expensive," said Gail.

"I've got some dosh," I told them.

"I think I'd rather just stay here." Gail looked to Sari. "Wouldn't you?"

Sari hesitated. "Well…"

"I think that's best," said Gail.

So I went home.

And woke in the dark, to see a figure standing over me, a thin, gray smudge, silent, motionless—yet watching, all the while.

I froze. My heart raced. I gathered myself, got ready, then I leapt up, yelling—

And there was no one there.

I searched the flat. The rooms were empty, front door locked, windows shut. Out in the night, a big truck rumbled by, then everything was quiet once more.

I switched the light out, lay back down, thinking I must have been mistaken. Some pattern in the shadows, maybe, or the remnants of a dream…

I didn't sleep again.

Y ou think only the dead have ghosts, but that's not true. The living are the scary ones. The living are the ghosts you need to fear.

It wasn't a voice, exactly. Not to start with. More, as if some notion came into my head, and I'd wonder: was that mine? Did I think that? It might be something that on any other day I'd find familiar, something I'd likely said myself a hundred times; yet now, the meaning seemed to shift in some unsettling, subtle way I couldn't fully grasp.

The superior man needs no morality.

Well, that, I recognized. We all talked like that. Me, Pete Briggs—even Gail and Sari. Conventional morality was meaningless, mere cant, hypocrisy, social control—

To hell with that.

You can do anything you want.

Yes! Now, *that's* what I liked to hear. I sat up straighter, felt the thrill rise in my belly, and knew that I'd been right in everything I'd done, in every choice I'd ever made.

Society, with all its pressures, all its expectations—it was garbage. It was fake, phony, full of shit. You slaved for someone else until you died. I could be free of that. I could do anything I wanted, anything that came into my head—

And by this time, it really *was* a voice, like someone talking in my ear, inspiring me, lifting me up—

You can do anything you want, it said again.

Then two more words:

To anyone.

And that's where things went sideways.

It was like a wedge being driven slowly, bit by bit, into my brain. First the thin end: the flattery, the praise, the uplift and encouragement, and thanks to that, I kept on listening, and hardly even noticed when the tone turned darker, till it was saying something so disgusting, so vile, I wanted to just shut it out, wipe it from my mind—except by then, it was too late. It was already in my head.

A child. Pleading, whimpering, begging me *not to, no, no, please—*

Calling for her Mum. Calling for help, for anyone—

A memory.

Not mine.

But real. And worse—I felt the relish in it, the sense of power in hurting someone smaller, weaker than yourself.

In hurting *kids.*

Hurting them until they flinch when you go near, every time you lift a hand, or glance at them—hurting them until they cry, and scream, and beg, beg, beg, because they know, you have complete control, you choose what happens during each remaining second of their short, short lives.

And it promised me, the voice.

If I'd just listen, just a little longer, to a little more.

It coaxed. Cajoled.

The rules can't bind you.

That's what it said.

But again, this time—it felt different.

It took me back to childhood, seven or eight years old, picking on the red-haired kid at school, pushing him around, laughing at him—

Felt good, didn't it?

"No."

But it had. Of course it had. Or else why do it?

The playground bully. The ugly archetype of childhood, both feared and despised. I'd had my turn at it, and the voice was right—I knew *exactly* how it felt.

And the wedge went in a little deeper, and the voice talked about other things.

Worse things.

Sex and death, Gail had said. Sex and Death.

But this wasn't sex, no matter how it looked. This was violation, torture—dominance.

While the voice made sure that it felt personal.

Manchester's a student town. Young kids, fresh from home. Trusting, vulnerable. And me, just walking down the street and watching them, these boys and girls, when the voice came back, weighing up each of them, lovingly, delightedly: *The blond there, with the pigtails. See her? The way she laughs, always a bit behind the others. Uncertain of herself. You see that, don't you?*

And it began to talk—about the possibilities. The opportunities, the likelihood, the chance—

You could, you know.

I didn't react. I wouldn't react. And the voice…went into details. What I could do. How I could do it. All I'd need would be a length of rope, a good, sharp knife—

"Shut up."

You want to, don't you?

I walked faster, tried to push her face out of my mind.

But the voice kept on, explaining what I'd do, and how I'd feel, and—

"Shut up!"

I yelled out loud. People looked at me, then quickly looked away.

See them? They're sheep. What use are they? To men like us, they're Playthings. They're toys for us to do with as we wish. We break them to our will, don't we? Don't we now?

If I set eyes on anyone, even for a moment, it would start up, telling me how to approach them, how to act as if I needed help, to get them on their own, and then—

Girls. Boys. It didn't matter which.

I looked at the ground, looked at my feet. Tried not to look at anyone, but sometimes—sometimes, I just couldn't help it.

You want to, don't you?

"No."

But you do. Everyone does, deep down. You know they do.

"They don't."

They do.

"You go to hell."

Did it laugh at that? Did it honestly laugh?

I wasn't walking anymore. I'd stopped dead, without even realizing, my fists up, shouting at somebody who wasn't there.

The crowds passed, pretending not to see. I backed against a wall.

You're excited.

"No."

Your breathing's getting heavy.

I hit my head against the bricks. Deliberately. Repeatedly.

You're getting hot now, aren't you?

"Fuck off! Fuck off fuck off fuck off—"

And—silence. Like a door slammed shut.

I looked around. I took a breath.

An ordinary street, with ordinary people—not sheep, not victims.

Just people.

What I felt then, besides the horror, and the fear, was something much, much more banal.

Embarrassment.

I put my head down, dug my hands into my pockets, and I fled.

I sat in All Saints park, smoking a cigarette. Blossom on the trees, white petals drifting in the wind like snowflakes.

All I wanted was some peace, a chance to be alone.

But I was never alone now. Never.

Even when I couldn't catch the words, the whispering was constant, like a radio playing in another room, nagging at me, picking at me, goading me, all the time.

Break every rule.

That's how it started, full of promise and rebellion, the vision of a new life, without boundaries or limits. Teasing, seductive. Then every time, at some point, it would twist, shift, turn into something ugly, broken…wrong.

I doused my cigarette. Stood up, quickly.

Walked off, like I was trying to leave the voice behind.

Or leave myself behind.

Whichever one came first.

G ail was alone. Sari'd got a job, she said.

"She's cleaning for this family."

"Uh-huh."

All the weeks that I'd been trying to catch Gail on her own, and now I had, but the timing was off. I felt awkward, uncertain of myself, and she seemed…distant, somehow, her mind elsewhere.

"That séance," I said, handing her a cigarette. "You think it went OK? Got a bit funny at the end, don't you think? You felt it too, eh?"

"It's like that sometimes. Why?"

"Well…"

It's stupid, but, like I say, I fancied Gail. I didn't want to look weak. I didn't want to say, *I've got a problem.* So I tried to look strong, confident—*manly*, if you like.

It was a long time back. A lot's changed since.

"He never answered, anyway," she said, a little mournfully.

"No?"

"D'you think he did?"

"No. Definitely not."

Yet through it all, the voice was there, telling me, telling me—

Telling me that I was bigger than she was. Stronger. More powerful. *The strong don't ask, they take.* How could she stop me? If I'd only had the nerve—the courage—if I'd only been a *real* man—

I left her a couple of cigarettes, told her, "Got to go. I'll catch you later, OK?"

Out on the street, I yelled and swore.

"I do *not* want that! I have *never* wanted that!"

I whirled around, certain somebody was following me, but I couldn't see them, no matter how I strained my eyes. I crossed the road, crossed back again. I stood a moment, helpless, looking back and forth—just one more crazy, one more loony on the loose.

And it got worse from there.

Maybe they were just coincidences.

Flukes, accidents.

Maybe.

But magic's all about coincidence, the inner and the outer worlds combining, meshing and becoming one.

As above, so below.

I put the telly on and got a documentary about Nazis, Brady's big obsession. In the pub, someone was talking about Saddleworth, the moor where the bodies were buried. But who? I looked around and couldn't see the speaker. Had I just imagined it? A woman I knew slightly came in with her hair bleached, and for one appalling second, I was staring straight at Myra Hindley. Then her face changed, grew cheery and familiar, but in that brief moment—

He was swallowing my life, Ian Brady, piece by piece; my world was turning into his, and there was nothing I could do to stop it.

"Si." I called him from a pay phone. "Your lot. They do exorcisms, don't they? That right?"

"Ooh, now that's a question. For what?"

"You know. Possession, demons—usual stuff?"

"Well, Master says that's mostly myth. It's schizophrenia, or—"

"But what if it's not?"

He paused a moment, then, with a note of suspicion, almost glee, he asked me, "Why?"

"Nothing, really. Friend wants to know. He's a bit, y'know. Bit loopy."

"He could try a priest...?"

"Yeah, I saw that film. Didn't end well, I remember..."

We're the last true heroes. We defy society, we scorn its empty values, spit on its most precious goals. We're the last true rebels, the only ones with guts, nerves, the courage to fight back—

A void. A vacuum. A black hole trying to fill itself with

meaning and significance.

Sometimes, I could almost see him, pacing in his cell, thin as a bone from hunger strikes, brain clenched like a fist.

And I wanted to tell him. I wanted to tell him what he really was.

You killed kids. That's what I'd say. *You picked the weakest, most vulnerable victims you could find, and got your girlfriend to go out and fetch them for you.*

You're a hero?

You killed kids.

And slowly, bit by bit, a plan began to form. It was sneaky, ramshackle, and very likely wrong, but it was all I could come up with.

Either that, or I'd go mad.

Everybody knew the secret knock. *Everybody.* I even sang along with it: "Da da da daa!"

"Pete, mate! Can I come in?"

Pete Briggs stood in the doorway, blocking me, like a bouncer at his own exclusive club.

The pause, to let me know that I was there on sufferance, and not by rights.

Then he stepped back.

Pete was a short guy in his thirties with a goatee and a bald stripe shaved down the center of his skull. He'd probably been shy and nerdy as a teenager, but now, he was the guru, the magus, and he'd got his little gang around him; there was always something going on at Pete's.

Music. Chatter. Air thick with draw and stale tobacco smoke.

"Word in private?" I said.

He weighed me up. Was I worth it?

Yes. It seemed I was.

"Could do," he said.

He took me to a side room—mattress on the floor, Giger poster, tell-tale stink of unwashed laundry. And I talked. I talked like I had never talked before, flattering him, teasing, trying to sell him on a single, big idea.

"You'll like this, mate. Soon as I heard it, I thought, this is for you." A sly smile; a little flicker of the eyes. "You're into serial killers, right?"

My first mistake.

He sighed.

Too *passé*, too old hat.

"I'm interested in…extreme psychology," he said.

"But this is different. Supposing you could…make contact, right? I don't mean interview the guy, I mean, have him in your head a while. For real. Can you imagine that? Seriously?"

He scratched his beard.

"Go on," he said.

So I made my pitch. I steered the conversation, took care to ask him questions, and bow to what, in his view, was his own superior knowledge.

Let him think that he was finding the ideas himself.

I said, "I've seen it done. I know people who do it."

He acted skeptical, dismissive.

So I pushed my next point home.

"It's a pair of girls," I said, and held his gaze.

Misogyny's a useful tool, used at the right moment.

"I tell you. Scared the life out of me, no mistake."

"I'm…curious," he said.

"It's a step beyond. And these girls—"

He put a finger to his lips.

I'd got him.

We went back to the main room, where the members of his crew lay scattered like discarded children, and he moved amongst them, pointing his toes, making his selection— tapping a shoulder here, a hand there… "You. And you. And—" swinging round, inspecting the faces, "you."

Oh, there was disappointment. One little creep even sidled up to him and asked to be included, but Pete, with practiced hauteur, simply turned his back.

"Downstairs," he said.

Downstairs was the temple.

It was a big, dark room with a sweet, spicy smell. Candles stood on saucers scattered around the floor. Pete gestured for an underling to light them. Then he lit the incense burner, muttering a prayer to—someone, I suppose. Probably himself.

"Breathe," he told us, pacing out a rhythm with his hand.

So we breathed, and Pete explained it all, like it was his idea. I didn't interrupt, and only when one eager acolyte began to gush about Ted Bundy, I drew Pete aside and told him, "I think we'd have more luck with someone closer, don't you? Local connections, and all?"

He frowned, pouted; but he took the hint.

Here goes.

It was a gorgeous week, the best of the spring weather. Trees in leaf, flowers in bloom, and even in the city, you could smell the earth. I took long walks. I did no magic. I smoked a little draw, but not much. I even cut back on the cigs. I sat there in my fifth floor flat, the windows wide, delighted when a small thrush came and perched upon the windowsill, bobbing and jerking in its own peculiar dance.

The voice was gone.

Now, looking back, I don't know whether magic works or not, the way we did it; but it *seemed* to work, and that's more than any of the other nonsense that we tried. So maybe we were all just kidding ourselves, and I'd been listening to my own thoughts, not a "voice" at all—and maybe, deep down, I really was the monster that the voice insisted I become.

But I don't think so, I don't think so at all.

I'd realized that I'd never get the voice out of my head. Not on my own. It was dug in, stubborn. But maybe, I thought—maybe I could find it someone tastier, more in line with its way of thought.

Maybe I could get it to move house.

Before I'd gone to Pete's that night, I'd done a sigil working. It's a common practice. Just one more way of focusing the mind, getting the juices flowing. I'd drawn the sigil on my skin: chest, thighs, upper arms, even on my back. Felt-tip pen, biro. I dropped a tab of acid, left the flat, and ran. Fast as I could. It's a clumsy way to get things going, but the best I could come up with at the time. The running was the main thing. Like I could see the city change around me, the streetlights strobing past, small cars smearing into great stretch limos, everything losing its shape, becoming soft and pliable…

Magic.

The sigil's essence was a simple one.

Get out and stay out.

I waited in the stairwell at Charles Barry Crescent, catching my breath and centering my mind.

Then I went up to Pete's.

We stood in a circle. Five of us.

The candles lit us from below: throat, top lip, orbits of the eyes.

Turning us all into ghosts.

I'd no regard for Pete as a magician. To me, he was a con artist, a bully with a nose for other people's weaknesses. But I'll say this: his sense of drama was exquisite. He set the mood, he got us all fired up, and then—he started chanting.

Softly, to begin with.

"Bray-dee. Bray-dee. Bray-dee…"

The rhythm got you. In your belly, in your bones. Repetitive, insistent. I could feel my own lips moving in response: "*Bray-dee. Bray-dee.*"

A pulse. A heartbeat. It throbbed in the air, grew louder, then louder still, until I felt like I was part of it, that it was in my blood, and my whole body shook with it.

"*Bray-dee. Bray-dee.*"

Pete set us off. Then—deliberately—he left the circle. He slipped through the shadows, a strange, slow-motion dance, hands weaving patterns in the air. It shouldn't have bothered me, I knew, but I felt my skin crawl, my belly hollow out, my heart rate rise.

The sigils itched like fresh tattoos.

Moving with the rhythm of the chant, his shadow leapt across the walls, over the ceiling, jumping and spinning while the candles flickered, and soon it seemed the whole room was in motion, flowing round us, rolling, liquid. The walls melted away. The floor was like a river. Nothing was fixed, nothing was safe.

Pete threw his head back and he howled.

"Come into me!" he boomed. "Come into me!"

He clapped his hands—a bang like a gun going off.

I jerked in shock.

And it was over. We fell silent. Faintly, I heard music from the room above; but the room above was in another world.

Pete hung there, bent up, like he'd been gut-punched. He uncurled slowly, looked around as if reminding himself where he was, then reached a hand to something—someone— no-one else could see, and in a creepy, put-on voice, said,

"Hello, Myra."

The sweat was cold in the small of my back.

But I knew then: I was free.

Days passed.

I rang the bell at Gail and Sari's, and I waited.

No mobile phones back then; only a handful of my friends even had landlines, so catching someone home was always hit-and-miss. Presently, though, I heard a movement, and Gail appeared, slimmer than ever, her cheekbones jutting, eyes too large.

"Oh—hi," she said, like she'd expected someone else.

"Got a cup of tea?" I asked her. "I've got cigs."

We sat under the clock with the backwards hands, me in the armchair, she on the sofa.

Sari wasn't home.

"She's out a lot," I said.

"She's busy with her job."

"The cleaning job?"

"Mm."

A fly buzzed round me. I blew smoke at it.

"Sounds like a lot of work," I said.

Gail didn't look at me.

"She just thought…you know. She wants to make some money."

"And you're left with the killers."

I nodded to them, taped to the chimney breast: newspaper

cuttings, photocopies—a couple looked like they'd been torn from library books. All this was new. Sutcliffe, Nilsen, Bundy, Dahmer. Brady and Hindley, pride of place, right in the middle.

Torturers, murderers, rapists, cannibals—

Totems.

Gail wrinkled her nose.

"I don't really do that anymore," she said. "It got…you know. It got harder, and…"

"I know." I wanted to sound sympathetic, and show I understood. "Sometimes…it's like you're not getting results, yeah? Or not the right results."

"Um."

I watched her profile: the turned-up nose, the delicate precision of her lips, the cleft in her chin. She was beautiful in a way so nearly not beautiful, so close to being strange or even ugly, if any aspect of her features had been altered slightly—but she *wasn't* ugly, and oh, God, I ached for her.

"Shoo! Shoo!" She flapped hands at another fly, and to me, complained, "They're everywhere. I don't know where they come from."

"'Where do the flies go in winter?'"

"What?"

"You know? It's an old…joke, or something. I dunno. But they always come back in spring, eh?"

"Um." She seemed distracted, uncertain of herself. It wasn't like her.

"Use your loo?" I said.

There was a hallway linking the rooms. I passed Gail's door, then Sari's. There was a bit of a smell here, like the sewage pipes had backed up. It was in the bathroom, too.

I peed, washed my hands, checked myself in the mirror, and flicked my hair up at the front. Then I went back to the lounge and, this time, sat on the sofa next to her.

"So…when's Sari due back, then?"

"Late, I think. D'you need to see her?"

"No. Just curious."

We chatted, idly. Or I chatted. She didn't really say much. I nodded to the row of portraits on the chimney breast. "How come the Americans all look like film stars, and ours look—I dunno. Like they're inbred or something?"

It was hard, just getting her attention. Getting it and keeping it. Eventually, I said, "Fancy a drink? I've got some cash."

I hadn't told her about Brady. Or Pete. I wasn't sure how she'd react—whether I'd look interesting, resourceful, or just nuts. Best to keep quiet, perhaps.

"I'll get a bottle, yeah? We'll have a few drinks together. Be nice, that. Drinks and a chat, eh? What d'you reckon?"

I stood up.

"Pop out for Popov. That should be their slogan, don't you think?" I laughed, awkwardly. "I'll use your loo again before I go."

I went into the hall. The smell was still there. I called back, "You need to phone your landlord about the plumbing. I think there's a leak or something."

"I'll sort it," she said.

The hallway. Gail's door. Sari's door. I saw a movement near my foot, and a black spot spiralled up towards me. Another bloody fly! Christ sakes! It had come from under Sari's door, I was almost certain. And here was another, crawling out, pushing through the thin pile of the carpet, flexing its wings…

I put a hand on the door, but didn't open it.

I went into the bathroom. Couldn't pee. When I came out, I stood at Sari's door again, but again, I left it closed.

I looked in on Gail.

"Sari," I said. "She's had this job—what? Couple of weeks?"

"Mm. 'Bout that."

"But, like, you saw her this morning, right?"

Only now she turned to look at me, looked me right in the eye. She was so, so pretty.

And she was lying.

"Course I did," she said.

I left, then.

I didn't go for booze. A breeze sprang up, rattling the trees, lifting the traffic fumes and city smells, but it made no difference: I couldn't get the stink of Gail's place out of my nostrils, or the thought of it out of my head.

For some people, sacrifice can be a big part of their magic practice. Take the thing you value most. The thing. Or the person. Or…

It's a different city these days, like I say, and the ghosts don't show under electric light, but listen carefully, and maybe you can hear them whispering, telling their stories, remembering how things used to be.

If I'm around, I'll see you there.

END

—

TIM LEES is from Manchester, England, where he lived for some years with a very nice Crowleyite magician, quite unlike the characters in the story. He now lives in Chicago. He is the author of the much-praised historical fantasy *Frankenstein's Prescription* (Brooligan Press), and the *Field Ops* books for HarperVoyager (*The God Hunter, Devil in the Wires, Steal the Lightning*). His latest story collection, The *Ice Plague and Other Inconveniences*, is available from Incunabula Media https://incunabulamedia.com/, as is *The Other Country*, his account of working in a psychiatric hospital. He contributed "Amsterdam" to this volume's predecessor, *Winter in the City*. When not writing, he has held a wide variety of jobs, including film extra, conference organiser, warehouse worker, teacher, and lizard-bottler in a museum.

Manchester itself was sadly destroyed in the great magical wars of the '90s, but a ghost of the city now haunts its original site, and can be readily accessed with the appropriate rituals. Enter at your peril.

TEL AVIV

Jonathan Papernick

It had rained shrapnel all winter, but now that spring was in full blush, Tel Aviv was alive with a hopeful hum of renewal.

Lovers strolled hand-in-hand through the picturesque streets of Neve Tzedek, the sweet scent of red bougainvillea and jasmine filling their noses with memories of better days. In Florentin, young Bohemians and startup entrepreneurs walked their dogs along the hipster streets, walls covered with bright graffiti. Shoppers crowded the pedestrian mall at the Nahalat Binyamin market where artisans sold their wares twice a week: a filigreed silver hamsa to guard against the evil eye, a stern mezuzah carved from golden Jerusalem stone, a menorah fashioned out of old Kinley soda cans. The cafes and restaurants along Dizengoff Street were packed with boisterous patrons. Tourists had returned at last, eager eyes on the utilitarian whitewashed structures created by the great architects of the Bauhaus School who had fled Germany a century earlier.

There was still a tremendous hole in the ground where an apartment house had collapsed on Mapu Street after a direct hit from a ballistic missile. A makeshift memorial marked the spot where the alloy tail of an intercepted cruise missile crushed a man on his way to work in Ramat Gan. Shuttered shops with dark, dead-eyed windows and empty shelves, out-of-business signs hastily posted, punctuated almost every block.

"See you in the World to Come," one handwritten note read outside a once-flourishing *sabich* shop.

The skies had been clear for weeks, the haunting wails of the warning sirens silent. It seemed the recent offensive in the North had finally brought a delicate peace to Tel Aviv.

Tzlil had spent so much time that awful winter in the cramped shelter beneath her family's apartment on Pinsker Street, that Tzlil knew she would have died of boredom if not for the cartons of musty old comic books some tenant had left behind years ago.

Within the yellowed pages of *The Incredible Hulk* #256, Tzlil had discovered Ruth Bat-Seraph, whose alter ego was Sabra, the brave Israeli superhero, gifted with superhuman strength, amazing speed and the ability to fly, thanks to her gravity-defying cape. Sabra appeared with Spider-Man, teaming up against Dr. Octopus, fighting alongside the X-Men, gracing the cover of *The New Warriors* #58, a blue Star of David emblazoned on her headband; in the pages of another she single-handedly kept the Western Wall from collapsing after the supervillain Krona set off devastating earthquakes across the globe.

An Israeli actor may have played Wonder Woman in the movies, but Wonder Woman, with her Lasso of Truth was an Amazon. And though the fearless Hannah Senesh was a real-life hero Tzlil had learned about in school, Tzlil couldn't ignore the fact that the polymath poet and parachutist was arrested behind enemy lines in 1944 where she was imprisoned, tortured and executed by firing squad.

How many times had Tzlil imagined herself transforming into Sabra, like a butterfly bursting from its chrysalis and taking to the air to fight the enemy as rockets and missiles and drones exploded in the sky above her beloved city? Tzlil filled page after page in her lined school notebooks, drawing Sabra catching any threat that slipped through the Iron Dome and flinging it with ease back to where it came from. Soon she manifested her own almond-shaped face, framed beneath a high-tech tiara configured to process her commands, firing energy quills at the speed of sound to paralyze enemies and save her terrified friends in *kita vav*.

Throughout the winter Tzlil suffered terrible pain, her thighs and calves throbbing with unthinkable agony, worse than when she had fallen on her face rollerblading on the Tayelet with her best friend, Roni. Her mother said it was just growing pains, as she applied a heating pad and massaged Tzlil's aching legs the way her own mother had done for her when she was young. But the pains persisted and Tzlil knew it was something more.

Tzlil's mother wouldn't be home from work for hours and she told Tzlil not to go outside in case there was another attack. But the day was so perfect, she couldn't sit locked up in their apartment another minute. She had the Red Alert app on her phone in case she had to run to the safety of a shelter, so off she went.

She slipped her white hair band emblazoned with a Star of David over her unruly hair, and soon her long, coltish legs carried her to the beach, where she splashed through the shallows carrying her pink Chuck Taylors in her hand, the warm sand soothing her bare feet.

Shirtless young men released from reserve duty preened and played *matkot* on Frishman Beach, the *pok-pok* of the rubber ball thwacking against their paddles a constant soundtrack as the cool blue waters of the Mediterranean rolled softly in and out. The ancient port city of Jaffa glimmered in the distance against a faultless sky, the bell tower of Saint Peter's Church rising above the square stone structures like a ladder to the heavens.

Tzlil took a deep, appreciative breath, the cleansing salt air washing away so much despair and fear, anticipation building with every step she took, a season of renewal and possibility free of terror and sirens and shelters unspooling beneath her feet.

Then Tzlil stepped on something stinging.

When she looked down, a transparent flying-saucer-shaped jellyfish pulsed steadily beneath her foot like a heartbeat.

Meduzot usually didn't haunt the beaches of Tel Aviv until June or July when the waters were warm and welcoming, but rising sea temperatures meant they came earlier and earlier in the season. A bloom of *meduzot,* hundreds of them, rolled in with the tide, and Tzlil was about to rush to the lifeguard station to tell of the coming swarm—they were multiplying, everywhere along the beach, *meduzot* as far as the eye could see—but the throbbing in her foot was too much. She fell to her knees just in time to see an enormous ball of flame flash across the sky, so blinding in its intensity that people who witnessed it would continue to see its burning form ablaze behind their eyelids for weeks when they closed their eyes to sleep.

There was no warning, no alert at all, just a brilliant blaze like a streaking meteor, a trailing tail of gyrating sparks igniting the sky with its long wake. A colossal, earth-shaking boom thundered throughout the city as the air filled with acrid smoke and debris, mushrooming high into the sky. Car alarms shrieked. Distressed dogs howled. A Levant Sparrowhawk tumbled from the sky like a stone dropped down a well. The world turned sideways, and Tzlil fell into the poison embrace of the swarming *meduzot.*

Tzlil slipped in and out of consciousness for the next four days as her mother kept vigil at her bedside in the trauma ward of Ichilov Hospital.

There, Tzlil floated beyond gravity's pull through a

bioluminescent darkness, the iridescent formations of the jellyfish glowing with their mysterious beauty, beckoning her onward and onward, past a rhythmic chorus of undulating shapes, some pink, some blue, some yellow, some vibrant purple, trailing tentacles waving slowly as she passed, their stinging cells scoring her skin, imprinting some arcane code within her. Each time she touched a gelatinous bell-shaped form her body flooded with a rush of sensation and light and sound as if she were downloading the universe from its source, electrical jolts surging through her limbs and organs. Something ancient and eternal had come to life within her, a primordial network of neurons firing as lightning thrummed through her veins, cortisol and dopamine and adrenaline surging throughout her body like the culmination of the sixth day of creation.

Tzlil awoke to the clacking sounds of a keyboard and a muffled laughter in her head that echoed throughout her whole body.

When she asked her mother what happened, her mother said she should rest.

When Tzlil asked her mother if everything was okay, her mother began to cry.

Tzlil had been stung by a swarm of nomad jellyfish, their payload of venom enough to shut down her organs and stop her heart from beating forever. She was found by a lifeguard who treated her at the scene. But she couldn't be seen by a doctor for hours because of all the injured and dead from the attack on Azrieli Center, a complex of three glass skyscrapers which included a large shopping mall, one square tower, one triangular tower, and one circular tower, the tallest climbing forty nine stories into the air.

843 people died in the attack. Only a deep chasm remained, flooding with seawater and gasoline from ruptured fuel pipes.

The Defense Minister was unable to explain why the Iron Dome or David's Sling wasn't activated, or any of the other air defense systems put in place to keep the people of Israel safe.

The Prime Minister admitted he didn't know where the fireball came from. Advanced radar systems said the attack wasn't launched from any of the many countries that wanted Israel erased from the map. It just appeared out of nowhere. The Prime Minister called reserves up to service, activated the Home Front Command, and scrambled warplanes to patrol the skies.

Rumors quickly spread that clerics in the distant city of Qom had summoned a vengeful *djinn* tasked with destroying the Zionist Entity. The Ayatollah himself appeared on television, mocking the idea that such magicians exist in his country, declaring that witchcraft of this sort is against all precepts handed down by Allah's messenger Muhammad.

An anonymous message appeared on telephones across the city of Tel Aviv, warning: "If you don't leave the city you will die. The fires of vengeance will continue until the city is empty or destroyed."

Most Tel Avivians believed the message was just another psychological operation crafted by one overwrought enemy or another and most went about their business as usual. There was a rich tradition of apocalyptic hyperbole in this part of the world, and many remembered the so-called "Mother of all Battles," launched more than three decades earlier by a bully who found himself eventually at the end of a rope.

Some chose to flee the city, but the endless traffic jams on the Ayalon Highway made it certain that few escaped before the next fireball struck.

This time it was the Kiryah, the heart of Israel's defense establishment, destroyed by a gargantuan fireball.

Next, it was Mossad Headquarters housed in northern Tel Aviv.

On the fourth day, a grandfather of two named Doron, kayaking on the Yarkon River saw the fireball strike the Reading Power Station, the calm waters of the Yarkon boiling and angry in an instant, nearly flipping his kayak as short-tailed Kingfishers rained from the sky, their orange bellies flashing amid their blue feathers as they pelted the waters around him. Nearby, the limp body of a Great Egret sank beneath the murky surface, followed by a Gray Heron and a flight of dive bombing Cormorants.

When Tzlil learned what had happened to her city she leapt out of bed declaring, "I have to stop this," pulling tubes and wires from her body and flinging them to the floor.

"*Chaim sheli*, you're not well," her mother said.

"I feel amazing!"

Some magnificent force lived inside her now, giving her strength she could never have imagined. Her body felt light and lithe, her muscles and tendons and sinews strong like steel cables.

Her mother reminded her that she was still heavily medicated, and this feeling of euphoria was false. She was a very sick child. "Look at yourself! You're covered in sores."

Tzlil stared at herself in the mirror and saw her once-pristine skin scrimshawed from neck to toes in stippled patterns of scarlet arabesques, tributaries and branches forming bands around her arms and legs, bracelets of crimson circling her limbs.

Again, she heard derisive laughter echoing through her skull as if trying to shame her for the way she looked. But she shut it down, saying aloud in response, "I'm a bad ass bitch."

"What happened to my little girl?"

Tzlil slipped on her pink Chuck Taylors.

"Where do you think you're going?" Tzlil's mother said.

"I need to help."

Dr. Hadid, who had grown up in the northern Arab city of Uum al-Fahm and had once dreamed of being an opera singer and playing La Scala, appeared as Tzlil was about to make her escape. He wore large-framed glasses to correct an astigmatism. His eyelids drooped with exhaustion beneath thick, friendly brows. A stethoscope was draped around his neck.

"What are you doing out of bed?"

"She thinks she feels better. She wants to leave," Tzlil's mother said.

"I've never felt better!" Tzlil said.

"Get back in bed," her mother shouted.

"Never, never, never," Tzlil said.

"You've had several grand mal seizures." The doctor adjusted his stethoscope. "You've suffered some serious trauma."

"Haven't we all?" Tzlil responded.

"*You ain't seen nothin' yet*," a voice in her head mocked. The voice was in English and it sounded the way the radio does when stuck between stations, far off and fuzzy so she couldn't be sure she was hearing what she thought she was hearing.

"She thinks she's going to leave the hospital," Tzlil's mother said.

"You've been here a difficult few days already," Dr. Hadid said. "Please let me check your vitals, just to make sure everything is *sababa*."

"And then I can go?" Tzlil hopped from foot to foot, bursting with energy. Tzlil's mother grimaced. Dr. Hadid squinched an eye at Tzlil's mother in what was intended to be a wink. He called a nurse to assist him as he checked Tzlil's vitals.

Tzlil's body temperature was impossibly high, but her skin was cool to the touch. Some patients' temperatures tend to run hot, but Dr. Hadid had never seen anything like this. Nobody could survive such a high temperature and certainly no patient would be lucid or ambulatory the way Tzlil seemed to be. The full body rashes were consistent with multiple *meduzot* stings, but Tzlil wasn't sweating and she wasn't experiencing chills or shivering. Ordinarily, the doctor would have called for further testing, but Dr. Hadid had been told by hospital administrators Ichilov General Hospital could be hit by the next fireball, and as many patients as possible needed to be released or moved underground, or to smaller hospitals in the outlying suburbs less likely to be targeted. The frantic rumbling of hospital beds rolling down the hallway outside reminded him that the patients needed to be moved to safety as quickly as possible.

When Dr. Hadid checked the jellyfish stings enrobing Tzlil's body they had hardened into some sort of flexible armor-like shell. Tzlil felt no pain when he palpated the stings, and when the doctor said he should make sure there were no signs of bacterial infection, Tzlil said she was leaving now.

"What's the hurry?" the doctor asked.

"I need to save Tel Aviv."

Again a crescendo of laughter filled her skull, but Tzlil knew that self-doubt was a monster she could tame simply by ignoring.

"Enough already!" her mother screamed.

When the doctor asked Tzlil if she really believed she could stop a fireball burning through the sky at Mach 5, Tzlil said yes.

Dr. Hadid turned to Tzlil's mother and said he needed to order a full psychological workup assessing her daughter's mental health, which suggested she was in the throes of some kind of grandiose delusion.

The doctor lowered his voice and asked Tzlil, "Just between the two of us. Tell me, do you really believe you can save Tel Aviv?"

"Of course."

"That's very honorable." Dr. Hadid paused. "And how do you know that you can do this?"

"I just know."

That ineffable feeling in her body told her everything she needed to know.

"Are you hearing voices?"

"Voices?"

"*Loser*," a voice inside Tzlil's head said. It was loud and clear now.

"No…" Tzlil hesitantly responded to Dr. Hadid. "Why?"

"Is something or someone telling you that you are some kind of…savior?"

Tzlil said no again and rolled her eyes.

"Tell me, if I release you to your mother's care…what do you plan on doing when you return home?"

"I'm going to stop the next fireball."

Tzlil's mother shrieked, "Stop being crazy!"

"Tzlil," Dr. Hadid said. "I'd like you to speak with Dr. Bookshtein. He's a very nice man and an expert in advanced PTSD care. I believe he can help you."

"I don't need help."

Dr. Hadid was about to ask whether Tzlil ever thought about hurting herself, but the laughter in her head was making it difficult to think, so she burst out of the hospital room before he had a chance. Tzlil ran down the hallway, her gown flying behind her like a cape, her mother calling for her to wait.

Despite the stay-at-home orders, Tzlil's mother was able to get a taxi for her and Tzlil. A fine particulate haze shrouded the city: the milky, ghostlike air dense with its oppressive weight, the vibrant colors of billboards and street signs washed out and dulled, an eerie silence overtaking the usual hustle and bustle. Mournful music played from the cab's radio, and Tzlil stared out the window rather than look at her mother. Tzlil was eager to try out her new body, which she knew was indestructible now, the blood rushing through her veins, screaming with restive agitation to DO SOMETHING! She could have run home in a matter of minutes, she could have flown, but her mother, who always worried too much, began to cry, so Tzlil had agreed to the taxi ride home, calling her mother an *Ima Polania* who was afraid to let her only daughter grow up.

The cab stopped at a flickering red light, its glow diffused, almost blurred as if uncertain of its purpose. Broken glass from shops and apartments littered the sidewalks. An abandoned lotto stand sat desolate beside the idling car, the lifeless bodies of so many birds strewn across the ground.

Tzlil's heart broke for what had happened to her city.

They arrived home and Tzlil leapt out, surprised to see that the entryway of their apartment house had been painted red as if with blood.

Tzlil asked what happened, and her mother told her gangs of yeshiva students from Bnei Brak had descended on the city, and, in the tradition of the ancient Israelites, marked unsuspecting Tel Avivian's doorposts with the blood of a lamb so that whatever evil was striking their city would pass safely over their homes.

Tzlil's mother told Tzlil to put on some clothing so they could go down to the shelter without her looking like an escaped mental patient.

"Do you think a shelter will save us from the next fireball? It destroys everything in its path."

"Just get dressed."

Tzlil's room looked smaller than it did just a few days ago, more childish, her teddy bears and pop star posters shockingly infantile. Her school textbook was open to a page on Ilan Ramon, the first Israeli astronaut, who died when the Columbia space shuttle disintegrated on reentry to the earth's atmosphere.

Tzlil took a pair of her mother's fitted black yoga pants off the clothesline strung outside her window and slipped them on. At the back of her drawer she found an old black t-shirt featuring a jagged exclamation point that looked a little like a pink lightning bolt. It was small on her, but she loved the way the bold graphic matched her shoes and how the shirt hugged her skin. She was just brushing out her long hair when the entire building shook as if the tectonic plates were shifting beneath the sands of Tel Aviv.

Tzlil's mother burst into her room, face streaked with

tears. She threw her arms around her daughter, kissing her on top of the head and telling her how much she loved her.

"I know, I know," Tzlil said. "Just stop it."

"Those poor people. How many more have to die?"

"I'm going up to the roof to see what happened," Tzlil said.

"It's not safe."

"It's as safe as it's ever going to be. We know there won't be another fireball in the next five minutes."

Her mother spat three times "*pthu, pthu, pthu,*" to shield her daughter from the powers of the evil eye and then said, "Fine, but don't be long. I'm going to check in on Saba and Savta."

The air smelled of scorched metal and bleach, sweet and pungent and charged, that slightly sentimental aroma that sometimes appears after a storm. A furious column of fire lit up the far distance, piercing the dome of the sky, the wailing of countless rescue vehicles performing their macabre symphony. The target might have been Tel Aviv University, with its many research laboratories. Tzlil just knew she had to get there as quickly as possible.

The voice inside her kept telling her to give it up, give it up; she was useless. But Tzlil knew she could fly and that it was her duty to save Tel Aviv. She found an old Goldstar Beer beach towel beneath the water heater, tied it around her neck as a cape, went to the far edge of the roof and took off running as fast as she could across the blacktop. She leapt into the air with all of her strength, and for the briefest of moments, she was flying, the street far below, her hair flowing behind her, arms outstretched like Sabra!

And then Tzlil was bobbing in the sky like a helium balloon, drifting, a gelatinous pulse throbbing throughout her. She moved with a maddening torpor, her boneless form undulating as she torqued her body, twisting and turning to leverage herself into flight. She tried flapping her arms like wings, but her muscles contracted and relaxed, contracted and relaxed, propelling her forward in a slow, rhythmic dance. She floated above the streets, losing altitude with every pulse, her body finally coming to rest a block away outside the gates of the nearby Trumpeldor Cemetery.

She rushed back to the rooftop and tried again, achieving little more than a weightless buoyancy which she could more or less control by squeezing her abdominal muscles and swaying gently back-and-forth. She tried again and again, knowing that she could fly, and that she alone would save Tel Aviv. She knew it with fanatic certainty. The voice in her head was silent now, replaced by an insistent clacking.

Each time she made her way back to the roof she passed piles of dead birds scattered across the roads and sidewalks, some gruesomely hanging from branches of trees where they had fallen, their songs silenced forever. When it became clear she wouldn't be taking flight, Tzlil knelt beside the broken body of a black stork that had dropped from the sky midway through its yearly migration from Africa to Europe. Tzlil picked up the graceful body and cradled it in her arms for a moment, its long red beak slack, her eyes filling with tears at the pity that such a creature would never fly again. She unfastened the Goldstar Beer towel from her neck and placed the bird inside it. She then proceeded to gather as many birds as she could into her makeshift sack and headed up the street to the Trumpeldor Cemetery.

Though it was just around the corner from her apartment, Tzlil had only entered the cemetery once on a school trip to honor the nation's modern founders, the great thinkers and giants of Hebrew literature buried beneath heavy stones. There was no grass anywhere in the cemetery and the ground was made up of stone tiles forming narrow paths between the grave markers. Just a few scrubby bushes and trees meant to offer shade from the unforgiving Middle Eastern sun dotted the crowded landscape.

She quickly found the grave of Israel's national poet, Haim Nachman Bialik, a large, pale cube towering over a smaller stone belonging to his wife Manya. Tzlil had had to recite part of Bialik's poem "In the City of Slaughter," for school, written to memorialize the brutal massacre of Jews in the Moldovan city of Kishinev 120 years earlier.

Now, Tzlil lived in the shadow of new massacres but she refused to accept them as her birthright.

The surface of the stone was covered with pebbles and rocks from visitors honoring the memory of the great poet. Tzlil moved them aside and laid out the birds. Since Tzlil didn't know any prayers, she stood respectfully over the winged bodies and began to recite the first lines of Bialik's poem "Alone."

> *Wind blew, light drew them all.*
> *New songs revive their mornings.*
> *Only I, a small bird, am forsaken*
> *Under the Shekhina's wing.*

She began to sob, hot tears streaming down her face in salty rivulets. She had been a fool to believe she could do anything to stop the killers that appeared every generation, determined to obliterate her people. *You're all going to die,* the voice taunted. As her tears fell onto the lifeless birds, a slight stirring kindled among the broken bodies. She blinked her eyes, believing her mind was playing tricks on her, and then she heard it, the first cheeps of life, and then, a chaos of flapping wings, a babel of birdsong filling the air with its tangle of sound.

The black stork was the first to take flight, followed by a clutch of warblers and then a common swift. Before long, the sky above the cemetery was full of the appreciative cries of the birds as they disappeared into the afternoon haze.

Tzlil's heart pounded in her chest, and she rushed to gather as many birds as she could. She repeated Bialik's words, sanctifying the birds with her tears even as the mocking voice in her head proclaimed: *There once was a little girl named Tzlil, who thought her powers were real…* But Tzlil raised her own voice to the heavens and the birds took joyously to the sky. Tzlil repeated the ritual a third and fourth time. Each time the air above the cemetery fluttered with life.

One bird, however, remained perched on Tzlil's forearm, tilting its head with a sense of knowing anticipation. Its orange crown of feathers tipped with black stood proudly erect. It nudged Tzlil with its slender, pointed beak.

"You're free to go, *motek*," Tzlil said. "You're alive! Go!"

She tried to shake the bird loose but it looked at Tzlil and cried, "hoop-hoop-hoop," and spread its wings to display beautiful black and white striping. The bird nudged Tzlil again, its avian swagger on full display.

"What do you want?"

This time the bird jabbed Tzlil with its sharp needle-like beak, and was preparing to do so again when Tzlil grabbed at the bird, catching it around its torso.

They lifted into the air, Tzlil gripping the hoopoe as they rose higher and higher, her body weightless and profound, loosened from the constraints of gravity's relentless grip. Her heart raced as the wind rushed against her skin, her hair flowing behind her like a wave. The air around her was charged, alive with the embrace of the sun's warm rays. The stone squares of the gravestones below disappeared in the haze as Tzlil continued to rise. The hoopoe was much too small for Tzlil to ride on but she quickly learned she could direct which way the bird flew just through the simple energy pulses she sent into the bird's wings.

They flew above the somber city and its glass towers and boulevards, the pulsing vein of the Ayalon Highway, the blue eye of the fountain at Dizengoff Square. Tzlil saw the raging inferno where the university had stood, and the terrible gaping holes where fireballs struck on previous days, immense sorrow filling her with grief and determination.

Down below, the wail of sirens filled the air, alerting the citizens of Tel Aviv of an incoming threat. The bird cried, "hoop-hoop-hoop," and Tzlil turned the hoopoe towards Jaffa and its ancient port, where the prophet Jonah had boarded a ship bound for the remote city of Tarshish.

Tzlil didn't see the interceptor missile coming, but felt the concussion of its explosions nearby. She tumbled in a dizzying freefall, her hair burning behind her like a comet's tail. The city spun kaleidoscopically beneath her and it seemed she might crash to earth before she caught herself, pulling back on the hoopoe's wings. Together they raced westward, diving into the sea beyond the stone breakers, into the cool blue water to extinguish herself, clutching the hoopoe in her hands.

Beneath the surface of the sea she felt the pulsing of thousands upon thousands of *meduzot*, millions even, transmitting their primeval dictate. Her burnt clothing peeled off. She knew the hoopoe would die if she stayed under any longer, so she clutched it to her chest, its sharp beak pressing into her sternum, where it pierced the flesh and disappeared inside her.

A longboard surfer named Niv, respecting the stay-at-home order enough not to trek out to Bat Yam or Herzliya, was in search of waves in the waters beyond Dolphinarium Beach. He may have been high on Lebanese hash, but that wasn't enough to explain the glorious creature that burst out of the water nearby, a golden crest of feathers topping her head like a flame.

The skin of Tzlil's arms billowed out like a sail, feathers covering the entire surface, her hands transformed into deadly talons, her eyesight sharp as an eagle. And now she was flying for real, gliding above the sea, the salt air surging into her lungs. The sensation of flying didn't feel strange to Tzlil. It was as if she had always had the power to do so, as simple as breathing or tying her shoes, the air surrounding her giving just enough resistance for her to feel its embrace. The instant before the next interceptor missile took to the air, her heart fluttered and she cried out, "hoop-hoop-hoop," as she shot into the sky like a rocket.

This time she escaped the aftershock of the interceptor missile, flying up, up, up, the entire coastal plain consuming her field of vision. A great wind followed each flap of her wings, leaving a swirling vortex in her wake as she rose higher and higher. Sweeping red blankets of kalaniot flowers spread out beneath her as she rose above the Negev Desert. The Dead Sea and the Hashemite Kingdom of Jordan just across the brief expanse of salt water and minerals. Lake Kinneret and Lebanon to the north; its neighbors Syria, and Iran, and Iraq all appeared far beneath her, impossible to differentiate without the artificial lines set by European colonial powers more than a century earlier. Tzlil swung her attention to the leaf-shaped island of Cyprus, where her parents had married to escape the religious strictures of the orthodox rabbinate. Then south, where the verdant green of the Nile River Delta contrasted with the sandy triangle of the Sinai Peninsula, a desolate land bridge connecting Asia to Africa where Tzlil's ancestors once wandered for 40 years.

The sun became brighter as the air thinned and turned frigid. Tzlil's breath froze in crystalline clouds, delicate ice crystals forming as soon as the water vapor in her breath hit the air. She flew on, the sky around her a dark inky blue, the sun, an intense disc of white pulsing before her like a beacon. Soon, dancing streamers of purples and reds and greens rippled against the velvet curtain of the sky, undulating sheets of color shimmering in ghostly display. She didn't know where she was going, except that she had to go higher and higher, pressing ever onwards, towards what, she did not know. As she passed beyond the magnificent light show, Tzlil was swallowed by a dense eternal blackness, only the distant eye of the sun, dazzling in its intensity, hypnotic in its relentless pull, lighting the way.

Tzlil was wondering how far she was going to have to fly, and whether she would ever be able to find her way home again, when she saw at the far edges of her vision a towering figure of swirling blue fire—equal parts shadow and flame; an enormous, menacing beast with depthless black eyes and hungry teeth bared with razored intent. The monster floated in the sky, a long, whip-like tail of sulfurous fire and brimstone flicking wickedly back and forth across the endless expanse of black. One sweeping arm gathered spearlike beams of sun, bending and weaving them into a spinning sphere of flame which hung suspended before the beast, growing in size and intensity with each pass of the giant creature's arm.

Tzlil's neurons lit up with the understanding that this fiery behemoth had first burst into being billions of years before the separation of darkness and light, emerging from the formless chaos of the void to bring mayhem and destruction.

Tzlil flew as close to the beast as she could, its fiery breath a burning furnace, setting her feathers alight. She tumbled down, falling, falling forever, pursued by the maniac laughter of the voice in her head.

Finally, Tzlil managed to right herself, and she began her long fruitless ascent.

Tears filled her eyes because she knew she could not stop this creature, and that everyone she knew and loved would be incinerated by its molten flames. She imagined her mother reading a book in bed, the way the tip of her tongue slipped out of the corner of her mouth, and how her brows furrowed when she came to a particularly tense passage. She thought of her saba and savta arguing at their kitchen table over who had cheated at the latest game of shesh besh. She saw her friends laughing and eating chocolate pretzel ice cream at Golda. She thought of the old man with the numbers on his arm who lived in the building across the way, playing the saddest songs on his piano she had ever heard. She even thought about Hezi, the watermelon man at the Carmel Market, who knew just where to tap the fruit to determine which one was the sweetest.

She shouted in her most piercing voice, but the creature took no notice of Tzlil as if she were just an insignificant speck of matter floating through the darkness. It continued with its grim task of weaving the radiant blades into the seething fireball.

"Stop! Stop right now." But her voice could find no purchase in the thin air of the upper atmosphere and her words disappeared into nothing, like a candle snuffed out.

Tzlil tried again to raise her voice, to roar in defiance! but before she could do so, wicked laughter filled her head, echoing off the walls of her skull. The laughter was cruel and pointed, and she knew it was aimed at her and her failure to vanquish the beast.

The monster twisted and braided the radiant power of the sun into a monumental projectile, larger even than the ones terrorizing Tel Aviv.

The voice inside her head spoke: "*Are you ready to meet your maker?*"

Before Tzlil had a chance to consider the question, she was rocketing downward through the darkness, the pressure in her ears intense, her eyes wide and watering as she descended. Soon she was flying west over the Mediterranean, and then the Atlantic Ocean opened up before her, the scream of jet engines regularly breaking the silence somewhere beneath her. Soon the East Coast of the United States appeared, and she passed over cities she had always wanted to visit, their lights glittering below like jewels. She was low enough now to see that a small city was approaching, the ordered gridlike pattern of its tree-lined streets unfolding beneath her.

And then she was crashing through the window of a ramshackle house, landing at last in a pile of dirty laundry on an unmade bed.

The first thing Tzlil realized was the room smelled thickly of something sweet and fruity and chemical. As she climbed off the bed, she understood she no longer had deadly talons; her feathers had been replaced by her mom's yoga pants and her T-shirt with the pink lightning bolt exclamation point, to match her pink Chuck Taylors. Her Star of David headband held back her unruly hair.

She was greeted with a cackling gale of laughter by a boy of about 18 years old who sat before a bank of computer monitors in a high-backed swivel chair, his blue dye job faded to an ashy grey. Posters calling for liberation and resistance covered his walls.

"You made it!" the boy said. He wore a checkered headscarf around his neck and had silver snakebite piercings on his lower lip. He took a hit off his vape pen, a cloud of vapor obscuring his pale features.

"Where am I?" Tzlil said. "What's going on?"

"I'm Kyle. And you're Tzlil."

"What am I doing here?" Nothing made any sense.

"I summoned you." Kyle took another hit off his vape pen. "Just like I summoned Dakhsara, who I believe you've met."

Tzlil's head spun. The presence of Kyle seemed stranger and somehow more unlikely than the discovery of the creature.

"I low-key didn't think it was going to happen. It took me a fuck ton of time, and I ran thousands of AI models, but I found the code to summon Dakhsara from the darkness. And you of course."

Tzlil's jaw dropped open in confusion.

"The code needed me to include a hero to counterbalance Dakhsara."

"Code?"

"Technically, yes, but really a magic spell."

Humiliated, Tzlil felt like collapsing into herself and disappearing. "Why did you choose me?"

"I saw your stupid TikTok, you and your spazzy friends dancing like fools to stop the rockets. It was the most pathetic thing I've ever seen. So I chose you to be the hero. I mean, look at you: nerdy girl badly in need of braces and a nose job. Who could be more useless than that? And look how you're dressed. Pretending to be a superhero. It's so sad. It's almost adorable."

That laughter again.

Tzlil balled her fists, but her superhuman strength had left her. "Why are you trying to destroy my city?"

"I've seen your terror," Kyle said unsmilingly. "And it's beautiful."

"People are dying!"

"People have always died and will always die. Why not have some fun?"

"This isn't some video game."

"For me it is." He took another hit from his vape pen. "I'm

just a keyboard warrior." Kyle laughed again, as if he had said something funny.

"You have to stop this."

"It'll all be over soon."

"What do you mean?"

"Dakhsara has just been playing. The next fireball will finish the job."

"No!" Tzlil screamed, lunging at Kyle.

He simply spun in his chair, offering his back. The monitors continued flashing with endless lines of code filling the screens.

Tzlil tried to appeal to Kyle's reason. "You're committing genocide."

"You want to talk about genocide?"

"Who told you to do this?"

"You don't follow @WalidDaqqasDeadBaby? He's super righteous. He put out the call. And I answered."

Kyle turned back to the keyboard, scanned the monitor and typed in a string of code. "I'm working on a number of operations all over the world."

"Real people are dying," Tzlil pleaded. "This isn't a game."

"You had your chance to take that up with Dakhsara."

"How can I..."

"You were chosen to be your people's champion and you took the L."

"What?"

"You lost. It's over."

"It can't be," Tzlil tried to roar, but her voice broke. "How do I stop him?"

"Them. How do I stop *them*."

"How? How? Just tell me how."

"You'd have to input the code and tell it to kill itself. But I programmed it so your fate and Dakhsara's are bound together, which means if they die, so do you."

"Give me the code," Tzlil said, glaring at Kyle with a killing stare.

"Ooooh, I'm scared. You look like you're going to cry."

Kyle took another hit of his vape and blew the poisonous vapor into Tzlil's face. "It won't be long now. Why don't you stay for the show? I'm connected to cameras all over Tel Aviv."

Kyle clicked a button and one of the monitors filled with a grid of live videos. Some of the images were grainy, and some were clear. It was morning, and the sun was shining. Tzlil could see a couple strolling hand-in-hand along the tree lined walkway of Rothschild Boulevard; another showed clusters of young people keeping vigil in Hostages Square.

"You want some popcorn," Kyle said, standing up for the first time since Tzlil had crashed through his bedroom window.

He wasn't that much taller than Tzlil, slightly built with a subtle curve to his spine.

Tzlil felt a flutter of wings in her chest and then she cried out her war whoop, "Hoop-hoop-hoop," and punched Kyle right in the nose.

Kyle dropped to the floor like a bag of wet sand.

Tzlil grabbed Kyle's phone off his desk and opened it with

his battered face. She found the code at the top of his notes app because Kyle was the kind of person who would do that. Tzlil typed it into Kyle's computer.

She looked at Tel Aviv one last time, basking in the glorious spring sunshine, said goodbye to her mother and her saba and savta and all her friends, and input the instruction to kill Dakhsara.

Tzlil hit the return key.

END

—

JONATHAN PAPERNICK was born and raised in Toronto, Canada. He is the author of the acclaimed short story collection *The Ascent of Eli Israel*, another collection, *There is No Other*, and the novels *The Book of Stone* and *I Am My Beloveds*. His work has received starred reviews from Publishers Weekly and Library Journal and has been translated into Spanish and Italian. Papernick has taught fiction writing at Emerson College since 2007 and serves as Assistant Professor in the Department of Writing, Literature and Publishing. He is currently at work on *The Oppressor Professor: A Novel of the Tentifada*.

MONTRÉAL

Su J Sokol and D.F. McCourt

Grey snow blankets the mountain, looking whiter and whiter as dawn creeps up. Under the snow is garbage and shit and filth, and maybe everyone else in Montréal can pretend it's not there when winter is wrapped around the city's shoulders like an old wool scarf, but JC has always been better at seeing things. Clambering up onto the low stone balustrade of Kondiaronk lookout, he sees the squat buildings of Pine Avenue and Sherbrooke Street huddled at the base of the mountain like sick stray dogs, shivering and mange-ridden and ready to bite. He sees the tall icy towers of de Maisonneuve and Sainte-Catherine jutting out of the frozen earth like shards of bone through broken skin. As the first sliver of orange sun breaks over the river, JC pulls open his fly and pisses a hot stream out into the cold air of the void, leaving a ragged scar of yellow across the snow of the southern slope.

Then, before the first self-satisfied morning hikers can crunch,

crunch up the footpath, JC hurries down the steep switchback stairs, muttering to himself the whole way. His thoughts always get a little more voicey when he hasn't slept. He's been walking all night, keeping the blood flowing because, even though it's April, the dark is killing cold in the open.

It's been twelve hours since the SPVM cruisers rolled up, since the jackboots spilled out with their matraques and their box cutters, slashing through the canopy of the tent Smriti gave him.

"You don't need no tent, Jean-Claude," he says to himself as people begin to stir in the sick-dog buildings. "Got an apartment now, remember? Be move-in day before you know it."

He walks slowly, favouring his bad foot, and the sun is full up by the time he's through downtown and across the bridge to Pointe-Saint-Charles. There it is, Tour Victoire, fifteen stories of hard steel, fresh-poured concrete, and pristine glass windows, blinding bright in the morning sun that's even now beginning to melt the snow. His home. Somewhere in there. He'll need to ask Madame Smriti again which window is his.

JC approaches through the park behind the building, where the encampment had been. The slashed tents have mostly been hauled off; the cops have even smashed up the little palette-and-tarp lean-to Annick built against the dumpster. He pokes through the wreckage for anything of value. Annick still owes him two bucks or half a beer, and who knows when he'll see her next? He's not sure which window is hers, either.

All he finds is a single salty quarter in a bootprint, probably dropped way back in December before the real staying-snow came. Lots of things are going to start showing up with the melt, he thinks. They always do. JC pockets the quarter and magnanimously subtracts it from Annick's debt, even though she surely had nothing to do with it.

He's looking with his true-seeing eyes now and thinking how Annick calls it his divine sight, though there's nothing godly in what he sees. "Garbage and shit and filth. And quarters."

Over at the base of the tower, behind the dumpster, JC finds Annick's rosary beads with the finger-worn pewter crucifix. He curses the cops because the crucifix so rarely left Annick's hands that she must've been truly terrorized to have dropped it. He bends down to retrieve the rosary from the dirty snow piled against the tower wall, black and yellow and melting slower than the rest. And then he sees something else.

There's a cancerous growth, the size of his head, bulging out from the smooth poured concrete foundation of his future home. The whole tumour is slick and grey-pink like a stillborn rat, with a tracery of blue running across it like veins.

"Get out," JC tells it. "Go away. That's my home you're growing on, câlice."

In response, a deep, dark shape within the tumour stirs, its movement wrought as a sickening ripple across the fleshy surface.

Patricia Abernathy exits her two million dollar Westmount pied-à-terre and walks in long, confident strides towards her black Mercedes, anticipating the triumphant rev of its turbocharged engine. The sun is high in the sky, melting the remaining snow on the sidewalk. Maybe the accursed winter is finally over. People complain about global warming, but Patricia would not be sorry to never again see snow outside of the kitschy snow globe her secretary gave her for Christmas.

She notes that the immigrant she'd hired to shovel out her car didn't show up today. Fortunately, most of the snow has melted. Even as she watches, thick, wet layers of it slough off her car's roof like white flesh from a bone. She shivers, thinking of the last time she saw her father at the hospice in Florida, the cancer eating away at his body, his once-firm flesh loose and sagging. She decides to call an Uber.

Exiting the car, Patricia slips on some dog shit exposed by the melting snow and tumbles to the sidewalk, coming nose to nose with a crushed water bottle, a flapping candy wrapper, and a takeout container spilling congealed, vomit-coloured rice. Lazy, good-for-nothing garbage men and their pointless strike!

The turbaned Uber driver rushes to her side. "Pourrais-je vous aider à vous relever, madame?"

"Thank you. I don't require assistance." From you or from anyone.

Patricia rises on her own and brushes herself off, hurrying

to the press conference. She smiles, imagining the deferential reporters, the obsequious officials from the Office Municipal d'habitation de Montréal, and even that adorably naive social worker, Smurfy or whatever, all praising Patricia for the social housing she's promised to include in her most ambitious condo project to date. Promises are easy to make.

"… to not only build housing for hardworking families and individuals in need but provide them and their neighbours with a revitalized community!"

Smriti watches the sun slip out from behind the clouds to light the sidewalk where they're all gathered for the press conference. As though Abernathy had paid off even the weather to conspire with her. Smriti glances across the street at Abernathy's last "community project"—a string of ugly high-rises that displaced the lower-income residents of this quartier—and it's all she can do not to gag on the nakedly fake community sentiment.

"Can you comment on the claim that the building is non-compliant with city by-laws concerning construction on brownfields?" asks a reporter from RadMots, a well-known socialist journal.

"Absolutely false," says Abernathy. "Not only have we followed every by-law to the letter, we've gone beyond the minimal requirements to provide both private and social housing units that are not only safe but spacious. Tomorrow, a senior member of the Régie du batiment will do a final inspection, and I am fully confident of the result. Now I pass the parole to Sm…to a representative of Se soulever de la rue, whose community support of this project has been invaluable."

The reporters turn to Smriti. She takes a breath and begins her own statement, first in French and then in English. She tries to bring enthusiasm to her voice by picturing her clients safe and warm in apartments of their very own. When she finishes, a few easy questions are lobbed her way. She answers them mechanically, a smile pasted to her face, wondering what Alyx would say. Probably something about collaborating with the devil or using the master's tools. Then the reporter, generally an ally, repeats the question about the structural integrity of the building.

"As a grassroots organization working with the unhoused, we don't have expertise—"

"Madame Smriti! Madame Smriti!" a familiar voice calls.

Smriti turns and spies her client, Jean-Claude Lacroix, limping his way over to her, his gait unbalanced, maybe by his meds, maybe by withdrawal from not taking them, maybe by diabetes sores on his feet, or maybe just from having gone on a bender.

Smriti waves to him, then returns her attention to the reporter. "As I was saying, the municipal inspectors—"

"Madame Smriti! It's Jean-Claude! I need to tell you about the building. It has cancer! I saw the growths this morning—"

"Jean-Claude, not now. A building can't have cancer," she says, putting up her hand to keep him from coming into camera range. She faces the reporter to finish her response.

Once she's done, Smriti finally searches for Jean-Claude, hoping to reassure him. He's nowhere to be found. The only sign of his presence is the butt of one of his hand-rolled cigarettes, crushed into the dirty, melting snow where he'd just been standing.

Smriti kicks slush from her boots as she climbs the stone front steps of Alyx's apartment, trying not to feel taunted by the "À Louer" sign in the window above the corner dépanneur. She doesn't have the fortitude right now to find out how much they're asking.

Stepping through Alyx's front door, Smriti briefly closes her eyes and wills them not to be home, even though she saw their green single-speed locked up out front. Alyx rarely goes anywhere without their bike, even in the coldest months of winter.

Sure enough, their singsong voice comes lilting from the back room. "Hey honey, you're home!"

Smriti squeezes her eyes more tightly closed lest she start to cry. "I'm not your honey, *babe*. You broke up with me three months ago, remember?"

She really needs to get her own place before Alyx's unrelenting tenderness kills her. This would be so much easier if they'd just had the decency to kick her out when they broke her heart. Now that she thinks about it, it's way past time for that fight.

"You know," Smriti says as she finally opens her eyes. "It's kinda cruel that—WHAT THE FUCK?"

There's a dead mouse at eye level, not four feet from Smriti's face. The mouse is clasped between the bright green-toothed leaves of a Venus fly trap so Little-Shop-of-Horrors-huge it can only be the result of one of Alyx's "experiments."

"Oh," says Alyx, drifting into the living room in a pink muumuu printed with black pentacles. "I see you've met Laurence."

"Is Laurence the plant or the dead fucking rat?"

"I didn't name the mouse," they say. "Maybe I should have?"

Smriti flops onto the corduroy couch, not even caring about the bottle of sage oil that falls to the floor, rolls across the pine boards, and disappears under the antique Singer sewing machine. "Why the hell is my vegan ex keeping mutant carnivorous plants in our living room?"

"All plants are carnivorous," Alyx says. "It's only a question of how patient they are."

"Think you can get one of them to eat Patricia Abernathy for me?"

Rather than answering, Alyx drifts across the room to the attached kitchen, patting Laurence affectionately like a cat as they pass. They start the electric kettle and then pull a series of unlabelled glass jars from the shelf, each filled with the dried leaves and stems of a different herb or weed.

"So the press conference went badly, I take it?" Alyx asks, placing a hot cup of tea in Smriti's hands and settling down onto the couch, so close that Smriti can feel the warmth of their thigh. The fragrant steam rising from the tea casts a spell that tries to rob Smriti of her well-earned anger and frustration.

"Obviously," Smriti says, fighting the witchy vapours. "I'm certain that awful woman has no intention of letting even one unhoused person move into her building. At this point, I'm almost ready to believe she delayed through the winter on purpose, hoping they'd all just die in the snow. I'm fighting so hard, Alyx, but I just can't win."

Alyx lifts a hand as though to gently stroke her hair, but Smriti catches their fingers in an awkward clasp.

"Apparently, Tour Victoire has cancer anyway," Smriti sighs.

Alyx pulls their hand free and gets a serious look in their eyes. "The building has cancer?"

"It's just something Jean-Claude was yelling about," Smriti says. "He's having a rough time. It's nothing."

Alyx stands, visibly agitated. "Jean-Claude sees things better than you realize, Smee. Those chemicals they dumped on the mountain in the fall, the garbage they piled in the parks, it's been festering beneath the snow all winter. There's a sickness under the skin of the city. But I didn't think it would spread so fast. What exactly did Jean-Claude say?"

"He said he saw growths on the building," Smriti says, and as soon as the words are out of her mouth, Alyx disappears into their bedroom. "Their" singular now, Smriti reminds herself. Alyx reemerges moments later, shoving the hem of their muumuu into the top of a pair of brown overalls. They grab their bike key from the windowsill.

"You're not going to Tour Victoire?" Smriti asks, alarmed. "Please don't make things worse for me."

"Smee," they say as they step into their boots. "I love you, but you'll have to trust me."

"Please don't—" Smriti calls, but they're already out the door.

Smriti sighs and slumps further into the couch. "Please don't say you love me."

Every fibre of Alyx's being is urging them towards Tour Victoire, but they resist. If the rot is there, it's elsewhere, too. They'll find it without tracking mud through Smee's world.

Instead, they go to the grounds of Maison St. Gabriel to visit the great willow tree that resides there. As Alyx pedals the path of Parc Marguerite-Bourgeoys, splitting the slush into tiny tsunamis with the bike's thin tires, they can see the broad winter-bare canopy of the wise old willow—spreading countless sensitive fingertips across the sky—well before the Maison itself comes into view. The willow—called Salix and Óse in older tongues—will be among the first to leaf out when the weather warms. And, with roots spread invisibly in all directions, reaching below and beyond the steel ribbons of train tracks that separate the grounds from the river, the willow will know what host rides in with the spring.

When Alyx reaches the willow, they find they're not alone. A young nun they know well—Sister Marie-Hélène—is gathering snowberries from a row of nearby shrubs. The berries are poisonous, Alyx knows, but also full of medicinal potential, much like the willow itself.

Alyx dismounts the green bicycle, leaning it against a low wrought iron fence. They nod to Marie-Hélène and then wade through the snow to the base of the willow tree. Placing one hand on the red-gray lichenous bark, they close their eyes in communion. There is a deep sadness in the tree and also a deep conviction. Alyx can feel the willow gathering its strength, preparing itself for an unprecedented mast year, for a spring it expects to be its last. A great battle is coming, and it cannot be won; it can only be lost with dignity.

"The plants can sense things we don't, n'est-ce pas?" Marie-Hélène says.

Alyx opens their eyes. "Yes. But they're willing to tell us some of their secrets if we listen."

The nun purses her lips and looks out across the train tracks. She thinks for a long time before speaking again.

"I heard you and Smriti broke up."

Alyx laughs sadly. "Who have you been spilling tea with, Sister?"

"I see a lot of her people at the soup kitchen on Saturdays. We talk. What happened?"

"She loved me too much," Alyx says, speaking the truth they could never voice to Smriti. "And I was worried a time would come when her love for me would keep her from doing what she needed to do. It's better for her if she hates me just a little."

Marie-Hélène frowns. "Shouldn't that be her choice?"

"Probably," Alyx admits, knowing as they say it that their voice betrays them for a snowberry. Alyx has so desperately wanted to be wrong, wanted Smriti to be right. The world would be a far better place if Smee's unending empathy and gumption were enough. But deep down, Alyx has always known they wouldn't be. Still, Alyx refused to stand in the way as Smriti tried. No matter how much it hurt both of them. Alyx still hoped to be proven wrong.

But the willow tree continues to speak through the palm of their hand. Telling them they'd been right all along. Alyx can feel the rot very close all around. But they still need to see it for themselves. They suddenly remember there's a gas station at Wellington and Bridge. If it's anywhere, it will be there.

Alyx whispers a thank you to the willow and retrieves their bicycle.

"And what about you?" Sister Marie-Hélène asks as Alyx mounts the bike. "Won't love stay your hand?"

Alyx pedals hard and fast towards Rue Wellington, calling back over their shoulder. "I hope not, Sister!"

Patricia notices something disturbing the clean, straight lines of Tour Victoire. A globular, tumescent shape where man-made squares and rectangles should reign. She grabs a metal pole sticking out of the nearby dumpster—probably from one of those homeless-people tents the social workers were giving out to those vagrants in the park before she put a stop to that—and pokes at the quivery mass tentatively. It undulates, making her stomach turn, but Patricia does not back off. Like her father always said, "If you push and you still don't get what you're after, push harder."

Patricia stabs at it viciously. It undulates again, but this time, rather than return to its former shape, it stretches and contorts, like a snake eating an egg in reverse. Then, it divides, giving birth to a second ugly lump.

Now, two pinkish-grey cysts cling parasitically to the base of her building. A phlegmy discharge splooges onto the sidewalk beneath them. It reminds her uncomfortably of those images of her father's cancer cells she'd demanded his doctor show her. And there was that crazy homeless man at the press conference, she recalls, claiming her building had cancer. She decides to call Smurfy, find out the man's name, and ban him from the building forever.

Just then, Patricia spots the inspector she's supposed to be meeting. She tries to intercept him, but it's too late. His eyes widen as he notices the cysts.

"I can explain," Patricia says as the inspector squats beside the growth to touch it tentatively with one gloved fingertip. "It's…vandalism," she declares.

"Vandalism?" he says, standing. "Je ne suis pas imbecile. I may have fallen on hard times, but I know my métier."

"And I know mine," Patricia says, standing tall. "This is not my first condo development, and it won't be my last. And if you know what's best, you'll honour our agreement."

"It's one thing to ignore certain overly bureaucratic regulations. It's another to turn a blind eye to…to that! Tabarnouche, the foundation of your building is bulging!

A pot-de-vin, even a large one, is not enough to make me overlook such a thing."

"Monsieur, I understand your position, and just as you record the results of your inspections, so have I recorded the many conversations we've had on this subject."

Patricia nearly laughs at the look of shock and betrayal on his face.

"Of course, no one will ever know," she continues, "so long as you don't cross me. Écoute, I am not unsympathetic to your situation. My husband tried to milk me of every last cent when we parted ways. I know the marital home is a bone of contention between you and your ex. With housing prices as high as they are, perhaps I can sweeten the pot."

Patricia digs around in her bag until she finds the item she's seeking. "Voilà!" she says, brandishing a shiny silver key.

"What is it?" the inspector asks warily.

"This opens the deluxe penthouse apartment. Would you like to see it?"

Without waiting for his response, Patricia heads for the entrance to the building. The inspector obediently follows behind her.

There's a feverish warmth radiating up through the asphalt and concrete everywhere JC goes. The snow is melting fast now, rivers of sweat heavy with floating refuse flooding the streets.

In Parc Arthur-Therrien, the air is cooler, but those who

spent Montréal's long winter in warm houses with mulled wine and YouTube mindfulness seminars are nonetheless out in droves. They're jogging along the footpaths and tossing frisbees between the mountains of uncleared garbage left over from the sanitation grève in the fall. No one but JC seems to notice that the trash piles are breathing, that the great oceans of melt are streaked with bile. A toddler clad in high-vis shakes a tupperware of raw zucchini happily at JC as he stumbles past. JC rushes towards the bramble of water birch and phragmites at the river's edge.

As soon as he's through the dense wild growth, looking out at the quiet towers of Île des Sœurs rising from the high spring waters of Fleuve Saint-Laurent, JC pulls his tobacco pouch from the pocket of his jacket, so he can finally think.

As he rolls his cigarette, he watches water vomiting endlessly from the storm drain outlet a dozen paces downriver. The huge bag of netting the city workers have fit over the pipe like a condom is swollen to bursting with trash, a great sausage of filth bobbing and writhing in the water. Something flesh-brown and incongruous catches his eye in the mess. He blinks and sees a hand tangled in the netting, two broken fingers splayed out at horrific angles, and a wrist that disappears into a blue wool duffle coat JC sickens to recognize. With a small spasm of the river, the trash net rolls and then Annick's dead eyes stare out at him, seeing nothing.

JC jumps to his feet, the breeze scattering his tobacco across the water.

"We were supposed to be neighbours," he accuses miserably. "Osti de crisse de tabarnak, Annick."

He needs to find Madame Smriti and tell her everything he's seen. Annick always believed he could see true and now he'll have to make Madame Smriti believe too. She wasn't ready to hear it yesterday, but today she will have to.

JC is wheezing and dragging his bad foot when he finally reaches the office of Se soulever de la rue. But the lights are all off, and the door is locked when he tries it.

He collapses on the doorstep and pulls out Annick's rosary, squeezing the crucifix so tightly he can feel blood seeping from his palm. He opens all his eyes. Though this little rue—all century-old duplexes filled with families and the occasional street-level converted storefront—seems mostly untouched by the spreading sickness, JC can perceive the cancer in the blood, rolling down the road disguised as SUVs and subcompacts.

He watches a woman driving a little imported pustule pull over as the vehicle shudders beneath her. Suddenly, the hood flies open, and a geyser of black ichor spews from the radiator, scorching the air and sizzling on contact with the wet asphalt.

JC jolts to his feet and staggers as fast as he can away from the dying thing and the crowd that gathers around it. From the end of the block, JC sees a terrible angel bearing down on him.

Their hair is a dense tangle of thorny twigs, and there's a green fire burning bright in their eyes. They fly down the street like a vengeful revenant. JC blinks. The angel is a person now, riding a green-painted bicycle.

"I know you," JC says to them, voice thin. "You're the witch."

"Yes, Jean-Claude," Alyx says. "You see me right."

"It killed Annick," JC says. "It's everywhere. You have to stop it."

"I'm trying, Jean-Claude. I'm going to the mountain now. You should come with me."

"No," JC says. "I have to go home."

Alyx stands on their pedals as they climb Rue Peel towards the mountain. They wish they could have spent more time trying to convince Jean-Claude to come with them. They fear that the rosary they'd seen dangling from his hand would not be enough to protect him in the face of an armageddon waged between forces orthogonal to the concerns of young human gods. But if Alyx is going to save anyone, they can't waste time trying to save everyone. As the way grows steeper, they only hope they aren't already too late.

Mont-Royal has always been a three-headed beast. When a fourth peak formed by the illegal dumping of toxic garbage began to rival the first three, Alyx knew it was time for an intervention. Alyx had sown the first battalions of their herbal army back in the autumn and had equipped them with the strength they'd need to reclaim the mountain from its long despoliation. The toxic waste seeping through the mountain soil would not hinder the growth of Alyx's green-stemmed darlings. It was a source of nutrition for them, and the plants' appetites would only grow the more toxins they absorbed. Once Mount-Royal was cleansed, Alyx had intended to transplant contingents of their legion to the other smaller parks around the city where similar affronts had occurred.

Alyx had not been certain their plan would succeed. When prey becomes predator, there's always a moment of transition in which it could go either way. Alyx is encouraged, however, by what they see. While the city slept beneath snow and ice, Alyx's hungry plants have matured and grown, feasting on an endless banquet of viscous fluids and metals.

Around the perimeter of Mont Royal, the transformation has not yet taken hold. Alyx leans their bike against the scored trunk of a maple tree. The bike will be safer here; the hungry new plants like steel too well. Alyx continues on foot.

As they approach the towering young forest of grasping, long-vined beauties, Alyx breathes in a heady mix of odours, green and juicy, a humid, almost meaty, stench trapped within a heavy floral haze. Alyx revels in this wild, savage perfume as they climb higher. The plants are taller and stronger here. Alyx stops to stroke the smooth, baby-green leaves of a particularly healthy specimen. It turns its tulip-shaped lips towards them. Alyx fishes their cell phone out of their pocket—they won't need it anymore—and places it within the plant's pink, salivating petals. The plant closes around this delicious morsel, seeming to tremble with ecstasy before rubbing one of its spiked leaves gently against Alyx's hand.

When Alyx reaches the highest summit, Colline de la Croix, they see that the new life form has eaten away most of the giant cross that had gazed down paternalistically upon the city all these years.

"Sorry, Sister," Alyx murmurs. "It was only a thing of steel."

Alyx thinks of Jean-Claude's rosary and knows that Marie-Hélène would understand. The meek shall yet inherit the earth.

But not without help. The horrors Alyx had seen at the gas station had been easy as entrails to read. The rot is no longer confined to the parks and the mountain. It is spreading even now through the whole length and width of their beloved island of Tiohtià:ke. It is in the lines and the pumps and the sewers, invading and growing stronger in the city's energy-sucking glass and metal towers, its guzzling, spewing cars and trucks. And it will not stop there.

Beside the place where the cross stood is the plaque, which marks the burial place for a time capsule filled with messages from children to be found by later generations. Alyx digs up the missives of peace and hope and sets them aflame, one by one. Calling upon their strongest magic, Alyx cuts their own arm, combining their blood with the ashes of those children's dreams. To that potion, they add the pollen and seeds of this new hungry flora that grows at the very top of the mountain. Soon, a tiny green shoot begins to emerge from the soil of the offering. In moments, it goes from sprout to juvenile, to full maturity, to seed, until it finally resembles nothing so much as the gigantic seed puff of a preternatural dandelion.

Alyx lifts the seedhead into the air and calls upon the wind to scatter their children throughout the city. Sometimes, the seeds of rebirth must also contain the seeds of destruction.

"What the hell is Alyx up to?" Smriti asks Laurence, who she could swear has tripled in size over the last twenty-four hours. She pours some water into his pot, opens the kitchen window against the fetid, unseasonable heat, and resumes her pacing, sweat beading on her neck.

"Meow."

For half a second, Smriti thinks she's losing her mind. Talking *to* plants is one thing. She narrows her eyes and wonders if Alyx has insinuated feline DNA into Laurence. That would explain the mice. Then she sees the black tail swishing on the kitchen counter and realizes she let the neighbour's half-feral cat, Minuit, in with the breeze.

Before Smriti can shoo Minuit back out, her phone rings. Private number.

"Alyx?"

"Hello, Smurfy," says a singsong voice on the line. "I hope I didn't bother you."

"Madame Abernathy?"

"I have wonderful news," Patricia says with a whisky-soaked giggle. "The city inspector has approved Tour Victoire for immediate occupancy."

"That's…great!" Worries about Alyx vanish from her mind.

"Come and celebrate with me, dear. I just opened an 18-year-old and—"

"You…you did what?"

"Scotch, dear. Come, it'll be fun."

Smriti can't tell if Patricia is taunting her or hitting on her. She's not thrilled about either possibility. "I'd really love to, Ms. Abernathy, but I have work to do."

"Don't be such a stick in the mud. Or, think of it as work. I've been going over the tenant list. That crazy homeless man, the one who said my building had cancer? I really do think a mental health facility would be more appropriate. And there are some other names—all clients of yours, I believe—who I may also need to strike from the list for…various reasons."

"Ms. Abernathy—"

"Patricia."

"Patricia. Please don't do that." Silence. "Alright, I'll be right over. We'll look at the list together, and we'll come to an agreement—in writing. Where are you?"

"Why, I'm at the Victoire, dear. In the penthouse. I'll look forward to it."

"Fuck," Smriti says as soon as the line goes dead. She rushes into the study, now doubling as her bedroom, and grabs her most conservative blouse and jacket from the laundry pile on the floor.

Passing back through the living room, she's startled to notice that Laurence's planter sits empty, a track of potting soil leading towards the kitchen. She glances over just in time to see him disappear out the window, trailing a swollen green cat-sized pod.

When Smriti arrives at Tour Victoire, she's surprised to see thick, emerald ivy covering the exterior of the lower three floors. One vine has even infiltrated the lobby, propping the front door ajar. None of this was here yesterday. Weird as hell, but landscaping is not Smriti's most pressing concern.

As she rides the glass panoramic elevator up to the penthouse, smoothing her jacket and searching for the words that will fix everything, Smriti watches Pointe-Saint-Charles fall away below her. It is green everywhere. Too green. New ivy climbs the walls of every high and mid-rise in sight. Over by the train tracks, a huge willow tree towers in full leaf, taller than any tree she can remember seeing there before. And where the gas station at Wellington and Bridge should be, a great knot of vines seems to thrash like a pack of coyotes on a fresh kill.

The elevator opens with a soft chime, and Patricia Abernathy is waiting for her with glassy eyes, a sloppy grin, and two cut crystal glasses of amber liquid.

"My father would turn in his grave to see me drinking this vintage on ice," Patricia says, waving Smriti in and placing a cold tumbler in her hand. "But I prefer it this way, and I refuse to apologize for my tastes. Try to appreciate it to the extent that you're able."

Smriti represses the urge to throw the glass across the room and through the huge picture window. Instead, she swallows the Scotch in one caustic gulp.

"I want to talk about Jean-Claude and the others."

"Of course, of course," Patricia says with a chuckle. "But there's no rush. We have all evening. Slàinte Mhath!"

Patricia tosses her own drink back and then plucks the empty tumbler from Smriti's hand, carrying both over to an obscene walnut and granite bar where a half-full bottle sits next to a bag of dépanneur ice.

Smriti accepts a refill in a nightmare trance. She sleepwalks over to the window and gazes out at the city she loves, wishing it would for once let her help it. A tracery of green passes in front of her eyes. She steps back from the glass in alarm. The ivy is growing so fast that the vines branch, grasp, and sprout huge fresh leaves in the space of a breath.

"Sorry I can't offer you anywhere to sit," Patricia is saying behind her. "The new tenant will be moving in shortly. I understand she has very particular tastes in furniture and knick-knacks."

Smriti turns towards Patricia just as the filigree copper ceiling panels above her begin to split. The crack in the ceiling yawns wider and wider as Patricia sips her Scotch with a self-satisfied sigh.

"You know," Patricia begins after a moment, "I do admire your spirit and hard work, dear. You're…delightfully innocent—"

Her speech is cut short by a vine from above that lashes around her face faster than any living thing should be able to move. More tendrils shoot down and wrap around her limbs, lifting her bodily from the hardwood floor as her eyes go wide and her cheeks redden.

Smriti takes a quick step forward, certain she should help though she has no idea how, and then the vines convulse and tear Patricia Abernathy apart, showering Smriti in blood and viscera.

Smriti retches and stumbles for the elevator, but as soon as she presses the call button, the power goes out. A sickening groan of steel reverberates all around her, and then the picture windows shatter all at once. The taut vines of ivy outside have grown thicker than tree trunks, and they squeeze like the tentacles of a kraken.

She tries 911, but the system is overwhelmed. Using the phone flashlight, she finds the emergency stairs and rushes down and down until, after three floors, the stairwell becomes an impassable jungle of snaking vines.

Smriti bursts out into the dark twelfth-floor hallway, gasping and sobbing as the building trembles around her. At the end of the hall, one of the doors swings open, and a silhouette of a man steps out, holding a bic lighter aloft.

"Madame Smriti?"

"Jean-Claude?"

"The door was open," Jean-Claude says. "I couldn't remember which apartment was mine, so I just picked one. I hope that's okay."

Smriti grabs Jean-Claude by the hand as she runs past him into his apartment. There's a sleeping bag on the kitchen floor and three cans of soup on the counter, one of them dented from where it's been used to hammer a bent nail into the wall. From the nail hangs a crucifix.

Smriti drags Jean-Claude to the balcony, where she is horrified to see downtown in flames. A vast cloud of ash and dust obscures the mountain. The huge skyscraper of Place Ville Marie is pulled down in slow motion before her eyes.

Green ropes of ivy cocoon all around them, and before Smriti can react, two vines lasso out to encircle her. She screams, remembering Patricia. The vines tighten and lift her from the balcony.

In the corner of her eye, Smriti sees a furry black tail swishing from a green clamped-tooth maw. It's not the building-crushing vine that has grabbed her. Laurence's embrace is firm, but she knows in her heart that he isn't here to hurt her.

She tries to pull Jean-Claude to her, to enfold him, but he pulls his hand from her grip and steps back through the balcony door.

"I live here," Jean-Claude says. "This is my home."

Laurence falls free of the building, Smriti swaddled in his runners. He spreads his broad tarpaulin leaves and glides through the muggy apocalypse sky. Smriti averts her eyes as Tour Victoire begins to crumble. She feels a small leafy tendril gently stroke her hair, just like Alyx used to.

Alyx cycles from one newly verdant neighbourhood to the next, regarding their handiwork. No, not *their* handiwork. Alyx had held the brush and mixed the paint, but every artist knows that once the œuvre is released out into the world, it's no longer yours. It belongs to everyone, and it morphs and twists and grows as it will. Perhaps that's for the best.

The survivors of the spring equinox—human and otherwise—gather at the foot of the mountain, inexorably drawn to the powers that dwell there, and this, too, is as it should be. Alyx does their best to help ragtag wanderers to safety. Communities are already beginning to coalesce as groups find their way to shelter-like clusters of plants that Alyx assures them are safe. Alyx has harboured no ambition to be a leader, but they recognize this new world yet needs more from them. They will return later to give more guidance. But first, they must make sure Smriti is okay.

For a neighbourhood so far from the mountain, Point-Ste-Charles's transformation from a place of rot-riddled structures to a leafy green triumph has been rapid and comprehensive. The great willow stretches above like a monarch, and Alyx veers toward it instinctively. At the base of the tree, several dozen people are huddled like refugees. Alyx recognizes a woman clutching a frayed sleeping bag as one of Smee's clients.

"Have you seen Smriti?" Alyx asks.

The woman stares at Alyx in numb shock. An adolescent—maybe the woman's child—puts an arm around her and says, "I think she might've been at the building. You know, Tour Victoire. We all heard it collapse, but we're scared to get closer."

Alyx suppresses a pang of fear and hurries towards the

nearby street where the building had stood. They notice that many of the group, including the parent and child, have risen to follow them. Alyx does not slow.

Alyx spots Laurence from a block away. They can't keep themself from smiling at how large Laurence has grown, how dark green his broad leaves, how red his maw. Then they see Smriti tangled in Laurence's understory.

"Smee!"

Smriti looks up at the sound of Alyx's voice. She sees relief on their face.

"I'm glad you're alright," Alyx continues.

Smriti still doesn't respond.

"I saw Jean-Claude earlier today on my way to the mountain. Did he—"

"He's dead," Smriti says, finally freeing her legs from Laurences's leafy grip.

"I'm so sorry," Alyx says, bowing their head.

"Sorry as in, 'I'm sad for you and your client' or sorry as in, 'I fucked up?'" Smriti asks.

"Smee, a lot of people were going to die either way. Jean-Claude is one person. Come to the mountain. It would mean a lot to me."

"Why? I'm only one person too."

"Please, Smee. You could do good there. There's work ahead that I'm not cut out for."

"I could do good here," Smriti says. She almost leaves it

at that, then thinks of Jean-Claude. "This is my home. Plus, I don't want to live with you anymore, Alyx."

Smriti is shocked at how easy those words are to say. Disentanglement had seemed an impossibility for so long, but now it feels laughably simple.

Alyx opens their mouth to reply, then sighs, turning to make their way back to the mountain. Most of the group follow Alyx, but some remain behind, too exhausted or hurt or disabled to make such a climb. Smriti has always been drawn to the vulnerable and the marginalized, to their strength and stubborn resilience. As Alyx fades into the green distance, more people emerge from nearby ruins and homes. People who never could have considered leaving to begin with. She sees Sister Marie-Hélène carrying an elder with a badly broken ankle through the rubble as though they weigh nothing at all. She sees the RadMots reporter handing out bottles of water.

A hot rain begins to fall as Smriti takes in the magnitude of the devastation all around. Her mind begins to spin with a list of people who need to be checked in on, medicines and supplies that need to be located, committees that need to be formed. This is a warzone relief effort, Smriti realizes. And she fears the war isn't over. Smriti will never go to the mountain, but the mountain might yet come to her. As the horror of this thought percolates, she feels a leafy tendril wrap her calf.

"Get off me!" Smriti tries to kick Laurence away. "Go up to the mountain with Alyx."

Laurence doesn't budge except to raise a broad leaf above her head to shelter her from the rain. All at once, shock and fatigue hit her like a wall. Smriti's legs wobble and she starts to slump to the ground. Laurence catches her, supports her, helps her stand tall. Smriti lets him.

Smriti sees all the gathered eyes turned her way. She takes a deep breath. "Okay, everyone. Écoutez tout le monde. We have a lot of work to do."

END

—

As a working journalist, **D.F. McCourt**'s writings have appeared hundreds of times in publications such as *Maclean's*, *The Montreal Gazette*, *Chatelaine*, *The Toronto Star*, and *The Calgary Herald*. His short fiction has recently appeared in *Toronto Journal* and *The Ex-Puritan*, and is upcoming in the *Best Canadian Stories 2026* anthology from Biblioasis.

Su J Sokol's short fiction has been published in various magazines and anthologies. Sokol is also the author of four traditionally published novels including *Cycling to Asylum*, longlisted for the Sunburst Award for Excellence in Canadian Literature of the Fantastic. Its sequel, *Five Points on an Invisible Line*, was published in September of 2025.

LONDON TOWN

Troy Seate

Spring 1888–Whitechapel

Upon leaving a bawdy display at a brothel, Daniel Connor whistled as he briskly strolled along the cobblestones. To his annoyance, a woman stepped from behind a poster plastered kiosk and blocked his way. She wore a dusty velvet bonnet and a bustier to accentuate a bosom that threatened to overflow its mooring of frilly lace, typical of the trollops who roam Whitechapel. Her spindly fingers reached up and brushed the man's cheek.

"Kind Sir," she crooned. "I saw yer comin' from the Madam's. I recognized you right off, I did. Never imagined I'd come face to face with the likes of a famous personage such as yourself. "

"What do you want?" the man said, anxious to be on his way.

"I can read, yer know. I've read everything you've put to paper. I 'ave one of your books just here in me pocket, if you'd be so kind as to sign it."

The man flashed the briefest of smiles, just enough to hide his irritation. "I have a pen. Produce your book. I'll sign it and you can be off."

"And if you'd be kind enough to pitch in a few bob, I could do them things they do at the Madam's a might better. Give you a night yer won't be soon forgettin'."

"See here, Miss. I don't believe you have a book for me to sign at all."

"Most surely I do, Sir. Ere it is." From within a skirt pocket, the woman produced not a book, but a carving knife with an eight-inch blade. A sardonic grin accompanied her words. "Ere yer go." She rammed the weapon into the man's belly.

Eyes bulging, his tongue protruded as if seeking the answer to the age-old question: *Why?*

"Like I said," the woman added, "won't be forgettin' me any time soon, I wager."

During the pre-dawn hours two days hence, a second man of means awaited a hansom to carry him from Whitechapel as a woman approached.

"How about one for the road, Govn'r?"

Edward Henagar never picked up women from the street. He preferred the confines of Madam Francois' relatively safe pleasure house. He looked at the hooded woman with some amusement. "I'll give you a shilling for swill if you'll be off."

"Add a crown and I'll show yer me teats and cunny."

Edward smirked. "A shilling and not a pence more."

"Perhaps you'd fancy a kiss then."

"Let me see your face."

"By all means, 'ave a good look."

The man's eyes opened wide, not at what he saw, but what he felt—a knife plunging deep into his torso. His jaw moved up and down like a ventriloquist dummy as the blade was pulled free. His mouth spewed not words, but blood. The woman's arm moved quickly. The blade tore through the skin beneath Edward's jaw, sped through the roof of his mouth past his nasal cavity, and reached the base of his brain. He fell in a heap. The woman worked over the corpse quickly before leaving the rest to the rats.

Morality is often the topic of the age. Most believe that crime is a deviation from the norm, exhibiting the basest of passions. I concur with this belief with one caveat: one man's crime is another's crusade for savagery. My acts are the rational result of moral corruption.

Do you know what it's like to feel immortal? When we create we are nearest the Creator, are we not? A lofty platform is reserved for those who take the reins of life and death and place them into their own capable hands, much like a painter or wordsmith who attempts to embellish creation with passionate sonnets, or swirls of pigment on canvas. Like these artisans, I have dreamt of being a remarkable man, tall in stature, revered by my colleagues, and hailed for my contributions to mankind, a man basking in the light of success and praise.

Taking a human life while avoiding detection takes superior intellect and wit. It is unquestionably art in its purest form and I am pleased to say my dream has been realized, even if it must hide amid a blanket of shadows. My acts have been given to a phantom the public fancies as Leather Apron as well as other colorful monikers. I rather fancy Jack the Ripper from the wags working for the London tabloids. These publications, written by naïfs who can never understand villainy's artistry, profess that I have filled the city with horror. I am described as a fiend, in league with nights pillowed in fog, who haunts the darkness, waiting for the moment to burst forth from a secret place and latch on to some hapless victim. On the contrary, I hunt only those intent on performing atrocities of the most heinous stripe. I seek to cleanse the squalor that haunts London's lowest places of excess, much like killing your children to spare them from an evil world. Not an unredeemable act in the slightest. The conception of my acts, though tantalizing, cannot equal the challenge of completion, my propensity for unorthodox solutions notwithstanding. The fact that I derive satisfaction in the process does not diminish the effort and, truth be told, the world craves someone like me. I am a repository for all that is dark in society.

But no matter. My work speaks for itself. *Jack the Ripper Strikes Again,* the presses print without any thought of the craft employed to render the service. Be that as it may, my accomplice and I find our crusade compelling—the hunt, the tracking down, the snare. It is only right that these escapades result in the procurement of extraordinary sensations.

The ill-fated women who are nearly invisible—unnoticeable, and hence unmemorable—stand before me. I study their unremarkable faces haloed by silly hats held in place with scarves that are the most vivid thing about them. They breathe with less than saintly sighs as I approach. The authorities believe I attack from the rear, unseen until they are cut, but that is not the case. I want them to see the man who will end their miserable lives. I watch their hands reach for their throats, trying to stop the arterial spray. Blood gushes out onto streets where sounds, despite their tenor, dissipate in the haze of a darkened pathway.

Ahhh, those moments so sublime when my blade slashes through muscle and sinew. A fierce joy flows through me as these disciples of degeneracy crumble, eyes rolling back into their heads while wretched heartbeats fade. I focus on the body inside the veneer of shabby clothing, the tissue beneath the penetrable frame. Then I carve and vivisect with exactitude, my blade in control, doing what is not allowed in the hospital, although I have often been tempted to put certain patients out of their misery. But for now, ladies of the evening suffice. The knife is what they need, the only way to salvation.

I exhibit no rage, only solemn commitment. I respond to a haunting siren's call, sometimes humming a Polish tune my mother sang when I was a child while I whittle away the pathetic shells of wasted flesh.

Unfortunately, self-preservation then comes into play and I must leave my canvas behind, but not without a memento. I take some small part of the dead thing with me. I deserve that much for immortalizing the body from which the organ is removed. My accomplice and I once again become mere mortals, players in the continuing farce of existence.

I shall not name myself. Jack the Ripper will have to suffice, but I will tell you that I witness the ebb and flow of life on a daily basis, not unlike the mighty rivers winding through the cities of Europe in which I have lived. My chemical dependency began in Warsaw, my native home. At first, it was something to help me through the long hours of cadaver study, and later, to stomach the sufferings of living patients with twisted faces and tortured wails. I have seen the scourge of syphilis and consequently, have formed no intimate relationships.

My first residency was at the School of Medicine in Glasgow. From there, I made my way to London. In so many western cities, immigrants of all types and flavors flood in, but none quite like me. My slight Eastern European accent gives me an added quality of mystery which comes in handy now and then. How I've managed to finance my travels and ongoing education is a tale for another time, but should fate ever cause for my detainment, it will all no doubt come to light.

I live simply. I seldom eat…oh, an occasional kidney pie and an ale in a tavern, but it is my other appetites that sustain me—my work, my barbiturates, and my proclivity for carving. No piles of books or knick-knacks clutter my room in the boarding-house owned by an elderly spinster. Within my sanctuary, my world is tidy and straightforward. I often sit alone and play out scenarios to my life, try on different outcomes, guess at what my reactions might be. My life as a physician is one that requires dedication, yes, but my other compulsions require a change of scenery every few years.

There is little ornamentation to my life other than the admittance of a young woman to whom I have provided a bit of adventure. She is a prostitute and turns tricks in her own lodgings far away from my residence, and equally far from redemption. Still, I have shared more than narcotics with her. I have allowed her to watch as I butcher. A female as an accomplice is the perfect ruse, you see, and like me, fear is no longer an emotion she carries. It was stripped away in her youth.

My accomplice and I hide in the shadows like vigilant wolves looking for prey, waiting for the smallest sign of vulnerability, a victim straying from the herd. Then I strike, each subject a player waiting to perform their role in the tapestry of my production. London's audience does not have to linger long. Mary Nichols was put down in Buck's Row. Annie Chapman in the backyard of Number 29, Hanbury Street. Elizabeth Stride was a different situation. Had it not been for my accomplice's alert, an approaching passerby might have walked right upon the scene. On that occasion, I had to settle for slitting her throat and fleeing in the rain. The interruption hadn't set at all well, my sense of elation unfulfilled. It was left to Catherine Eddows to complete my mission that same night at Mitre Square.

When the work is finished, I remove my blood-spotted coverlet and cram it into my accomplice's tapestry bag to be laundered later. Then I place whatever part of the woman I've chosen in a piece of cloth within my own black bag. I keep them only temporarily, long enough to indulge myself in the privacy of my austere abode. I do not leave false clues. The words written on a wall; that was my accomplice's doing.

Then the two of us are off. On one occasion, we passed strolling bobbies who showed us courtesy by touching their fingertips to the brim of their helmets, just a man and his sinful companion walking away from what in the dark appears to be no more than a bundle of rags. My harlot returns to Spitalfields. I flag a hansom and, within its cabin, slowly come down from the rush of achievement as the horse clip-clops toward my boarding-house. That is all there is to it. Yet, reports are filled with elaborate rumor while churches and pubs give my handiwork joyful embellishment. How exquisite it all is.

It seems Scotland Yard is talking to every known sex offender and all the blokes arrested in Whitechapel for drunkenness, with little result. The authorities are fools, trying to make sense of the macabre spectacles before them. They occasionally need to be stirred up, have their noses tweaked to stew in their contempt and terror.

I spend time walking the city, but it isn't peaceful contemplation I seek. I pick up a handful of publications to see what terrible calamity they are either reporting or forecasting. The collective mania suggesting the worst for the remainder of the century intrigues me, all the more so since my own exploits have gained considerable recognition. Even tales told in the Penny Dreadfuls seem tame compared to my endeavors.

London has its share of impressive edifices to dazzle modern man, and would have him think of order rather than chaos. But it is the ravages of an age I see. Dead women's bones speak to me. Voices of runaway hungry girls who thought little of themselves, their eyes dark sinkholes of despair, lives spent without meaning. Many have grown into something less than human, something that ignores the sense of danger for a few shillings, with no one to come to their rescue. My obsequious accomplice has expressed it. "Once the worst has happened, the place where fear begins is lost. Only scar tissue remains." I am able to relate, and only I have come to *her* rescue. Only I have shown her other possibilities. I plan to see her only twice more. Once in my lodgings, and once in…

But now she has arrived, standing in my room with a small package. It could be anything—a pair of gloves from an emporium, something from the bake shop. But it is neither. She places it on a table before me, her eyes shining with conspiratorial pride. I open the package, unfold the cloth, and smile at what is inside.

"Better than a kidney, as good as a womb. No internal cutting necessary. You did well, missy."

"Tit for tat, yer said."

"Indeed. Tit for tat. How did you feel?"

"At the moment they breathe their last, I feel like I might be the Queen of England. I stand over them until, inside of me, it becomes like nothing." She paused, reliving the moment. "Then I finish my bloody work just as yer instructed."

"Men who fornicate in darkened alleys or in filthy beds are no better than the strumpets that please them. If something needs to be done, might as well thrill to its completion," I told her, knowing how easily one can become infatuated with such extremes. She is realizing anything can become pleasurable if done often enough.

Only once has she offered a disparaging word to me during the course of her transformation. "You 'ave the coldest eyes I've ever seen," she said. I took heart in telling her they were merely calculating, a distinction for those of us who see a great purpose to our lives—acts that define our nature.

It was on London's east side that our paths crossed. I saw a girl growing old before her time, her soul lost in the pit of debauchery. Yet something burned inside, something pleading for more than the life of harlotry. That spark of want convinced me to take this waif under my wing and give her a sense of mission. Provide her with the chance to be something astounding.

She has come a long way from the dirty faced urchin, little more than a liquored up marionette stumbling into my path. I found her amongst the miscreants prowling the dimly lit streets of Whitechapel and Spitalfields. But beneath the grime, I also saw the appealing hardness and resentment of her status. Away from the dustbins, a pretty face with eyes the color of Burmese Jade lurked there as well. I am no fool. I insist she wear a cloak with the hood held tightly around her face when she visits. She is to speak to no one. Let anyone who might take notice think her a woman of mystery, but I doubt anyone has. In boarding-houses, people come and go like ants scurrying about in their underground labyrinths.

She has committed two acts alone, first a writer and now a banker. The slightest of smiles creeps across my face as I study the package's contents with admiration, for nothing is more satisfying than an apt pupil. Well…almost nothing. I can only trust she has learned my methods of stealth.

Her syntax speaks to more than a common slut. My interest in her was validated by her sharp mind and tongue. I have prepared the narcotics for her visit. This is an occasion to celebrate. Just as my nocturnal activities are a righteous dalliance, my accomplice's taste for blood has become equal to my own. She has both killed and maimed. In the package lies the proof.

"Are yer pleased with me acquisition?"

Returning from my reverie, my attention moves from her prize back to her. "Of course, but it is an uncertain retribution. How much better to give them the blade, see the expression of terror and then the ebbing of their lives. That is the just punishment. But I must say, you have a knack for symbolism."

"Let their privates rot away, I say."

"Take it down to the furnace and destroy it," I tell her. "Keepsakes are not for us. We are not fetishists."

She notices the daily laying on the table next to her parcel. "Anything in 'ere yet?"

"Read for yourself."

She picks up the paper. "Look 'ere. It says, 'with callous cold-bloodedness,' and 'ere, 'dispassionate evil.'"

"I'm amazed you read so well considering your humble beginnings."

"Didn't start out where I ended up, but yer know that, knowing everything 'bout me like yer do."

It is true. I know her inside and out, everything except her methods of false passion when she plies her trade. There was no doubt she would welcome me between her thighs as quickly as anyone who offered a pound or a pint of ale for her charms, but a seduction is not my métier. The night she kissed the back of my neck, I knew it must end. Physical intimacy or even infatuation has no place in our partnership.

I recently turned thirty-two years of age and have rutted with only two women, both prostitutes. I did not achieve orgasm on either occasion. That release was arrived at only through self-abuse, which I prefer to the acrobatics of intercourse. I found the liaisons to be little more than expeditionary, my harlots' passageways too often entered. This was but one more proof that women are of little use other than to procreate, and most of them have no business doing that. I killed them both.

My third victim was in Scotland before coming to London. I took a part of her with me, soon learning that nothing quite satiated my passion like the aid of one organ or another after a kill.

My trained eyes take note of everything as I tramp along the cobblestones into areas of London where the neighborhoods grow ever more shabby and sordid, those grimy with age and unspoken violence. I am no demon, no compulsive madman like the rascals here who roam streets and tenements brutalizing each other. Along my path are tatty storefronts, followed by a string of roach-infested flophouses, surrounded by the smell of rotting garbage. I pass humans scuttling about like rats, and drunkards shambling along with unstable waddles.

These are places where evil thrives, where narrow pathways consisting of towering structures seem to lean ominously inward like great sleeping beasts, enveloping the pathways below, allowing only minimal sunlight to find buildings coated with industrial soot. Alleyways sparsely lit by faulty gas lamps fan out like spider webs where people who have sunk to their lowest level might debase themselves further. Yes, this is where I can perform my services to mankind, locales in which the dwellings are little more than dungeons where hopes and dreams struggle to survive.

My accomplice's tactics have worked on unsuspecting swells from uptown, but my work on the curmudgeons who live in the East End is a horse of a different color. The virtuous and unstained may go their way unharmed, for they are not to be found where I prowl. Better to make an example of those who wade through life dallying nightly in vulgar activities. Although my accomplice's aptitude is quick and cunning, and her company amusing, I cannot depart London without the *fait accompli*. Her knowledge is her death warrant and I shall treat myself to a final display of my craftsmanship before moving on, this time to America where a new life awaits.

I do not deny my vanity and admit to some derision in my motives. Perhaps I just like the rapture of killing and observing the critical moment of transition. The unwritten pages of my life will play out and eventually tell an intriguing tale. America, with its bustling industry and burgeoning metropolises, is sure to provide as fertile of hunting grounds as London—a series of fresh canvases upon which to paint tableaus of violence. A cleansing of alley sluts from slums will always be required, for I know, as surely as winter yields to spring, I shall accomplish what is needed. These plans are unknown to my accomplice, and for one evening, I am offering her the world.

"I'm going to let you assist me tonight, Mary Kelly. You may help the master at his work."

With my words, she at first looked shocked, and then gleeful. I knew she had not expected such an honor, but her time has come.

"I'll collect you around midnight."

My accomplice lives in a squalid, rented room. She has been off and on again with a lowly fish porter, but that appears to be over. I resent the unselfconscious way harlots go about their lives, and detest the catchy nicknames they give one another. Mary has her share: all of them beneath her, if that is possible considering what she is. More than once, I have questioned my good sense in forming such a relationship.

At present, Mary shares her room with another trollop, but there is to be no one there whenever I visit, for it is from her room we set about to perform our nocturnal deeds. Even though I have convinced her I am sending her fellow gutter-sluts to a better place, I have not encouraged her to stop plying her trade. I have no intention of supporting her, or humoring the possibility of our strange partnership becoming common knowledge. Believing in the rightness of my convictions, she wants to experience the same rush as I—something even better than the euphoria that comes with the injections we share—and I have provided such a stimulus. Convincing her that the men, the procurers of women's bodies, are as guilty as the recipients of their lust, she desires to exceed my body-count. I understand the longing to do it again, only better. The more blood she spills, the further she is removed from her guilt. Tit for tat.

Her two killings were a noble start, but they lack a flair for the dramatic. Great artwork cannot be explained. A professional can always surpass the tactics of a mere amateur or hobbyist. Genius cannot be summarized. Those without a true gift will be prenticed all their lives rather than gaining transformation from the human condition onto angel's wings, turning them from a monster into a god, such as myself. Besides, Mary is still one of *them*—cleaner and prettier perhaps, but a harlot, nonetheless. She would eventually reveal the face behind the mask. It can be strenuous to play a role continually. How easy to make a gaffe that would betray her most recent proclivity, leading to shackles, and possibly to her mentor.

I will be remembered here, but a change of venue is called for. Self-preservation dictates I find a distant shore where a wrathful hand may continue its work. The time is right to checkmate dear Mary and move on to a chessboard far from London. My gamesmanship did not begin in this city, nor will it end here. Although facing a mechanized future of sweeping change, the desire for violence is in the make-up of all nations. I am but one cell in its bloodstream. How glorious might such a future odyssey be, with heroic pages yet to be written? All things are possible if you have the ruthless courage to obtain them. My mind is possessed by such thoughts as I rush to Miller's Court off Dorset Street in Spitalfields.

I no longer see the sense in having an assistant, for this is no magic act. Still, I plan to honor her peculiar position of someone in my confidence with a hallmark to savagery: a lasting impression for Londoners to remember me—and her—by.

So I go to her room where a crucifix bearing a suffering

Christ hangs. It is accompanied by two candles, one bearing the image of the Virgin Mary, and the other, the likeness of some anonymous, grimacing saint. The scene is always worth a chuckle. These are not symbols of love and peace, but representations of the eternal battle with evil, the fight that festers in every man to one degree or another. God…the Devil: two gods competing for the minds and souls of men. Is the Dark One any worse than Catholics who believe bread and wine become the actual body and blood of Christ, thus turning themselves into cannibals? I think not.

The Irish are a superstitious lot. Her room's sainted companions will have something different to see this night. I will tell her to have no fear. If there is a Hell, it is surely overflowing with those she knows and loves. She shall be in good company.

Death, the fulcrum of our relationship, must now come full circle. As truth is available only on a need-to-know basis, this will be a climactic scene unrevealed to her, the end of the three-act play that will lead to her inevitable destiny. When I arrive, her blood will be racing excitedly through her intricate network of veins just under the skin, waiting to be set free. I will make her death quick as always, but not the ceremony to follow.

As my soul will not compromise, the time has come to create, the planets aligning in my favor—the night my friend. I occupy an entirely unique place at the center of the universe. I am truly godlike, for I am good at what I do. Tonight, I might even sing while I work.

But first, I shall deliver magic from inside my black bag, its gravitational pull already calling my name. We will chase the dragon together. Then I will provide her with the supreme horrifying experience. Her neck will open with a dark wet smile. The entire room will be transformed into a crimson wound—a poignant closure. She will become a sacrifice on the altar of a decadent society—my finest work to date, a sublime artifact for all to see.

The Daily Telegraph:

Early this morning, the body of a man, brutally murdered, was discovered in Miller's Court off Dorset Street in Spitalfields. Passerby initially assumed the man to be inebriated or asleep before authorities were notified. A medical bag at the scene revealed that its contents were likely used to dispatch the victim whose identity is not as yet known. Most shocking is the fact that the victim had been castrated and the male organs are missing. The manner in which he was murdered, with similarities to the deaths of two other male victims, has led to speculation that this may be the handiwork of Jack the Ripper, or perhaps a second party mimicking his savagery.

Scotland Yard appears to have its hands full as unsolved murders continue at an alarming pace.

END

—

TROY SEATE stands on the side of the literary highway and thumbs down whatever genre comes roaring by. His storytelling runs the gamut from *Horror Novel Review's* Best Short Fiction to the *Chicken Soup for the Soul* series. His memoirs and essays report fact, while his fiction incorporates fantasy, suspense, or humor featuring the quirkiest of characters. Troy's latest short story collection, *Gallery of Souls*, can currently be found on Amazon.

LOS ANGELES

Amanda Cecelia Lang

THE END

In these final *déjà vu* minutes before the city trembles and the stars die, the Witch ascends to the top of the HOLLYWOOD sign. Corrugated steel, box-office glitz. She popped champagne when the shrine was erected in 1923, and now, the Fates have summoned her back.

An unnatural wind shivers the sagebrush, snaking down the midnight hill while doomed soundtracks boom inside her bones. The Witch opens her inner eyes, already mourning as she peers between distant skyrises and boulevards and crescent-moon hills.

Somewhere, inside a hollow studio backlot, or a sleazy V.I.P. nightclub, or a swanky yesteryear hotel, casting-couch bigwigs waggle cigars while the very last of L.A.'s disenchanted starlets swallow their tears and unfasten their bras. For the last time, a waitress slips her headshot to a gatekeeper in a power suit; for the last time, a small-town nobody staggers off a bus. Smog and sunset, limelight and special effects. Down there, they worship the fickle goddess of fame and illusion; they chase fools-gold immortality across silver screens.

And now, as THE END begins, like sudden cursive letters scrawling across the screen, Tinseltown gasps for dramatic effect, just as the Witch always envisioned.

First, the stars go dark. New and ancient constellations popping like flashbulbs, trailing a billion smoky afterimages into the sudden sky-vast darkness.

Down on the Walk of Fame, sidewalk stars rumble, terrazzo cracks, and molten lava erupts from the seams. The Witch has a star down there. Her inner eyes watch it collapse into a sizzling void. Divine chaos sounds, and glittery phantasmagorical waves wash down Hollywood Boulevard. Theaters and costume shops are swept away in a fury of starstruck prayers that were never granted. From there, a power-grid blackout creature-crawls outward through the L.A. basin, plummeting the cityscape into darkness as sparkling fuchsia lava branches down infamous roads, molten rivulets lighting up the city like a tourist map of broken dreams.

Perched on the HOLLYWOOD sign's corrugated W, the Witch raises her glamours in desperate supplication to the Fates. Whirlwinds of projector light flickering from her pores, she summons the heroic immortal souls of every character she's ever played in this town—thousands across the century. Genies and queens and goddesses…

Eddies of smoky light sparkle around her gown and red-carpet curls, forming a protective bubble before expanding across L.A. in haunted prismatic gusts. They deserve a happy ending—the extras, the day players, the unrelenting hopefuls. Hollywood sang its siren song to them all. Then, in a game of audition roulette, watched their aspirations crumble. One by one by millions. They can't build a shining city atop the artifice of fame and fortune and expect it to stand forever.

Molten retribution carves a path from Sunset Boulevard to Rodeo Drive, boiling gold and plastic façades. The downtown skyline topples with the precision of choreographed stunts, and studio backlots ignite in technicolor flames. The very real screams of the expiring mingle with the hollow howls of crumbling soundstages.

Ever-shining and safe inside her protective glamours, the Witch reaches for all the bit-part mortals as they scurry and tumble. But celluloid flesh crisps away, injected lips liquify and elongate, tungsten-lamp eyes fizzle in sockets. A vast breathlessness blows between rubble-bone mansions and the slant of palm trees. With a final dramatic shudder, Tinseltown collapses in on itself like a low-budget studio set.

And everything fades to black.

DING-DONG, THE WITCH IS BORN—1896

Despite one-thousand starring roles, she has always been the Witch.

Born of mortal parents, from her first radiant breath, immortal magick dazzled her veins. The small-town nurse who birthed her dropped her onto the farmhouse floor—and whatever mystery she witnessed flickering inside those eerie newborn eyes would derange her until her dying day. A devil's portal, a mesmerizer's wink—or so the local legends went. Behind whispers and troubled stares, the Witch became famous long before Hollywood's siren-glow snaked from the reels and took her hold.

She grew up knowing she was different, but never dared imagine she might be special. During her early years, inside her hollows, she sensed twinkles of curious powers. Misty bravados, touchable daydreams. She often danced inside the flickering gossamer bubble of her lonesome imagination, plucking rainbows, chasing bluebirds. And sometimes, when she wished it, new stars appeared in the sky.

Even so, her clothing hung brown and limp, and when the pains of the Great War echoed through her cornhusk town, her fingers ached in the munitions factory, and her hunger cramped, same as the venom-tongued gossips. But then the Spanish flu appeared. While her neighbors and parents died, delirium and sepsis and hemorrhaging lungs, the Witch never caught a fever. She thrived through every tragedy. She glowed while others dulled.

Because long before the Witch had a name for them, the Fates graced her. As the swirling grave-dust of wars and pandemics settled, they granted a wish she hadn't even known she'd made.

And one golden spring evening, the traveling picture palace arrived in town.

The Post-Credits Ruin

The ashen aftermath of 3.8 million dreams settles, and all the city is a graveyard.

A-listers and D-listers and nobodies alike, creatures mighty and meek, their hollow chrysalises and mortal bones litter the ruins of mansions and studio apartments and gridlock roadways.

In THE END, mortals become the reality of their lives. Everything else falls away. They take only truth, journeying wherever mortal souls journey upon death. The pain, the love, the heartache, the people they touched, good deeds and evils. They take it with them.

Yet, unrealized fantasies slough away like unworn skin— champagne wishes and caviar dreams. Because how can a soul be something it never was? Lost dreams aren't people. At death, they're merely seeds that never took root. Ashes.

Now, those ashes fill the silent city.

Protected inside her gossamer bubble, the Witch climbs down from the HOLLYWOOD sign's W. As far as her inner eyes can see, this W is the only limelight relic untouched by the Fates.

The haunted ash of millions of dreamscapes flutters around her. She reaches toward the hazy starless sky, catching fragmented seedlings that invoke fragmented theaters for her inner eyes.

A heroine clicking her ruby slippers…lovers dancing in the rain on a lamp-lit street…an uncanny count rising from his coffin…

Such wishes these scenes inspired, such illusions.

Choking on futile anguish, the Witch brushes the visions from her hands, lets her inner eyes go empty.

"Is anybody there?" Her cry echoes everywhere all at once, boulevards, backlots. Not a single soul responds. She's the last, as she knew she would be.

She's always lived alone.

In cornfields, in Studebakers, in luxury, and now…

She drapes a hand across her forehead and closes her eyes.

Reopening them, she stands in a glitzy white-fur penthouse atop the tallest downtown skyscraper. She glimpsed enough aftermath to know this building now leans as a smoldering steel skeleton. But like the Witch, her home is untouchable, swathed in the same protective bubble she always used to ward off fans; the same protection she'd been unable to extend the city.

She closes red-velvet curtains, eclipsing her smoldering view of L.A.—an unwanted glimpse of HOLLYWOOD's W there in the distance, a single jagged tooth in the city's battered face. The paparazzi would love that.

Too bad, they're all dead.

The Witch swallows a sleepy tonic of champagne and mystic melancholy. It makes her wobbly. Disconnecting, she entombs herself inside a satin shroud of bedsheets. Immortality forbids eternal sleep. Yet the Witch prays to escape inside an endless trance. No genies, no queens, no goddesses. Just herself and the silhouette of a man she once knew. But when she closes every eye, shadow-scapes slip through her like smoky tendrils, ephemeral, ungraspable.

She's forgotten how to dream.

Eternities pass; dusty emptiness possesses her, impossibly profound. She once believed nothing could be as barren as fame in a city where everybody loved her yet nobody knew her. But, debuting with the apocalypse, is a void to consume all voids.

And yet, outside her curtained windows, something slowly echoes. Spring rains, fertile decay, mortal yearnings twisting upward from tumbledown bones.

A soundtrack of growth.

The Dream Weaver—1923

The traveling picture palace rolled into the Witch's town like a dazzling one-truck circus, Hollywood in the back of a Studebaker. In a freshly-sowed cornfield, while a violinist tuned his instrument before the gathering crowd, the Projectionist erected a vast bedsheet and the golden machine he called his Dream Weaver. Darkness swelled with the stars as the Witch approached. Unseasonable fireflies flickered above earthen rows, and local gossips kept a sour distance on folding chairs. Admission cost 15¢—but for the Witch, a blushing kiss on the Projectionist's cheek.

He bowed at the waist and popped a rose from his sleeve, and never had the Witch felt so un-alone. His smile erased years of cruel scorn, skittish whisperings—this was something earnest, something enchanting.

"Let's see what marvels we might see!" Snap of fingers, the violin swelled, and his Dream Weaver ignited, reels spinning, and upon the bedsheet flickered an equally heady magick.

A black-and-silver dreamscape.

So vivid, so dynamic, surely the Projectionist had cast fantastical glamours—just like the Witch.

The townsfolk gasped in artless unease. But tears awed the Witch's inner eyes. Like the vampire spying his prey, it was love at first sight. The loyal hero and his flower-garden heroine; the harrowing snaggletooth count rising from his coffin!

Though nobody else would, the Projectionist sat beside the Witch the entire film, caressing her hand while the vampire indulged his final bloody sips, dying with the damsel in the sunrise so the hero might live. Only the sudden scrawl of THE END shattered the spell.

She blinked, sitting back in stunned transcendence—and the Fates blew sequins into the Projectionist's next words.

"You could do that…"

She could barely speak. "Do what?"

"You could be a star."

Be a star? A new effervescence tingled through her.

He showed her an array of films that first yet strangely final night. Swashbuckling musketeers, moon-traveling epics…

The Witch's blood spiraled in rhythm with the reels. Inner eyes glowing, she scarcely glanced away. When the next silent-screen hero appeared on his pathécolor horse, misty light trembled from the Witch's pores. Magick flashed, and the musketeer's buttercup yellow horse trotted off the screen into the cornfield, kicking up dirt, circling the gasping audience. The violinist cut to shocked silence. The townsfolk bolted from their seats. The impossible steed whinnied silently, and they scattered in abject panic. Always running from her, always afraid.

But the Witch, bewitched, didn't notice.

All night, the movies played on—played *through* her, breathtaking set pieces sparkling to life around the cornfield.

After the final reel hummed to silence, the film's rocket-struck Man in the Moon still dazzled the sky.

"Never seen such wonders," the Projectionist whispered, dissolving her loneliness with a soft gaze and awed baritone laughter. "How do you do that?"

"Do what?" She smiled coyly, already grasping the wiles of cinema minxes.

He exhaled, euphoric. "I think I'm in love…"

Instincts swirling like moondust, she looped arms around him. "Let's see what marvels we might see…"

He kissed her, dramatic, thrilling, like a hero in the final frame, and movie-prop stars sparked from her soul, haunting the predawn air as silver-feather bluebirds sparkled around them.

Oh, that kiss.

Her every immortal day, the Witch would recall that kiss as a montage of the happily-ever-after that could've been. Dazzled by this man, her inner eyes witnessed her wedding lace and an open-air ceremony beside his Studebaker; she saw breezy nights in picture-palace cornfields while the Dream Weaver spun and toddlers waddled in the light; she saw their hands entwined, growing old on a farmhouse porch painted golden with sunsets and grandchildren.

All this in one sweet, miraculous kiss.

She returned his kiss, kissing him deeper as her magick painted their fading nightscape in lush broad-strokes of future color. Passion, laughter, companionship, a three-act lovescape.

They lived a lifetime in that kiss.

When the sweetness broke, the Projectionist's eyes star-fell upon hers, and she knew he wished for her, too.

Yet, his Dream Weaver had shown her another future, glowing in the west—her magick the envy of millions. And oh, to be witnessed, to be universally adored…

His smile drooped, the light abandoning his eyes. He sputtered, collapsing to his knees even as bluebirds circled.

The Witch fell upon her knees, too. He said she could be a star! Clutching his hands, she tried wildly to prop up his life even as his forehead slumped dead upon her shoulder.

Kneeling with his corpse, pores weeping starlight, desperate for both callings—true love, fame—she screamed and snatched a bluebird from the sky. Snap of neck, fizz of glitter, she clutched its limp feathers against her Projectionist.

When sunrise came, the pitchfork townsfolk circled the cornfield, but couldn't break her protective bubble. Terrified, they spat vitriol and veiled jealousies, even as they watched in awe.

All day, the Witch clutched her dead Projectionist and her dead bluebird, wishing he might have a starring role in her chosen future.

But the Fates never grant gifts without also taking.

At sunset, something limp and dead twitched inside the Witch's clutch.

A chirp of birdsong, and the Projectionist's corpse collapsed to the dirt. The bluebird took flight from her hand. In a flicker of projector light and magick, the dream-creature feathered westward, leading the way, chasing the siren call of Hollywood.

Cue the Light

Birdsong wakes her.

A dawn chorus warbles beyond her dreamless fugue and penthouse windows. Spritely, impossible. Everything out there is dead.

Too sick of heart to open inner eyes, she opens the curtains.

An ash-smog of apocalyptic ruin blackens the cityscape.

Darkness so profound, it inflicts its own gravity, crushing

hope. Nothing could survive such oblivion. Film critics always swore she glittered so fabulously new constellations appeared. The genie, the queen, the goddess. Now, the city of sun-kissed angels will never shine again. And yet...

High beyond the darkness, that birdsong persists.

She steps onto her balcony, extending skyward hands. Blackout clouds explode open with swooping, flickering wings.

A silver bluebird?

It alights upon the Witch's hand. Fluff of wings, pecking at the darkness, it leans forward with an offering.

A luminous golden crabapple, gleaming with lacework radiance. The fruit trembles in the Witch's palm. A gift from the Fates?

Opening inner eyes, she bites in.

Sunshine explodes from the juices.

Molten, glorious, right on cue, kaleidoscopic light rushes through the blackout void—L.A.'s rubble shining like reels of lost dreams. The bluebird takes wing, swooping low, racing the sunshine as it blossoms across 3.8 million newborn colors. The dream-seeded ruins have flowered into a surreal spring.

"How lovely..." The Witch leans over the railing. To see what marvels she might see.

WELCOME TO HOLLYWOODLAND–1923

The pretty young hopeful who went before her was still crying when the casting assistant called the Witch's name. Sobbing, actually. Poor mortal thing, she'd barely been in there twenty seconds before scurrying back into the cramped lobby where thirty other pretty young hopefuls watched her vacate the casting office. Not pretty enough?

Practically choreographed, thirty wide-eyed girls smoothed their skirts. The assistant had to repeat the Witch's name.

Only two weeks had passed since the Witch arrived in the Projectionist's old Studebaker, but already her name felt distant as her cornhusk town. Folks in this dusty land of orange groves and studio lots never stared or gossiped—at least, not with abject horror like back home. Here, the men had love-eyes like her Projectionist. She'd forever grieve him, the stranger she loved inside a kiss and a vision.

"Alright, doll, nothing to it." The assistant hurried her forward. "Walk across the room, do a little twirl, don't speak unless spoken to, and keep that smile on full wattage."

To reach the casting office, the Witch had entered through the studio's marvelous art deco front gate, then crossed a sprawling backlot through a dusty old west town, costumes and carriage horses. But inside that office, she found nothing so dramatic. Just four blank walls and tungsten floodlights.

"You a vamp or an ingénue?" barked a disembodied voice.

"Pardon?" The lights blazed with such intensity they smudged the masculine silhouettes seated at the table.

"Vamp or ingénue," the voice repeated. "You selling sex or innocence?"

The Witch was here to be a star. Damp fingers kneading

her skirt, lips aching for her dead Projectionist, she trembled. "Both?"

Laughter echoed, and gooseflesh rippled.

"Come closer, cupcake, let's see if you crumble in the lights. Lift that hemline, we're trying to see what you're working with."

Something sour shivered inside, but she obliged. She remembered the little twirl, the room twisting, ears filling with electric dizziness.

"You're the one my producer spotted dancing with the jazz band at the Cocoanut Grove, drinking up everyone's giggle water."

"He said I cast an entrancing profile." She angled her face. "Plus, I laughed at his jokes."

More laughter echoed, wolfish, slathering on for an overbright eternity. The Witch knew what the voice would say before he opened his greasy mouth.

"I'm not seeing it. Beaky nose, chubby gams, boring chest. Where's the razzle-dazzle? Where's the magic? *Next!*"

The Witch froze, hell-storms crashing inside like every cruel isolation she'd endured back home. She was bigger than life, a force unto herself—she shouldn't feel so alone! In her bones, she wanted to be loved. Loved, adored, worshipped for the miracle she was. When the assistant nudged her toward the exit, something ignited.

She tossed her arms up high, cocked her hip, and golden projector light blazed from her pores, transforming the drab office into a shimmering Hollywoodland premiere. A red carpet unrolled, and a towering theater marquee rose at her back, her name in shining lights. Not her real name. The name they'd one day scream in droves.

She chased the red carpet, her wool audition dress melting into a gown that hugged suddenly sleek curves like liquid fire. Phantom paparazzi appeared, cameras popping, immortalizing her measured grace as she approached the casting table. The voice sunk low in his chair, gaping up at her, his cheeky color draining to gray, ill-prepared for the special effects of her soul.

"How's this for razzle-dazzle?" she purred, luxuriating in the spectacle.

He clutched his chest. Not love. On cue, he slumped forward, forehead smacking the table. His silent film was slated to be called *Ragtime Hero,* and they needed a ragtime heroine. The Witch would've elevated the schlock. Shame it'd never get made. Like the casting director, his studio wouldn't even survive to see the erection of the Hollywoodland sign in the coming month.

But the Witch knew, without a dazzle of doubt, that she would land her next audition.

BACK ON SET

Atop her penthouse balcony, the Witch walks L.A.'s ruins as a ghost of blazing inner eyes, everywhere and nowhere at once.

Colorful dramatic scabs of invasive dream-flora sprout from rubble wounds and toppled landmarks. Iridescent vines, colossal ethereal blooms, bizarre fruiting trees like eerie creations on the soundstage of an exotic alien world. Swaying technicolor tall grass blankets ever-gridlocked highways, and glowing crescent-moon blossoms tangle the stucco remains of hillside mansions, bowing in her passing ethereal wake.

The Chinese Theater's grand pagoda leans half-collapsed atop its forecourt of celebrity handprints, weeping lustrous willow fronds and diamond-studded branches. The Hollywood Bowl's acoustical dome sits egg-cracked, and a neon yolk of slithering vines creeps from center stage, dragging bulbous fruits. Around the slumped accordion shell of the Capitol Records Tower, simpering trumpet flowers echo with phantom jazz-time melodies.

Everywhere the Witch's gaze walks, she finds mortal skeletons nestled amid leafy overgrown ruins. Snapped bones and skulls with grins turned on full wattage—more like props than extras, nevermind vessels that once contained souls.

Souls that once contained dreams.

Dreams that have, after a century of futile heartache, taken root. An enchanted post-apocalyptic Neverland. It's all so lovely, and monstrous. The Witch closes her inner eyes, returning to her flesh and balcony.

She steps back, but leafy vines constrict, binding her wrist to the railing. A fruiting flower snakes into her open palm, plumping with an offering of sequined grapes. She samples one. Her inner eyes blur with visions, movie reels spinning in reverse, greenscreens, soundstages, backlots…

Out amid Hollywood's ruins, something once-lost rumbles, rising again.

And out there, beyond the rubble-echo, the Witch imagines she hears voices. Survivors?

The vines release her, but as she stumbles across her penthouse's threshold, the ozone shimmers, and her bedroom crossfades into the next scene.

All around, tungsten floodlights brighten an open-air stage.

She stands in the courtyard of an Arabian palace. Sprawling minarets, arches, marble columns made of plaster and chicken-wire. Fog machines push mist between papier-mâché palm trees. And sudden shackles jangle the Witch's wrists, her beaded chiffon costume billowing dramatically.

This is where she filmed *Shadow Lamp*, her first movie, the first time her immortal magick burned itself onto celluloid. Behind the palace, a matte painting transforms L.A. into a sand-dune oasis, painted camels framed against an oversized full moon. Backlighting makes the stars twinkle—but it was the Witch who breathed magick into the film.

The tale of a projectionist who searches a mysterious bazaar for exotic films only to discover a whole new magic with a genie in a lamp. A script practically written by the Fates. The lonesome genie trapped inside her prison of magic—the projectionist who frees her. First day on set, when the Witch arrived to attend a blocking rehearsal, she nurtured secret wishes that her leading man might truly be her fallen Projectionist. Resurrected from his grave, here to shine by her side.

But the Fates never give without also taking.

The actor who greeted her was a boorish studio-puppet who thought she existed to grant his wishes in real life, too. He embodied all the leading men who would romance her in the coming century. Their dramatic final kisses shone enchanted on the screen, but no costar ever sparked visions of happily-ever-after like her Projectionist had in that cornfield.

As for this open-air palace—along with its silk-fire lanterns and the love the Witch once hoped to rekindle here—it was torn down a century ago. It shouldn't exist in this dead city.

Unless the city being dead is exactly why it exists.

The Fates take, and they give.

Approaching the faux-marble fountain where she first met her long-ago costar, she doesn't dare hope. Can old wishes come true? Certainly, a dream manifested for the Witch when the director called "Cut!" that first time on this set. The man sat frozen, eyes bulging with the ethereal afterimages of her genie performance. She feared another heart attack. What if the special effects of her soul were too much for *any* mortal?

But instead of collapsing dead, this director sprung to his feet.

"Did you get that?" The Witch can still remember him shouting at his cameraman then tripping over a hookah. Righting himself, he swept the Witch onto his shoulder and cheered through his bullhorn. She was magic, she was transcendent, she was going to be the brightest superstar ever to dazzle theaters!

The rest, as the title cards sometimes said, became the thing of legends.

And when the old ladies from the gossip rags knocked on her dressing room door, inquiring about fame and fortune and love, the Witch would smile coyly and promise she was madly in love with Hollywood.

Now, beside the palace fountain, she traces fingertips through her ageless, rippling reflection. Her heartbeat feels stagnant, but from nowhere, rose petals cascade around her. Like a gift pulled from a lover's sleeve.

She gasps, looking up.

The petaled rain washes away the palace, minarets crossfading into the ruins of modern soundstages. Poof!—her genie costume dissolves. Only palm trees remain, papier-mâché dissolving, revealing the lava-charred palms that occupied the backlot when THE END came. Starry indigo vines swirl around blackened trunks, and nebulous flowers pulsate at the top. The silver bluebird gyres overhead, landing on a vine with plump coppery fruit.

One falls. Half-plum—half-genie lamp?

The Witch catches it, nearly falling to her knees. Whatever swirls inside the tarnished fruit, it weighs more than the moon. She squints with inner eyes, straining to believe the shadow-show inside. Dream Weavers and kisses in cornfields—a man with enough magick rooting his grave to defy death. She doesn't dare hope. Fingertips denting the fruit, she presses it against her lips.

A quick kiss to pay her ticket price, then her teeth burst through the flesh in a fabulous rush of juices. Genies, queens, goddesses. Her vision fast-forwards, every onscreen kiss, every love scene—even as sweet moonstruck magick backlights the constant vaporous memory of her Projectionist. He bows and pulls a rose from his sleeve.

Standing alone between the tumbledown soundstages, the Witch swallows.

And somewhere in the dead city, voices echo out.

Mortal Stars—1960

"**L**adies and gentleman, our queen has arrived!" The tuxedoed emcee gripped his microphone, pointing toward the street. Spotlights crisscrossed the red carpet, and Hollywood Boulevard's jam-packed terrazzo sidewalk detonated with cheers and flashing bulbs.

Flaunting glamours only she could summon, the Witch emerged from a silver-mirrored limousine. Inspired by her latest role, her chiffon gown twinkled behind her like a comet tail. Glitter-dusted fog machines transformed the Walk of Fame into an alien dreamscape, and fans in silver go-go pants lined the barricades, waving posters of *Crimson Cosmos*, the Witch's latest film. In it, she reigned as an intergalactic queen who bathes in the technicolor blood of her planetary servants, absorbing their alien life-forces.

T.V. cameras rolled, and reporters shouted questions about

the sidewalk star she was there to receive, about her enigmatic love life—and, of course, her sci-fi box-office smash that was delighting critics with its controversial debauchery. Electric smile, the Witch ignored questions and scribbled autographs. Flourish of pen, her signature crackled with effervescent stars that leapt into the air like tiny fireworks.

The fans cheered, greedily swallowing her magick into their eyes.

Atop the emcee's podium stage, Hollywood's handpicked elite lined up to greet her, smiles burning full wattage. The most gorgeous, charismatic, powerful souls—of that decade, anyway.

For all but the Witch, fame was a revolving door.

Hitting her mark beside the emcee, the Witch winked at her crowd. Twitch of hip, her chiffon gown went supernova, burning away to reveal the futuristic gold-plated ballgown she'd brandished during the climax of *Crimson Cosmos*, when her queenly powers became too magnificent and she destroyed her own planet.

The fans exploded in riotous applause. The emcee had to repeat his opening line three times before they quieted to a low rumble. "Tonight, we unveil a star for the queen of film! Almost forty years, she's transported us from our mundane lives into fantastical worlds that pulse with electricity…"

His voice blurred with the crowd's bland voices, myriad faces swarming the boulevard. Forever surrounded, but the only face the Witch longed to see never appeared. Instead, the emcee handed the microphone over to her costars and sycophants.

"Her beauty's ageless…" they gushed, stepping up, one by one, to ooze their respects. Perhaps the closest thing to a funeral the Witch would ever have.

"She's everything this town desires…" "Eternal youth…" "Eternal sex-appeal…" "Eternal fame…" "Eternal box-office diamonds…" These accompanied by wolfish, slathering laughter.

"And oh, ladies and gentlemen, how coyly she hides her secrets!"

"She glows while others dull…"

The Witch scanned the faces, forever searching. In that long-ago cornfield, she never dreamed true love would be her one-hit wonder. But of course they loved her, didn't they? Just look at them. So many giddy faces tilted her way. They couldn't consume enough of her, couldn't get close enough. Her orbit, her gravity, they longed to be a part of her universe, like she longed for roses and Dream Weavers.

These same faces had flocked her for forty years. Naturally, the souls inside changed like the fashions, decade after decade. But their awe, their envy always reeked the same.

Now, she recognized a face, here and there. Faces of all the pretty young hopefuls who bubbled and begged in auditions, who hiked their hemlines only to be told they were too ordinary, too plump, too dried up… Where's the magic, where's the razzle-dazzle?!

"Now, for our spectacular reveal!"

Down on the sidewalk, two Walk of Fame custodians who would never live in mansions, two nameless extras following the script written by the Fates—they pulled back a red velvet shroud, unveiling the Witch's mortal-carved star.

Pink-coral terrazzo, her name in brass above a brass movie camera—tears crosscut her vision, blurring it with the silhouette of a projector.

The crowd applauded, and a stinging, buzzing dizziness spiraled through the Witch. How could a queen feel so alone in her own kingdom? All those shadow-cast faces. The dreamers who, for lack of sufficient limelight, would spend tiny lives withering in the Witch's insurmountable shadow. Flashbulbs reflected off her gold-plated ballgown, and endlessly rejected faces stared back at themselves, rabid and dazzle-eyed.

After the Witch's thank you speech—every word a silent scream for her Projectionist—someone onstage popped a bottle of champagne. Only enough glasses for the elite. But a wise queen knew how to pacify her subjects.

Bubbles overflowing, she blew an effervescent kiss into the crowd and—*poof!*

Champagne glasses appeared in everyone's hands.

Above Hollywood Boulevard, fireworks ignited a new constellation across the sky—and within these stars, they saw their own faces.

How's that for razzle-dazzle?

On cue, everyone cheered and toasted her.

But strange, unbalanced energies skittered inside. A spidery otherness, all too reminiscent of her old cornhusk town. The creature features of the '30s hadn't been far off with their torches and pitchforks. The Witch fought to keep her breath steady, her smile celestial, but her inner eyes stung inside the crowd's secret pounding hearts.

They didn't love her, she saw, not like her Projectionist. Endless mortals surrounding her from a distance, and they didn't love her. They loved what she was.

They wanted to *be her.*

They wanted to unzip her like a costume and luxuriate in her skin. They wanted vast unachievable dreams—unachievable because the vastest, starriest wishes only came true for the Witch. If they could, they would slit her immortal throat and bathe in her blood, absorbing every sizzling drop of her magick.

The Witch raised her champagne glass. She dared them to try.

THE DREAM REAPER

The voices echo from somewhere in the tumbledown city: sometimes weeping, sometimes whispering like a hushed theater. Survivors? The rebirth of a dream? Baritone laughter joins them, entices her closer. Could it belong to her Projectionist?

The Witch grips her half-eaten plum. But it seems her inner eyes have gone blind. Chasing that elusive long-ago voice, her vision fogs. She can summon countless spectacles, but recalling her Projectionist's electric touch feels like grasping at mist. She takes another sweet gushing bite, heartbeat swelling like violins.

Somewhere out there, that voice sounds again.

She hurries forward, but instead of crossing a mystic threshold to discover who's calling, a cramp fizzes inside her ribcage. Her feet crunch soundstage wreckage.

The Fates want her to find her Projectionist on foot?

It'll be an adventure, she decides, like the silent costume pictures that debuted her career.

Walking, sometimes stumbling, she follows disembodied laughter through thickets and immense valleys carved between stucco and iron husks. Pulsating indigo vines twist amid the Walk of Fame's terrazzo-and-brass debris. Over 2,700 illustrious names obliterated, replaced by fuchsia star-flowers that scrape her ankles, filling her with classic vaporous visions.

A boy on his bicycle silhouetted against the full moon…a bombshell on a subway grate with a billowing white skirt…

She doesn't look back.

Walking for a virtual century: her bare soles ache, then blister, then bleed. Even in the most dangerous stilettos, has this ever happened?

But the Fates take and also give.

She finds the voices between the vine-choked carcasses of a one-hour photoshop where hopefuls developed headshots, and a diner where they slaved to pay the bills.

Holding her breath against hope and hellos, she invokes a gossamer bubble—but it flickers, fades. The protections she once summoned to hide from her fans fail. Quickly, heart rioting like stage fright, she dips behind a palm tree.

Moments later, a shabby little girl climbs out from under the diner's half-collapsed roof, followed by a mousy middle-aged woman and a paunchy man. He chuckles, a sleepy baritone drawl, but he isn't *him*.

The Witch swallows a gasp of painful disappointment, breath scratching her chest. Yet, she's seen these mortals before, sure she has.

These are the too-plain, the too-chubby, the too-old. Scars mar their limbs, and the woman slings a rifle over one shoulder.

A stage prop. An empty threat for an empty city.

The Witch draws back into the gnarled shadows. Where did these mortals come from? Are they survivors, newborns… a peculiar combination of both?

"What's the haul?" the woman says. The man lowers his knapsack and the three gather around, clearly starving. They sort a meager collection of cans.

"Can we open one now?" the little girl asks. She looks tiny amid the immense sky-reaching ruins.

The man nods. "Take your pick."

The girl selects a can with a pull-top. But when the lid pops, there's nothing inside. Another stage prop.

The woman curses under her breath, tossing the hollow can aside. "They can't all be empty, but let's get home first. Darkness soon."

"And no stars…" The little girl glances skyward, cowering.

The Witch follows them, keeping a nervous, limping distance. As the sun vanishes below a brilliant moss-painted horizon, they arrive at the art deco remains of a mansion in the hills. Hollywood intuition tells the Witch the house wasn't originally theirs—not unless they occupied the servant quarters.

Loss knots itself tighter inside her chest. Why did the Fates lead her here? The trio duck inside their hovel, and birdsong rises. The girl cocks her ear. "Wish we could find it."

"Oh?" says the woman. "For a pet?"

"No, silly. To eat."

The Witch lurks closer. An iridescent tree pulsing with all manner of dreamfruit grows from a cracked swimming pool. Why bother hunting birds and empty canned goods when L.A. hangs ripe with edible fantasies?

But suddenly it's obvious. The gossamer flowers, the thronging fruits sagging on vines…mortals can't see them! Not unless she shares her limelight, pollinating these orchards with immortality. Her razzle-dazzle, her magick. A single bite could change their lives, grant their dreams…

The Fates reopen her blurry inner eyes, one final future vision to spin her blood. Citrus perfumed with genies… berries haunting of queens…stone-fruit born from brave-heart goddesses… myriad magick awaiting the harvest.

The birdsong hushes beneath the starless night. Amid the glittery vine-twisted wasteland, the Witch plucks dreamfruit; then she faces the ruined mansion.

"Let's see what marvels they might see."

AND THE AWARD GOES TO–1973, 1998…

In 1973, the Academy presented her with the Honorary Award for exceptional lifetime achievements in the motion picture arts—but never the art of love. During the afterparty, the latest crop of fleeting A-list starlets roller-skated topless under disco-ball lights, while grindhouse grit sprayed from projectors, and wilting legends surrounded the Witch like tangle-weeds. "Fifty years ruling the limelight," they buzzed, sniffing cocaine off her flawless supple curves. "Tell us, gold dust woman, isn't it time to share…?"

In 1998, the Academy presented her with the Honorary Award for exceptional lifetime achievements in the motion picture arts—but never love. During the afterparty, the latest crop of fleeting starlets moshed topless in strobing grunge pits, while clueless chick flicks sprayed from projectors, and wilting legends entangled the Witch. "Seventy-five years," they hissed, sucking ecstasy off her timeless matte-velvet lips. "Surely, babe, you don't intend to live forever…?"

Just this year, the Academy presented her with the Honorary Award for exceptional lifetime achievements in the motion picture arts—never love. During the afterparty at an ancient art deco mansion in the hills, the latest crop of fleeting starlets wore shimmery superhero capes and posed for selfies with the sleek tech-sexy motorcycle the Witch rode throughout her latest cinematic universe. The *Indigo Goddess* trilogy already cracked a box-office billion, and the Witch's mighty shadow loomed ever-vaster over Hollywood's parched, weary façade. "One-hundred years," the tangle-weeds hissed, twisting bony fingers in her curls, high on vape pens and *Rotten Tomatoes* scores. "Soon you'll star in the requels of the reboots of the remakes of your silent films. Shouldn't someone else shape the stars…?"

The Witch replied as she always replied: "I've lost too much to lose Hollywood, too."

Except that was a lie. At the end of *Indigo Goddess*, her caped deity bent time backward for love. In reality, the Witch could only peer forward. In reality, she'd always known without a dazzle of doubt what would happen at THE END of her Act Three.

When an unsmiling butler with a headshot in his tuxedo invited her into the mansion's infamous private theater, she followed the winding breath of the Fates without question. Downstairs, casting couches from the '20s still luxuriated, every seat occupied with narrow eyes and fame-starved bodies. The Witch's blood hummed, and millions of restless, forsaken ambitions shifted under the mansion and grumbled under the hills. Bitter jealousies, siren-lured heartaches, disenchantments untold. Intuition prickled.

The splash washed through the Witch's void-filled life decades before the washed-up scream queen waiting in the shadows tossed the bucket of water.

Drenching her gown, drenching her resolve.

Because how else could they kill a Hollywood witch?

Cue the mob. Everyone, it seemed. The dream-dashed

waitstaff, the one-hit starlets, the has-beens, paparazzi and endless covetous fans, faces expressive as silent-screen ghosts. Disappointed that the Witch, dripping, didn't melt.

Flaming stakes…falls from high cliffs…a century of onscreen witch hunts dizzied inside her. She wondered if her Projectionist was watching from wherever mortals went when they died—just as she'd wondered during every barren heartbeat spent on a set or a red carpet. Did he forgive her for trading the love they would've had for this razzle-dazzle illusion of a life?

After all, despite her magick, Hollywood's siren call had beguiled her. And buried beside a century of broken mortal dreams, the Witch had a graveyard all her own. Festering under the city's starry terrazzo crust was a simple life traveling town to town, spinning the Dream Weaver. Buried were the wedding lace and the grandchildren on the farmhouse porch. Buried was a love that could've been simple and real and never hollow.

The mob closed in.

"You promised us immortality," they hissed. And it was true. With every onscreen glamour, she sowed wishes that would never feel the sunlight. Not beneath her shadow.

Their love became hatred, echoing the skittish gossips from her old cornhusk town. Endless eyes taking notes as she grieved forsaken love. Because like her Indigo Goddess, like all superheroes, the Witch had a secret kryptonite.

The Dream Weaver shuddered when they rolled it out.

Antique, golden, but surely not the same one…

Reels spinning, light spraying, they resurrected that long-ago silent vampire—and from the Witch's pores, a restless swaying cornfield expanded outward, superimposing bluebirds and starbursts atop the intimate crowd-choked theater.

And standing on the horizon, a blurry love-at-first-sight silhouette bowed at the waist. The Witch raised her hand, and he dissipated like ashes.

For all her magick, the Fates had ensured one glamour would never stick.

She sobbed.

And the mob laughed, riotous cruel cackles spreading like applause. It was the glee of it, their self-satisfied pleasure at her pain, that cracked her uncrackable façade.

A seismic fracture. Everything shuddered, rising up, their heartbreak and her heartbreak colliding like waves.

Molten sobs crumbling foundations; dispirited gravities extinguishing illusions.

She saw their terror and their awe.

Like too much champagne, the Witch didn't recall leaving the afterparty. The ground was already whimpering when she found herself staggering along the hills. She sensed the Fates nearby, and couldn't control the howling regret in her blood—or the wreckage boiling below the crust.

And in those final *déjà vu* minutes, before the city trembled and the stars died, the Witch ascended to the top of the HOLLYWOOD sign.

THE END AGAIN

When the sun rises, a basket of dreamfruit waits glittering on the ancient mansion's porch.

With her last flickers of inner sight, the Witch sits atop the surviving W, watching the little girl discover the gift. The fruit reflects like miracles in the girl's eyes.

The man and woman join the child around the basket, laughing happy tears.

"May I?" the girl asks.

They nod.

Her first bite, a victorious juicy burst, sends luminous waves exploding outward. Across the hills, across the L.A. basin, the glitzy ruin of an opulent century trembles and stirs like reverse gravity. Terrazzo and stucco debris rewind and crossfade into a clean, reborn dreamscape. Dusty roads and studio lots, the silent era town as it sparkled when the Witch first arrived. Though instead of oranges, a vivid cosmos of dreamfruit tangles the groves. The HOLLYWOODLAND sign quakes, rises, resolidifies—and with ebbing strength, the Witch climbs down from her W, lest she tumble from great heights.

Below, the art deco mansion gleams, healed and whole. The man and woman raise fruit to their lips. Their juicy bursting bites wash indigo twilight across the sky, resplendent, swirling, igniting old constellations. In the valley, the tangled bones of countless theaters knit together, marquees rising, spotlights crisscrossing the sky. Dizzy afterimages bedazzle the Witch's fading eyes. Goddesses, queens, genies…

The next bites bring bravura auditions and big breaks, paparazzi and red-carpet fans. And as dreamers and hopefuls flock from premieres, electrified and starry-eyed, they pluck fruit from vines, and the magick multiplies. Champagne wishes and caviar dreams…

Atop her hill, the Witch slouches, each breath a gasp. If she had the strength, she'd tell them they're wishing the wrong wishes. The magick of movies isn't just the razzle-dazzle and applause.

It's the marvelous moving visions movies inspire for real life.

Real-life adventures, real-life romances, real-life heroines and heroes writing their own scripts. But this glittery truth hiding inside Hollywood is a lesson they'll have to reap in their own third acts.

For with every bite, every wish granted by the Fates, the Witch dulls, and she sighs, washed-up, at peace. They take, they give. Let others spread immortal magick through the centuries.

Inside her, violins swell, the final credits cue up, and as her vision fades to black, a silhouette appears against a backlit matte painting of eternity. Bowing before her, he pulls a rose from his sleeve.

And when she reaches, her Projectionist doesn't dissipate. His hand closes around hers, and he tugs her happily into the sky.

Where together, they become stars.

END

—

AMANDA CECELIA LANG is a horror author and aspiring silver-screen witch from Colorado. As a diehard scary movie nerd, her favorite things are meta-slashers, '80s nostalgia, and the rise of a fierce final girl. Her scary stories haunt the dark corners of many popular podcasts, magazines, and anthologies, including *The Deadlands*, *Ghoulish Tales*, *Uncharted*, *Cast of Wonders*, *Gamut*, and *Darkness Beckons*. Her short story collections, *Saturday Fright at the Movies: 13 Tales from the Multiplex* (Dark Matter INK) and *The Library of Broken Girls: Stories of Survival* (Gateway Literary), are available everywhere nightmares are sold. You can stalk her work at amandacecelialang.com—just don't be surprised if she leaps out at you from the shadows.

OSLO

Ross Baxter

Inspector Kristin Vestvik breathed a sigh of relief as she saw the cluster of police vehicles ahead and the uniformed officers blocking the entrance to the small bay at Hvervenbukta. The drive out from central Oslo had been difficult; the roads clogged with those wishing to escape to the mountains or fjords for the weekend, given the forecast of good early spring weather.

After showing her identification to the police blocking the car park, she swung her unmarked Volvo to park by one of the black vans of the Oslo Coroner's Office. Despite the sunny forecast, the skies remained dark grey and overcast, and ice still covered much of the bay, now closed by her colleagues. Grabbing her cap and heavy jacket, she left the car and trudged towards the gaggle of officers huddled from the chilly wind behind a large police incident tent by the shore. Two police inflatables chugged slowly between ice floes in the bay, with divers on board chatting and drinking hot coffee. An officer by the tent saw her approaching and quickly broke off to meet her. She recognized Sergeant Alendal from his shoulder insignia and shock of ginger hair poking from beneath his police cap and smiled a greeting.

"Long time no see!" Vestvik said, shaking the sergeant's gloved hand warmly.

"Too long," smiled Alendal. "I appreciate you coming over."

"Well, Hvervenbukta in March is not top of my bucket list," she replied, glancing at the empty body bags laid out on the icy beach. "The last time I was here with you was when we were cadets, what, twenty years ago?"

"Twenty-one years ago," Alendal corrected her. "Back in the time when all cadets were brought here during basic police training to toughen them up by seeing lots of dead bodies in multitude states of decay. It's not in the curriculum now."

"Thank God," Vestvik muttered. "I had nightmares for months afterward."

"Me too," the sergeant conceded. "But I now work for South Oslo Police District, so Hvervenbukta is part of my patch. I have to do this every spring now."

"It still amazes me that almost anyone lost in the Oslofjord usually washes up here in this small bay. They say it has something to do with the tides, currents, and underwater geography, but it's still pretty strange. Then comes the fateful day in spring when the ice melts, and nearly five months' worth of corpses from around Oslo are recovered here in a single day. All the suicides and accidents; it's a very harrowing day for everyone."

"It is truly the worst day of the year," Alendal agreed. "No one in the South Oslo District wants to be on duty today."

"Which is why it's a bit strange, after not being in touch for years, that you ask me to come to this dreadful place to meet you today." Vestvik frowned.

Sergeant Alendal's face reddened a little as he looked back towards the large white police tent on the icy shoreline. "The dive boat just recovered the last body. How many corpses do you think are lying in that tent?"

Vestvik followed the sergeant's gaze. She shrugged. "Twenty-one years ago, there were twenty-six. Oslo has grown since then. My guess would be around thirty?"

"Wrong. We've only recovered nine."

"That's good then, isn't it?"

"Two years ago, we recovered thirty two bodies," Alendal replied. "Last year we only found fourteen, and this year just nine. Yet the population of the city is at an all-time high of one point one million. Accidents around the water and suicides have both increased in line with the growth of the population, in fact more. But today we've recovered less than a third of the expected corpses, and, strangely, only two were male."

The inspector stared at the tent for a few moments in contemplation. "Then the decrease in numbers must have something to do with the hydrography of Oslofjord. Maybe the currents have changed, maybe less water is coming in from the mountains, maybe something has to do with global warming?"

"Not according to the University of Oslo. They say nothing significant has changed in the fjord in the last thirty years. The tides, currents, water temperature, and salinity are all the same."

"So, are the South Oslo Police District looking into this? Vestvik asked.

"That's just it," Alendal said, shaking his head. "I've tried to raise it a number of times as an issue, but the senior team is ignoring it."

"Well, maybe there's nothing to investigate," Vestvik offered with a shrug. "If the South Oslo workload is anything like our workload in the National Criminal Investigation Service, then this would be way down the list."

"I need to show you something in the tent."

"I'd rather not," muttered Vestvik, wrinkling her nose. "Decomposing corpses will put me off supper tonight, and my partner is making raspeballer."

"Please. You'll then understand why I'm asking for your help."

Vestvik frowned. "I didn't know you were asking for my help."

"Help, advice, or guidance," said Alendal. "There is something amiss here, and it's being wilfully ignored. Even if you could point me in the right direction, being an inspector in the National Criminal Investigation Service, you must know someone at a senior level who would be interested."

"Well, show me what you need to show me, and I'll tell you straight if I can help," she sighed. "Although, I will hold you accountable if I have to throw tonight's meal in the bin."

Alendal nodded his thanks and led her towards the stark white incident tent. The small gaggle of grim-faced junior officers parted to give them access, and they passed through the thick polyester flap. Inside, nine corpses in varying states of decay lay face-up on aluminium gurneys.

"Shit," muttered Vestvik, holding her hands over her mouth and nose against the sickening stench.

Alendal moved to the cadaver on the second gurney and pulled the wheeled table out a little over the flat pebbles forming the floor. A middle-aged man in swimming shorts lay on it, his ruined skin all shades of green and grey. Having been encased in ice for months, the corpse showed only minor signs of carrion predation, although the eyes were long gone and numerous blackened holes in the torso marked the burrows of ragworms. Most striking was the absence of the left leg from midway down the thigh. The shattered yellowy femur extended a little beyond the blackened, putrid meat of the stump, encased in green decaying skin. Vestvik felt her stomach heave.

"The fourth one along has a similar wound and is missing the entire right arm," said Alendal matter-of-factly.

"So?" mumbled Vestvik, trying not to vomit.

Alendal gently took her arm and led her out of the tent, walking with her a dozen meters along the icy beach, into the fresher air.

"Both the corpses with missing limbs are male, the other seven are all female, and none of those are missing appendages. Nothing mechanical could have caused the loss of the leg or the arm. Not a powerboat, not a jet ski, nor the propeller of a larger ship," explained the sergeant.

"Isn't that a question for the coroner?" asked Vestvik, gulping large quantities of chilled air.

"All those corpses are known deaths. They are people who took their own life or had an accident in the last five months but whose bodies were not recovered. As such, the coroner does not undertake a full autopsy, just identifies the corpse before releasing it back to their families for burial. So, how the limb was lost is not investigated."

"Just cut to the chase!" Vestvik ordered testily, fighting her nausea and eager to escape the dreadful beach.

The sergeant withdrew a mobile phone from his winter jacket, flicking through a few screens to find an image he held up to Vestvik. "That is the stump of the arm which was taken from the man on the fourth gurney. If you look closely, you can see teeth marks on the skin."

Vestvik peered at the image but felt unconvinced. "Not necessarily."

Alendal flicked to the next image, showing the screen to the inspector. "Here is the stump of the leg from the guy in swimming shorts. Look to the left."

To Vestvik's untrained eye, teeth could have made the marks, but again, she could not be sure.

Alendal zoomed into the yellowing, splintered bone

extending a few centimeters beyond the putrid flesh. "Those two parallel lines on the bone could only be made by teeth."

"Look, this is not my area of expertise. I've no idea," Vestvik replied. "You need to take this to the coroner."

"I did last year, but I just got ignored. Then, three days ago, a body got washed up near here, a paddleboarder who had been reported missing in late November. Both legs had been taken, and bite marks could be seen. I went to the coroner, and she told me directly not to interfere. When I returned to the station in South Oslo, I received a stern talking-to from my station officer. When I tried to explain, I got a reprimand and received a written warning. I have never had anything like that happen in my twenty-one years on the force. Something is wrong here, and I don't know what to do about it. That's why I contacted you."

Vestvik looked back at the sergeant's phone and the marks on the bone. "Okay. Give me a few days, and I'll try to make some discreet inquiries. Have you any theories on any of this?"

The sergeant's face reddened. "I do, but I'd prefer to see what you come up with first. I don't want you to prejudge anything."

"Fair enough. I'll give you a call sometime next week."

"Thank you," said Alendal.

Vestvik returned up the stony path to her Volvo, unsure whether or not she could stomach any food that evening.

She arrived early at the office to start the new week, partly in an attempt to beat the Oslo traffic, and partly to get a head start on her heavy workload. Leaving the lights off, she walked through the empty six-floor office to the windows, looking at the pink glow over the hills to the east of the city that heralded the start of a new day. Spring was a beautiful season in Oslo—the snow still heavy on the surrounding mountains but the snowdrops bursting from the ground in the parks and gardens, and the bright sunlight turning Oslofjord a twinkling sapphire blue.

Returning to her desk after grabbing a bitter-tasting coffee from the machine, she powered up her laptop and got to work.

"Early start for you, Kristin?" came a voice behind her.

She turned to see Superintendent Leif Foss walking through the open-plan office. She had little time for Foss, a small-minded man who valued the process of police work over the actual gaining of convictions. The early rays of sunshine lit up his gold epaulets and shone from his zealously polished shoes. She groaned inwardly.

"Morning, sir," she said, faking a smile.

"I'm glad you're in the office today," said Foss. "There's something I wanted to talk to you about."

Her heart fell. Luckily, she avoided the self-important superintendent most of the time, as her boss had the particular pleasure of reporting directly to him. Her few dealings with Foss always left her frustrated at how someone so noisome could reach such a senior position in the National Criminal Investigation Service.

Foss moved to stand in front of her desk. "I've been told you were asking many questions at the Coroner's Office on Friday?"

She looked up at him, trying to hide her surprise. "A few questions, yes."

"Concerning which investigation?"

Vestvik frowned; talking to the coroner was not unusual for a police inspector, which she had to do relatively frequently. "I had a few questions on something. That's all."

"Concerning which investigation?" Foss repeated tersely.

"Is there something I should know about?" Vestvik challenged back. "Going to the coroner's office is an everyday occurrence for the team and me. I'm interested to know why you are asking."

Foss's face reddened. "I'm asking because I'm a superintendent, and you're just an inspector. I don't have to justify my questions to you!"

Vestvik raised her eyebrows. She momentarily debated whether to tell the pompous fool where to stick his questions, but decided against it. "You don't, sir, no. My visit to the coroner's office was not about any current investigation. I had a hunch about another possible crime, and I wanted to check something out."

"I'm also told you visited the annual spring corpse recovery at Hvervenbukta last week. Was that anything to do with your hunch?" Foss demanded.

"No, sir," she lied. "I just wanted to catch up with an old friend."

Foss looked at her darkly. "Given the current high

workload of your department, I'm surprised you have time to run after hunches about other crimes, or catch up with friends on police time."

She took a breath, determined to stay calm. "Point taken, sir."

"It better be," warned Foss. "In the future, stick to your own investigations and don't meddle in other departments' work."

"What other departments' work? Whose toes am I stepping on?"

"Are you being deliberately insolent?" Foss spluttered.

"Not at all."

"You've been warned, and I'll be sure to mention your attitude to Chief Inspector Hovda when he returns from his holiday."

She watched him turn and march through the desks towards the door, shocked at the superintendent's strange and officious outburst. Her surprise quickly turned to anger, and she went down to the canteen and took a long, leisurely breakfast at the expense of the department's current high workload.

The shrill ringtone of her cell phone cutting through the silence of the public library made her jump. She picked up, quickly walking to the exit followed by the accusing stares of the handful of other people in the reading room.

"Kristin?" came the voice. *"It's Sergeant Alendal."*

"Hi, Otto."

"*Sorry to bother you, but I was just wondering if you had any thoughts after our meeting at Hvervenbukta bay last week?*"

She moved further into the corridor. "Well, I got warned off by Superintendent Foss. Told to keep my nose out."

"*Oh, I see,*" said Alendal, disappointment clear in his voice.

"Which made me even more curious," she continued. "Which is why I'm doing some research in Oslo's Central Library."

"*Oh,*" said Alendal, this time sounding more upbeat. "*What sort of research?*"

"When we met last week, I asked you if you had any theories on what we saw on those gurneys. You said you did, but that you'd prefer to see what I come up with first. Now I think it's time for you to share your hypothesis."

Alendal replied after a moment of silence. "*I think there is something…something supernatural at work. And I also think that there is some sort of cover up going on on a senior level in the police, and possibly government.*"

"When you say supernatural, what do you mean exactly?"

"*I thought you were going to laugh at me.*"

"No, not at all," she assured him. "What do you think it is?"

Again he paused. "*I'm just a simple policeman, and this is completely outside of my experience. I've tried to come up with a rational explanation, such as a serial killer or a cult, but I can't make the pieces fit. But I can deduce that it is something with a taste for males rather than females. Something that lives in or around water, and lures its victims to their death. Something possibly akin to the folklore surrounding sirens, nøkken or nixe.*"

"Is that not a big assumption?" she questioned.

"If it were a serial killer, or a murderous cult, then the police, the government and the press would be all over it. However, that is not the case here, and so I believe there is definitely some sort of cover-up going on. The folklore of Scandinavia and Northern Europe is full of shapeshifting water spirits using song or music to lure people to drown. They are even mentioned in the fairy tales of the Brothers Grimm."

"I'm not sure why there would be a cover up if there is some sort of supernatural explanation behind this," she mused.

"So you believe me?"

"As a Detective Inspector, I have to be open-minded," she replied. "I'm not ruling it out, but I need more time. My suggestion to you is that you keep your head down over the next few weeks. In the meantime, I'll do some digging, and we'll see what develops."

"But the longer we wait, the more people it takes. I'm close now to finding out where this thing lives. You know Oslo has many rivers and lakes, and Oslofjord itself is huge, but over the months I've narrowed it down significantly."

"Look," she said flatly, "we don't want to be on the wrong side of a cover up. Just have a bit of patience and bear with me."

"I'll try," said Alendal. *"But if I find it I'll have to take action."*

"I understand, but I recommend that you don't. I'll call you later this week. I'm going now. The library closes shortly," she said, ending the call.

With her partner away on business in Bergen, Vestvik settled down to a lazy evening watching TV with an excellent red wine. After her early start, and the late finish at the library, she felt she deserved the vintage bottle. Just as she sat down, a knock sounded on the door, and she irritably rose to answer it. She opened the door to find her boss, Chief Inspector Atle Hovda, standing in the cold outside, resplendent in a bright yellow ski jacket.

"Atle," she said, surprised. "I thought you were skiing in the mountains."

"I am," he muttered. "Or was. But I need to talk to you urgently."

She led him into the lounge and pointed to a seat on the sofa. "Coffee?"

"No, thanks," he said, remaining standing. "Superintendent Foss called me today, Kristin. Evidently, you pissed him off."

She recounted the morning's encounter with the superintendent, adding it was certainly not worthy of disturbing his holiday.

Hovda nodded gravely. "You know my thoughts on Foss, Kristin. He's a jumped-up prick. But we must be careful with him; he's highly connected and has career-ending power."

"I know that, but I'm not sure why he has a stick up his ass about me going to the coroner's office. I can't believe he called you on holiday about it."

"It's about Hvervenbukta," said Hovda in a half whisper.

"I can't tell you any more about it, but I want you to forget whatever you're looking into. Just drop it. Do you understand?"

"Yes, but Sergeant Alendal, from the South Oslo District, brought my attention to it. I think he's right; there is something strange going on."

"Strange or not, you need to drop this, Kristin," Hovda retorted. "Tell him you've found nothing, and tell him to drop it too. I don't want you to leave the force, and lose you from my team."

"I'm not going to leave the police," Vestvik assured him.

"You're not listening to me. Drop this, or you'll find yourself retired early."

She looked at him in consternation; despite being her boss, the chief inspector had always been a friend, and she hugely respected him. The current conversation flew in the face of everything.

"You have to be kidding me!" she blurted, although she already knew the answer. "This is twenty-first century Norway, and a police force which is as open and honest as it can be."

Hovda shook his head. "It's…complicated."

"Look, seventy percent fewer bodies were recovered from Hvervenbukta this year than the usual average. However, I checked the figures, and in the last twelve months, the number of suicides in Oslofjord has doubled. Doubled! And a higher proportion of the bodies were not recovered than in previous years. The few male bodies recovered seem to have bite marks on them, but the coroner will not share or release any records. Something needs investigation here, and yet that self-important ass pulls you back from your vacation to tell me to drop it!"

Hovda closed his eyes and took a deep, tired breath. "If I tell you any more a line will have been crossed. It would be better for us not to cross that line."

"Sir, I've worked for you for many years," Vestvik retorted. "You know I can't walk away from something like this."

"Fine," he sighed, opening his eyes and fixing her with a hard stare. "What do you know about Nixe?"

"Nixe? Malevolent water spirits from Scandinavian folklore?"

"Yes."

"Not much more than I've just told you," she lied, her eyes narrowing.

"Nixe are indeed malevolent water spirits from Northern European mythology. Shapeshifting entities who can appear as mermaids, violin-playing humans, or even horses, and who lure their victims to drown in nearby water. Well, we think we actually have one living in the waters in and around Oslo."

"I don't think this is a good time for jokes," she shot back, trying to sound surprised.

"It's anything but a joke," Hovda assured her gravely. "We have a mythical creature luring people to their deaths and possibly eating some of the bodies. Hence, the increase in suspected suicides and reported accidents, and falling numbers of bodies recovered."

"OK," she replied evenly. "I know the increase in suspected suicides and accidents, and the fall in recovered corpses, is all true, but surely there has to be a more rational explanation. Eastern European gangs, drug wars, weird religious sects, or something like that?"

The chief inspector shook his head. "No, I'm afraid not, which is why all the secrecy. Our government does not know how to tell our citizens and the rest of the world that mythical creatures exist. It would be akin to saying that UFOs and aliens are real. The concern is that if we officially acknowledge the existence of the supernatural, it would lead to a rapid and dangerous erosion of core beliefs and value systems in society, with consequences that no one is prepared for. Religion, science and everything the social order is based on will be questioned. They're scared to open Pandora's Box, and are trying to deal with the nixe without it becoming public and causing wide scale panic, and worse."

"That doesn't make sense," she challenged.

Hovda shrugged his shoulders. "That's how things work at the highest levels."

"So, how many people know?"

Hovda looked even more uncomfortable. "Less than three dozen. Only a select few in the government, some senior commanders in the police, and a small team dedicated to keeping it from the press and social media. I'm the most junior rank who knows, and that's only because of my contacts with the media."

She looked at him and nodded. Then her cell phone

began ringing from the coffee table where she had left it. She reached down, glancing at the illuminated screen.

"It's Sergeant Alendal."

"Put it on speaker. Tell him you've found nothing, and strongly suggest, as a friend, that he drops it," Hovda ordered.

Vestvik gave him a pained expression.

"Trust me, Kristin. Please."

She nodded, answering the call with a flick of her thumb, and turning on the speaker at the same time. "Hello?"

"Kristin, it's Otto Alendal. I desperately need your help!"

Vestvik glanced at her boss, who shook his head discouragingly.

"I'm off duty. What's the matter?"

"I'm technically off duty too, but I followed a hunch and I'm at the south end of the Oslo cruise ship terminal at Filipstad. I think I've finally found the cause of all the missing corpses and the teeth marks, but I need some backup."

"I'm not on duty. Just call it in, Otto."

"I can't. With all this cover up and conspiracy happening, if I call it in, I don't know what will happen. I've found what I think is some lair right here in the heart of the city! I'm waiting for it to return, but I'm not sure I can handle it alone. My theory is that it only preys on men, that it has some sort of hold on them. You might be immune."

"Just get out of there!" she commanded. "That's an order!"

"I can't, I think it knows I'm here. I'm hiding in some old crates, if I make a run for it it'll see me. There's a hole in the fence behind an old shipping container at the end of Filipstad Road. You'll see

my old Saab parked there. Please help me, Kristin, I'm not sure what I'm facing and I can't do this alone."

She looked at Hovda, who again shook his head, this time more vigorously.

"I'll be there in twenty minutes," she said, ending the call.

"Shit!" Hovda cursed.

"You don't have to come," she replied, "but a fellow police officer has asked for help. And if Superintendent Foss won't deal with it, I will."

"He'll have our badges," Hovda muttered.

"Your choice," she shot back angrily.

Hovda shook his head. "I'll drive. But bring your gun, I don't have mine."

Hovda pulled in behind Sergeant Alendal's tatty Saab, the only vehicle at the end of the deserted service road by the port. With the start of cruise ship sailing season still a month away, the area stood forlorn and empty, waiting for the temperatures to rise.

Vestvik handed Hovda her spare torch and jumped out of the car into the dark chill of the early spring evening, her breath condensing in white clouds. Her boss locked the car and followed, his bright yellow ski jacket seeming very out of place in the drab surroundings.

She quickly found the hole in the chain-link fence behind a rusting shipping container and squeezed through, turning on the powerful torch to illuminate the darkness ahead.

Overgrown with weeds and strewn with rubbish, the area starkly contrasted with the clean and wealthy city that lay just a few hundred meters beyond the empty dockyards. Hovda followed, taking his time to get through the rusting fence, careful not to rip his glaringly bright jacket. They crept along an unkempt path, the wet undergrowth soaking their trousers. After a short distance, they stepped out behind a low, unlit building onto the slippery concrete of the dock. Vestvik shone her torch along the wet apron, stopping on a small dark object twenty meters away.

"Is that a gun?" Hovda whispered.

Vestvik did not answer but cautiously approached, stooping down to examine the discarded weapon, a police-issue Heckler & Koch P30 pistol. She looked up worriedly at Hovda, then picked up the weapon and checked the magazine.

"It's not been fired. It's Sergeant Alendal's I think. We may be too late," she muttered, seeing the Chief Inspector gazing off to sea.

"Can you hear that?" Hovda said. "It's beautiful."

Vestvik stood, straining her ears. "I can't hear anything."

"The singing. So clear, so perfect."

She looked at him in confusion, hearing only the sound of distant traffic from the Oslo ring road. "We need to call for support. Alendal has dropped his weapon and he is nowhere to be seen."

Hovda held a finger to his lips, his eyes fixed on the dark waters beyond the dock. The torch fell out of his hand and clattered onto the rough concrete.

Vestvik grabbed his shoulder. "What's wrong with you?"

Hovda ignored her, moving slowly towards the edge of the dock. She pointed her torch towards the dark, still water, scanning the glassy surface. Then she saw the wake of something moving towards them. Hovda shook her hand from his shoulder and took another faltering step forward. She focused the torch at the front of the wake, watching in horror as something rose from the water. Long, dank, straggling hair fell over a thin grey face, a visage of death itself, yellowy eyes over a maw stuffed with needle-sharp teeth.

"She's beautiful," Hovda rasped, drool running down his chin.

This time, she grabbed both his shoulders, dragging him backwards over her outstretched leg and causing him to tumble heavily down to the wet concrete. Memories of childhood fairy tales of the nixe flooded back: a malignant spirit taking the form of a beautiful singing nymph, luring men to a watery grave. Whether her gender made her immune to the trance, she was unsure, but the creature now headed straight towards her, its ghastly putrid eyes fixed on her own. Rising half out of the water, two skeletal arms and a slick snake-like torso appeared in the torchlight. She whipped her pistol out of her jacket pocket, levelling it with one steady hand at the advancing horror. Her first shot smashed through the teeth in the gaping maw, the next two hitting the forehead and left eye, sending the creature whirling back. She then emptied the remaining seven rounds into the writhing scaly body, which stopped the advance but did not knock it down.

It opened its mouth wide to emit a bellow, but she heard no sound. Hovda screamed in agony on the dockside behind her, clutching desperately at his ears. Dropping her own pistol, she grabbed the sergeant's P30 from her pocket and sent another nine bullets into the nixe's head. The creature fell backwards and slowly sank from view, its blood leaving an oily slick on the water's surface.

"What happened?" Hovda croaked, looking around dazed and confused.

"I've sorted Oslo's nixe problem out. It's a good thing it's you here and not Superintendent Foss. I may have been tempted to act as slowly as he has been acting all these months, and let the nixe take him as it took the good sergeant. Now, let's go and see Foss and discuss his forthcoming resignation."

END

—

After thirty years at sea, **ROSS BAXTER** now concentrates on writing sci-fi and horror fiction. He originally started writing Westerns to while away the long hours at sea during the lengthy night watches, the wide open spaces of the Old West distracting from the close confines of a warship of the New West. His varied work has been published in print and Kindle by a number of publishing houses in the US and the UK. Married to a Norwegian and with two Anglo-Viking kids, he now lives in Derby, England.

DETROIT

V.L. Barycz

"When spring has sprung through sidewalk cracks, Mr. Splitfoot is brought back. Born to Detroit, misfortune sown. Blood for blood, he'll take what's owed."
—Ms. Edna Coleman, 1977

Mr. Hobert was off his meds again. He stood, naked as the day he was born, on his porch, making a fuss at something in his yard. That was the curse of Detroit in March when the air could be ripe with garbage the city was too busy to collect one minute, or bone-rattling cold the next. Filamena "Filly" Moore, at fourteen, understood this ailment—the heat, the smell, and Mr. Hobert losing his medicine—was something to be endured, not broken. This curse was eased by the infrastructure her father talked about over the dinner table, eyes fiery but smiling easily when any of his girls' asked questions. No, Filly didn't believe in dragons or knights or curse-breaking. She believed in collective bargaining, the importance of literacy, and getting

Mr. Hobert to at least put on a pair of shorts.

By the time she got to the chain link that blocked entry to Mr. Hobert's front yard, he was sitting on his stoop, muttering hotly as he pointed to some spot on the lawn. His head was low, his dark curls flattened on one side and bursting out from the other as if in fright.

"Hey there, Mr. Hobert."

"He stole it. Took it right off m'porch."

That was a new one. "You got a thief, Mr. Hobert?"

He glanced up, "He's mad I don't got a better tribute this year."

Filly's excitement deflated. Not real. Well, it was real to Mr. Hobert, but it was not something she could take to the Watchers.

"Did he steal your pants?" she asked sympathetically. "Notorious for it, if I remember correctly."

He stared, his brown eyes sharp for a second even as the yellow around them crowded in, "Don't be stupid."

"Then what's your excuse?" she said, "Because you ain't got nothing on, and we got kids on this street."

"Oh damn," he said in wonder as he looked down. "My apologies, Miss. Filly, this ain't right. Not right to be sittin' out here like this."

He covered himself, and Filly bit her cheek as he stumbled back up the steps. She shouldn't have been sharp. "Edges like sandpaper," her auntie would say with no venom, just facts. Filly wished sometimes, she could be like her little sister Gracie, who let most things roll off her with a shrug and a smile.

The door creaked open, wailing on its hinges before it cut off with a click. Silence filled the street, interrupted in fits and starts by the hum of traffic on Martin, but Filly just brushed her hands together and made her way through the yard. The block raised itself, taking pride despite the exhaustion of the residents. It was the whole reason Filly suggested the Watchers in the first place, when she found Ms. Jimenez asleep in her car after a double at the hospital. She knew how hard the block worked—saw how tired its brick and mortar was. Even her own stoop, with its welcome mat and brightly potted flowers, held spots of crumbling concrete.

There was dinner to think about, and books still left on her spring break reading list, but the warm weather was a welcome reprieve, so she laid her cheek against the wrought iron guardrail. She hadn't quite made it to Gran's level of delusion, that if you closed your eyes and listened to the hum of traffic it sounded like the ocean, but the bump of stereo bass down the block was soothing nonetheless. When her father pulled up, stretching out of his car with long limbs and smelling of automotive grease, he only blinked before settling beside her.

"Anything to report?"

Filly smiled and curled her toes against the edge of the crumbling step. "Nothing much. Ms. Cassie finally caught the raccoon getting into her garden; someone forgot a dollar near the dead-end gutter, and Mr. Hobert—"

"Again?" he said.

"Yep, said he's got a thief. I got him back inside."

Her father's hand was gentle on her shoulder, and she pressed her cheek to it.

"Good looking out, Filly. The early heat always makes it worse."

Mr. Hobert had lived in that same house since he was a boy, never leaving the street even after his parents passed. It was a common point of gossip that by some miracle of the Good Lord, Mrs. Hobert, previously Miss Edna Coleman, had fallen for the peculiar Ernie Hobert when they were children no older than Filly. They seemed like an old mismatched salt and pepper set, Mrs. Hobert in her Sunday best and Mr. Hobert in his white tank and shorts. But if she hadn't, the block whispered to each other, then who knows how quickly he would have fallen apart? Yes, it was a miracle and Mrs. Hobert, an angel. But now, Mrs. Hobert was two years in the ground and Mr. Hobert naked in his yard.

"We should get inside and get dinner started."

Filly nodded, "Gracie's lost that tooth."

"Did she—"

Before he could finish, Filly lifted the loose brick near their feet. They both stared at the tiny white tooth sitting in the crushed mortar.

Her dad's sigh was as long suffering as her own when Gracie wiggled that tooth at Filly earlier. "I'll speak to Gran again. She knows that story scares y'all."

"It scares Gracie." Filly said, "Doesn't stop her fussin' about getting that butterfly braid bead as her prize."

"Friday, I'll take her down to Char's and let her pick out the exact one. You want a change-up before school starts back?"

She patted her tightly bound buns and considered, "Nah, I don't want to sit that long right now."

In amusement, her father shook his head and pulled her up to her feet. "Remember, it's break; you're allowed to relax."

Filly nodded her agreement even as she went over the next day's schedule in her head. It was easier than people thought, watching once you knew what to look for, and they were all mostly outside during break anyway.

As she followed through their brightly painted red door, she glanced back towards where her sister's tooth lay hidden before ducking inside.

Rasheed Thompson hated basketball. Such thoughts were sacrilege, and he couldn't admit it to anyone besides Jonah, who was a lost cause. It was the stupid shoes, that incessant squeaking as ankles rotated left, then right, before cutting left again. Spring was a reprieve from it, mostly, as the street scraped at rubber soles instead of shrieking on the glossy court. Still, it's why Rasheed asked for the morning Watcher shifts, so by the time he was done, he had an excuse to miss the early afternoon game.

Besides, from the window of his duplex's bedroom, he had one of the better sightlines of the street even without the binoculars Filly gave him when he accepted the role. Well, accepted was an understatement he could admit only to himself, and even that made him cringe. He'd been listening so intently, he'd nearly eaten concrete while walking to the bus stop, when Filly detailed her plan.

"You want to watch the neighborhood?"

"I want to keep everyone safe," she said, pointing at the streetlights. "The city started, got those fixed, but it's up to us to maintain."

It was his moment; he had trained for this all his life. All thirteen years of his life.

"So, we're gonna be like Batman."

That earned him a look that might have made him wither if he hadn't been born to his mother.

"Jonah already said he'd help, you know. I don't actually need you."

"Please, like he's getting taken seriously on the block. He's practically new."

Even if Jonah had been born to the block like the rest of them, he'd still be the odd one out. He hated basketball openly and liked collecting bugs, for what purpose no one knew. He wore sweaters that covered his arms, and chewed on his pen caps. He also happened to be the unknowing recipient of Rasheed's unending devotion. Not that that amounted to much, Rasheed could admit to himself, but he had plans. This was gonna be his year.

"I've got binoculars."

Rasheed scratched at the recently sprouted chin hairs he coveted. "If I get the binoculars, you got yourself a Watcher."

Jonah Wiśniewski needed spring over. Everything was wet and wanted a piece of you. The mud that came from dogs running the same chained paths sucked at your feet, and the heavy air could be rancid or bitterly cold, depending on the mood that blew down the block. If he had his way, he'd sleep through spring, curled under his blankets, instead of walking the Watchers beat that Filly had outlined for today.

The block was quiet, still muted in color by the pummeling of winter. The grass, which valiantly survived, was the tone of a mottled bruise, and as if in solidarity, Jonah rubbed at the one similar on his wrist before pulling his sleeve down over it. No one was on their porch midday, too busy with work to be idling, but at the end of the street, Jonah saw Mr. Hobert dragging something from the bed of his truck.

Dodging as many dips in the sidewalk as he could, Jonah made his way to the older man, cataloging the amount of straw stacked and the three bottles of lighter fluid.

"Need any help, Mr. H?"

The old man froze, eyes wide in his narrow face, as if keeping them open allowed him to see everything simultaneously. When he didn't respond, Jonah nodded and lifted the bale for him.

"It's okay, Mr. H. I had a bad day yesterday; didn't feel like talking much either. Why don't you show me where you want these, and I'll get them moved for you?"

With a nod, the old man led the way. If the house had seen better days, the fence would have been a relic from another time. What once provided privacy from peering eyes now, like Mr. Hobert's mouth, held gaps that allowed for glimpses into the yard. Jonah followed and grimaced as the mud slurped the soles of his shoes.

"You getting a dog for the yard, Mr. H? Is that why you got all the straw?"

Mr. Hobert hadn't had a dog in years, and even then, it was a house dog, a tiny yorkie that eyed anyone who came close with suspicion. He'd never heard of Mr. H wanting a yard dog, but there wasn't much else this amount of straw could be for.

"Buildin'."

Jonah looked up from the mud, trying to steal his shoes, and almost dropped the bale. It was a man woven from straw and loose bits of wood. He only had one arm, tightly bound to his body with what looked like torn cotton, the color of blood.

Rasheed would have cursed. Filly would have immediately written it down in her log. Jonah only stepped forward and gently set the bale down. Mr. Hobert didn't bother waiting for privacy; he just began pulling straw and shaping it into the gaping void of the straw man's side.

"What's he for?"

"Mr. Splitfoot. He's coming back."

Jonah nodded like he understood, "You buildin' for him then?"

Mr. Hobert paused, brow furrowed as he stared. Jonah stared back, hands curling into the sleeves of his shirt. He saw the minute the man's eyes flickered on his wrists.

"He can help with that if you ask him. Helped me. Helped most of the block before."

Jonah shoved his hands into his pockets. "I'll go grab your straw for you."

Hunching his shoulders, he returned to the truck, writing his report in his head, wondering how much more he could pump Mr. H for information.

"Whatupdoe!"

Jonah felt his stomach flip even as he grinned. Rasheed, lanky as a skeleton, with hands and feet oversized enough to make him look like the Hamburger Helper mascot, jogged towards him.

Jonah motioned to the straw, "Helping out."

"He got a dog?"

Jonah shook his head. "Want something to yell at Filly about?"

Rasheed's smile went wide. "Always."

"Grab a bale," he said. "How was morning watch?"

Rasheed rolled his eyes, "Boring as fuck. Nothing ever happens when—I'm sorry, the fuck?"

The laughter caught in Jonah's throat as Rasheed left him behind, his long legs eating up the distance between them and the straw man. Without preamble, Rasheed launched the bale and immediately began inspecting. He poked at the cloth-bound joint, lip sucked between his teeth.

"Gonna burn pretty quick," he said, then gripped its finished hand. "Godspeed, my friend."

"Don't be touchin' unless you want trouble." Mr. Hobert said, shooing at them. "Go on now."

"Why?"

"I don't have time for questions." Mr. Hobert said, "Your boyfriend listens just fine, but you—always yappin'."

Jonah shrank back at the term, but despite the red of Rasheed's cheeks, he—in fact—continued yapping.

"Nothing wrong with asking questions and now I'm gonna be sendin' Filly your way, Mr. Hobert." Rasheed warned, pulling Jonah away and around to the front of the yard, "One, what the fuck, Jonah, and two, what the fuck, Jonah."

"I'm not the one building it."

"No, just referring to it by its Christian name. Have you eaten?"

Jonah jerked a little at the change of subject. "Why?"

"Means no," Rasheed said, and tugged on him. "Come on, I'll get you fed."

"Sheed."

"Your hands are shaking."

The duplex door shuddered as Rasheed shoved at it, the crimson poinsettia wreath barely hanging on for dear life. Even as his friend barreled up the stairs, Jonah gently shut the door before jogging to catch up.

"Ma! You home?"

For a second, there was silence; then a woman popped her head out of the doorway down the narrow hall. Akea Thompson was tall like her son, skin the same warm brown, dark curls sheared short.

"Why are you yelling in my house, Sheed?"

"The Lord gifted me this voice," he said and grinned at her. "You told me that I should use it freely."

"Not to be a menace," she said, and stepped out into the

hall. "Jonah, you know he's trouble. You should just leave while you can."

Jonah knew she was teasing by the way she gently hip-bumped her son on the way to the kitchen. She was like Rasheed. Soft despite their demonstrative height. Safe despite the loudness of their voices.

As always, Rasheed pulled Jonah with him. "Mr. Hobert's on about Splitfoot again."

While Jonah rarely was aware of his own shaking or the whisper of his peers, he knew adults. He saw the little bursts of fire in their eyes that meant a fist would be raised, or the way a setting of a dish on the table at 5:01 could be an act of war. So he saw Akea's hand freeze for a second, the red threaded bracelet on her wrist swinging at the abrupt stop.

"I'll have to ask Filly's daddy to talk to him," she said, then finished her coffee pour. "He shouldn't be scaring you kids with tales."

"We ain't scared." Rasheed said.

His mother's eyes narrowed again, but she nodded, "Jonah?"

She always asked. Whether it was for his opinion, preferences, or just his food order, she never forgot about him.

"I'm alright. I just—who is he?"

"He's foolishness," she said. "A story from the block to get kids to behave. My mother used to say there was a time he was a Nain Rouge, more mischief than malice after the thaw, but that was before the fires."

"Then he came back as Mr. Splitfoot," Rasheed said, lowering his voice and wiggling his eyebrows. "With teeth so ground down from fury he had to take ours, skin blood red. He no longer gave miracles, only deals."

Jonah swallowed hard and tucked his thumbs to his palms, letting his sleeves cover his cold hands. *He can help you with that. Helped most of the block before.*

"So, what happens if you don't?" Rasheed asked and nudged Jonah. "She tells this story every time I misbehave."

At that, Akea rolled her eyes. "I told you, Jonah, my son is a menace. We *used to say,* he took Tone Jame's gold teeth right out of his head after he broke the deal they made. And that he made Elisha Cole's baby sister disappear because her mama didn't live up to her end of the bargain."

"Did he?" Jonah asked.

Akea's face softened, and where her voice had been firm with her son, it was gentle with his friend.

"No, honey, we was just being kids. Tone James owed people money and Elisha's mama—well, she wasn't right all the time. It wasn't a Nain Rouge baby, just desperate people being people."

"Well, Mr. Hobert thinks he is," Rasheed said as he went for the cookie jar. "He's got himself a straw man all built up in his yard, said he's gonna burn him."

"Don't tell stories." She said, giving his hand a swat. "Food first, leftover pizzas in the fridge. I gotta make my shift. I'll be home in the morning. Be good."

"I'm always good," Rasheed said even as he smacked a kiss

to her cheek on his way to the fridge. "You watch out for Mr. Splitfoot."

"You're lucky I love you," she said. "You need to eat too, Jonah."

"Yes, Ma'am," he said.

He listened as she collected her bag and keys, humming a little tune Rasheed mimicked as he warmed pizza in the microwave. Soft. Safe.

"You just wait till tonight," Rasheed said, his fingers tapping the beat he stopped humming. "The Watchers are gonna put out a fire."

"**F**illy!"

Even as Filly made a mental note to invest in earplugs, she didn't look up from packing her backpack. She wanted to make sure that they had a little bit of everything tonight, since Mr. Hobert hadn't wanted to listen to reason. She had tried everything, tapping her foot like Gran, coughing loudly like Dad, but he hadn't even looked up from that stupid straw man.

"Where is it?"

Filly marked bug spray and a lighter off her list, "What did you lose?"

It was the wrong thing to say, something Filly seemed to be getting increasingly better at the older Gracie got. Even from the corner of her eye she could see her sister's hands slapped onto her hips into what Dad affectionately called chicken wings.

"I didn't lose anything. Someone stole it!"

More likely, whatever it was, would be found in the dirty clothes hamper, so Filly moved on to packing her favorite notepad.

"Filly!"

Dropping the list, Filly gave her a look. "Fine, what are we lookin' for?"

"My tooth. It's not under the brick anymore."

"Gracie, I do not have time for nonsense right now. The Watchers are working tonight."

"I'm a Watcher, aren't I?" she asked. "And I got a problem!"

Pushing a breath through her nose, Filly slung her backpack over her shoulder. It would have to be good enough. "Fine. Let's go look."

She led the way, checking the windows and back door quickly since she'd be leaving Gracie alone till the bonfire was done. On their way out the door, as they always did, both girls pressed two fingers to the picture of their smiling mother, her hair adorned in red flowers.

"I'm telling you, it's not there."

Filly just shot her another look and kicked at the brick, flipping it with the toe of her sneaker. Just that morning, the little tooth gleamed white against the decaying concrete. Now she just stared at a single butterfly bead, not purple, red.

"Yo, Fila-dough!"

She looked up at the boys approaching her. "Don't call me that."

Rasheed grinned back, unperturbed. "Can't. It's too cool a name. Whatcha looking at?"

"I got a bead for my tooth!" Gracie said, and plucked it from the crumbling concrete. "Mr. Splitfoot left it!"

"*Dad left it.*" Filly said. "But he got the color wrong, remember you wanted purple?"

"Oh, right," Gracie said. "Huh, well I bet I can find the tooth in Dad's room. Tell him I lost another one so I can get a red *and* a purple!"

"A con artist after my own heart," Rasheed said. "We got a plan for tonight?"

"We are going to watch, and if it gets out of control, call the fire department," Filly said.

"Boooo!"

"She had me unroll a hose from the side of his house and fill buckets earlier," Jonah said.

Rasheed fist pumped at that, narrow hips shimmying enough that his shorts almost slipped down. "I knew you had it in you, Filly!"

Filly often felt like the only person responsible in the world, but she couldn't help smiling. "Gracie, go back in and lock the door. We'll be back later."

"You gonna tell Dad I was snoopin' in his room?" she asked with narrowed eyes.

"Not if you stop wasting my time."

The chicken wings sprouted again, bony elbows pointed out, palms on tiny hips.

"Rude."

"Get."

The slam of the door would get her a slap on the bottom

from Gran or a steely look from Dad. Filly just shook her head and started down the steps. Even though the street was deserted, they crept across the alley pass between Parkwood and Waldo. The far end of Mr. Hobert's fence was bent forward, as if winded from a long run, and with two boards missing, they had a perfect viewing spot. The straw man stood, visible in the rapidly descending darkness, as Mr. Hobert approached him.

"Welp, guessin' the nagging you gave him didn't work," Rasheed said.

As the older man moved, the floodlights on the back of his house bloomed, spreading across the yard. Filly shoved the boys down.

"He's got the lighter fluid," she said. "He's dousing it."

Before anyone could answer, the floodlights cut, the timer expiring. Blinking against the darkness, they watched a single flare of light pop into existence. The glow bobbed through the air, then towards the earth.

The match caught the straw; its crackle was more like phlegm-choked laughter than fire, but the light emanating left no doubt. The straw man didn't struggle as smoke curled around his legs, nor when it swept past the first red cloth-bound joint of his hip. Mr. Hobert, however, couldn't seem to stay still. His hands fluttered, and they could hear him speaking, but distance swallowed the words.

The straw man shivered in the flames. Then, as if by some trick of light, he stepped forward. Except he didn't. Another figure, bent and crooked, flames licking it, stepped towards Mr. Hobert.

"Are you guys fucking seeing this?" Rasheed said.

Both Jonah and Filly nodded mutely. The creature was hunched, and the flickering fire cast a red glow against his skin.

"Yo, this ain't right. Filly, this ain't right," Rasheed said.

"Shush." Jonah and Filly said in tandem.

There was a sharp snap as if a bundle of twigs broke, and the creature's head whipped around to stare at the fence, head cocked.

"No way he can see us. Just keep quiet," Filly said.

Mr. Hobert must have spoken because the creature turned back in his direction. In the dark, Filly leaned forward and strained, but could only hear the tone of her neighbor's voice, ripe with panic.

Refusing to blink, she narrowed her eyes, trying to focus on the creature's face. The firelight flickered or maybe his face did, like his flesh had to catch up with the quickness of his movement. Then he grabbed Mr. Hobert by the neck. A sickening crack, too wet to be wood, split the distance, and they all watched their neighbor's limbs go limp.

"Did—did he just—"

The words were quiet, only a breath Jonah and Filly should have heard, but the creature's head whipped in their direction again. Before they could swallow, Mr. Hobert's body hit the ground, and the beast was coming.

"Run!"

Like bullets, they flew, feet scrambling over broken asphalt and things left behind. Rasheed quickly passed them both, leading the way back to the street's front. The crackling of fire was louder now, harsh glee, and Filly could have sworn she felt the soles of her sneakers melting into her socks.

"Safe House!" she said. "Safe House, Rasheed!"

"No shit!" he said and took a hard left.

The house looked the same as the others on the street. The squat block foundation with its half a dozen steps, and the siding a faded cornflower blue. What was once the pride of Ms. Judith Simmons had, since her death, lain dormant while her children fought over it in probate downtown. The house wasn't worth its weight, but the land would sell. So, the house was left to lose the war to weeds and wear.

He hopped the small fence that outlined the front yard and immediately shot up the steps, skipping the one he knew wouldn't hold weight. He grabbed the key tucked under the mat and had it in the lock by the time the other two caught up to him.

"Inside, inside!" Filly said and shoved at the boys. Last in, she slammed it behind her and pressed her back against the wood as she slid to the floor.

"I'm just gonna say it," Rasheed said, "I'm the fastest kid within ten feet."

Even as she swatted at him, Filly felt the hysterical laughter bubbling in her chest. He dodged it easily and plopped down next to Jonah, who had pulled his knees up to his chest.

"Okay, okay, so none of us is crazy," Rasheed said, nodding as he talked, "and only Jonah needs glasses, so at least the two of us know what we saw."

"I don't need—"

"You squint at the whiteboard at school."

"Hush!" Filly held a finger to her lips as she turned her ear to the door. Even through the thick wood, she could hear the creak of the first step. Rasheed slid on his knees to the window, fingers just grazing the bottom of the curtain so he could peek. The second step was even louder and Filly looked to Rasheed, who held up three fingers.

The wood cried out as the creature stepped again, a high pitched dry crack as the third step gave way. Heat burst through the room as the creature shrieked.

"Pit trap," Jonah whispered.

During the winter, boredom overtook common sense, and Rasheed had found old pieces of rebar, so they built the stair trap. Jonah suggested it, and crawled under the broken piece of lattice that blocked entry to the under porch to hammer rebar into the frozen earth, so they stuck out like sharp nails from an unyielding hand. A first defense, he explained, in case anyone ever came after the Watchers. Safety.

The creature continued to shriek, and Filly pushed away from the door.

"Do we call someone?" She said as she paced, "do we call the police?"

"And tell them what? Be real, Filly, like the sixth precinct gonna come down here at this time of night with any urgency," Rasheed said, eyes glancing around, "I'll be right back."

He scampered off, pushing on all fours for a second, and then he was through the back hallway into the darkness.

Quietly, Jonah eased up onto his knees and took the window position, but instead of looking out, he turned to Filly.

"Rasheed's mom knows about this thing."

"What?"

"You don't have to believe me, I know I'm not block, but she knows. She called it a story but she was lying."

"How do you know?"

He looked at her, face smeared with dirt where he must have tripped running but his eyes were hard and clear. "Adults lie. She said you can make deals with it for stuff. That's what Hobert said too."

"Got my bat!" Rasheed declared as he sprinted back. "Are we gonna go out and end this thing or what?"

Filly didn't shift her gaze from Jonah, searching for a second then nodding to the window. Jonah pushed the curtain aside.

"It's too dark, but I can hear it."

She could too, now that she focused, a wet whimper that sounded like a wounded dog. "Sheed, you sure you can do this?"

"Of course," he said, gripping his bat tighter, "probably."

It was as good a response as could be expected, so she turned the knob. The door wailed on its hinges and single file, they stepped out, heads whipping from side to side, taking in the empty porch. Slowly, gingerly, they crept towards the wound in the stairs they created and stared down. Blood was splashed, like the time Gracie had dropped a can of Prego, painting the empty rebar that reached out towards them a gruesome chunky red.

"He's not there."

"Now, what the fuck do we do?"

"Guys," Jonah said, voice wavering as he pointed.

In the pooling of the light from the street, its skin was a slick crimson as if dipped into a fresh nosebleed. Matted dark hair ran down its body, ending at the two split hooves it stood on. As it cocked its head it smiled at them, exposing two rows of glistening teeth.

"Back in the house," Filly said, voice low as she grabbed both boys' shirts. "Now."

She expected it to chase them, but it only watched, head turned, smile wide, as they quickly backed up through the doorway. Filly once again shut the door and pressed her back to it.

"Filly. We need a plan."

"And I need a minute," she said, "Sheed, did your mom make a deal with him?"

"My mom? What?"

The tapping of glass from deep within the house had them all jumping and Rasheed swinging his bat. Bewildered, Filly glanced around, but Jonah nodded.

"Back door."

Filly went to move but Rasheed caught her hand, "It could be him."

"Help! Please, is anyone home?"

Filly and Rasheed scrambled at that, tripping over each

other on their way to the kitchen, shoving the sliding glass open, and immediately hauled in Mr. Hobert. The side of his head was bloody, his chest moving with a flutter, and his left arm hung twisted like a green limb on a tree.

"We got you," Filly said. "We have supplies. Rasheed, check his vitals like I showed you. We thought you were— we saw—we thought we saw—"

Mr. Hobert reached out a trembling hand. "Bless you, Filamena."

As Mr. Hobert spoke, only Jonah seemed to stay back, moving towards Rasheed's abandoned bat. Without taking his eyes off the man, he eased down and gripped its handle.

"Don't touch him, Rasheed."

Even as the others looked in confusion, Mr. Hobert started to smile.

"Oh, a smart one," he said, tongue flicking out to wet his lips, leaving a streak of blood at the corner. "My bet was on the girl."

"Mr. Hobert doesn't have a gold tooth," Jonah said.

"Right again," he said. "Nor does he have this lovely little baby tooth I picked up this morning."

He opened his mouth wide, jaw cracking to expose the second row. Nestled in between two mismatched molars was a single gleaming white tooth, tiny and perfect.

"What do you want from us?"

At that, his head cocked curiously. "What do I want? It's what one of you wants. That's how it works. You ask, I give."

"None of us asked for you." Filly said.

He eased up onto his hands and knees, and the kids all scuttled back. Even as he pushed to his feet, Mr. Hobert's skin draped, a suit too big, before sliding off completely to the floor. It slapped against the cheap linoleum like a hand against a cheek.

"I'm gonna throw up," Rasheed said.

"I know it wasn't you," Mr. Splitfoot said, his yellow eyes on Jonah. "Your parents haven't even said hello to me since you came to the block. And yours," he pointed at Filly, "well, your father's too stubborn after that unfortunate misunderstanding with your mother. So, I'm thinking, it's you."

Rasheed looked at the others, then down at his chest. "Me? I didn't—"

"Oh, but you did."

He opened his mouth to argue, then slumped. "I shook your hand," he said, looking back at his friends, "I was doing a bit."

"While I have been called for far worse things than a comedy routine, it doesn't change the facts," Mr. Splitfoot said, taking a step forward, "a deal must be made."

"I have a deal for you."

Stepping forward, Filly pushed Rasheed back towards Jonah and held her hand out. Filamena Moore didn't believe in curse-breaking. She believed in researching problems, in town hall discussions, and that when you had to raise a fist instead of offering a hand, you were prepared to live with the consequences.

"Five years," she said. "I want five years of you off my block."

"A martyr."

"A rest," she said. "The block deserves it."

"Hmmm. And what do I get for it?"

Swallowing hard, Filly let out a wavering breath, then opened her mouth to show her teeth. "Take your pick."

Mr. Splitfoot's smile grew wider, eyes darting from tooth to tooth, his tongue running over the mismatched set in his own mouth. "That's a lot of time for one measly tooth."

"What about one from each of us?" Jonah asked, eyes darting to Rasheed, who nodded. "Three teeth, four since you already got Gracie's. Four teeth for five years."

The beast's lips pulled, the red flesh of his cheeks curling up behind his ears as he leaned forward to inspect his prize. "Open up and let me see."

Filly sat with her swollen cheek against the cool iron guardrail of her stoop, watching as the police wrapped the gate of Mr. Hobert's house with neon yellow tape. Her jaw throbbed, but she let the ice pack Gracie brought melt against her leg, dripping darkened splotches onto the steps. Every so often, an officer would glance her way, but she just stared back. She wanted to close her eyes, to try to hear the traffic on Martin and pretend it was the ocean, but she realized outside of tv, she wasn't sure what the ocean sounded like. It wasn't until her father's car gently tapped the curb that she felt a little piece of herself come back, the familiarity of his parking, his stretching, his voice the first thing to feel real.

"Looks like something big happened, huh," he said and settled next to her. "Anything to report?"

Filly curled her toes against the edge of the crumbling step and turned so he could see her swollen cheek. Immediately, his hand was there, cradling, a thumb pushing up her chin so he could get a better look.

"Baby wh—"

Filly opened her mouth to let him see.

END

—

V.L. BARYCZ became a writer when her elementary school convinced her that words were more constructive than fists. Since then, she's written for *Foliate Oak Literary Magazine*, *Gravel Magazine*, and *Empty Sink Publishing*. Her debut novel, *A Promise of Sirens*, is now available through Outland Entertainment. When not hoarding notebooks to write in, V.L. can be found somewhere in Detroit collecting the things people discard.

CHESTER

Die Booth

Then:

"Llanfair…pwllgwyn…"

"Is he OK?" Jake's whisper comes out louder than he intended, but Dave doesn't hear him or doesn't care.

Owen says, "Yeah. He does this when he's stoned."

"Gyllgogery…chwyrndrobwll…" Dave lets out a low-pitched giggle as he rocks gently back and forth on the flagstones. They're all tucked up someone's path, a side entrance to the pink flats by the old bridge, the chalky bubblegum hue of the pebbledash overhanging them leeched grey by the hungry night. Jake flashes Owen a look of alarm, and Owen grins and hands him the joint, loosely wrapped and ashy. "Llantysilio…gogogoch…" Still rocking, Dave looks, despite his hazy smile, worryingly pale in the darkness.

"Just, he looks like he's about to whitey—"

The second Jake says it, Dave executes the mildest yet

most effusive vomit that Jake's ever witnessed, spraying in a golden fan across the dirty flagstones. The girls squeal and rocket to their feet, quick enough to make Jake's head spin: he takes a showy drag on the joint, purposefully not inhaling too deeply, and passes it back to Owen, checking to see if he's looking.

"Oh god, it's running downhill," Emma says. Dave smiles softly, still rocking.

Jake says, "C'mon. Let's get the drinks." He needs a walk to clear his head and escape the smell. And he gets to give Owen a hand up as he hauls himself to standing.

It feels a little mean to leave Dave there, but only a little. "He'll catch us up," Owen says, zig-zagging the width of the walkway as Jake tries to bump into him but make it look accidental. It's almost pitch black now, this side of the river. They navigate by familiarity and the few lights spangling the high dark waters from the street on the other side, like glitter tossed across satin. When they get to the bushes by the suspension bridge, the crossed iron latticework of the bridge tower is barely visible, silhouetted against a midnight-blue sky. The air here smells clean again. Clean green leaves, budding. Sweet, damp mud, the sluggish brown river scent still cool enough to be fresh. By instinct alone, Jake digs in the deep leaves just inside the dome of foliage until he feels the clink of his nails against glass and comes up with a bottle of Thunderbird. "Ladies."

"Cheers." Vicky takes it and passes the next one to Emma. Groping through the undergrowth, Jake digs deeper. Feels a fleeting gut-drop before his fingers finally close upon his bottle of cider. Not stolen, then, while they were all at the pub. He pulls it out, brushing off the leaf mould and cradling the three litres like a weighty baby as they all follow Owen beneath the bridge.

"Not here." Emma looks up, and for a brief second, the lights across the river catch her eyes like a cat's. "Conifer tree." She carries on down the way, plonking herself in a clear space on the slope of grass leading down to the lower path directly bordering the riverbank.

"What?"

"Belinda," Owen says, and Jake can hear the smirk in his voice.

"Who's Belinda?"

"You know. Belinda, Belinda, beware, beware."

"Shut up, Owe." Emma actually sounds a little anxious. Jake watches her take a long pull of wine, shuffling closer to Vicky on the grass.

And Jake does know. He's not heard that chant or thought about that name since primary school, but the lore is lodged deep in there, tucked up in his memory as cosy as any innocent bedtime fairy tale. "The girl who hung herself in the tree?"

"Hanged herself," Owen says, and Jake punches him in the arm. Even that small contact feels warm on the chill spring night. "And if you walk three times around her conifer tree saying the words, then her skeleton appears in the branches, and...I dunno." Owen rubs his arm slowly. "Kills you, or something. Belinda, Belinda, beware..."

"Shut *up*, Owen!"

"That was a tree at Mill Lane," Jake says. Carefully avoiding the green spikes of daffodils already emerging from the earth, he finds a space on the slope to sit. "It's not just *any* conifer tree. She can't teleport or something; that makes no sense. Ghosts haunt the place they died, right."

Vicky says, "It was Our Lady's High, anyway," as if teleporting is the biggest logic problem with a ghost story.

Jake shakes his head. He says, "Our lady's high. I bet she is," aiming a sideways grin at Vicky. Close beside him, Owen laughs, and it pools a warm, syrupy feeling into his guts. He's drunk already, but he could be drunker. The plastic of the bottle dimples and pops beneath his fingers as he twists open the lid with a crack and takes a chemical-scented swig. He catches Emma's eye. "You have to walk around the tree and do the rhyme. She can't just turn up."

"Or *can* she?"

"Shut up, Owen." They say it at the same time. Jake grins and leans forward to link pinkies with Emma. "Jinx."

"I wouldn't be scared of ghosts, anyway," Owen says. "I'd be more scared of drinking from plastic bottles. You know you can spike a plastic bottle with a syringe."

"Whatever, man." Jake takes another swig, purposefully long, to prove to Owen and himself just how much all the horror stories about spiked drinks don't bother him. The lights on the water twinkle, beckoning, as a breeze stirs the trees and ripples the black surface of the river. He offers the bottle to Owen, and feels just the tiniest prick of rejection when Owen shakes his head.

"Dawn Hunt's cousin said a girl from her school sat on a syringe hidden in a cinema seat, and now she's got AIDS," Vicky says.

Jake shivers. Wipes the back of his mouth with his arm. "Bullshit."

"Don't believe me then, it's just what I heard."

Emma says, "Yeah, but you know about the corner shop on Beckett's Lane when they found pins in the Pick n Mix…"

Jake closes his eyes, forces the shadow of anxiety from his mind, letting their voices sludge together into white noise, tidal as the river Dee beyond. The cider is taking hold, making his mind fog and his belly churn, and he hopes that he's not going to show himself up by puking like Dave did, not in front of Owen, except it's an abstract sort of hope, as if he's floating far above his thoughts and nothing matters anymore. It's kind of relaxing. Shuffling down on the slope, he lies back and can somehow feel every individual grass blade through the fabric of his hoodie, cold and prickly, as if he's becoming part of the earth, the night air like a piece of silk laid over his face.

"Jake?"

When he opens his eyes, there's nothing but darkness. He feels no panic, but for a moment he's confused, until he focuses on twinkling distant pinpricks and remembers that he's lying down and staring at the sky. If he tilts his head backwards, he can barely make out the tops of the trees, black on black. A figure, flickering like heat haze, drifting up there, just about visible even in the dark.

"Jake!"

Jake sits up. He feels lightheaded in the weirdest way, like he's high: OK then, he's probably definitely just high. The others are yelling, but he's never felt so mellow, a marrow-deep peace like the warm touch of summer sunshine on this cool spring midnight. "What's up?" Nobody answers him. He looks down. Someone is lying on the ground, the four others crowded around. "Dave?" He knows he should be worried, but it all feels so fine. Dave's just stoned and passed out, and it's going to be alright. Wait—*four* others?

"Don't move him!" Emma says, her voice high and panicked.

Vicky shouts, "We need to call an ambulance."

They huddle together, the three girls looking pale and scared. Emma and Vicky, and—

The stars shine brighter, telescoping tunnels through time. Choked voices on the wind. Wailing. Crying. Footsteps, further down the path: a figure coming closer. Jake blinks. Rubs his forehead. He tries to catch up through his confusion, and like skipping film frames Dave reaches them. Says, "What's wrong with Jake?" Owen, eyes wild and tearful, rolls the figure into the recovery position on the grass, dark fluid spewing slack from its mouth. From *Jake's* mouth.

It's him. It's *his* body down there. Jake stands dumbly, watching as the wails warp into sirens and others appear, moving too quickly to seem real. It feels fine. It's OK. He watches it like it's happening to somebody else on a TV screen. *He's-not-breathing* is stretchered away up the path to the side of the suspension bridge, his four friends following in spurts and sobs, ebbing up the steps to the main road.

Jake watches them go. At the last moment, Owen looks back. His cheeks are tear-tracked and his eyes are haunted, and for a moment Jake is certain that they lock gazes. That an understanding passes between them. Then, Owen reaches the top of the steps and disappears from view.

The riverbank is quiet with an early morning stillness like a released breath, like a homecoming. He's not alone. She's still with him—the third girl, pale and glowing and unearthly as a pearl. Standing by his side, she says nothing. Nothing needs to be said. Silence heals the night. Fingers brush his, dry as conifer needles, and he takes her hand. Her bones aren't cold. They're warm as belonging.

Now:

This time of year always reminds him of Jake.

The white sky clings to winter, a low sun struggling to climb again, shadows stark and frozen long. But the glitter of frost has turned to a sparkling spring, varnished with frequent misty raindrops that stipple iridescent rainbows across Owen's phone screen as he checks the clock. Burrowing his hands back into his pockets, he quickens his pace. He doesn't want to be late.

Time passes so slowly and so quickly. Owen wonders precisely when he became the type of person who goes to school reunions, let alone one at The Rooftop Social. The answer, he supposes, is that he isn't that type of person at all.

The rain threatens, misting from a ruffled, pigeon-coloured sky. Gulls whirl above the waters, diving at a tree root stuck on the churning weir like a giant, curled spider, as he crosses the old bridge. There are crocuses on the grass in front of the flats, a swirl of violet and gold, but the flats are no longer the pink of his youth, painted instead a dull, invisible grey that matches the milk-glass clouds.

Passing beneath Bridge Gate, he slides down the alley to the right and onto the walls, one hand skimming red sandstone blotched green and white and black with moss and age, the old soft stone rounded by time. From above, the Dee is high and slow, gorged with brown flood water. He can see across it a perfect view of where Jake died. He can remember that night like it was yesterday. He thought that Jake—

He bypasses the Wishing Steps in favour of street level. No wishes today.

He can remember. He thought he saw—

This is why he needs to go to this reunion. To see the others. To see if anyone else noticed, too.

Past the Albion with its jingoistic flags and jaunty chalkboard caps promising "A ZERO TOLERANCE PUB!", the row of Nine Houses lean in, low-doored, treacle-beamed, lion-knockered. What were once alms-houses are now unaffordable, for all they're towered over by the ugly, angular rise of the multistorey car park next door. Old, overshadowed by new, encircled by old. This city has forgotten itself.

No matter how much they've tried to scrub down the stairwell walls of the car park, they can't quite exorcise the ghost of piss. Owen greets the surprisingly friendly bouncer with a nod and tries not to wonder why there's a bouncer on the door at four in the afternoon as he ascends the corkscrew concrete steps to the top floor, his knees creaking.

The top floor is loud. More like a food court than a bar, with kids running about and day-drinking office parties playing pub-Jenga in plywood booths along the walls. It's like they moved the market to an inconvenient location and doubled the drinks prices: you can't even see the view over the built-up beer-garden walls, smothered in plastic ivy. Gritting his teeth, he hands over seven quid for a pint of lager and looks around. Wonders if he'll even recognize anyone, then instantly does.

"You look…*great*." Owen gets a whiff of something floral and vanilla as he hugs her. "You look exactly the same!" He doesn't need to specify when she looks the same as, eerily so, a shiny kind of facsimile of her teenage self, like augmented reality, her teeth white and skin tanned in a way seventeen-year-old Emma's never was.

Emma smiles, the expression oddly neutral. "Cheers hon! You look like shit." She adds a raucous laugh that Owen assumes is meant to signify she's joking (he can't quite tell from her face), but it's a fair cop.

"Yeah. Not been sleeping great."

Emma rolls her eyes at Vicky. "Oh, try having three toddlers." They perform matching giggles. Owen feels like he's disassociating. These aren't the girls he knew in sixth form. Something has changed. Maybe it's him; Jake's death shaped him into somebody more cautious and afraid than his younger self had ever been. In just ten minutes, he can tell the people he once knew have grown older with no memory of what it's like to be young and scared. He's come here for nothing. He'll stay for one drink.

"You doing anything special for Valentine's, Owe?" Vicky asks.

Owen shakes his head. "Nah. No. I just broke up."

Vicky pulls a sad face. "No! Did she bin you off?"

"He."

The women exchange a look so quickly he might have imagined it. Emma says, "Oh, I always knew. With you and Jake…"

And there it is.

He thought that Jake—

"I wanted to talk to you about him." Another quick look passes between the women, this one more panicked than the last, but Owen has just downed a pint, and he ploughs on. "That night."

"Yeah, that was awful," Emma says.

Owen says, "Did you…see anything?"

"See anything? What d'you mean, babe?"

He thought that Jake had felt the same way about him.

He thought that he saw another person there with them that night Jake died.

"Belinda," Owen says.

He isn't sure what reaction he'd expected, but laughter wasn't it.

When Emma and Vicky recover, Emma says, "Oh my god! Fucking Belinda!"

"Who's Belinda?" Emma's husband must be six foot four, with an immaculate flat top and fade, and the exact same shirt as at least ten other guys in the room.

"Matty, you know I told you about that kid that died, and I was there?" Emma says. Vicky's husband, Andy, has tuned in too at the mention of tragedy. Matt nods. Owen thinks, *that kid*. Jake, who will never become an adult shadow of himself. Who has become just an anecdote now, to people who once knew him. "There was this creepy story we all used to tell about this girl what hung herself in a tree at our school, and you had to dance 'round it and say her name three times, and she'd appear."

"What's that got to do with the kid you seen die?"

The kid. Jake. Their friend. Owen's head pounds. Because Jake's death might have been written off as aspiration after too much to drink, but he could swear that he saw Belinda that night, an extra head bent there next to Vicky and Emma.

Emma doesn't answer. She squeals, "Dave!" and runs to greet someone across the crowded room.

This kind of evening can go many ways, none of which Owen had the foresight to predict. They find a booth and order overpriced pizza and more drinks. And more drinks. He catches up with Dave, who works in PPI claims now. He mouths the words to the conversations he's had a hundred times with a hundred people, and now with the ones he once painted his youthful hopes for, who have somehow become strangers to him. As the sun fades outside their bubble of electric light, Emma says, "We should do Belinda!"

"Wahey!" Dave says, loudly drunk, and Emma smacks him on his arm, grinning, and Owen feels, just briefly, a glimmer of what once was.

"The summoning thing! We should summon her. C'mon. For old-time's sake. It'll be well funny."

"I dunno," Vicky says, her expression unreadable.

Emma says, drunkenly insistent, "As a tribute. To Jake."

The sun disappears without fanfare just as they make it to the street. No orange sunset or gilded clouds, just a sudden fading of the white sky into darkness. Across the road, rainbow lights strobe in the window of Off The Wall, the hum of music and voices a contrast to the silent Roman ruins it overlooks.

"Where shall we do it?" Vicky asks.

Emma says, "We need a conifer tree." She points, in through the gates of the Roman Gardens on their right, the mosaic floor mural at the entrance quilted in a drift of ballerina blossom from the trees that flank it. "There's a big one."

Andy, getting into the spirit of it, shakes his head. "Too close to the road. People could see."

"You scared of looking stupid?" Vicky says.

Andy says, "Ghosts don't show up if they're being watched." And a slow, sick feeling slides down Owen's spine.

They carry on, crossing Souter's Lane to the amphitheatre. Dee House looms on the right, standing derelict and blank-eyed, abandoned by a council that only cares for history-that-earns. It's never quiet, even when it is. The traffic rumbles steadily. Saturday night stragglers shout. St John's broods red and squat, embraced by its older ruins, its crisp concentric arched entrance gated and barred in black iron. As they reach it, the clock tower strikes six sonorous dongs.

Vicky slips her hand through Andy's bent arm. Both her and Emma wobble in their heels on the cobbles. "The park's less private than the gardens."

"We're not going to the park," Owen says. He can tell that the others don't believe in this, not a bit. They're just drunk and bored and desperate to feel even briefly what it was like to be their high school selves one last time. He's not even sure why he's going along with it, except something feels like it's pulling him, magnetic and inevitable.

Through the ruins, evergreens arch. It's darker here, down the side of the church, but the city sounds are still strangely present, as if superimposed over a different time and place. They pass beneath the coffin in the wall, the wood worn and warped by weather and long years being mounted up there in the old stonework. Owen expects someone to say something, but nobody does. They're all intent, excited to finally be allowed to play again. As they round the corner to the back of the church, someone has left a pair of lost gloves slipped onto two spikes of the iron railings, waving a welcome. Or a warning to turn back. In front of him, the party piles up, Emma and Vicky giggling, all fear of ghosts lost in the past.

"Conifer tree!" Emma points to where a lone little Christmas tree has been replanted, devoid of its decorations, in the lawn next to the church.

"No," Vicky says. "Not that one. The big one."

Past the church, and the path, and the benches, is a long patch of grass overlooking the river from a height, cut off from the main street and the path that connects the park and the Groves below. You can hear the river from here, and just about see the white tips of the suspension bridge peeking over the rise of the hill. Owen folds his arms, hugging himself, but his beer jacket is suddenly useless. It seems darker here, the wind colder, everything turned down. In the centre of the grassed area, a huge pointed tree looms, black and sombre.

"Well. It's private enough," Owen says. Something is curdling inside him, a mixture of beer and fear, apprehension, and something strangely close to hope.

He climbs up the little wall that borders the path, Dave in tow, silent. Goes to stand next to the tree to wait for the others, who've gone the long way round to avoid the climb. Standing and looking up at it feels more like greeting an old friend than he's felt during the reunion so far. It's vast. Hollow and shadowy inside, with a lattice of branches that look horribly like ribs. The needles are dark, a glossy green paling to yellow at the tips. From the close-growing, teardrop-shaped bulk of it, one long, swaying branch reaches out, like a skeletal arm groping above their heads.

"Shit!" Emma says from right behind him. Owen turns to see her and Vicky both staggering, their spike heels sinking into the soft ground. "This is a stupid idea."

"It was *your* idea," Vicky says, and they both start laughing again, the sound rippling around like dominoes until everyone but Owen is amused.

"What's up with you?" Matt says.

Owen frowns. "I just don't think we should be…" Laughing? Disrespecting her? "I dunno. You know. People died."

Matt snorts. "I don't think there was actually a Belinda, mate. It's just an urban legend."

"Jake died."

Matt raises an eyebrow at him, annoyingly cool. "She didn't kill him though, did she? From what Em told me he choked on his puke, like Hendrix. Rock n' roll."

"He was a person!" If Owen was braver, maybe he'd hit Matt right now. Instead, he says, "He was our friend." If he was braver still, maybe he'd say it: *and I loved him.*

"What happened to 'it's a tribute to him'?" Matt says.

The arm of the tree waves. Owen thinks of Jake, reaching out to him across the decades. He presses his lips together. "Yeah. Alright."

"So," Emma is animated, tipsy-excited. "We've got to go around the tree and say her name three times. Like Bloody Mary."

"That's not it." Vicky starts to walk, towing Andy by the hand. "It's not just her name. It's the words. You've gotta say the words. Belinda, Belinda, beware, beware. Three times."

"Not the words three times. Three times around the tree." Owen can't help it. He has to follow until they're all following, like little kids playing ring o' roses, trooping around the tree and chanting, a blooming crescendo.

"Belinda, Belinda, beware, beware. Belinda, Belinda, beware, beware. Belinda, Belinda, beware, beware. Belinda, Belinda, beware, beware."

It feels unreal. Like the words have lost meaning, only the sound and cadence and action remain, powerful in repetition. Perhaps the words were never the point at all—maybe they could be anything, just sounds to carry the intent of summoning. Owen glances up, up, up, at the top of the tree, shaking like an angry fist. It pounds in his ears like a heartbeat: the roar of the river, roar of the wind in the vast blank sky, the tree creaking like a door opening, like a voice waking.

"Belinda, Belinda, beware, beware. Belinda, Belinda, beware, beware."

A blackbird trills in panic, breaking cover in a flurry from the shivering branches. The roar of the weir goes rush, rush in Owen's ears, the chant lulling him to a stupor, rewinding time. The tree is too tall to see the top of it when you stand close. Too broad around to see the person in front as you follow. He stumbles after Emma, but he can't see her anymore. The scent of pine is sharp and strong in his throat. The stray branch overhead seems to quest and grasp, searching, with clicks and squeaks and whirrs, an alien language. Invoking her, inevitable as the seasons.

Owen chokes on his own breath. His skin goes cold, despite the mild evening, a sudden dump of adrenaline, as he sees. For a second, freezes.

Not the sad shade of a hanged schoolgirl. She is the spring. A spirit that never lived and never died, made of the tree itself, ages old, a force that resurrects year on year when the crocus come, who wants nothing more than to remind them of the fears and magics of youth that they have so wilfully turned their backs on. She looks like Emma, she looks like Vicky, she looks like Owen and Jake and everyone he ever knew, she looks like this city, she looks like the land—like the land before it and after it—she looks like birth and death and rebirth, she looks like rebirth and death.

Owen runs.

His feet slide on the damp grass, going too fast, wild instinct overtaking thought as he jumps down from the tallest part of the wall, stalling as his knees buckle. When he looks back, he sees them transfixed by her dawning light, all six of them. Emma and Vicky. Matt, Andy and Dave. And Jake.

He could stay. He could be reborn into death with them, like Jake was all those years ago, a sacrifice to the new season that centuries of so-called progress explained away into a trite urban fable and named "Belinda." He could join Jake again, become part of the fabric of this land they all grew up and forgot. It feels like a long time, a moment suspended, as he hesitates. Long enough for Jake to turn and see him. To shake his head with a smile. Then Owen is moving again, the smack of his boots against the cobbles loud and real as he pelts through the ruins and back out into the lonely safety of the brightly lit street.

END

—

DIE BOOTH is an indie author who likes wild beaches and exploring dark places. When not writing, he DJs alongside his boyfriend at Last Rites—the best (and only) goth club in Chester, UK. You can read his prize-winning stories in anthologies from Egaeus Press, Neon Hemlock, Flame Tree Publishing and many others. His books, including his cursed novella *Cool S* are available online, and he's currently working on a queer coming-of-age folk horror novella. You can find out more about Die's writing at http://diebooth.wordpress.com/ or say hi on Instagram @dieboothwrites or Bluesky @diebooth.bsky.social.

CAPE TOWN

Rich Larson

The night air is muggy when Elsie limps out onto the terrace to make her phone call. The sky was gray all day, swollen with dark, cancerous clouds, but the spring storms she was promised have yet to arrive, and even the usual sea breeze is nowhere to be found. The distant silhouette of Table Mountain is all but invisible in the evening fog.

She thumbs the call button, her thumb leaving an oily whorl of sweat. The phone starts to ring. Elsie has only one saved contact in her new SIM card: her grandmother, whom she calls each night at 22:30 SAST, which is 15:30 EST across the ocean.

The conversation is always the same. If she wanted, she could recite it by heart.

Hello? her grandmother will say, sounding out of breath and disjointed, even though the phone Elsie bought her lives right beside her easy chair.

Hi, Oma, Elsie will say, with the same intonation every time, drawing out the diphthong of the *i.*

Elsie! her grandmother will say, and Elsie knows she should be grateful to be recognized. *Where are you?*

Cape Town still, Oma. How are you today?

Cape Town? A moment of baffled silence because, in her mind, Elsie is still young, still lives with her parents in Boston, then: *Oh, I'm all right. Still kicking. And you? How are you?*

Elsie sits down in her usual plastic deck chair and waits, rubbing the blister on the bridge of her foot.

After four rings, her grandmother picks up.

"Hello?"

"Hi, Oma."

"Elsie! Where are you?"

"Cape Town still, Oma. How are you today?"

"Cape Town?" The pause is a little longer than usual. "Oh, I'm all right. Still pecking. And you? How are you?"

Elsie knows specifics will be forgotten within minutes, but she worries emotions might linger—so she lies and says she is doing well. She says her article is progressing, that she is deep in research, speaking with experts and locals alike, sponging up every drop of folklore she can.

Every night, Elsie's grandmother is surprised that Elsie is a journalist and worries that it's not a steady income and that it takes her too far from home. But there's a hint of pride, too. That used to be why Elsie called: to make her grandmother feel proud for an instant, happy for another, even if new memories slid off her like oil on water.

But recently, she uses her grandmother's faulty memory as a panic room.

"When are you coming home, Elsie?" The eternal question is laced with reproach. "Why go so far away?"

Elsie rubs more furiously at the top of her foot, skin flaking off against the heel of her hand. "I'll be back in the summer," she says. "Like always. It's late here, Oma. I have to go to sleep."

Another lie. She has not slept all week because whenever she shuts her eyes for too long, she sees the Baby.

Elsie came here to write about the folklore of Cape Town and its surrounding localities. There is no substitute for oral tradition, is what she told herself. No amount of research, whether in online archives or physical libraries, could replace the personal flourishes of a story twisted and sharpened by generations of repetition.

Elsie came here for the tokoloshe, which ranges from a small hairy mischief-maker to a terrifying shrunken corpse, eyes gouged out and reanimated for vengeance. She came here for the nocturnal nagloper, the serpentine grootslang, the bathroom-dwelling pinky-pinky.

More than anything, she came here for Antjie Somers: a melding of Khoisan and European legends, originally a highwayman disguising himself as an old woman, mutated through years of retellings to become a classic child-stealer archetype, a haggish figure armed with a burlap sack, hunting for babies left unattended in their cradles.

It's always nice to have someone to blame.

Insomnia has turned Elsie's days into surrealist films. Part of it is the silence: she's staying in a student residence, but it's mid-term vacation, and most of them have gone back to their families. The lime green hallway is empty, all doors locked except for hers. The televisions in the common area are dark, dead mirrors. The scarred-up billiards table, which normally provides a knocking-clacking chorus no matter the hour, is mute.

From the time she crawls from her sweat-slicked sheets to the time she descends into the city, she doesn't see another human face. There are radio susurrations when she passes the guardhouse, but the man inside has found the perfect angle at which to place his plastic chair. Unless Elsie intentionally cranes her head through the doorway, she can't see any part of him but his propped-up feet.

She limps east along Lion Street, past Bo-Kaap's multicolor block houses—this neighborhood was spared the bulldozers during Apartheid but still suffered. Families were forced from their homes. On her first night in Cape Town, a drunk young man, who worked on cruise ships but grew up in the Cape Flats, said *if you want to write about horror, write about those days: District Six, Apartheid.*

When she told him it wasn't her place to write about real-world tragedies, except as they intersected with legends and folklore, he shrugged, took a suck off his vape, and said *maybe the grootslang, then. It lives in the river and causes thunderstorms.* When he exhaled, the neon red light of the bar sign turned the smoke into a billow of blood. The sight of it made her body heave.

That first night feels impossibly distant now. Her sense of time has been stretched on a rack, the usual joints of sleep and wake brutally dislocated. This morning route along Lion Street, the dip onto Wale's wide cobblestoned artery, the passage through two glass-strewn alleys to rise back onto Chiappini—it seems like she's walked it for years.

Yesterday's clouds dispersed without giving up their rain; now, the sunshine is strong, punching her shadow thick and dark against the dusty pavement. It scuttles along between her legs like a bat. Otherwise, she is alone. This high on the slope, Cape Town's roaring traffic is barely a murmur. She can hear her shoes slap and crunch.

She passes a cafe just opening, an employee sliding the rattling burglar bars to one side. The bandage on her foot slides back and forth, soggy already, and she is thinking of going back to the residence to reapply it when she hears something else: first a scraping, a shuffling, then the thin wail of an infant, lasting only an instant before something cuts it short.

Fresh sweat pours out of her armpits. She smells her own sour fear. She does not break stride.

22:32 SAST. Elsie walked all day, because when she walks long enough, traveling the same route over and over, she can almost stop thinking. The blister has swollen again. She fears popping it, so she scratches only the surrounding skin. Her grandmother picks up on the sixth ring.

"Hello?"

"Hi, Oma."

"Elsie! Where are you?"

"Cape Town still, Oma. How are you today?"

"Cape Town? Oh, I'm all right. Still pecking, still clawing. And you? How are you?"

Elsie is distracted by the feeling of something wet under her nails. She looks down and sees blood and pus blossoming from the bridge of her sweat-studded foot, the blister rent open. She thought she was done bleeding. Her stomach clenches at the hemoglobin smell, and in her memory it mingles with another: the chemical lavender of the washroom where she realized everything was coming apart.

"I'm doing really good," she says.

She swathes her whole foot in bandages and medical tape and walks to the V&A canal. Today, clouds break and swirl across the sun, toggling Bo-Kaap's colors bright, then dull, then poisonously bright again. The wind chops at her hair. Dust and bits of trash whirl up off the paving. On the corner of Wale Street, she watches a plastic bag escape a second-floor window: it extrudes through the burglar bars like a collapsing organ, reinflates, and floats away.

Before she actually came here, Cape Town occupied a Schrödinger's box in her imagination. It was vibrant and beautiful and as safe as any big city; it was crime-ridden, dangerous, specifically harrowing for women. She spent two sleepless nights online, rewording her queries like rolling dice, reading endless anecdotes before she realized it was performative, and booked her nineteen-hour flight.

Now she's really here, but the city feels more imaginary than ever. Part of that is the way it goes from teeming to empty in an instant: she takes the footbridge over Buitengracht's busy double lanes, skirts a writhing traffic circle, descends a stone ramp—and suddenly it's quiet again. She limps alone along the edge of the sparkling green canal, picturing the grootslang uncoiling below the surface.

She knows cities are at their most dangerous when you look around and see nobody. But the canal is hemmed in by financial buildings and luxury apartments, an oasis of wealth patrolled by security guards with reflective vests and tired eyes, a bubble she can enter unthinkingly thanks to white skin and designer sunglasses.

The clouds burn away as she walks, leaving the sky a shocking blue. The sun drums at her skull, counterpoint to the throb in her foot, and she feels a familiar migraine coming on, the one that curls up behind her left eye socket. She finds a bench in the shade and sits down in her sweat. A fly buzzes up to drink the corners of her mouth.

Apart from its chirring wings and the soft keening in her head, the world is silent. She stares into the sunlit canal until its dancing photons sear her eyes. She pushes her cold metal thermos against her temple. The smell of clean metal is the smell of a clinic. When she opens her eyes again, she sees something far stranger than the grootslang.

At first, she thinks it's a boatman poling his way down the canal. But the shape is wrong, and the sunshine makes no differentiation between the craft and the figure rising from its stern. Both glisten like raw meat. As the thing approaches, she realizes they share a spinal column, too: the figure is legless, an elongated torso extending from the stern.

Its face is a nightmare, bony, vaguely avian, eyes hidden in abyssal sockets. The pole, clutched in clumsy, puppet-crude hands, is only for show. Elsie can see muscular flippers, like those of a seal, churning below the surface of the canal. The water is no longer clear: thick dark blood, clotted with bits of tissue, is clouding outward from some invisible wound on the thing's underside.

Elsie doubles over, clutching hard to her abdomen. When her gaze moves to what she thought was a prow, she finds the creature's second head. This one is larger, pudgy-cheeked, almost cherubic, but equally eyeless. The Baby sees her anyway and starts to wail.

She stumbles up from the bench. She runs.

2:18 SAST. Elsie calls early because she spoke to nobody today, and that always sharpens her craving for a familiar voice. She calls early because of the creature she's nearly certain she saw in the canal—even though when she circled back, using a tour group like human shields, there was no trace of it. Her grandmother picks up on the third ring.

"Hello?"

"Hi, Oma."

"Elsie! Where are you?"

"Cape Town still, Oma. How are you today?"

"Cape Town? Really? I'm all right. Still crawling and scratching. How are you?"

"Still crawling and scratching?" Elsie echoes, realizing the script has changed.

"Good," her grandmother says, misunderstanding. "I'm glad. Where are you, Elsie? When are you coming home?"

The next day, or maybe the day after, Elsie goes to the Zeitz MOCAA, threading her way through a roundabout jammed with decal-splattered taxi vans and Ubers, breathing air tangy with exhaust. Normally, the museum's concrete womb is wandered by at least a handful of tourists; today, she has it to herself. She takes the glass capsule elevator to the bottom floor. When she looks up at the ceiling of the ancient grain silo, she feels like she's in a cathedral. Her head starts throbbing again.

She distracts herself with the art. Most of it centers on atrocities past, oppression present. She recalls that first night, that bar conversation about the intersection of real-world tragedy and folklore. She has learned, since then, just how deeply entwined they are here. The tokoloshe suffocates its victims on winter nights, an explanation for carbon monoxide poisoning in cramped Bantu rondavels. The pinky-pinky favors the girls' washroom over the boys'—a warning against rapists lying in wait.

Even one version of Antjie Somers, the child-stealer, comes with a starkly human origin: Andries Somers is an enslaved fisherman who, during an altercation, accidentally kills a member of his crew. He dons his sister's clothes as a disguise, then flees to the mountain with his long knife and his burlap sack, and there goes mad with guilt and grief.

Elsie feels some kinship with that version. She finds herself stopped in front of a photorealist painting on the third floor, her left foot rubbing stork-like against her right calf. The painting shows a man in a bowler hat, turned away from the viewer, with metal calipers extending from his face. From the height of them, she knows they emerge from where his eyes ought to be.

The quiet is absolute. No distant echo of footsteps, no hum of electricity, no liquid hiss of aircon. She watches the man's neck muscles bunch taut beneath his shirt collar. Waits for him to turn his head.

The quiet shatters. The cathedral feeling roars back with the buzzing of her sacrilegious phone. She fumbles it from her tote and slashes out the unlock pattern. She stares down at the screen, disbelieving. Elsie calls her grandmother every day at 15:30 EST. Her grandmother never calls her, not for years and years now—but there it is, the number her fingers have memorized.

Elsie's heart starts to pound. It's 11:32 SAST, which is 02:32 EST. She answers on the fifth ring.

"**H**ello? Oma?"

A familiar labored breath, then: "Elsie?"

"Yes, Oma. It's Elsie." Her dry mouth sticks to itself. "Are you okay?"

"Of course. Why wouldn't I be?"

Something scrapes in the background of the call, a staticky knife in Elsie's ear. She tries to picture the scene, crossing ocean and time zones: it's the middle of the night in her grandmother's tiny apartment, and she missed taking her sleeping pills somehow. She woke up confused, lurched her way to her easy chair, picked up her phone, and returned the last call by sheer chance.

"It's late where you are," Elsie says. "Isn't it?"

"Oh! I'm calling you late." Her grandmother makes a clucking sound. "It's just that I found a note—my handwriting, so it must have been me who wrote it—I found a note saying to call you on the sixteenth. And today was the sixteenth. The nurse marked my calendar."

Elsie has tried so hard to lose track of the date. She took

it off her phone display and her laptop display. She ignores her emails and her socials, letting the messages accumulate, foaming up behind a digital dam. She speaks to nobody back home except her grandmother, who is safe to speak to because her memory is as slippery as a hydrogel.

"Elsie, my dear Elsie—" Her grandmother trails off, uncertain. "Aren't you at twelve weeks today? Aren't you expecting?"

Elsie forgot to charge her phone in the night. It dies, if it was ever alive.

She would have been at twelve weeks today, but the pregnancy ended at nine, and nine weeks is nothing. Elsie has told herself that over and over. It's nothing compared to her mother, who delivered Elsie's small stillborn sister and watched her buried in a casket the size of a breadbox. It's nothing compared to her grandmother, who had four living children and lost three in between them. There is a reason she told almost nobody.

There is also a reason she fled New England, where the trees were turning to rusty skeletons, and came to Cape Town, where the seasons are inverse, and she would find birds hatching, flowers blooming, spring storms roving wild across a beautiful city. Now, as she staggers back along Lion Street with the sky turning dark overhead and the wind whipping her hair, she sees nothing but terrors:

The hairy tokoloshe shambles out from under a parked

water truck; she recoils as it darts across her path. The emaciated nagloper peers through the burglar bars of a shuttered shop, jolting her. The slick-skinned pinky-pinky crawls on its belly through the gutter beside her.

When she reels away, looking up the dusty slope of Signal Hill, she sees a figure descending toward Bo-Kaap with a stained burlap sack. For a moment, her spine is drenched by icy certainty. But the figure is not heading in her direction. Antjie Somers pays her no mind. Neither do the others. She remembers she is only a visitor here, transient, irrelevant.

The only thing that can hurt her is the one she brought with her. She hears it now, scraping along the cobblestones behind her. She cannot help but turn.

The creature has adapted, exchanging flippers for sinewy arms. Its body looks more predatory, lithe and compact. The awful bony face that was once the boatman's now has a gaping mouth with teeth like a saw. The creature stalks forward, quadrupedal, leonine. Elsie moves backward. She hopes that the second head is gone, shed or resorbed.

Then the creature flips up onto its front arms, heaving its body up behind it like a jester or gymnast. The Baby stares eyelessly at her from its new perch. Elsie's head throbs. Her heart slams like a leathery fist against her ribcage. She smells blood in the air again, metallic, pungent.

The bulging clouds overhead finally buckle and split, and it comes pouring out of the sky.

She thought she was done bleeding, but now she runs through a red torrent with the two-faced creature in pursuit. The downpour turns Bo-Kaap's cobblestones sticky here, slippery there, and drenches its colorful houses a uniform crimson. It spatters hot on her scalp and stings in her eyes. She sobs and gasps, but there is not enough air in her lungs to scream.

The Baby screams for both of them. Its wail pierces the rushing wind, the machine gun rattle of rain striking tin roofs. The sound grows closer, closer, but the residence is closer still. There is only one thought in her panic-fogged mind: if she can make it up the sloped drive and get the metal gate shut behind her, she'll be safe.

Her shoes lose traction as she reaches the fence. She slams her knee and skins her palms, but her blood is everywhere already, and she barely feels the sting. She scrambles up the incline on all fours, clawing for the cracks between the stones, her bag bouncing against her hip. The creature comes scraping behind her; she imagines its dragging nails as metal calipers.

The guardhouse door is open, the chair in its usual place, but no propped up feet to be seen. The sliding gate is open, too: Elsie lunges through, gripping the bars for balance as she pulls herself upright. She turns, twists, and tries to force the gate shut. It screeches in its groove, unwilling. She looks through the bars. The creature is on all fours again, teeth gleaming moon-bright; every other part of it is coated with coagulating blood. Even so, something in the shape of its face looks horribly familiar.

She gives the gate a final useless heave, then flees up the tiled steps that lead to the terrace. Her shoes slip and slide, and she sprawls up the last few stairs and collides with an empty laundry rack someone left near the top. It clatters and implodes like a model skeleton. She stumbles over it, reaches the dormitory door, and grabs the knob with a trembling hand.

It's not locked; it's never locked, but the blood makes the knob too slippery to turn. She squeezes, pleads, howls, surrenders. To the edge of the balcony next, to judge the drop—too far, too far. She can already picture the bend and snap of her shin bones, the creature making its leisurely way downward as she lies paralyzed in the dirt.

But if she were to dive headfirst, it would all be over. One long fall from the terrace, a smashed skull, and she'll be insensate when the creature eats her. She'll never feel its saw teeth or any other kind. No more endless, aimless wandering through cities that can't be hers. No more endless, aimless conversations with a confidante who will recall nothing. No more scratching, crawling, bleeding.

No more spring, whether here in Cape Town or back home in New England. The finality howls at her. There is nowhere to run, so Elsie turns to face it.

The creature is upright again, walking on its hands, presenting both its heads. At the top, the Baby: silent now, almost serene, its malformed mouth puckered shut. At the bottom, its jaws hinging wider and wider, its bony face a warped mirror: another Elsie, one that will devour her if she allows it. She dumps everything from her threadbare bag except the heavy metal thermos. She wraps it tight, hoping she might be able to swing it like a club—

The creature is on top of her before she can move. Its nails rip through her shirt, through her skin, gouging deep. She falls backward, the creature's sinewy arms bearing her down, its slavering mouth somewhere near hers. A wash of hot, stale breath hits her face, all metal and liquor—hers smelled the same the night she decided to fly.

She twists, flails, thumping it with her fists, clawing at it with her own ragged fingernails. The creature's body is a rippling jigsaw, bones and tendons attached at angles that make no sense, but it can feel pain: when she manages to drive her thumb into the hollow where the other Elsie's eye should be, it shudders and slackens its grip. The wailing of its other head pauses for just an instant, then doubles in volume.

She jabs again, deeper until she reaches something warm and liquid like she's digging a hole at the beach. The creature's body spasms. Contorts. It's wrapped around her now, both faces in view: the squalling never-was-infant, the ravenous nearly-was-mother. The wetness trickling from its empty socket is tears, not blood.

The saw teeth gnash in her ear. Her heart pounds. She worms her other arm free and reaches—not for her doppelgänger, but for the Baby. She claps a hand to either side of the wailing face and pulls it inward. The creature writes, struggles. She strains, pulling so hard she fears the Baby's head will tear free, curving the creature's pliable body into itself one centimeter at a time.

The other Elsie's nostrils flare, as if catching a brand new scent. Her maw snaps suddenly shut. She cranes forward, past Elsie, and presses her scabbed lips to the Baby's forehead. For a moment the monstrous body is a perfect loop. Then the saw-toothed mouth gapes open once more, and the creature devours itself.

The work starts with snapping jaws and ends with stranger forces, the last of the creature's flesh collapsing inward like a black hole until there's not enough left to fill a cup, never mind a burlap sack. Elsie shuts her eyes for just a moment, and when she opens them, even that is gone. She splays back in her usual plastic deck chair, weeping, then laughing, then weeping again, exhausted in every cell of her body.

The rain is relentless but clear and cool again. It floods the terrace clean, chasing swirls of blood over the edge until only a few soft pink tendrils remain in fractured puddles. The gouges on her arms, hands, and collarbone are not deep. They gradually stop pulsing and slowly stop bleeding. The throb in her head goes, too, leaving it curiously empty.

Eventually, the distant grootslang tires: the rain dribbles to a halt, and the sky opens up. She finds her dead phone safe in its waterproofed case and takes it inside to charge, tracking wet footprints down the empty hall. She goes online, at last, returning the most worried messages. She writes a concise opening paragraph. She finds her bandages and rubbing alcohol and does what she can for the scratch marks on her skin.

At 22:28 SAST, she limps back out to the terrace. The sky is clear overhead. When she looks up, she sees a scattering of stars, more than she gets in most cities. When she looks over the balcony, she sees Cape Town, glossy from the rain, its yellow-orange lights spilling toward Table Mountain.

She thumbs the call button.

Her grandmother picks up on the second ring.
"Hello?"

"Hi, Oma."

"Elsie! Where are you?"

"Cape Town still, Oma. How are you today?"

"Cape Town? Oh, I'm all right. Still living. And you? How are you?"

"Still living," Elsie echoes. "I love you, Oma."

"I love you, too, Elsie," her grandmother says, sounding puzzled but pleased. "What day are we today? I found a note."

The scratches on Elsie's arms begin to throb. Her head keens. She envisions a future in which she explains this over and over every evening, but she swallows the fear whole.

"I was expecting," she says. "You were one of the only people I told. I thought I could handle losing it, but I couldn't, so I ran away."

"Oh, Elsie," her grandmother says. "I'm so sorry. Ran away where?"

Elsie breathes.

"Still Cape Town, Oma," she says. "But I'll come visit you soon."

END

—

Rich Larson was born in Niger, has lived in Spain and Czech Republic, and is currently based in Canada. He is the author of the novels *Annex* and *Ymir*, as well as over 250 short stories—some of the best of which can be found in his collections *Tomorrow Factory* and *The Sky Didn't Load Today and Other Glitches*. His fiction has been translated into over a dozen languages, among them Polish, French, Romanian and Japanese, and adapted into an Emmy-winning episode of *LOVE DEATH + ROBOTS*. His latest book, *Changelog*, drops September 2025. Find him at instagram.com/richlarsonwrites and patreon.com/richlarson.

NEW YORK CITY

Jeff Enos

I closed my apartment door and scraped a big, sticky clump of purple flowers off the bottom sole of my runners.

I exhaled, still catching my breath from my morning jog.

The flowers amongst the goo resembled tiny sunflowers, with lavender petals and a big royal purple center that almost looked like a black void the longer you stared at it.

It was spring in New York City and if TikTok was to be believed, this was the year of invasive species. A spider from Australia. A moth from India.

And this mess of purple sunflowery goo.

They smelled like my stepmother's godawful perfume—too sweet and too musky at the same time.

The odor seeped into every crevice of my tiny one-bedroom apartment in Queens, the apartment I'd been living in ever since I dropped out of Columbia Law School a year ago against my father's wishes.

"You can't survive in New York without a plan, Teddy," he'd said. "This city will eat you alive."

But however angry he was, I wasn't blind to the hint of pride behind his eyes—like he was secretly rooting for me, like he respected me for trying to forge my own path, my own identity.

After a year on my own, I feared that maybe he was right. Twenty-three years old and working six nights a week waiting tables, just barely paying the rent on time. I was good at it, even though I hated it. I'd lived amongst "polite society" on the Upper East Side for most of my life, so I had plenty of practice smiling and gritting my teeth around people who thought they were better than me.

I uploaded a photo of the purple sunflowery goo to Instagram and went to type the caption "Stepped in Thanos's snot this morning," but stopped. That was Rick talking, not me.

I decided on the caption "Stepped in Ursula the Sea Witch's snot this morning."

I hopped into the shower, still able to smell the flowers.

My stepmother, Nora—she of the pristine blonde Upper East Side ponytail and pantsuit combo and the your-father-and-I-are-too-busy-to-make-plans attitude, Esquire—was the first to like my Instagram post.

My father had always lovingly called me a gentle giant—tall, muscular, just like my real mother. Still, if there was anyone who could bring out the beast within me, it was my stepmother.

"Bitch," I muttered.

It was an unusually warm day for early spring, so I dug out my summer clothes from the back of the closet.

A Polaroid from last summer fell out of the pile of clothes: Rick and I at the top of the Empire State Building.

I stared at the picture blankly for two whole minutes before opening my dresser junk drawer and stuffing it underneath a stack of journals—gifts I'd received from Rick but had never written inside of. They reminded me of my mother's journals, with thick leather-like covers and a long strap that wrapped around the cover twice.

I remember my mother keeping her journals all over the apartment when I was little. She wrote everything in them—poems, recipes, workout routines, summaries of what she was watching on tv that week. When she died, the journals disappeared. I asked my father about them, but he just ignored me. I was a bashful eight-year-old; I was easy to ignore.

I rummaged through the pile of clothes, picking out a yellow tank and tight black shorts. The warm weather allowed me to show off the one thing I'm proud of—my physique. It gives that shy little boy the confidence he was severely lacking.

I packed a small lunch, a blanket, and a book, and made the subway trek from Queens to Manhattan, to the only place any self-respecting twenty-something would go on their day off on a nice day in New York City: Sheep's Meadow in Central Park.

I spread out my blanket in a half-shaded corner of the vast

lawn, kicked off my shoes, and lay down, propping my head up on my bag.

I started in on the same novel I'd been trying to finish reading for the past six months, a historical romance about two men who fell in love on the Titanic. A part of me didn't want it to end. Just ignore the iceberg.

Across from me, a man my age with glasses and a cute side-part kept eyeing me. He was reading a graphic novel. He reminded me of Rick—small and a little nerdy, with a boyish smile that never seemed to vanish from his face.

I shifted on my blanket, trying to avert his gaze. Sheep's Meadow could turn into a cruising ground on days like these; I'd forgotten. I wasn't ready for sex, wasn't ready to start dating again after what happened with Rick.

"Hi," side-part said, walking up to me. The eternal smile on his face wavered a bit. He shoved his hands deep in his pockets, hunched.

I looked at him, not unkindly, and waited for him to speak again.

"I knew Rick," he said.

My heart dropped. Of course he'd known Rick. He looked like his clone. They'd probably hung out in the same tech circles, maybe even worked together.

He continued. "I wasn't close with him, but I remember him talking about you. He really loved you. You gave a beautiful eulogy at his funeral, I just wanted to tell you that."

The muscles in my throat tightened. My mouth went dry. And time seemed to stop…

Rick…

We met at a Broadway show, aka gay church. He sat next to me, and I accidentally spilled his drink with my foot. Rick joked that I owed him dinner. He was charming, polite, unthreatening. His hair, short and auburn, reminded me of my mother's hair, long waves of scarlet red like a Disney princess.

He asked for my number.

I'd always been hesitant about love, about being loved. I don't know why. Maybe it was my mother's death when I was younger, maybe it was my well-meaning but distant father—maybe it was my evil stepmother.

But something about Rick seemed to make all that go away.

He'd come to my restaurant and wait until my shift was over, even if I had to work hours past closing time. We'd walk around Central Park late at night in the moonlight, gazing at the city views. We'd go to the movies: he'd drag me to his superhero movies, I'd drag him to my Disney movies. We'd laugh at the crazy things we witnessed on the subway together, shaking our heads. That's New York, we'd shrug at each other.

He supported me when I decided to drop out of law school. He helped me move my stuff from my father's penthouse to the apartment in Queens.

I could still picture that day last summer at the top of the

Empire State Building. We'd been dating for a little over two years at that point. He had brought the Polaroid camera I bought him for his birthday.

That was the last picture we took together.

Rick had bad headaches. Sometimes he'd go off in a dark, quiet room for hours until they resolved. But the headache he got that day was unlike anything I'd seen before. His eyes were red and tearing, his brow was twitching. I held him tight against the railing, looking down at the city below, amazed at how peaceful and quiet it looked from up there. The only noise, chaotic and buzzing, seemed to be inside Rick's head.

The headache died down, and that's when he told me.

"I have a brain tumor." He'd been diagnosed two and a half years prior, just before we'd started dating.

He'd been in and out of hospitals over the past year. He'd hid it from me well, mostly using work as an excuse as to why he wasn't available on a particular day or time.

As I listened to him, suddenly the city didn't look peaceful and quiet anymore. Suddenly it screamed. Suddenly it turned on me. Just like my father said it would.

Rick's treatment options were limited. The tumor was too far along, and all he could do was enjoy the little time he had left.

Rick had no one else but me. He'd come from a deeply devout family, and they'd disowned him after he came out. I tried to get him to tell them about his situation, but he was stubborn, insisting that they wouldn't care, insisting that he didn't care.

Rick didn't want to die in a hospital, didn't want to be hooked up to machines. I told him he could move in with me, I'd take care of him when the end came. I didn't realize how soon the end would be.

As I prepared to care for Rick, I had visions of my mother during her final days. Glimpses of a weakened body behind a cracked bedroom door, stillness and whispers in the gloom, all lost in a flurry of my father's business activities. Big, fancy attorneys and their ilk spilled into the house like locusts—Nora (my future stepmother) the biggest one of them all.

My mother was taken to the hospital, forgotten. Two whole weeks she was there and my father only took me to see her once. She died alone, and I've never forgiven my father for that.

I wouldn't let that happen to Rick. No matter what, I would make him comfortable, I would be there for him.

Rick had a good amount of savings, so I didn't have to wait tables while I was caring for him. He died just a few months after that day at the Empire State Building.

Toward the end, I was exhausted, overwhelmed, and a little numb. I started to have dark thoughts. Thoughts like maybe Rick had never loved me, maybe the only reason he went out with me in the first place was so I could take care of him when he was dying.

The thoughts lurked underneath kisses and I love you's and long sleepless nights and never-ending trips to the bathroom. And underneath the keys of my laptop as I wrote his eulogy for a small ceremony he'd already planned.

Rick started to have hallucinations toward the end, talking to no one in particular, reacting to things that weren't there.

Sometimes I wondered if the hallucinations were contagious. It was hard to believe some of the things I saw. Rick would cough up blood, but it wasn't like any blood I'd ever seen before. It was thick and black, shiny like oil. It reminded me of illnesses from the olden days—the Black Plague.

And then I started to question whether Rick was being honest with me about his diagnosis. Was it really a brain tumor, or…something else? Was it contagious? Was I going to be infected? Was that my future, too? And the smell…

I awoke from my thoughts just as side-part started to walk away. I stopped him.

"Please. Would you like to join me?"

His name was Hal. He fused his blanket with mine and sat across from me. We talked about the weather, our love-hate relationship with New York, our favorite movies and tv shows.

Hal was a self-described comic book nerd. "I think I have enough comics in storage to open my own shop." He reminded me of Rick in that way. In every way. His interests, his attitude. And his smile. Innocent, like he truly believed a man with a cape could fly.

He was easy to talk to. One topic bled into the next, and soon we were discussing deeper things—our jobs, our passions, our hopes for the future.

I told him I was considering going back to school, doing something like physical therapy. But I was scared. I'd already left school behind once, I didn't know if I could go back.

Hal was a computer engineer and worked for a big tech company. He was smart, probably too smart for me.

I got out my lunch and shared it with him.

It started to feel like a date, and I could feel myself withdrawing the more we talked.

I studied Hal, trying to find some flaw, any sign of illness or weakness, a funny-looking mole, discoloration in his eyes.

I found nothing.

Then Hal said, "Tell me about your family."

I went quiet.

Hal changed the subject, catching my hesitation. "These things are everywhere," he said, twirling a stem of small purple flowers he'd picked from the grass. The same ones I'd stepped in earlier during my morning jog, the tiny sunflower-like ones with the lavender petals and the purple-verging-on-black-void center.

I found my voice again, slowly snapping out of it. "TikTok says they're an invasive species. I think they're from Japan."

"They're beautiful. Too beautiful for New York," Hal said.

We both laughed.

Hal gathered a bunch of them in a small bouquet and slipped them behind my left ear. "Not too beautiful for you, though."

I grinned, my face turning pink. "Thanks."

I couldn't deny that it felt good to be seen, especially by someone who'd known what I went through with Rick.

"It's a nosegay," Hal said.

I looked at him, confused. "A what, now?"

Hal laughed. "A small, handheld bouquet of flowers—a nosegay."

"Well, if the shoe fits," I said, modeling my nosegay, and we both laughed.

It was silent, and then I said, quite quickly, "Are you free tonight?" The words just slipped out, like the barrier between my unconscious thoughts and my mouth had disappeared.

Hal nodded, smiling.

I walked back to my apartment with the nosegay still tucked behind my ear. Everything in the city seemed brighter, more inviting. Spring was springing and for the first time since Rick died, I felt optimistic.

Hal and I started dating after that. A few weeks in and I was already falling for him hard. I didn't know why. Maybe because it was Spring. Maybe because he reminded me of Rick. Maybe because I was finally ready to move on.

Being with Hal was almost as if Rick had never died, as if Rick had been reborn in Hal's body and we'd been given a second chance.

Still, I wanted to leave Rick behind, tuck him away in the back of my memory, close that door and toss away the key.

The purple flowers continued to spread throughout the entire city. They covered the ground, making it impossible to avoid stepping on them. They popped up in between the cracks of the sidewalk, in the dirt of empty lots waiting to be filled with concrete, in every single greenspace in the city. Residents embraced the flowers, bunching them up in vases, in bouquets, in nosegays.

The flowers became a symbol of my relationship with Hal. Every time he came over, he'd bring me a new nosegay. I put them in little jars and vases, filling the apartment with them.

Things were going great with Hal, and I actually felt happy. I should have known something would come in the way. I should have known the city would find a way to bring me misery. I should have known (as my father had said) that the city would eat me alive.

It happened one day after a lunch date with Hal. I came back to my apartment in a hurry, already late for work.

That's when I saw it.

There was a pool of black oil by the front door. Something in my apartment was leaking out into the hallway.

I opened the door to find what looked like an oil spill. A thin black lake coated the floor.

Dumbfounded, I touched the substance, rubbed it between my fingers. It was smooth, and smelled sweet and musky, exactly like the purple flowers, exactly like my stepmother's perfume.

I looked up at the window by the kitchen counter, at the living room table, at every single surface where there had been purple flowers. The vases and jars remained, but the flowers were gone, and in their place was black oil. Pools of it overflowed and spilled onto the floor.

Had there been some kind of burst pipe in the building? A leak from the apartment above mine?

Confused, I grabbed my phone and called the landlord. When he didn't pick up, I left a message. I was just about to call a plumber when I heard a voice coming from the other room.

A whisper.

I stood still, slowly putting my phone in my pocket. Silence. Quietly, I crept down the hallway.

"Hello?"

Another unintelligible whisper.

My heart stopped cold when I got closer to my room.

"Teddy," the voice said. It was Rick's voice. I'd heard that same exact whisper near the end of his life when all he could muster were soft mumbles.

My body told me to leave the apartment, to go downstairs to the coffee shop and wait until I got a hold of a plumber or the landlord, but curiosity got the best of me.

When I got to my room, what I saw in front of my bed should have sent me running, but I just stood there, frozen in place.

It was a man-shaped figure coated in the black oil. He seemed to grow from the lake, and smelled like the purple flowers. A lush garden of the flowers grew at his feet.

"Teddy," he said, holding out his hand.

"R-rick?" I shook my head in disbelief.

Before I could move, he lunged at me, grabbing my arm. I tried to escape his grip, but he was too strong. The oil smeared my shirt, my arms. It was hot, burning my skin.

"I never loved you," he whispered in my ear. "And he'll never love you, either. Everyone you've ever loved dies, and he'll die, too. He'll leave you all alone."

Then he kissed me, smashing his lips against mine. His breath reeked of the flowers, death and sweetness at the same time. The way the apartment smelled not six months ago, as Rick lay there dying, and I desperately tried to cover it up with air freshener and scented cleaning supplies.

Somehow, I managed to break free, running out of the apartment and into the sun. I wanted to scream for help, but couldn't. All around, the city took my voice. A woman in neon pajamas blasting her music on a Bluetooth speaker. A short animated Greek man arguing with the bodega cashier over a price. The blare of car horns. The incessant cooing of pigeons picking at discarded trash in the street.

I bumped into an angry homely-looking mother of two walking down the sidewalk.

"Watch it, kid," she sneered at me, pulling her toddlers closer to her.

I tried to explain, but all that came out of my mouth were jumbled words. She brushed right past me, sighing and shaking her head.

A homeless man sorting through a garbage can paused to look at me like I was crazy.

I didn't know what to do, who to turn to. How many

times had I ignored the eccentric ramblings of strangers on the streets of New York City? It was something you learned living here, a necessary skill.

I didn't have anyone to turn to. So, I ran.

I must have gone twenty blocks before finally stopping in a public restroom at a small sculpture park near the East River.

I washed my clothes in the bathroom sink, ringing out every last drop of black oil.

I got dressed and sat dripping on a bench. The sun washed over me, warming my skin and drying my clothes over time. I tried to calm myself down.

I stared at the river for what seemed like hours, trying to make sense of what had just happened. I wanted to text Hal, but I didn't want him to think I was crazy.

I tried my landlord again, but there was still no answer.

I thought about calling my dad, but I didn't want him to think I needed his help. I hadn't asked him for anything for the past year, ever since I'd moved out. Not even when I was taking care of Rick. I didn't want him to think the city had swallowed me whole, even if some days it had.

The image of the man-shaped figure, Rick, came back to me, standing there covered in the black oil, taunting me.

I couldn't go back to my apartment, but I needed a place to rest, to think.

Finally, I texted Hal and asked him if I could come over. He responded quickly, saying yes.

Hal lived on the Upper West Side, so I made my way to

the nearest subway station and waited on the underground platform for the train to arrive.

There was a delay. The platform started to overfill with people. It was approaching rush hour, and the crowd was antsy.

The air thickened with typical subway fumes cloaked in the scent of the purple flowers. As the scent intensified, the crowd turned angry. Grumblings turned into shouts. And then people began to take their frustration out on each other.

A middle-aged businessman to my right glared at me. His eyes were pitch black and shiny, just like the oil in my apartment. And when he spoke, the stench of death and the purple sweetness.

"It's never going to work out with Hal, because he's not dying. Those last few months with Rick were the best of your life. You felt needed, wanted. But no one will ever need you again, not like that, and that terrifies you."

"No," I said, shaking my head.

Then he touched my ear and pulled a flower out of it.

I grabbed my ear, and what I felt there horrified me. A sprig of flowers had grown there, the stems deeply rooted in the skin around my ear. I clawed them out frantically, praying that the plants hadn't already taken root inside my head.

My hand was full of purple sunflowery goo.

I ran down to the other end of the platform, pushing my way through the growing, growling crowds. Behind me, the man did not follow, but that didn't stop him from yelling at me.

"You can't escape! It's coming for you, boy!"

My head was like an impending avalanche, one wrong step and everything would come crashing down.

My chest tightened, my breathing shallowed. When I reached the other end of the platform, I inhaled and exhaled slowly, again and again, trying to calm myself.

I was mid-exhale when a few rats on the track below caught my eye. Growths of flowers like purple tumors covered their bodies, sprouting wildly as the rats scurried about.

It was then that I realized the purple flowers had completely conquered the city.

I scanned the crowded subway platform—a growth of purple flowers on the lips of the woman standing next to me, on the neck of the little girl beside her, on the nose of the man behind them. All around me, purple loomed.

The smell was sweet, too sweet. The odor stung my nose.

My phone vibrated with a call from my stepmother. She was just about the last person I wanted to talk to, but I answered it. Any respite from the horror I was experiencing.

"I'm at the apartment," she said. She sounded annoyed, more so than usual. Then she hung up.

I called her back, but she didn't answer.

The apartment? She couldn't be talking about my apartment? What would she be doing there?

The train finally arrived, the doors opening to a horrific sight. What had once been a subway car full of people was now an overgrown purple forest. Terrified faces were scattered throughout, human flesh indistinguishable from the foliage.

Instead of retreating, the crowds on the platform squeezed

into the subway car like a hungry mob, anticipating the moment they would merge with the forest like the other passengers had.

People pushed past me.

I ran away, climbing the station stairs back up to the street.

I hailed a taxi, jumping inside.

We drove past throngs of tourists in Times Square. Everything appeared normal. The flowers were still part of the city landscape, but they looked benign. They didn't seem to be having any negative effects on anyone I could see.

Hal lived on the fourth floor of a four-story brownstone. He buzzed me in and I ran up the stairs. I pounded on his door.

"What happened to you?" He asked as I burst into the apartment. He touched the purple goo on my face. It had since turned black.

Hal's apartment was surprisingly sleek and clean for a self-described nerd. A few framed classic comic books gave the living room some character. There was a giant monster-like starfish on the cover of one of them. I stared at it, almost expecting the purple flowers to grow out of its legs, waiting for the black oil to drip down the frame, to slide down the wall.

"We need to leave the city right now," I said.

"Calm down," he said.

Hal sat me on the couch and brought me a glass of water. Then he got a hand towel from the kitchen and began wiping my face.

He sat down across from me, a skeptical look in his eyes.

I could see the gears turning in his head, assessing me like a scientist would assess an unexpected lab result.

Hal's face softened the longer we sat there, the longer I was unable to speak.

"What is this?" Hal asked, looking at the black oil. "It smells like—"

"Death," I said. "It's the flowers, the invasive species. They're taking over the city, changing it somehow."

"What do you mean, changing it?"

I talked a million miles a minute, telling Hal everything I'd witnessed, everything from the black lake in my apartment to the apparition of Rick to the chaos on the subway. Hal looked at me like I was insane, delusional, like I was having some sort of mental breakdown.

"Should I call someone?" Hal asked slowly.

"I'm not crazy," I said. "I can take you there…to the apartment."

I started to shiver. My teeth chattered.

"Come on, let's lie down," Hal said, wrapping me up in a blanket he'd grabbed from the couch.

He started to lay me down, but I protested. "No, I have to show you."

"Let's just lay here for a bit," Hal said, cradling me.

"No!"

Hal stopped.

"Please," I said.

Hal didn't object this time. There was a look in his eyes, a cautionary expression, but a curious one nevertheless.

Whatever was bothering me, he wanted to know.

"Ok," he said.

We took a taxi straight to my place and walked up the stairs to my apartment. I fought with my body as we approached the front door. Every muscle seemed to tense in place as I guided my hand toward the door handle.

Before I could open it, the door opened on its own. I leapt back, nearly knocking Hal over.

"There you are," my stepmother said, huffing at me. She looked me up and down, scoffing at my outfit. My shorts were too short, my shirt too tight. It wasn't proper.

"You," I said accusingly. "What are you doing here?"

I barged inside, pushing past her. The apartment looked completely normal. There was no black lake. There was no scent of death. And the purple flowers were intact and back in their vases and jars, no oil in their place.

I ran into my room to see if the man-shaped figure that looked like Rick was still there. He wasn't.

I came back into the living room and stormed at Nora. "What did you do? Where's Rick?"

Nora looked at me sympathetically. "Oh, honey," she said, her sharp fingernails grazing my cheek.

I flinched.

"Tell me why you're here!" I demanded.

"Your landlord called us again. This is the fifth time this month you've harassed him. It's one thing after another. Now it's black oil and zombie boyfriends. He wants you out of the apartment, Teddy. Your father is hiring movers as we speak.

You're coming home with us."

"I know what I saw." But as I looked around the apartment, even I couldn't argue with the fact that everything was in its proper place.

I looked back at Hal, but he wasn't there.

"Hal?" I said, looking around the living room. "Where's Hal?" I asked Nora.

"Who's Hal?"

"The man who was with me."

"No one was with you."

I felt dizzy. My mouth went dry. My ears hurt, I could feel pressure building up inside of them. I knew my stepmother was talking, but I couldn't understand her, couldn't hear her correctly. It all sounded like mindless chatter.

"We'll have to take the subway home," she said.

"The subway," I said. "No, I don't want to go back there."

"None of us do, honey. But that's the price of being a New Yorker."

Nora never took the subway. Taxis and rideshares were her primary mode of transportation. I looked at her, suddenly suspicious.

I began to slowly back away, one step at a time until I reached the bathroom. I slammed the door shut, locking myself inside.

The building pressure in my ears was now a volcano, ready to erupt at any second. In the mirror, I saw a small purple stem peeking from each ear. I pulled them one at a time. Long purple vines slid out. Blood coated them, followed by a thick film of black oil. When the last of it finally came out, it was like a veil had been lifted from my eyes.

I saw the world as it really was again.

I saw the black oil at my feet, this time it was up to my knees. It burned my skin. I opened the bathroom door to find that the lake had returned to the whole apartment, and my stepmother was nowhere to be seen.

In the center of the living room rose two gigantic coffin-like shapes. One molded itself into a man-shaped figure, Rick. The other remained a coffin, and a name formed upon it: Hal.

"You can't have him," Rick said.

I trudged my way through the oil and approached Rick. "You don't belong here," I said.

A humongous flower began to grow and bloom behind Rick. It was just like the others, sunflower-like with lavender petals and a large purple center, except this center was barely even purple, it was a large black void. Black oil started to pour down from it, filling the room all the more. The lake rose higher. The flower grew to the ceiling, reigning over the room.

Another coffin rose up from the lake beside Hal's, this one with my name on it. The lid opened and Rick said, "Get inside."

"No," I said, gritting my teeth. I wouldn't give in. I had to fight. I had to make sure I survived. For Rick, for my mother, for Hal.

For myself.

Rick just stared at me. "You need to get inside. It's the

only way you'll be able to rest. You don't have to take care of anyone anymore."

I looked at the coffin with my name on it, looked back at Rick, looked at the black void behind him that seemed to grow larger and larger by the second. Deep down, in a moment of weakness, I contemplated it.

Then I looked at Hal's coffin again, watched as the black oil dripped down his name.

Suddenly, I knew what I had to do, and I gained the strength to do it.

I punched my way through the coffin. Inside, I felt arms, a torso, a head. It was Hal. He was slick, slipping through my fingers. I grabbed onto him, tugged as hard as I could. Hal came tumbling out. I held onto him, cradling his limp body in my arms. I wiped the oil from his face, kissed him.

He opened his eyes.

"You're a fool," Rick said, and then he melted back into the black lake, the giant flower following him.

It took me a week to clean up the apartment. The black oil eventually turned translucent, so it was hard to know exactly how much of it remained sticking to certain surfaces and crevices.

What really mattered was getting rid of the flowers, but that was nearly impossible. They had taken over the entire city.

The flowers targeted certain people. Scientists tried to

figure out why. Much was unknown about the flowers' psychiatric effects, which only seemed to influence residents of the city. Tourists weren't affected. No matter where they grew, the flowers seemed to have no impact on people in any other place in the world other than New York City.

There was something different about New Yorkers, something the flowers took advantage of. Was it feeding off of our weaknesses? Our strengths? Our traumas?

The incident on the subway was fortunately isolated. Five hundred people died on that train. The subway station was closed, the NIH and CDC setting up shop around it. It was designated as ground zero for the strange abilities the flowers could hold over people. A theory was posited that a particularly strong responder had served as a catalyst for the incident. I always wondered if it had been me.

I could still smell the sweetness of the flowers most places I went, but the stench of death had dissipated.

Hal was never the same after the incident. Whatever he'd seen or experienced while he was in the coffin scarred him beyond repair. I tried to take care of him, tried to get him to seek help, but nothing worked. He left the city unannounced: no goodbye, no text, no voicemail.

I'm still in New York City. It's my home; I can't leave it, no matter how much I want to sometimes. Half of the city is pure purple forest now; it's something we'll have to adapt to, just like we've done before with countless other things.

I later found out that my stepmother Nora really had come over to my apartment that day. My father had asked her to check in on me.

My stepmother hasn't been seen since.

I keep the picture of Rick and I on top of the Empire State Building on my refrigerator.

Sometimes I think I can smell the faint hint of death whenever I walk past a freshly grown flower in the city. I still call them the purple flowers. I know they have a proper name, but I don't know what it is. I don't think I want to know. Whenever I smell it, I remind myself that I'm still here, I'm still alive, and that no matter how much the city may want to swallow me whole, I'll never let it.

My father came over the other day and gave me my mother's journals. He'd hid them away in storage after she died.

The journals are just like I remembered them. Random thoughts, ideas, poems, all written along fragile, thin pages. They are the writings of someone deeply creative, someone trying to find herself.

I took out my own journals that Rick had gotten me. I started writing in them, started to conjure up some sort of idea about myself. It would take time, but I could feel the hint of a plan forming. Maybe going back to school, becoming a physical therapist. I wanted to use my body to help people. It felt right, it felt like me.

One day, I sat at my kitchen table, perusing through my mother's journals again. There was a purple one on the bottom of the stack. I slid it out, unraveled the straps.

The pages opened reflexively to an entry in the middle

dated a few months before she died. She talked about going to the park, enjoying the spring air, feeling the warmth of the sun on her face again after a long winter. Pressed between the pages was a flower. It was dried and had no scent. It had been trapped in the pages for fifteen years, but I recognized it.

It looked like a small sunflower with lavender petals and a large royal purple center, but if you stared at it long enough, you could see a hint of the black void underneath, waiting to consume you.

END

—

As a young boy, JEFF ENOS was the kid reading under a tree (probably *Goosebumps* or Stephen King) while the other kids played. He got serious about writing in 2020, when we were all forced to re-examine our lives. He successfully completed GrubStreet's *Into to Fiction* course in the fall of 2020. Jeff has been published in *Allegory* e-zine. He lives in New York City with his partner, Arik. You can connect with Jeff on Instagram @jfreez and twitter/X @JeffEnosWrites.

ST. LOUIS

John Joseph Ryan

I see things that other people can't.

I don't mean I have excellent vision. I mean, I see shit that isn't really there. Or so others tell me.

But it is.

Some might call it a gift, a supernatural talent, to which I say, Yeah, right. You try having it.

But it could be proof of God to have that capability, they argue. Or at least a spirit world of some kind.

Well, it's proof of something. But not God.

Listen, before you protest or get all excited, let me just put all those notions to rest for you. See that woman over there, the one sitting outside the café? Naw, not the one in the Cardinals hat. The one who keeps waving a hand past her ear, swatting at some invisible bug?

There's an affliction demon squatting down above her, tickling her ear with the tip of its tail. It's feathered, not barbed. Now, hear me out! The quills are highly prized among goblin scribes. I'm not kidding! The less savory among them will buy them on the black market, no questions asked. Seems affliction demons are easily cowed by bigger demons, who pin them down and pluck out their feathers with about as much conscience as a fisherman cutting off a shark's dorsal fin and then throwing it back in the sea, alive.

How do I know this, you ask?

Because I don't just *see* them, I talk to them. Or rather, they talk to me. I don't seek them out. They seem *drawn* to me, like they know I have this so-called talent. And let me tell you, it's no picnic to be woken up in the middle of the night by a tattle wraith. Those suckers'll hunker down on your chest and won't let you move until they exhaust their supply of otherworldly gossip. And since the Otherworld is so vast, that takes a *very* long time. I've been kept up until dawn before being released. Sometimes, they sit a little way on your bladder. And look at me. I'm middle-aged! I have to get up to pee every night!

Go ahead and laugh if you like. No, I know you weren't laughing. Not out loud. But you were laughing inside. Yeah, that's right. I can read people's hidden emotions. Not perfectly. Not to the extent that I'm attuned to those awful creatures. But enough. Enough to add to my own affliction.

I can tell you think I'm crazy. Maybe you think I've had a nervous breakdown. Well, maybe I have. My head hurts. All the time. But that doesn't change what I know to be true.

Still not convinced? Then, let me tell you about an event that will bring my nightmare life home for you.

I didn't have this ability before. I was a fairly normal guy. Single, decent job working for Commerce Bank. I had my own condo in the Central West End, friends, and the occasional female companion. And I had the sweetest dog, Badger. I used to walk him around Forest Park almost every day. I didn't know it then, but that was probably the best time of my life. Damn. Well, one spring day, there was rain in the forecast. Radar made it look like a big storm, with lots of angry reds and oranges. I figured I better take Badger out quick before it hit. He used to get pretty scared by thunder and refused to leave our home for hours after a storm. I didn't want to step in a surprise gift of his in the middle of the night because of that, if you know what I mean, so off we went to the park.

Across Kingshighway, I could see the new leaves showing their gray backsides, the limbs bowing before this big beast on the western horizon. Now, if you believe me yet, this was no metaphorical beast. But more on that later. I got the pedestrian signal at the Laclede intersection but waited a few seconds. Sure enough, some shitmobile goes flying through the red light, rear bumper dragging, temporary tag flapping. I don't flip 'em off anymore after one guy pulled a gun on me. Anyway, the park. There was nobody really around. A few mothers were hustling their kids into cars, and a jogger or two were racing to beat the rain. You know the trail, right, that goes in a big loop, following Lindell? There's big sycamores arching over it. I figured even if I did catch a little early rain, it wouldn't be too bad.

As I rounded this turn, I saw a solitary car parked a little ways off the trail, right beneath this achingly gorgeous redbud. Even over the sound of the rustling leaves, I could hear its engine running. It was an old sedan, a little rusty, and the engine was knocking and revving. I could see someone was behind the wheel. The driver's side window was open partway. Some kind of tube or hose was hanging out of it, leading back to the trunk. I thought that was weird. As I got a little closer, the tube fell out of the window. The engine settled some, and suddenly, the door was flung open. I saw an older man stick his foot out. His face was angry, frustrated. As he stepped out, the wind blew his combover into his eyes. He thrust it back, then stooped down to pick up the tube. I watched him feed it through the open window, then he held on to it as he got in and closed the door again. The window went up a little more. Well, you've probably figured this out by now, but for some reason, I was pretty dense at the time. *Jesus*, I realized. *That guy's trying to kill himself!*

Badger was straining to pull me back towards the condo. I thought it was just the pending storm, but now I know better. I had to practically drag him as I raced over to the man's car. He saw me, his eyes widened, and he began revving the engine even harder. I could see exhaust filling the interior of his car. He started coughing, but he just kept revving harder and harder. I got up to his car and tried the door handle. It was locked. I think I beat on the window and started yelling at him. He just kept coughing, glaring at me, revving the engine. Badger was pulling like crazy, growling now. I looked down at him, and he was baring his teeth at me, something I'd never seen him do. I remember looking back at the man. His eyelids were starting to droop. But he kept revving. So I just grabbed the hose, yanked it out of the window, pulled the other end off the tailpipe, and ran across the road with it.

I wondered if I should find a rock or something to break the window in. I could see the man's head was up, so he wasn't totally overwhelmed. After a few moments, he opened the car door again, but stayed inside. For a minute, I just watched him. Badger had calmed down some, but he was stretching the leash, pointing his head towards home. I was tempted to just leave the guy and throw the hose away on my way out of the park, but I was too worried about him. Finally, he stepped out of the car.

He was wearing a tan suit and a really garish, florid tie. He actually buttoned the jacket and straightened the tie before looking over at me. I felt a welling of compassion at that moment. I can't describe it. The misery on his face, the terminal act he was about to commit, the embarrassment he must be feeling. I was a witness to it all. And not just that. Now, I was involved. And I could feel my involvement was about to deepen, almost against my will.

I think I called over with something banal like, *Are you all right?* He just shrugged and looked at the car like it would provide him an answer. The wind was picking up, and I felt the first few drops fall. *Listen, I just live a few minutes from here. You want some tea? We could talk.* He looked from me towards the approaching storm, and without taking his eyes off that roiling black sky, he said, *We better hurry.*

You better roll up your window, I said before I could think.

He smiled at that. It was a wry one, but it was a smile.

For being an old guy who had lost his will to live, he sure was spry. We got back to my place in half the time it normally takes. Most of the cars on Kingshighway were pulled off as an ambulance wailed by on its way to Barnes Hospital. Badger was still skittish, but moving in the opposite direction of the storm seemed to help.

When we got inside my condo, I showed the old man where the bathroom was and offered to make tea. He said water would be enough and went into the bathroom. I poured the water and went to sit in my living room, right near the bathroom door. I was straining to listen. I know a few minutes went by. I started running through what was in there: a disposable razor, scissors, medications. What if he was going to do himself in, still, only now in my house? It was enough that I stood up and put my ear to the bathroom door. Of course, right at that moment, he opened it. He didn't look at all startled to see me. He said something like, *Don't worry. I'm not going to do anything drastic in your home.* For some odd reason, I believed him.

I handed him the glass of water, and we sat down. The reek of car exhaust was all over him. He took a little sip of the water; then he practically gulped the rest down. I remember the first huge bolt of lightning flashed then, and the thunderclap was almost immediate. I jumped, and Badger scurried under the dining room table, but the old guy just wiped his mouth with the sleeve of his cheap jacket and closed his eyes.

What do you say in a moment like that? A dozen trivialities passed through my mind till I felt compelled to just take the matter head-on.

Why were you trying to kill yourself? I asked.

He opened his eyes and set the glass down. Before answering me, he craned his neck like he was listening to something. One ear faced my front windows, the direction of the pending storm.

The storm is talking to me, he said.

Oh, great, I thought, *Here we go*. This guy's had a serious breakdown. Suicidal, mentally unbalanced. I immediately went back on guard.

I know you think I'm crazy, he said, like he was reading my mind. *A few months ago, I would have thought I was, too. But what I'm telling you is true*. He closed his eyes again.

I was thinking at that moment that I'd better call 911. I was pondering a tactful way to do that when he opened his eyes and spoke again.

Don't call the authorities. I'm not going to hurt myself here. I'm not going to hurt you. If you just let me explain, I'll go on my way, and you can forget you ever saw me.

Something about him compelled me. Despite his down-and-out state, I could see in his bearing that he had been someone once, maybe an important someone, a successful business leader or a military officer. I had already invited him in. The hospitable thing would be to listen to his story.

I just couldn't bear it anymore. We've had more storms this spring than any previous year. Each one is a torment. You have no idea.

A torment, how? I wondered.

Here comes a lightning strike, was all he said.

And damn if another bolt didn't light up the windows.

That could be a coincidence, I said.

Nope. Hold on, he appeared to count down silently. *Now.*

Another bolt flashed as the thunderclap from the first one boomed. The old man covered his ears and winced. Badger whined under the dining room table.

I have to get his thunder jacket, I said. *Here, I'll get you some more water while I'm up.*

He didn't appear to hear me. He just kept his ears covered until the last rumblings of the thunder had passed. I got Badger suited up and tried to give him a treat, but he was trembling too much to accept it. I filled the water glass and brought it back to the old man, who had uncovered his ears but closed his eyes again.

Thank you, he said, taking the glass without seeing it. He just seemed to sense where it was. He took a sip but then set it down suddenly.

Here comes another bolt.

He covered his ears as, sure enough, a fresh flash illuminated the room. This time, the thunder followed more closely. The storm would be upon us in minutes. I looked out to see that the few errant drops running down the window were multiplying and enlarging.

You said before that the storm was talking to you. What did you mean by that?

He opened his eyes but didn't look at me when he replied.

Just what I said. It's talking to me. Not in one voice but in a legion of voices. A battalion of infernal tongues. I can't bear to hear it.

I decided to play along.

Can you understand them?

Yes. They're inhuman languages, and they overlap, but I can hear each one distinctly despite the cacophony. It is Hell. He finally looked at me. *By which I mean it is literal Hell.*

That chilled me. The wind beat the tree limbs suddenly, and the real downpour began. For a minute, we both just sat and listened. He was looking out the window with a grimace on his face. I kept watching him, trying not to stare, but unable to help myself. When the first pelts of hail began, he stood up. His face took on an anguished look.

I can't bear to listen to it! I just can't.

For the first time since we sat down, I worried again that he might hurt himself. He leapt up and started beating his fists against the sides of his head. Badger's whimpering became louder, more forceful. Pretty soon, he broke into a howl, a loud, sinuous, unbroken, pure one. That seemed to snap the old man out of his private pain for a moment. He stopped beating his head and looked over at Badger. Then he did the strangest thing on a day of stranger and stranger things. He made this high-pitched whistle with a kind of ululation at the end of it. I had never heard anything like it in my lifetime. But it calmed Badger down at once. He broke off his howl and even came out from under the table. He went up to the old man, who sat down again, and sitting himself, Badger offered up a paw.

How did you do that? I asked, incredulous.

You won't believe me, but I learned that technique from a faerie. He took Badger's paw absentmindedly. *It's one of the very few resources I have…against that.* He pointed towards the windows. *This is a good dog. I had a dog like him once. And a family. And a good career. It's all, all gone.*

I thought he might start hitting himself again, but he kept his composure while he petted Badger and looked at me.

I appreciate you helping me out and letting me try to explain myself. I haven't done a good job so far. Despite what I'm hearing right now, even as I speak, I'm going to do my best to overcome it. I owe that much to you.

He sighed and tried to center himself. Badger nuzzled him and jumped up on the couch next to him. Normally, I didn't allow my dog onto the furniture, but the old guy put an arm around Badger, and that seemed to anchor him emotionally.

I know what I'm telling you is hard to believe. Wait.

He paused and clinched as another lightning bolt fell, followed by an immediate, window-rattling boom of thunder. The storm was right on top of us. He shook his head from side to side and clutched Badger tighter. My dog seemed strangely unaffected by the giant thunderclap.

These more frequent, more intense storms have a scientific explanation. I know that. Nature is opportunistic despite—or maybe because of—what we've done to the planet. The supernatural is even more so. The Otherworld is getting closer and closer to breaching our own world. Every storm brings more and more eldritch creatures into our presence. They can't get through the natural barricades. Nature has had to adapt to the supernatural as well, and she did so over a greater span of time than we've been around to mess with her. But now our actions are weakening those barriers that took eons to develop. Massive thunderstorms, stronger hurricanes, unstoppable year-round wildfires. These are just signs of worse to come after that once-impermeable border crumbles.

He paused again. I knew, without him having to say so, that lightning would strike. He looked into my eyes and nodded as the bolt landed. Maybe I was becoming susceptible to what he was saying at that moment because I thought the light shifted just then, suffusing the room in a scarlet tone. The thunder sounded a few seconds later. *What do the creatures tell you?* I found myself asking.

He took a deep breath and held Badger harder before answering.

The message is the same, but the variations in its delivery are maddening. They plan to take over the earth and reign as they have reigned over the Otherworld. Each species has its own particular part to play, and none of them are shy about boasting about their plans.

He released Badger long enough to lean forward and look me straight in the eyes.

You'll be fortunate if you are merely enslaved.

That shook me. He continued to share everything these creatures would do to us. We would become their playthings: forced into struggles for life, tortured, served as food, compelled to do the foulest, most horrific things to the people we loved, and summarily killed in brutal, spectacular ways. Merely contemplating those foretold evils was enough to destroy any sense of peace I might have left after he finished talking. During the telling, his face had taken on many anguished expressions. But one last question showed him at his most vulnerable.

Do you believe me?

For a moment, I couldn't answer. Then I realized the storm was beginning to pass. The wind had abated, and the rain fell softly. Looking west through the windows, I could see the sky start to lighten, losing its gray-green cast. A low, distant rumble of thunder developed into a staccato pattern. As I listened to it I discerned a definite polyrhythm. After it tapered off, I felt I understood a message from it that I could never articulate. It spoke directly into my brain, if *speak* is even the right word. And right then I felt crushed by the knowledge that humanity is doomed. I didn't want to admit it, but I did believe the old man. It took everything in me just to look him in the eye and nod.

His enormous relief surprised me. He sprang up, came over to me, lifted me by the hands, and embraced me like a long-lost brother. He didn't let go for a long time, and I could feel him shuddering with sobs. Finally, I peeled him off of me, feeling embarrassed. He wiped his eyes and thanked me.

He left after that. I watched him through the window as he headed back to Forest Park through the slackening rain. When he reached Kingshighway, he didn't slacken his pace. For one horrible moment I thought he was going to walk straight into traffic, that I had merely delayed the inevitability of his suicide. Just then he stopped and his body seemed to go slack. He looked back at my condo. Even from my vantage point I could see he looked confused. He even scratched his head, his jaw slack. He looked up and down the block, took a few steps north, then stopped again. Other pedestrians gave him a wide berth. After a few moments, he sat down on the curb and just stared into the park.

I had made up my mind to go down to check on him when a young woman stopped to lean down and speak to him. Whatever she said seemed to revive him, give him direction. He stood up and embraced her, a big smile on his face. He turned that smile in all directions, looking like a lunatic. She backed off and scurried away. Then, he practically bounced over to the crosswalk.

I watched him wave at all the passengers in the passing cars before he got the signal to cross. I swear he almost skipped his way back to the park. Badger nudged against me and stood by the door, wagging his tail. I couldn't believe he wanted to go out. Whatever the old man had communicated with his strange whistle, Badger was almost a different dog now. I figured going out wouldn't hurt. I needed to try to process everything that had just happened—including the old man's strange transformation down on the boulevard. And I was too curious to see if the old man's car would still be there. In fact, I realized I had to see him again, that now questions and anxieties were frothing inside me.

The park was desolate, wet, and shining as the sun began to break through. Limbs lay everywhere, and trash cans were overturned. I found myself hustling to the tree-lined section of the trail near where I had spotted his car.

When I got there, it was gone.

I never saw the old man again.

I wasn't worried. That is, about him. I had a whole host of worries now.

That night, I hardly slept. When I did sleep, my mind made those nightmare scenarios the old man so vividly described take on color, form—and, worst of all, sound. After feeding Badger the next morning, I was grateful to take him out, away from my transformed living room, the site of the horrific telling. The scent of car exhaust would have surely dissipated, but somehow it was still present.

I remember it was a gorgeous day; it was clear, the air washed clean, and the world was sparkling and cool. And the dogwoods in the park! Like wedding cakes gleaming in the sunshine. I walked Badger over to the park and let him run off-leash. He was so delighted, so happy cavorting around the beds of daffodils, that I almost began to doubt my experience with the old man was real. That night, I had trouble falling asleep, but my dreams were untroubled. The next day, the whole encounter seemed less real, almost fabricated.

But that's when weird things started happening. At the

bank, I kept miscounting money, enough to merit a concerned conversation with my manager. Outside, I caught glimpses of people, just within my periphery, who disappeared when I tried to look at them straight on. Over the following weeks, I heard odd voices coming from air conditioners, rattling in the trees, and filtering through the agitated chattering of squirrels. I went on dates with a couple of women, but they never contacted me again. One blocked me on a dating site. Children avoided me in the park. Hummingbirds stopped visiting my feeders. But the biggest blow came when Badger ran away. He was off-leash at the park, and he just split. I don't want to talk about that, actually. I hope he's okay. He must have known what was going to happen. After that, those peripheral shapes took on flesh. And they weren't human after all. And that's when they began talking to me.

And they haven't stopped since.

So now you know my story. It's only been a couple of months since it all happened, but it feels like a lifetime ago, my previous life just a happy, evanescent dream.

Hey, this is my bus. I gotta go. But there's just one thing I have to ask you.

Do you believe me?

Let me make sure. Let me look at you. Hmm. Okay, I can't read you at all. Hey, good! Oh, good, good, so very good.

Now, I've just passed the talent on to you. Thank you.

Sincerely.

And good luck with what's to come. Good…huh… That's funny… What am I doing here?

Oh, buddy, do I feel good! Say, how do you do? Are you waiting on the same bus as me? What's the matter? You look concerned. Do you need bus fare? No? What are you talking about? I don't know you, sorry. What story? Huh? Hey, listen, I don't know what you're on about, but I've never spoken to you before now. Get away from me, this is my bus! Off of me! Let go or I'll let you have it. Driver, help! This guy's a lunatic! He's convinced there's a demon across the street coming for us! Let me on right now! Hurry!

There isn't much time.

END

—

JOHN JOSEPH RYAN's work has appeared in such places as *McSweeney's*, *Suspense Magazine*, and *Creepy Podcast* (U.S.), and in international publications such as *Mystery Tribune* (Canada), *Samjoko* (Republic of Korea), *Channel* (Ireland), and *A-Z of Horror* (U.K.). John's collaborative noir short, "Hothouse by the River," was published by the University of Iowa Center for the Book. He is the author of a noir novel, *A Bullet Apiece* (Amphorae Publishing Group, 2015). As a passion project, he created and hosted the YouTube series, *Creepy Poem of the Day*. John lives in St. Louis, Missouri.

BRISBANE

EJ Delaney

Week twelve, and the campus jacarandas were out. That meant time was in flux: gnarled, unruly branches furrowed with wisdom, lulabelle petals demure yet vivacious against a backdrop of old sandstone, dropping in ones and twos until each tree sported a lavender petticoat to match its shawl and bonnet. When the jacarandas blossomed, it was time to start cramming; that was the UQ mantra, adhered to in turn by decade upon decade of undergrad students: a gentle warning to all who had wiled away their semesters.

I wasn't such a person. I had not wiled; I had not frittered. (Though as I hurried from the Steele Building across the Great Court and through the Forgan Smith, I was forced to admit it made little difference.) I had rent to cover and the storm damage to Gran's house in Woody Point, plus whatever petrol I churned through while bending ends towards a straining approximation of meeting. Where others joined social clubs or went jogging alongside the river to flesh out their twelve contact hours, I devoted myself to more necessary activities.

None of which made me any less behind in my coursework.

Two hours to kill until the tutorial. I'd been late signing up, so had missed the ones directly after the lecture. If I had any sense I'd spend the time grappling with my ANCH2030 essay. At the very least I could read the extracts from Lucian, Pliny and Virgil.

Instead my phone pinged. A fare popped up and I broke into a jog, skirting the art museum and picking up speed down past the Curlew Habitat and the Hartley Teakle Building. "The Colander," I'd heard this called—the curvaceous slab masterpiece of some famous architect—though to me it looked more like a cheese grater.

It was funny what some people valued. Then again, I myself was working for Sh!honky (logo stylised to meld an exclamation point to the second "h"). If there was room in the world for a proudly third-rate Uber, then why not a slab-brick design eyesore?

I crossed the drawbridge to the multi-storey carpark and zig-zagged up the stairwell inside, then reversed my battle-scarred Daihatsu out of its customary, small-car-only space and rattled a helter-skelter out into the afternoon sunlight. I turned right—the wrong way—up the one-way feeder lane then left onto Sir William MacGregor Drive, past a brace of playing fields and down to the Eric Freeman Boathouse.

I found my fare waiting beneath the enormous siris tree.

She pointed across the river: 500 metres as the galah flew, twenty minutes by car.

"Just over there, please."

She could have cycled it quicker—taking the bridge to Dutton Park—or caught a bus the same way. But a job is a job, and so I drove her around past the glass Gotham façade of Toowong Village, following the river bend onto Coronation Drive with its rendered unit blocks and Queen Mother jacarandas. Bypassing the Go Between Bridge, I took us over the William Jolly and then struck through West End to Dornoch Terrace. Once we hit Highgate Hill my fare directed us down, then up, then down again, riding the contours through narrow, overgrown laneways to a renovated unit block standing one tier back from the river.

"Here's good," she said, waving at a stretch of guardrail.

Transaction settled, I moved on from the blind corner and pulled over to check the Sh!honky app. There were several fares going but none in my direction. Maybe that was for the best. Given the state of my assessment, I really should have been prepping for that week's *Medea* tutorial, but then a new job came up that would take me from Stefan's Skyneedle all the way over to Chapel Hill. I'd be cutting it fine but the Imp of Optimism sat cajoling upon my shoulder. *Go on*, it urged. *You know this part of the city; you can do it.*

Enamoured with my own skills, I swiped right.

Nemesis swiped left.

The drop-off went without a hitch—up the hill, right at the chapel; Neptune Street; Chantilly Lace; Big Boppering along—but my return to campus was ill-fated. It seemed so obvious in retrospect (Moggill Road a bumper-to-bumper purgatory) but I'd thought I could duck and dodge my way through. Unfortunately, my would-be shortcut down Witton Road and around towards the Walter Taylor was curtailed by blowback from the Catholic school. I took an impulsive left, wending my way back past Indooroopilly.

That's when I hit the scrub turkey.

I was driving too fast and it darted out in front of me with the neurotic abruptness for which the species is renowned. Running low, its plumage tucked back like the dark cloak of some crazed count, it dashed from one ancestral patch in search of another, contriving somehow to broadside my front bumper.

I hit the brakes. The turkey went *thunk*. I flicked my hazard lights on and got out to have a look. *Stupid bird*, I thought sadly.

I took it by the legs and dragged it to the far verge. Its yellow neck wattle hung pathetically limp, its head bare and red as though flushed from a lifetime's exertion.

"Stupid, stupid bird," I reiterated.

Feeling that my efforts had been inadequate, I shifted my grip on the ill-fated gweela and carried it further from the road, bearing it aloft like an op-shop dress on a hanger. It drooped upside-down, fusty tail feathers tickling my nose. I slung the remains, corpse-to-copse, into a scraggle of poor man's orchid—a nearby concrete manhole riser serving to mark the spot—then I hobbled back to the Daihatsu. I'd felt a stab of pain, holding the body up high like that: a sharp twinge just under my waistband.

"Great," I muttered. "'Why are you late, Maxim?' 'Oh, you know. I was with this bird and I pulled a groin muscle.'"

The rest of the drive was excruciating. Station Road was banked back and it took forever to clear the rail line; then St Lucia's leafy maze had me stamping in fits and spurts. By the time I parked and staggered up to the Michie Building, I was three-quarters of an hour late for a one-hour tutorial.

"Traffic," I explained. "Although, ironically, that helped me get past a block in my thinking. To draw a parallel with Hecate as protector of the household, it seems to me that Our Lady should be understood first and foremost as a woman and only then as the deity of man's imagining…"

The tutor was nodding along, as she tended to do whenever someone bemired themselves in the source material and couldn't get free. I took that as a participation grade snatched from the jaws of non-attendance.

"There's an intrinsic liminality," I concluded, "where male as mortal presumes to encroach upon the female divine. That's where I got to, anyway, and I think it's what Seneca was driving at."

Emphasising this with a hapless shrug, I sat back in my chair. The girl to my left leaned close and whispered:

"Our Lady?"

"Of Blessed Acceleration," I clarified. "Also, my car."

The words were glib. A pair of off-duty self-monitoring thoughts dropped their beers in dismay and leapt to the winches, clamping my jaw shut on some half-formed prattle about holy dualities. *For fuck's sake*, I berated myself. This was the poised girl I was talking to! Mediterranean skin. Meticulous updo hair. The only person in the tutorial who genuinely engaged with the course.

She regarded me for a long moment, an expert inspecting a brazen forgery.

Then, with the tiniest of frowns, she returned her attention to Seneca and Medea.

I slept badly that night, my dreams overrun by bachelor scrub turkeys charging pent-up and hell-for-feather across Finney Road. Again and again they crumpled under my bumper, jolting me awake as I braked and bunny-hopped through the early hours.

At last the dawn came scratching about. Hours passed, and I heaved myself out of bed.

I'd set the morning aside to work on my PHIL2300 essay: 1,700 as yet unmanifested words teetering at the vanishing point of a diligently wheedled four-week extension. *No excuses*, I told myself. No matter what else enticed me in the moment, I'd open my laptop, lock eyes with the screen and just write the thing: phenomenology, existentialism, the problem of being. Only—

The task stretched endless. A blank page, people said; so full of promise! Yet my document felt utterly devoid of it. My cursor lay adrift, treading water in a sea of off-white. When

I turned my mind to Heidegger—pitching an argument in terms of epoché, following the strands of eidetic variation—my thoughts merely took up the floundering.

I couldn't engage with this shit. I had sweet F.A. to say and no urge to pretend otherwise, and yet the famed Margraf-Jones instinct for displacement activity—which on other days would have propelled me behind the wheel and had me Sh!honking like a madman—seemed equally to have deserted me. That, in a sense, was the stranger of the two disinclinations. My phone buzzed but I didn't so much as clock on, let alone check for fares.

My groin ached, a dull throb abutting my right testicle, in my mons pubis or whatever muscle lay cushioned by that fatty tissue. As for my assignment, any insight I might have summoned lay cruelled by wobble board and the insistent refrain of Monty Python singing:

> *Heidegger, Heidegger was a boozy beggar*
> *who could think you under the table…*

As much as I wrestled with this earworm, it wrapped itself tight, constricting me with that single, cod-ocker loop. Before I knew it the morning was gone. I'd drained my laptop battery, skipped lunch—achieved bupkis.

And now I was late for class!

With an aggrieved squawk, I burst from my bedroom and blew past the latest flatmate, stopping only to check in with Sh!honky and snag an opportunistic fare: Latrobe Terrace;

pickup in Bardon; then down the guts past Toowong Cemetery; Sylvan Road, Coro Drive, the narrow, leafy overhang of Sir Fred Schonell. I dropped my fare outside the Avalon Theatre (unsafely on the turn; I must have driven past a hundred times without ever noticing it). Then I hit the multi-storey, clattered its stairwell and skittered across to the Llew Edwards Building, arriving just in time to be conspicuously the last one there.

The door did me no favours. It unsealed with a heavy click and an exaggerated hiss of pressure imbalance, admitting me just as the lecturer began speaking. I slunk past her elbow and up to the back row of poppy-red seats, conscious that I'd rocked up empty-handed: no pad, no laptop; nothing to indicate I had any interest whatsoever in Judith Butler or pandemic phenomenology.

Which, to be fair, I didn't. As the professor started up again, I felt a dark, sullen flash steal over me, blotting out my usual ambivalence. What was the point? Lectures, tutes, timetables. Essay topics that I intuitively parsed as pure flannel.

Brisbane was done up in its best blossoms, the campus a titivation of jacarandas and early-flowering poincianas, with the occasional flame tree in sequinned, party-girl red. Spring was in full force, yet I couldn't help feeling this was just a veneer. All that gladdened would fall away eventually, crushed underfoot.

What was it the insurance company had told Gran? *Roof older than twenty years; no documentation of maintenance.* Yeah, sure. And that after thirty-five minutes playing Louis Armstrong at her on the customer service line.

I glared around me. Under my baleful eye the lecture hall had grown shadowy. The professor's words turned oddly guttural: *intertwining* this, *grievability* that. *The pandemic as ethical meliorist, repudiating egological foundations and upending the bounded self...* I sat stewing throughout it all, increasingly disgruntled that I should be listening to such twaddle.

I clenched my right hand. Fixated now, I envisaged a club—a thick wooden drumstick weighted for bludgeoning.

My head swam. I—

Well, I'm not quite sure what happened next. Time went squidgy and folded up into an origami puzzle box: a miniature escape room with me trapped inside. Only after several aeons did I come to, released from my prison and raging across the University Drive greenspace.

"Maxim!" Even as I registered the voice, its owner caught up and brushed her hand across my shoulder. "Maxim, wait."

A part of me unknotted. My next step was faltering; the one after sloughed me of all momentum.

I turned and found myself face-to-face with the poised girl.

"Good," she affirmed. "Now, don't take this the wrong way. I've got a boyfriend, understand? Long-term. I'm in no way hitting on you. But—" She half dipped, half tilted her head. "I think we should go for coffee."

"How—?" I began.

But she was already steering me over to the Forgan Smith.

"I'm in three of your classes, Maxim. Your ETAs are chaotic but that's nine contact hours! Four days a week we've seen each other, plus History 22-20 and 2-3-12 last semester. I know who you are."

Thinking back, I realised it was true. Her presence had been a constant in my lectures and tutes: Demonology, The History Makers, Medieval Mediterranean, and all the rest. Unconsciously I'd baulked from engaging with her. (She favoured half-sleeve denim playsuits and her self-assurance made me feel like a schoolboy.) And yet I wasn't intimidated now. Meeting her outside of class, I saw some of the personality bubbling beneath her poise—the individual, not the type I'd assigned her.

And, of course, I knew *her* name, too, gleaned through osmosis while a numbing conflux of tutorials washed over me. As we crossed the Great Court, I dredged it to the surface:

"Charm."

"That's me! And my boyfriend's called Darcy, just to emphasise that point. Now, sit. What will you drink?"

"Frappé?" I ventured.

"At your peril."

She'd brought us down to Wordsmiths Café. An ibis picked over the only free table, but she shooed it away and scraped two chairs around before making for the tuckshop-style counter. I sat myself down. A pair of maiden-aunt poincianas spread their branches overhead, their sun-dappled canopy a profusion of ferny leaves and budding, goldfish-shoal flowers.

"So…" Charm returned with an order number. "Do you want to tell me what happened back there?"

"Um…?"

"In the lecture. You were—how do I put this? Spanging out."

"What?"

"Spanging. Slipping the rails. That's a placeholder diagnosis but if you came clean on the symptoms I could be more specific."

I wasn't sure this made sense. Which was fine; I didn't mind. My BA to date had been a molasses of sticky logic, so I could hardly complain if a girl wanted to talk to me along those same lines. Still, I felt myself grow edgy.

"Look," Charm said. "I have some experience with this kind of thing. In school I was—well, it's not something you put on your resumé. A bit like prefect only totally not. Anyway, I still get flashes. You've changed, Maxim, just in the last few days. There's a darkness…"

I shook my head. "No."

I kicked out at the ibis, which flapped clear in an outrage of abused brotherhood. I balled my hand into a fist.

"No," I repeated. "You're wrong."

"It's not a problem," Charm said. "Well, I mean, it *is*. But it's not your *fault*. And I'm pretty sure it's solvable. Like a rogue elephant or a dog with bindis in its paw."

"You want to tweezer me?"

"Well, possibly. To help, at any rate."

The way she was looking at me, I imagined she could see right through to the emotions within: anger, fear, frustration. I didn't believe her, of course. Who would? There was nothing the matter with me! And yet…

My vehemence was disquieting—my pre-emptive certainty on this very point. Like when I'd called the black ball "white" during a game of billiards and immediately become 100% convinced I hadn't, despite the testimony of witnesses.

Adrenaline sent me to my feet, prepped in equal measure for toxic aggression or neutered withdrawal.

"I have to go." I grabbed for my phone and swiped at the first fare: a potential hell ride from Mt Coot-Tha to Seventeen Mile Rocks.

"It's going to get worse," Charm warned.

"Yeah, if I don't get ahead of peak hour…"

"You know that's—" She was addressing my back now, raising her voice as I lurched away: "You know that isn't what I meant!" Then: "To be continued, Maxim." And finally: "What about your frappé?"

Groin twinging in protest, I took hold of the metal handrail and hauled myself back up the stairs past the Richards Building, through to the Great Court.

Gathering no moss.

The drive across-river just about did me in, but I pushed through it and funneled my frustrations into notching up fares: Sinnamon Park to Springfield Lakes; Camira to Coopers Plains to Carindale to Coorparoo; Norman Park to Newstead; Herston to Hamilton to Hendra, then Portside back to Paddington. I Sh!honked until there was no more Sh!honking to be done.

I woke late the next morning, my inner thigh stiff from too much jockeying of the accelerator. Rubbing at the tender spot, I opened my laptop and, channeling the dregs of fading nightmare, hovered above myself like some dissociated, self-immolating monk and hammered out the overdue PHIL2300 essay.

It was, I considered, a masterpiece: premium-grade bullshit, peeling back Heidegger through the world-linked sub/objective viewpoint of a scrub turkey. Churn it out. Turnitin.

If my luck held, I might just about scrape a pass grade after all.

Rolling with this thought, I snagged a packet salad from the Paddington Woolworths then Sh!honkied my way from Rosalie to Toowong and onward to my 2 p.m. tute.

Things started to go wrong along Sir Fred Schonell Drive. My crotch complained at being moulded to the driver's seat again. As I passed the first playing field the tufted, shaven-necked Dr. Seuss pines, which usually struck me as comically endearing, seemed preening, mocking and aloof. The leopard trees alongside the multi-storeys turned menacing in their guard of honour.

Charm's warning came back to me, nonsensical as it had been (the vaguest of "its" set to escalate in some non-specified fashion). I hunched over the wheel and gurned my way past the parabolic solar panels in their mounted tracking array, caged now as if to keep the assemblage safe from slavering hordes of Little John bottlebrush and Honey Gem grevillea. I hit the roundabout. With a blur like falling dominoes all the UQ foliage twisted through some dread plane of transformation, attuning itself somehow to Munch's great scream.

I choked back a cry. My heel spasmed and I fishtailed out of the roundabout and back in a squeaking loop, past revenant gum trees and grasping she-oaks, to take refuge in the multi-storey. Inside wasn't so bad. I ramped the switchbacks, flew like some early Wright Brothers prototype over the speedbumps, and swung screeching into my usual car space. But I knew I couldn't stay there—not with tutorial credit on the line, roofing quotes to chase up.

Abandoning the Daihatsu, I took the stairwell to Level 2. When I reached the landing some desperate part of me wanted to curl up and stay safe in its musty embrace. Instead, I pulled the fire door hard against its closer and scuttled through, the snap of its jaws coming muffled at my heels. As the echo faded, I ventured out across the drawbridge and crept cautiously up toward the Hartley Teakle—past the bamboo grove, which swayed and loomed and swallowed up most of the path. The slope itself wasn't excessive but the trail lay damp underfoot, reeking of rot and digestive fluid. Bird of paradise plants crowded around me. Frangipani pressed their flowers close—heady and hungry for contact.

Participation marks, I coaxed myself. *One small step from marginal fail to functional achievement.*

A crow swooped down at me. It was huge, dark and elusive save a whoosh of feathers as I ducked clear. This at least was normal. (I always forget about the Hartley Teakle crows; the attack stirred both a familiar panic and a tinge of relief—a bit like swotvac.) Emerging from the clutches of rampant, flailing greenery, I hit the flat concrete beyond ModWest and ran a new gamut past bark-encircled poincianas and other great, sprawling rancors, hurrying towards the Biol Library. I bypassed Darwin's at my usual trot, then tackled the broad stairs up to the Michie Building and through to room 217, which turned out to be empty.

"Tutes finished last week." Charm stepped from the alcove of the Antiquities Museum opposite. "Never mind, here's your coffee."

She held out a Styrofoam cup. Reflexively I took it.

"Ugh. Thanks."

Charm shrugged. "From the lows of frappé, tepid is up. Now, about this dark passenger of yours…"

"My what?"

"Dark passenger. Which, again, is something of a genericism, but if you've read your Jung you'll get the idea. Or watched any *Dexter*." She eyed the coffee cup. "If you want specifics, you'll have to be more forthcoming."

"Forthcoming, sure. Only I don't know what you're talking about."

"I think you do. Look, denial doesn't help anyone. Like I said yesterday, I can—Maxim, please don't run away."

I had indeed begun edging back down the corridor.

"I'm not," I lied. "This is me recognising the tute-lessness of the situation and directing my efforts elsewhere."

"I can sense it, Max. It's on you and it won't let go, not willingly." She took a step nearer. "I can help. I—"

"No!" The refusal roared out of me, loud enough to turn heads in the museum. It shook the glass door and, for all I knew, set lekythoi and neck amphoras shaking on their plinths. I blinked, stunned by my own outburst. "No, I—"

Without the slightest hesitation, Charm flowed into the breach. She took me by the wrist and unfolded my fingers, rolling back my fist to make a hand she could press with her own.

"Right," she announced. "Enough repartee. Maxim Margraf-Jones? Boyfriend notwithstanding, it is now absolutely imperative that you come home with me and get naked."

Which really wasn't playing fair—my brain declared a blissful state of emergency and dream logic then induced a retroactive sleepwalker's daze: Charm led me by the hand back down to the multi-storey, retracing my steps past docile crows and flaccid, comatose flora. I reversed the Daihatsu on autopilot, then followed her directions back along Sir Fred Schonell, up Brisbane Street, then right onto Carmody Road and down to a gum-lined park and playground. A cockatoo eyed me askance as we pulled up, one clawed foot pegging it to a poinciana branch, the other upturned, holding a half-nibbled passionfruit like a wine glass. Charm guided me across the road, clear of an oncoming bus, before letting us into a semi-detached share house; through the key-locked iron front gate; upstairs to the bathroom.

"Get clean," she ordered, and threw me a towel. "Soap. Shampoo. Put this on when you're done."

She wrenched the door shut behind me, battening it to

the frame as if sealing me inside a decontamination unit. I stripped down and stepped into the shower cubicle. The pummelling water did little to unfog my thoughts, but it did induce a languid, pre-sexual arousal. I dried off while staring at Rorschach-patterned wall tiles, then wrapped the towel as best I could.

"Right," said Charm when I poked my head back outside. "This way."

She dragged me down the hall and into one of the bedrooms. Belatedly my higher brain functions took an interest.

"Um, about your boyfriend…?"

"Darcy," she confirmed. "Don't worry, he's used to all this."

She took me by the shoulders and walked me backwards to the centre of the room, positioning me under the ceiling light. After a final adjustment, she stood close and combed her fingers through my chest hair.

"Valentine's Day, the semi-formal. It can't have been easy but he's always been really supportive. Right, hands up."

She brought my wrists together, elbows splayed at shoulder height, then she felt about in my armpits—which I would have thought more weird if I hadn't been distracted by the towel working its way loose. She spun me around just as it slipped free.

"Actually, Darce is down in Melbourne just now." She massaged her fingertips through my scruffy half-mullet, inspecting my nape. "He's trying to crack the pubs and clubs scene."

"Melbourne, right."

With Charm at my back and nothing in front now but her neatly made bed, the scenario took on a character both untamed and thrillingly clinical.

"Long-distance is tough, but we're making it work."

"Urhl," I gurgled.

Once she'd finished with my neck, she traced a four-fingered path down either side of my spine then across and under my buttocks.

"All clear," she pronounced. "Oh well, it was best to check. On we go then."

She rotated me back away from the bed and dropped to her knees on a shagpile rug the same royal blue as the Cookie Monster soft toy on her dresser. I couldn't help it; I let out a groan like an adolescent walrus.

"Max…" she chided.

She presented herself to me in duplicate: the back of her head reflected in the wardrobe mirror (hitched shoulders, a fletching of neck hair), and at the same time her face tilted in front of me, brow slightly furrowed, nose pert above watermelon-pink lips hovering close—*so close*—to my dick.

I didn't know where to put my hands. I reached out, hesitated—

"…I think I've been quite clear about this. Boyfriend, remember?" She brought my left hand across my erection. "Cover that, please, and keep it to one side. It's in the way."

Anguish warred with bewilderment as she walked her fingers through my pubic hair, teasing it aside as she searched for—

"Yes, I thought so. Look, here it is." At my inarticulate mewl, she glanced up briefly then brought her phone out and snapped a picture of my groin. "Yes, I know you're a boy; you have urges. I'm sorry it's such an ordeal. But see?" She rocked back and pushed to her feet, twisting the phone to face me. "Right there, where the skin's all inflamed."

I recoiled, one hand still cradling my balls. The image was blurry but I couldn't mistake the red, speckled rash where she'd pulled the pubic hair sparse—that and—

Something else; something dark and evil-looking. It was the size of a small blueberry and, judging from the curvature, had embedded itself some four-ninths below the surface.

"Wha— What is it?" I managed.

"I'm coining the term 'tick pic'. As to the parasite, it's a *Haemocriptor kurilpa*, the Brisbane Bloodruptor." She lowered the phone. "Nasty creatures. They take physical nourishment from haemoglobin but do the real damage feeding off your psyche. Not deadly *per se*, but they'll pull you out of shape, tip you towards your Hyde-side. Breaker Morant had one. Arthur Streeton, too, most like."

"And you, what? Collect them?" Confusion churned through me; a flood of thwarted sexpression. "That's why you brought me here, pretended to—?"

I gestured, my left hand coming away to mime an urgent, harried pileup. Here I was, nude as a newt in Charm's bedroom, towel around my ankles—and she hadn't even undressed!

My right fist clenched. It was worse than when Brad Zwisler pulled my togs down in grade six, and for the next fortnight whenever one of the girls had caught my eye we'd shared an instant, touchpaper acknowledgement of what had happened and what she'd seen, my cheeks undouseable in reliving the exposure.

Dacked in public; shunned in private.

Simmering impotence seized my jaw. "You can't just—"

"Maxim." Again, she laid her hand on mine. "I'm not pretending. I want to help you, just like I said. But the Bloodruptor, it messes with your perceptions. If we don't get it off you, you'll—"

"Fine." I yanked my arm away. "I'll go see a doctor."

"You can try that." She gave me half a beat to stalk from rug to door. "Be aware though: a doctor won't go down on you either, and they won't know how to remove it. This isn't an ordinary tick, Maxim. If any part is left behind…"

The way she said it drew me up short. She'd always had the knack of sounding credible: every tutorial, no matter which side of the argument she took. I stilled my hand on the doorknob, one twist shy of rattling its backplate.

"The problem is," Charm continued, "you can only work one loose if the host is calm—which you're most certainly not—or dead, which is likely how this one came your way. Given how late you're always running, I'd say you…hit a bush turkey?"

I swung around. "How—?"

"Turkeys," she explained, "are like free-range prisons. They've evolved to contain their dark passengers, to survive in our world even when their senses are attuned to another."

I saw myself back on Finney Road, carrying the dead turkey by its ankles, holding it high while its gormless, sunburnt head hung dead-eyed by my waist. That's when the ache had started, then the spanging fugue and Munch's Scream in Green.

"Christ," I muttered. I made to scratch but she forestalled me:

"Don't. The more you irritate it, the more it'll dig in."

"So, what? I just leave it there? Adapt?"

I heard the bitterness in my own voice, the seething volatility as anger flooded my erectile tissue, piggybacking distress signals from my pent-up balls.

"No," she countered. "But like I said, we can't do anything while you're—agitated. Take a breath, Maxim. Then we'll slow things down, ease you into the right frame of mind."

I squeezed my eyes shut. Like refreshing my internet browser, opening them again merely reaffirmed the original glitch: I was joystick-naked and she wasn't even planning to fire-and-forget me.

I slapped resentfully at my erection. "What about this?"

"That," she said, "will have to go. Your job, I'm afraid." She directed me with a tilt of her chin: "Bathroom."

"Right."

I turned, humiliated, and blundered back through to the landing. Thankfully there were no housemates around—only an overweight Birman, which gave me a disapproving look as I flounced past. It was still there a minute later when I made my escape downstairs, fully dressed and sexually unsatisfied, crammed into my chino shorts.

"Max, wait!" Charm urged. "This is what it does, the Bloodruptor. It stirs you up, sets you on edge. You have to fight it!"

But she couldn't stop me. I was through the front door and out the gate, across the traffic island—gone. I cast about for the Daihatsu and found I'd parked it under a stick-thin, junkie crepe myrtle.

"Max, please. You can't just 'she'll be right' this!"

But I could, and did, scuffing through a crush of coquettishly-shed blossoms. I keyed the ignition and revved my way up the hill. Right at the t-junction. I swerved once as a blur of bottlebrush trees leant weeping to embrace me, counter-swerved as a scrub turkey flung itself across the road. It weaved a paranoid arc, bolting low from one pocket of reality to the next.

I missed it by half an erection. The Daihatsu guttered out and clipped a wheelie bin, sending it tumbling.

This time I didn't stop.

Nightmare, nightmare, all is nightmare…
I couldn't be certain that was Shakespeare, but the gist seemed on point given my overdue ENGL2060 abstract and annotated bibliography (an assessment piece still to drag itself from the gloop of a human-skull inkpot). Butchered deadlines lay strung up outside my window, dripping blood onto the carport's corrugated iron roof.

I spent an hour with study lamp and mirror, probing at

the loathsome pustule lodged in my groin, then a further hour researching the two Bloodruptor victims Charm had mentioned: the painter Arthur Streeton, all mood swings and manic energy, pouring his visions into impressionist landscapes; and colonial antihero Breaker Morant, spurred on by whatever dark force had ridden him, penning bush ballads and growing more and more unhinged until main-chancing it to South Africa and losing his rag in the Second Boer War.

Beyond the carport, a rogue flying fox fell savagely upon the resident pawpaw tree's one ripe progeny. I fell asleep, lulled by the gruesome patter.

And so another dawn came scratching.

Thursday morning saw me planted once more amidst the poppy-red seats of Llew Edwards 116, spanging my way through a lecture on the decline—question mark?—of witchcraft and demonic possession in latter-day Europe and its colonies. Charm was there, her witchfinder's gaze set squarely upon me. Her hairpins glinted like pricking-needles but she didn't speak to me. Or perhaps she did; I guess I can't be sure of that. Time went all cosmic again and I found myself back in Cthulhu's puzzle box, lost to the drone and click of eternity.

This time when I came to, I was on the road to Gran's, ensconced in the Daihatsu and Sh!honking north through steady drizzle: Toowong to Nundah; Boondall to Brighton. I drove the last stretch alone, phone on speaker so I could run through her case with the lady from the AFCA. The Hornibrook Bridge lampposts, which used to play host to roosting pelicans, trundled by in bleak, birdless monotony.

Deterrent spikes, Gran had told me. *To stop them pooping on cars. But it's the pollies we need spikes for, not the pellies!*

Though sympathetic, the AFCA lady said she'd have to speak to Gran directly, and that nothing could happen until the insurer's internal dispute resolution came through, which could take up to 30 days.

"You could maybe claim an urgent action exemption," she suggested. "Health and safety concerns. But you'd need to provide evidence of unsafe living conditions."

"Like half the roof staved in and a Norfolk Island Pine bivouacked in the kitchen?"

"That sort of thing, yes."

Plain as a pikestaff, the Bard might have attested, but they'd still require documentation—an independent inspection. Even if we got the case escalated, no one would start work on repairs, not until the insurance people coughed up.

I clenched one fist around the rim of the steering wheel. Where the bridge petered out and the road split, I took the Esplanade around towards Woody Point. Rendered unit blocks crowded the left footpath, grey and ghoulish through what was now a downpour. Moreton Bay huddled equally dismal to my right. I forged ahead past older brick units and the caravan ground, then inland where the two big parks meet—hard right past the bowls club. Familiar old houses glugged by, their poincianas, palm trees, and pines wavering through watery glass.

When had I arranged for the building guy to come? I couldn't actually remember—and I doubted he'd show, not with the rain so heavy. I tried to call him—swiped Gran's profile by accident. What I did know was that I wouldn't make it back in time for my English lecture—likely not for the HIST2411 tutorial either. Great globules of participation credit sluiced from the windshield.

"Maxi? Maxi, is that you?"

"Yes, Gran. I'm coming up to Wharf Street now, okay? I'll see you soon."

Even that close to home, though, my inner satnav proved unduly optimistic. Aching where I couldn't rub, I chivvied the accelerator in lieu and surged past the cricket oval—a drenched frustration of paperbark trees stood lining the boundary, weeping out of their skins—then hauled left, just as an RACQ Roadside Assist vehicle (of all things) pulled up to the t-junction, a distorted rubber duck blinking to turn right.

"Christ!" I swore, slewing towards it on bald tyres.

I thought of the kamikaze scrub turkey—of me gunning with equal, wild gusto to meet my maker, of Gran left on her own, Charm inspecting my dead, naked body down at the morgue.

That's how easily a story can end. Parasite or no parasite. Instant bloodruption.

People say that during a near-death experience your life flashes before you. Well, I can attest to that—the last several days at any rate. Gamma rays riddle my brain (like mobsters machine-gunning a car—total overkill). Time slows: Achilles chases Zeno's tortoise—an over-cranking of memories where mistake tips into mistake and butterfly-winged domino chains go spiraling off around me, their ribbons tied to an unreachable future. I find myself thinking:

Charm could get me out of this.

The notion is pure whimsy, born no doubt of angst and regret. Nonetheless it feels true. With her in the passenger seat, I know somehow I'd shimmy an impossible correction; we'd fishtail past the RACQ vehicle, a lick of paint between seat-of-the-saddle folk escapade and coming mortally a cropper.

No ambulance, no hospital; no flatlining ER machines.

No wayfaring coma.

Charm, my brain keens. *Charm, I was wrong. I—*

Might-have-beens. Misgivings. All recollections to the contrary, my thoughts coalesce and suddenly she's there; she's come along to see Gran. Her posture is pure gravitas, anchoring one side of the Daihatsu.

The balance of the universe shifts. We slide gloriously aftwise of disaster.

Fuck <u>me,</u> I exalt, beatific in the comedown. Rain patters the windscreen as spent wipers shudder. Sirens fade into a still, distant never.

But, of course, she has a boyfriend.

We meet next morning down by the Therapies Building—a bleak, oddly utilitarian choice for English tutorials. Anaesthetised by a discussion on race and gender in *The Merchant of Venice*, I barely register the caged creak of the leopard tree in the Annexe courtyard, or the Medusa-head aerial roots snaking down from the overhanging fig.

"So," I ask, "how do we do this?"

Charm leads me through the gloom, up the narrow walkway to Slip Road.

"We bring it full circle," she says. "The turkey you hit, did it have much of a wattle? The dangly bit around the neck?"

"Like a saggy yellow scrotum."

"Male then, which means it probably had a nest nearby. That's where we go."

We trek the usual path to the multi-storey. It feels weird to disable my Sh!honky app, but I do as Charm says, and we Schonell without Sh!honking, down to Gailey Road then up through the Fiveways and along the ridge. Two-storey houses rest their chins at street level, interspersed with unit blocks that hog the vista north to Taringa and Toowong. The view to our left is even less accessible: a strung-out mass of greenery and dumpy old trees in floral-print house dresses.

Brisbane roils in my peripheral vision. The city has always been alive; now bandersnatches ripple and sway to the Bloodruptor's summoning. Shadows blot the springtime confetti.

My phone goes off as we hit Moggill Road: Patti Smith, *Redondo Beach*. I swipe to connect.

"Hello, Gran?"

"Maxim?" she quavers. "Maxi, are you there?"

"Yes, Gran. I've got you on loudspeaker. Is everything—?"

"Maxim? There's a man parked outside from Rothwell Roof Repairs. Should I let him in? Maxi?"

"Gran?" I raise my voice above the traffic. A siren wails down the line: the bullroaring wolf whistle of an ambulance. "Gran, can you hear me? Are you all right? Gran?"

But it's clear I'm not getting through. I promise loudly to call her back, then cast about for an opportunity to pull over.

"No, Max. Keep driving." Charm steadies my hand on the gearstick. "No distractions; not now."

"It's my Gran," I protest. "She might be hurt!"

"Or she might have the phone round the wrong way. One thing at a time, Max. You won't help anyone by rushing off willy-nilly."

She's right I guess. Evidence four semesters spent slipping about on an icy pass-grade, assignments flung to the wayside.

Still, it's my Gran!

Rebellious, I shoulder-check again for gaps. Charm prunes her face into an absurd Yoda impersonation and warbles:

"Complete your training, you must, hmm?"

It's so incongruous, I miss the turn onto Jackson Street.

I sneak a look sideways at her as we swing along Woodville and back around, but she's reverted—if not to her normal countenance, then to a slightly more open approximation: unrepentant, unembarrassed, uniting us in a shared secret. Though the moment goes uncaptured, I feel my agitation dissipate.

Trust her, I tell myself. *Follow her lead.*

The world continues to warp as I park us just off Finney Road, alongside a nest of jacaranda dragons and a high-rise apartment block whose bronze-pipe trappings call to mind a pneumatic delivery system.

"You're seeing that, too, right?"

Charm purses her lips. "Reality is mutable, but also sometimes it's neo-modernism on too many space cakes."

I take that as my cue to try Gran again. I tap her contact picture, but when the call goes through she still can't hear me.

"—axim?" She renders my name in plaintive post-aphaeresis, as if I've cut in on a tragic monologue. "Maxi? *Mijn haasje?*"

I try to make myself heard, but it's like that time up at Noosa Heads when I got stuck in a triathlon event and police kept directing me from one road closure to the next, Daihatsu steaming through an impossible Rush Hour puzzle.

"Gran?" I angle my phone skyward; squint at the reception bars. "Gran, I'm here! It's a bad connection, okay? Gran?"

"Oh, Maxim." She sounds tremulous, lost. "Maxi, my little rabbit. Why won't you answer?"

Charm lays a hand on my arm.

"Come," she says. "I'll keep trying your gran, but we need to move. Here."

Reluctantly, I give the phone over. She tucks it into her hip pocket then leads us down onto Finney Road: a modern-day Dorothy with tick-laden Toto, following the yellow no parking line.

We cross to where I dumped the turkey. Its body still lies amidst the poor man's orchid, feathers faded and beyond dead. (Rats and maggots have gone to work. The rancid whiff of its flesh cuts sharply through the more pleasant rainforest smells.) Stomachs clenched, we carry on through to what proves a hidden children's playground and, past that, a tract of bushland.

"No kids," Charm notes. "Just as well. We'll need you dick-out for this: full kit-and-caboodle."

She glances my way as if she's said that to test me. The thought does elicit a twitch—nothing I can't tamp down though. I remember hefting the dead turkey: the feel of its legs still warm in my hand—a tough, scaly brace paired awkwardly below the claws.

Yes, I'm alone again with Charm. The jacarandas are throwing their bouquets, the oleander and crepe-myrtle, too, stirring up the birds and bees and inciting their wedding guests to go at it.

But there's death in the air. My pulse comes in slow ripples, subverting my heart and answering instead to the dread presence in my nether regions. Scavengers from the in-between places size me up behind devil's teeth and reaper-scythe beaks.

An erection now would be fatal.

Platonic penis, I resolve (which actually is a pretty good name for a grunge band). Where turkeys flee, I'll channel my urges into stoic contemplation.

Charm nods. "Good. Now, let's find where your turkey lurkeyed, see if we can't restore the balance."

We head off into the brush and soon come across what looks to be a giant compost heap: waist-high at the apex, bark and dirt and leaf litter raked up from all around and wedged against a subsided tangle of paperbark trees. I picture a concrete mixer–truck backing through the undergrowth and emptying mulch from its drum.

"One bush-turkey shag pad," Charm observes. "Lovingly constructed by the male, scene of many a dalliance." She pulls me up onto the mound. "Maintained by the male, too. There's maybe fifty eggs in here, temperature-regulated by adding or removing layers. Turkeys have a sense-organ in their beak," she explains. "Like a meat thermometer. Right, strip down and in you get."

I lose my footing at the non-sequitur.

"Dig yourself in," she elaborates. "We need you incubating and immobilised. Up to the neck if you can manage it."

Which is utterly daft. For all I know, Gran's just had a fall. Even if she doesn't need attention, her roof does, on top of which I'm in arrears on both my rent and my coursework (40% essay due today on witchcraft and demons in early modern medicine). Now is not the time to pull a reverse zombie-rising. And yet…

In the back of my mind it feels like I'm already there. I slip my shoes and socks off; my chinos and Haiku Hands tee; my Tradie briefs. Even as I crouch down and start scooping vegetable matter from beneath my feet, I sense an existence outside of the bloodrupted here-and-now—an analogous state that I'm moulding myself into.

"That's it," Charm encourages. She takes my clothes and stands in attendance. "Deeper, down. Close your eyes, Max. Feel the warmth, the stillness without and within."

I do as she says. I insert myself further into the turkey mound, shovelling to make room then pulling the mixture back to me as I wriggle languorously into the hollow. Where the exterior is scratchy with twigs and bark, the lower layers are heavier, damp. My nostrils flare, my lungs giddy with the waft of leaf decay. My hands touch upon turkey eggs—rounded, gritty potatoes that I reapportion to share my self-entombment.

"There," Charm soothes, her words the soft starch of hospital linen. "Now, count backwards for me, from ten…"

The heft and humidity of the mound enfold me. I sink into a dreamy stupor. No tick, no Sh!honking, no Witchcraft and Demonology. Redondo Beach starts up again but the sound is distant, carrying as if from neighbouring share houses late on a Friday evening. I catch an odd gust of disinfectant as I hear Gran ask:

"Is it gone? Did you get it off him, this emo-conscriptor creature?"

Her questions are liver-spotted, cracked with concern, like that time when I was nine and she and Grandad sat by my bed through an endless night of fever-racked dreams. Grandad is five years passed now (the scents of the oncology ward bullrush the back of my throat: embalming fluid and sickly stewed beef; astringent greens asphyxiated beneath their tray-covers), but Gran is still the same old Humpty/ Jemima-doll I clung to in childhood.

Gran? I rasp; or try to. Just like I could never fully wrap my arms around her, the mononym won't form. My lips are slack, my head cocked on a pillow of empty seed pods.

"Haemocriptor kurilpa," Charm supplies. She's as assured in her nomenclature as everywhere else, running her tongue along a polished splice of Graeco-Latin and Turrbal. "We think so, Mrs. Margraf. It's a delicate procedure, but all indications are that we've extracted the physical taint. It's up to Maxim now." She orientates her voice towards me: "Regression or recovery, Max. Even with the Bloodruptor gone, your brain's going to be wintley, at least for a while. You need to stay grounded, okay? However unsettled you feel."

I nod, or at least, bob my chin imperceptibly as I float on my starched Lilo. Somewhere down by my groin an orphaned turkey chick breaks from its egg. It rests a few hours then struggles up through the vegetative fug, digging and clawing its way to the surface. The disinterment takes days. Exhaustion piles atop exhaustion—I doze and drift, only dimly aware—but at last the chick squirms free.

"There we go," Charm murmurs. "Godspeed, little gobbler."

The chick casts about, a tattered mismatch of beak and bearings. It's like David Byrne crossed with a newly hatched Skeksis, claws scritching to its own strange rhythms—syncopating realities. It collapses briefly in a dense, downy heap before picking itself up and darting from the mound, down into a thicket of lantana.

Born running, I decide. *Deadlines to meet, fares to earn.*

I hear my own heartbeat as if from far away: the recondite *skreet* of rainbow lorikeets; the wheeze of shifting camphor laurel. Charm's hand ghosts my brow as the fledgling turkey takes to its back-toes, picking a whispering path through the scrub.

Bearing its dark passenger.

END

—

EJ DELANEY is a speculative fiction writer living in Brisbane, Australia's River City. EJ's short stories have appeared in *Daily Science Fiction* and the podcasts *Cast of Wonders* and *Escape Pod*, as well as the *Reinvented Detective* anthology and in limited edition print collections from Air & Nothingness Press. EJ has thrice been shortlisted for Australia's premier speculative fiction accolade the Aurealis Awards, in 2021 winning in the category of Best Fantasy Short Story. EJ can be found online at www.ejdelaney.com.

VANCOUVER

Maria Haskins

Third Beach in Stanley Park is Emma's favourite beach, but she hasn't been back there since she drowned.

Instead, she's been taking the kids to other beaches around the city at least twice a week, no matter the weather. The coves near their home in Point Grey. The wide, sandy flats of Spanish Banks. Locarno and Jericho. Kits Beach. English Bay. Second Beach. If she could, she'd take them to the beach every day, but Iggy is five now and goes to kindergarten, and Teppo has just turned three and has preschool four days a week. Then there's dance and music, Parent and Tot at the Community Centre. And playdates, of course. Plus all the other activities they attend.

Emma takes them wherever they're meant to go, like a good stay-at-home mom should. She sits there in her jeans and hoodie, sipping Starbucks or Tim Hortons with the other parents, talking about the terrible twos and the even-worse-threes, and all the while, beneath the thin surface of her skin, the cold currents of the Pacific are tugging at her, rippling through her veins and arteries, eddying through her ribs, as if she were still there: below. As if she never resurfaced, was never pulled out of the water lifeless and unbreathing, was never resurrected by oxygen and CPR…

Today is a Friday but there's no school, and Emma is heading back to Third Beach for the first time since that day last July. Brian can't understand it. He's argued with her about it since she told him last night, and this morning he keeps the argument going in the kitchen while the kids mess around with their Cheerios and watch cartoons. "There are other beaches," he says and then, when all his other arguments have failed, "I don't think it's good for the kids."

Emma says nothing to that, just sips her coffee and waits for him to head to work. She can't explain to him why she is going back to Third Beach, at least not in a way that would give him the kind of answer he is looking for.

She's tired. Tired of the way he looks at her these days, tired of fighting, tired of herself and him. Most days—most nights too—they move through their lives, through the house, in memorized, well-worn patterns without ever touching each other. Emma can't reach him, and he can't reach her, because he is where he always was, above the surface, and she is still sinking.

Water always finds its way to the ocean, whether it's the early March rain swirling through Vancouver's storm drains, or spring meltwater flowing down the mountains into the

North Shore's creeks and rivers. It's the same for Emma. In the end, there is no other destination for her than the shore, the water's edge, the deep.

That's how it's been ever since she drowned.

Emma drives through Kitsilano, across the Burrard Street Bridge into downtown. These days, she feels the presence of water everywhere she goes. The flow and movement of it, is a tangible presence in her body, like a pulse, like the peristalsis of her own internal organs.

There is water everywhere in Vancouver. Besides the ocean, the Fraser River and countless creeks and brooks, there are hundreds of streams hidden beneath the city. Once upon a time, they flowed freely through bracken and tumbled rocks, caressing damp moss and fern. But when the city was built, the water was confined to culverts and drainage pipes, paved over with asphalt and concrete. Though their water has been detained, it is still there, just beneath the urban veneer of streets and houses, sidewalks and strip malls.

The city might have forgotten all that water, but Emma knows, and the water, well, it remembers everything. It remembers what it was and what it will be again. It remembers salt and storms, rain and snow, it remembers the inside of her body and the bottom of the sea.

It always finds a way.

Emma turns onto Stanley Park Drive. The one-way road winds through stands of tall cedars and hemlock and glossy-leaved rhododendron, past tourist buses, cyclists, early morning joggers, and cafés. She likes the reprieve the drive gives her. Usually, the kids are both busy singing along to the radio or looking at cars or doing something other than vying for her attention, and the hum of the vehicle is almost like a tide in her head, almost as soothing as the murmur of waves over sand. But not today.

"Mom!"

Emma turns away from the traffic ahead, keeping her hands steady on the wheel. She can tell from the tenor of Teppo's voice that he's been screaming for a while. She hasn't heard him until now. There are scratches on his face from Iggy's fingers, drops of blood forming on his cheek where her nails dug into his skin.

"Iggy." Emma tries to sound stern. "We talked about this. It is not OK to scratch your brother."

She knows she ought to scold Iggy louder, longer, make her apologize, but her heart isn't in it and the kids know it. Teppo cries noisily while Iggy bares her teeth at him, her face a mocking, menacing mask, her soft, blunt fingers curved into claws, scratching invisible patterns in the air. Emma turns back to the road, away from both of them.

"We're almost there," she says to them and to herself, trying to to use a glossy sing-song voice she's heard other moms use.

In the mirror, Iggy glares back at Emma, and Emma

can't remember if her daughter ever used to look at her like this before she drowned. There are so many things she can't remember from before. She vaguely remembers her old job at the university, watching television with Brian on the couch, having sex in their bed, club nights and hikes with friends before they had the kids, but she can't remember *how* she used to be back then, what she felt or thought about, or what the children used to be like around her. And some of the things she can remember are fuzzy and distant. Things that happened to someone else in a movie she's half forgotten.

"You scare me," Brian told her once after they'd had another one of their many arguments. "The way you get so angry. It's not like you."

Not like you used to be, is what he means.

It was after Thanksgiving dinner at his parents' place last year. They had argued in the car on the way home. Later, he and Emma stood in the doorway of the kids' bedroom, watching them sleep, their breaths barely audible in the dark, their shapes uncertain and undefined beneath the covers.

I scare me too, is what Emma wanted to say, but didn't.

"I'd never hurt them," is what she whispered, instead.

Brian didn't look relieved. He just walked away. Emma stayed and watched the kids as they slipped ever deeper beneath the surface of the world into a darkness where other creatures stirred, impossible to see in daylight, undulating shapes of fear and joy brushing against their minds. She thought of the softness of their skin, their bones wrapped in lingering baby fat. They were such terrifyingly fragile things, so easy to break, to lose, and the world was so sharp and jagged and loud. How could she be expected to keep them safe?

When Emma dreams about drowning, she floats above or swims below, watching herself struggle. She thinks, *Don't fight. Let it take you.* And then she reaches out for herself, for her own sinking form, but her hands are not her own; they are webbed, with claws, and all she wants to do is drag herself down, down, down, beneath the turmoil of the waves to the calm of the seabed where she can rest.

At the parking lot, Emma pays at the meter and unpacks the car while Teppo clings to her leg, whining about his cheek. She shivers in the lingering west coast winter rippling through the early spring air, the shade holding onto the chill, the buds of the trees still tightly wrapped in sheaths of brown. Out of the corner of her eye, she sees Iggy sprint across the lot, already immersed in some game that plays out inside her head as she ducks and darts between the few vehicles parked beneath the trees.

Emma calls too late for Iggy to wait, but that kid has never listened to her or waited for anything in her entire life. Teppo takes off too, chasing after his sister. Lugging the bag with their buckets and beach towels, Emma catches up to them halfway down the stairs leading to the Seawall and Third Beach. The kids have descended on a stranger and her jowly rottweiler, reaching out and petting the dog before Emma can arrive and warn them to be careful. "She likes children," the woman says as Emma approaches. The woman glances away from Emma, to the top of the steep, concrete stairs. Her lipsticked mouth is set in a sharp, judgmental line, and Emma half expects a scolding before the woman and her dog move on.

Once they've crossed the pedestrian walkway on the Seawall the kids take off in the sand, brightly colored buckets and shovels in hand. Emma walks slowly, trailing them as they use their plastic tools to dig, as they weave and wander, searching for rocks and exploring the tidal pools.

At first, she's watching the kids. Soon, she is only watching the water. Far off to the left is Point Grey and Spanish Banks. Closer, to the right, across the inlet, are the North Shore mountains and the fancy houses of West Vancouver. The horizon is strung between them where the Burrard Inlet opens up into the Strait of Georgia. The city itself, its jagged silhouette, lies far behind her, beyond the trees and trails of Stanley Park.

People who come to visit always say Vancouver is so beautiful. Emma doesn't know what they're talking about. She figures most of the time they're not looking at the city at all, but away from it. At the mountains. At the ocean. At the sky. The city has no beauty in itself. It is nothing but a jumbled mass of asphalt, concrete, and steel. It is too new, too sharp, too full of agony and anxiety to be anything at all. It has forgotten what it was before. It doesn't know what it is now.

"M om!"
Teppo is calling for her and pointing at Iggy who is clambering on the jumbled rocks of the jetty, bucket discarded somewhere, arms out like a circus acrobat on a wire. Emma knows that jetty, knows how slick those rocks are with algae and kelp, every cracked and creviced surface studded with barnacles. She should hurry over there. Tell Iggy that it isn't safe. But her eyes are drawn beyond the jetty, out to where the water glitters and heaves in the breeze. Something is moving. Something shadowy. Something like the butt of a deadhead log, maybe. Or a head, bobbing in the waves. It disappears beneath the surface, reappears, dives again.

"What is that?" Teppo asks, shading his eyes like she is doing, looking where she looks.

"It's a seal," Emma says and almost believes it.

A t family dinners and friends' barbecues, Brian likes to tell the story of how she drowned. When he speaks, the audience quiets, leaning in to capture every word. He has the story down pat, the twists and turns. The drama and the tragedy. He tells people how he panicked when he looked out at the water and could not see her anywhere. How he raced up and down searching along the beach. How desperate he was. How the kids were crying and screaming and clinging to him as he talked to the lifeguard. Later, his relief and dread when they carried her out of the ocean, laying her down on land.

Emma sometimes forgets the story is about her.

Brian thinks the only reason she is able to come back here, to Third Beach, is because she doesn't remember what happened. Truth is, she remembers everything. She remembers the caress of seaweed and bullwhips against her legs as she waded in deeper, the familiar pull of tide and waves as she started swimming, the heaviness of her limbs and the sting of salt in her eyes as she swam out farther, beyond the rocky pier. She remembers the current embracing her, and the excruciating pain in her leg before the cold water swallowed her. At the hospital, the doctor said the cuts on her foot and calf were likely from the rocks when she was dragged out of the water, but Emma knows better. She knows the pain came before she sank, and she remembers the sharp talons, the strong hand tugging at her ankle. She remembers the face, staring up at her as she sank.

In the sunshine at the water's edge, it's warm enough that Emma wishes she'd worn shorts and a t-shirt instead of jeans and a fleece sweater and a windbreaker. It's as if the city, all at once, is letting go of winter and rushing headlong into spring. Emma takes off her runners, tucks her socks into her shoes and puts them on a driftwood log before she rolls up her pant legs to her knees. The tide is most of the way out now, the wet sand baring ocean secrets and dilapidated treasures, broken shells and tiny crabs, a stranded sea jelly with trailing tentacles. Farther out, skimming the water, cormorants streak by, sleek and black and sharp.

The children are far away now. Iggy is still balancing on the jetty, Teppo stomps his feet to make footprints at the water's edge. On the rocks, Iggy's movements are intent and focused. She crouches to touch the water, then pops up, waving at the screaming seagulls circling overhead. Meanwhile, Teppo, all loose and ungainly, flaps his arms like wings as he runs in circles.

I would never hurt them. I'm not a monster, Emma tells herself and almost believes it.

This is where it happened. Out there, beyond the jetty. It was summer. July. Hot. Brian had taken the kids with him to the concession stand at the top of the stairs for ice cream. She was alone for once. It had been years since she'd gone swimming in the ocean—before the kids, before she got pregnant. The last time was probably back when she and Brian first got together, back when they first met, right here, on this beach. It didn't matter. Her body remembered the water, and that day she wondered if the water still remembered her.

She was in hospital for a couple of days after she drowned. Her heart and her lungs weren't quite right, they said, and she needed to be kept for observation. There were cuts on her hands and knees. Twenty-five stitches. The scars are still there, red fading into pink.

Emma is staring at the water beyond the jetty. Something

moves again. A silhouette against the sun-bright sparkle of the waves.

The thing she has wanted to tell Brian ever since she woke up in the hospital, is that she really did drown that day. Her body came out of the water, but she did not. She is not the same Emma who went in the water. She is something new, something old, something borrowed, perhaps. A stranger, even to herself.

Emma knows she should be watching the kids. She knows that's what a good mom would do, but it's the water that brought her here, and it's the water that calls to her now. She wants to shed her jacket and sweater, shed everything, every layer, and dive below. She wants to feel that touch again, that cold darkness entering her, that briny taste of life and death on her tongue and throat. She wants to swim until her body cannot swim anymore. Once she's spent, she wants to sink and see what waits beneath the surface.

She remembers how tired she was when she sank the last time, how exhausted she felt right before the claws gripped her, how her limbs seized up and stopped moving, how something dark and frozen grasped hold of her heart. What a relief it was to sink. Like coming home. Like resting. Like being back where she belonged.

When they carried her out, she had already left her body. She was hovering high above herself, above the beach. Looking down, she saw them working on her and tried to tell them to put her back in the water. Release her. Let her sink. She tried to leave that day, but they rescued her. And here she is.

Emma walks into the water until it laps around her ankles. All at once, relief bubbles through her like a fizzing, startling sense of joy, even as her toes go numb in the chill.

The water knows. It knows where she came from and where she's going. It knows where she has been. It knows what she was before she drowned and what she is now. The ocean remembers. It remembers holding her and pulling her down. It remembers the taste of her skin and the constriction of her lungs. It remembers the taste of her blood.

Emma keeps walking in the shallows until the water is up to her knees. The tide is coming in slowly but she feels the movement of it, the way it rises to meet her. She looks around. Here, from the water, everything looks different. Distant, small, insignificant. Somewhere, far away, another world and another life, Teppo calls out, "Mom!" but it's not her he's calling for.

She's up to her armpits in the water now, and her clothes are heavy, but she starts swimming. Her arms remember the strokes, remember their strength.

Gulls are calling to her, or maybe it's the kids. She isn't sure. Doesn't care. She keeps swimming, her movements certain and strong as she swims towards the last place she saw the dark silhouette in the waves. Then, she dives.

It feels so good to be back beneath the surface. It feels good not to have to breathe every single fucking second of every single fucking day. It feels good to let the current take her and pull her away. It feels so good to be herself.

Something stirs beneath her skin. Longing, darkness, and

something else, *something* that wants to come out. Maybe she will see the thing that reached for her, again. Or maybe she will find *herself* here in the depths, the white bones of the first Emma resting on the bottom in the swell and tide, caressed by undercurrents, her skull and ribs delicately picked clean.

As much as she tries to dive deeper, she cannot get farther down than a few feet. Exasperated, she bobs up to the surface, the waves heaving around her. Her arms and legs ache, but the water will not take her. It does not want her. Further out, just out of reach, the glistening shape watches her. A seal, that's what she told Teppo. Its eyes are dark and wet and Emma knows it is her sole companion. No one else has come.

She should never have left the first time. She should have stayed below the waves.

Emma puts her face in the water, and below, in the gloom and undertow, the moving waters seem to clear like a globe of glassy light, and she sees an illuminated face beneath her, lit by sun through waves—sharp teeth, wide mouth, webbed fingers. It's almost her own face, almost, looking back from a tangle of kelp, a sinuous body moving through the waters as if it belongs nowhere else. As if it knows exactly what it is and what it wants to be.

Take me back, Emma wants to say. *I made a mistake.*

She bobs up to the surface again. She has drifted closer to the beach and the jetty and can see Teppo. He's up to his knees in the water. She cannot hear him, but she knows he's crying. Crying for her.

Closer, at the tip of the jetty, Iggy crouches, clinging to

the rocks, one raised hand closed into a fist as if she's holding onto something precious, the other hand scrabbling for purchase on the sharp boulders. Iggy's mouth is open, her round eyes fixed on Emma, her face close enough that, even from the water, Emma can see the streaks of dirt and sand running down her cheeks and how the fierce and mocking smile her girl usually wears has crumpled into panic.

"Mommyyyyyyy!"

Teppo is wading out towards her, crying. He fights the rising tide as it grasps hold of his legs, forcing him back. His bright, panicked voice is a thorn and tether in her skin. Iggy is screaming too, both arms wheeling, a terrified windmill of a girl, wobbling on the rocks. Voice cracking, her cries mingle with the gulls, "Mom!"

Emma dips her head under the water, but there's nothing there. No glassy light, no face, no sinuous movement, no claws. Her mouth fills with brine. Maybe she's crying, or maybe she is just tasting the ocean. Her body is too tired, cramps stiffening her limbs, but she swims toward Iggy, toward Teppo. She swims to them because they're calling for her, and because the water does not want her. Not today. Not anymore.

As Emma wades through the waves, Iggy is waiting on the rocks, cheeks wet with tears, eyes wide, clutching something bright and smooth in her hand, the gleaming fragment of a shell or bone, polished from ages of being tossed about in the water. Together, they make their way towards the beach, Iggy holding onto Emma's soaking wet sleeve with one hand, knuckles white. Teppo is on the beach, out of the water, safe, but gasping and sobbing. He skinned his knee, stumbling through the rising tide, and it's bleeding. An older couple are with him, beachcombers in matching tracksuits. The woman is bending down, half embracing Teppo; the man, ramrod straight, stares at Emma and asks Teppo if he's OK.

Once they're back on the beach, when she's reached the driftwood log where she left her shoes, backpack, and beach towels, the kids can't stop chattering, their tears and panic already forgotten in the time it has taken to reach dry sand. The day feels suddenly too warm, too bright, like shards of glass glinting in the sun. Emma gathers up their things, water still dripping from her hair and clothes while the kids ask for ice cream and slurpees.

By the time they get to the car, winter has fully disappeared. It has somehow become spring, suddenly and undeniably, the air soft even as Emma shivers, and she feels new life stirring all around her, the same way she felt new life stirring in her body, painful and strange, when they carried her out of the water last year.

Strapping the kids into their car seats, she thinks of the face, below, and looks at herself in the mirror. Bloodshot eyes, wrinkles around the mouth, hair plastered to her forehead. Nothing else. No one else. Behind her, in the reflection, is Iggy's face, sun warmed and blushing, chocolate ice cream smeared across her cheek, singing along to the radio with Teppo.

On the drive back home, through the West End, Emma opens the car windows. There's the smell of fresh cut grass, green buds unfurling, and everywhere the blushing petals of cherry blossoms are turning the skeletal fingers of the trees into foamy pink. It's as if the world skipped ahead a month or two while she was underneath the water.

Driving, Emma feels the shivering presence of the forgotten streams rushing beneath the city, fiercely carving new paths through all the obstacles and devices used to contain and smother them. The water always finds a way.

"Is this your mom?" the elderly man asked as his wife quietly crouched to wrap an arm around Teppo's small, shaking body. A wavering, sharp edge of concern cut through his stern voice, and Emma wonders what she must have looked like there, on the barnacle-studded rocks, risen from the deep, waterlogged and out of breath.

Teppo looked at Emma. He was blinking away sunlight and tears, standing there with his scratched-up face and his skinned knee and sand rubbed over his runny nose and mouth. For all the world an abandoned child, a stray, an orphan.

"Yes," Iggy answered loud and sure when Teppo said nothing, stepping close and grabbing her brother's hand. An almost-smile tugging at her lips, as she rubbed her own salt-streaked cheek. "That's our mom."

In the car, Emma feels the weight of those words, the way they anchor her. Hold her in place.

She will try to forget, Emma tells herself. Forget what she saw, what she was, what she might have been if the water still wanted her. She will forget what is and what will never be. The water will remember it for her. It remembers everything. It remembers what was and what will be again. It always finds a way. And one day, maybe, it will welcome her again.

END

—

Maria Haskins is a Swedish-Canadian writer and reviewer of speculative fiction. She is a senior columnist and non-fiction editor at Ruadán Books, and a fiction editor at *Many Worlds*. Maria also writes essays and reviews for *Psychopomp* and a quarterly short fiction roundup for *Strange Horizons*. She is a certified translator between Swedish and English.

TAIPEI

Avram Lavinsky

For a little while, I feel free of the weight, Méi Lì behind me on the Yamaha, her arms around my waist, droning scooters surrounding us like a swarm of mechanical insects.

A family of four on a single scooter flies by in the opposite direction, the engine whining in protest. They're probably returning from the park, but the festival will continue until sunset.

Most people on two feet or two wheels wear masks. All the fuss people made about masks during the pandemic when I was in middle school back in Massachusetts seems hard to imagine here. Half the population of Taipei City has been wearing masks on the road forever. If you don't want to blow dark grey snot rockets all the time, you mask up. The dust and smog just kind of hang in the damp air, caught between the mountains, like a lobster in a trap.

To make a left onto Mingshui Road, I have to make a

J-turn, essentially proceeding to a white box marked near the far corner of the intersection, facing left, and waiting for the light a second time to complete the maneuver. It's a pain in the ass if you're in a rush, but a clever way to avoid some accidents on city streets where bikes and scooters might outnumber cars ten to one on any given day. It's a bit more of a pain in the ass today because two of Taipei's famous Smurf-blue box trucks have pulled up too far, bumper to bumper, blocking all of us left-turners and forcing us to make a right, followed by a very elongated U-turn.

Stoney gray clouds veil the sky, and the heat and humidity are oppressive even with the sun hanging near the horizon. The light turns green. I wait for the bikes and scooters ahead of me and finally get moving again, thankful for the air rushing against my trunk and evaporating some of my growing film of sweat. In the spring, this city doesn't cool off much until midnight.

We zip past a guy with four oversized propane tanks bungeed to the back of his motorcycle.

I'm not sure I'm ready to see the river, but then it comes into view, rusty grey, shimmering with reflected light despite the cloud cover. The dragon boats are scattered across the broad surface, a kaleidoscope of color against the sepia tones of the riverscape.

Méi Lì's arms stiffen. She wanted to come. It's only been three weeks since the pilot of a water taxi spotted Kǎi Míng's body floating in the shallows, a chain around his midsection, just a few miles from here, where the Keelung River meets the Tamsui. Maybe she wants to prove we can enjoy the festival despite all that's happened. I have those thoughts, too. We can't avoid rivers for the rest of our lives.

I find free space in the giant tangle of two-wheeled vehicles, park the scooter, and hop off.

Méi Lì dismounts, pulls off her helmet, slides the scrunchy down her ponytail, and shakes out her shiny black mane.

I lock the helmets in the compartment under the seat.

She hooks an arm in mine and forces her best consoling smile. She is beautiful, amber-skinned, dark-eyed, but her sadness—our shared sadness—draws me to her in ways nothing else ever could. It binds us together, the weight of all that's happened. It presses down on us, morbid and relentless, the way Kǎi Míng was in the end.

He wasn't always. Sure, he was always a fighter. He always stood up for Méi Lì and me, and not just to other kids. Last year, when our algebra teacher tore up my graphing test because he said it was too sloppy, Kǎi Míng stood and tore up *his* test, slowly, staring at the teacher as he did. He got himself suspended for a day because he thought a teacher was bullying me. How could I have ever known he would turn a much darker anger against his beautiful girlfriend and me?

Arm in arm, we weave through the crowd of families and tourists.

Méi Lì leans into me as we head out toward the pier.

I never knew so much happiness and sadness could exist together in my world.

We come to a stand, and I buy two zongzi. There are

a million kinds, and people eat them all year round here, but they're the traditional food of the Dragon Boat Festival. Supposedly, Qu Yuan, the ancient poet whose self-sacrifice the day celebrates, drowned in a river, and his followers threw zongzi into the water to keep the fish from eating his body. I slide down the strings, peel back the wrapping of bamboo leaves, and take a bite. It's the sweet kind, with a paste of red beans and peanuts at the center.

"They're good," says Méi Lì in Mandarin, chewing with a hand across her mouth.

Having grown up in Singapore, Méi Lì speaks both English and Mandarin flawlessly, plus a few other languages— even a little Taiwanese, which the locals here favor in less formal settings. Apparently, it resembles some other dialect her grandparents brought with them from Fujian province in southeastern China.

I take another bite and nod my agreement.

We walk as we eat, and the details of the boats come into view: the colorful and elaborately carved dragon heads at the elongated bow, the scales painted along the hull, and the graceful arch of the tail at the stern. Each crew wears its own colors, some with matching caps.

Where the boats are still at the pier, waiting crews hold their paddles vertically, blades up. Other boats glide leisurely along east of the pier near the Dazhi Bridge. To the west, the racing lanes are a matrix of buoys in the shadow of the enormous Grand Hotel with its golden, pagoda-style roof.

A horn sounds, and a race begins. Paddles stab deep into

the river, synchronized and machinelike. White foam streams from the raised bows of the vessels. The simple cadences of the drums mingle and echo in strange rhythms.

Before I can catch myself, I say, in Mandarin, "So slow."

A couple of college kids turn to look at me.

"I mean, compared to sculling," I say, lowering my voice and switching to English.

"We're not comparing to anything," says Méi Lì, bouncing my forearm playfully.

She's right. I just can't help myself. Back in Marshfield, Mass, I joined the youth rowing program the summer after fifth grade and loved it right away. I even rowed through the pandemic in middle school. The seats in those quads are just far enough apart that we could. If they offered rowing at the American School, I'd be all over it. Or at least I would have been before that last night with Kǎi Míng.

The drumming of the boats echoes off the buildings on both sides of the river and repeats like far-off gunfire. The paddles continue to plunge into the river, furious yet synchronized like the legs of some giant, many-segmented insects. They surge forward with each stroke. The flag catchers lay flat across the bow, balanced precariously on the carved dragon head, reaching impossibly far forward to snatch the pole with their team's colors. And in under two minutes, it's over, one flag catcher shaking her symbol of victory triumphantly in the air, the paddlers still, the boats drifting.

I can almost feel their exhaustion. It's true. You can't compare. Dragon boats are paddled, not rowed. They're beautiful, but they're built for tradition first and speed second. They're much wider than a sculling shell to accommodate ten to twenty paddlers side by side. The carvings probably add serious weight. So do the extra crew members, the drummer and a flag-catcher at the bow and the steersperson at the stern.

Méi Lì leads us away from the piers. We cross a vast grassy slope, leaving the crowds behind us, and making our way closer to the shore.

Her arm clamps tighter around mine. She's testing us both, and at first, I'm happy that we pass. Grass gives way to the pebbly riverbank that shifts beneath our sneakers. The sounds of the festival fade into the rhythmic lapping of the waves and the sharp clacking of stone against stone.

A faint patch of sun glows crimson between the steel-grey clouds. We are suddenly alone.

In the murky water nearby, I can make out a large stone and some fluttering debris. Then the stone turns, and I realize the debris is human hair, swaying like tentacles. Blackened eyelids part to reveal bloody empty sockets.

I twist away from Méi Lì and stagger backward, falling onto my back and scrambling up the bank on my elbows and heels, the vision seared into my mind. But even more terrifying is the sound, the gurgling shriek of his voice.

1

At my dad's apartment, sneakers by the door, slippers on our feet, we sit on the couch, drinking his vodka and orange juice. Méi Lì strokes my shoulders, trying to settle me down. There is no ignoring the weight now.

"I swear it was him," I say.

"I know."

I snap around to face her. "You saw it…what was left of him…there too?"

She sets her jaw and nods slowly.

"But you didn't seem startled."

"I guess I wasn't. That's because I see him all the time."

I take another sip from the rocks glass, the liquor clearing the haze from my thoughts—or maybe just numbing the fear from them. "Of course you do. I should have known."

"How can I not? Every time I walk to class, and someone stares at me or tries too hard not to stare at me, I see him… or hear him. Sometimes that's the worst. Why did he have to do it? I tried so hard to let him down easily…to tell him it just wasn't working." Her voice cracks. "I wanted a chance at happiness. I wanted *him* to have a chance at happiness, too. I just couldn't be with him anymore. He said he'd kill himself so many times I stopped believing him."

"It's not on you, Méi. You know that."

"I do. But maybe you and me are the only ones who know. And maybe Dr. Dilba," she says, referencing the school shrink.

"People know. Sane people know."

She laughs ruefully. "I never knew there were so many insane people then. You heard his mom."

Kǎi Míng's mom made no secret of blaming Méi Lì for his death. It wasn't a stretch after the suicide note that Kǎi Míng plastered all over social media, telling everyone how *he knew the ones he tried to love the most would be happier when he was gone,* how he couldn't *scream into the void anymore.* The woman erupted into screams at the funeral and threw Méi Lì out while the detective investigating his death watched impassively from the back of the funeral parlor.

Of course, I followed her out. I wouldn't have lasted long there anyway. The funeral music, with the gongs and the suonas, the traditional Chinese double-reed instruments, was starting to morph into something strange and terrible in my brain, the gurgling scream of Kǎi Míng the last time I was with him.

"He tried to own me," said Méi Lì, "even after I called it off. For a year of my life. I won't let him own me anymore."

"You shouldn't."

"*I choose* who to be with." She places her hands on my cheeks and turns my head to her. Her lips brush against mine. And again. And then she parts my lips, and we kiss deeply.

She leans away for a moment, her dark eyes locked on mine, urgent, desperate. She brings one thigh across my legs and straddles me.

My heart seems ready to pound its way out of my ribcage. She knows, or at least suspects, that I've never done it with anyone. I know she has had at least one lover in Kǎi Míng. We are both strangers to this moment, and yet we're not. Past and future seem to melt into each other. I've known forever that this instant would come. I was afraid to admit it all the times Kǎi Míng pounded on my dorm room door, all the times he talked without listening late into the night.

Her hands slide under my T-shirt and explore the muscles of my back. Her lips lock on mine. Our mouths open wide, tongues gently coming together.

I close my eyes, and the vision of the face in the river flashes in my mind.

She knows. "It's okay. Look at me."

I open my eyes. She kisses me harder, pressing my head onto the back of the couch. The canopy of her hair blocks out the world. Then she leans away and pulls her T-shirt over her head.

And he's there. Behind her naked shoulder and the black strap of her bra. The bloody eyeless sockets. The bloated face. The sand and marine plants caught in his hair. He is hatred. He is envy. He is loathing. He is accusation.

"Please," I say. "There's something I need to tell you."

She pulls me to her and buries her head in my neck. "No. Don't."

"I have to."

Her embrace crushes me, and her breath hisses in my ear. "Please don't."

"I was there. At the Dadaocheng Wharf. I was with him."

The mouth of Kǎi Míng's eyeless face twists into a knowing grimace.

I look away. "He talked me into drinking some of my dad's liquor. But the more he drank, the more he talked about you, and the more he talked about you, the angrier he got.

"He kept on like that when we went down to get our scooters. He ran onto the pier. And I thought *it's just all talk; he's not going to do anything.*

"He hopped into the little boat. He took out his jackknife. He cut the line from the anchor and chain and took it back to me. It wasn't real heavy. Most of the weight was in the chain, but I was thinking it was just heavy enough to do the job; maybe he's serious.

"And I say the same things I always say. *Get through the day. Get help. Move on. Live your life.* And he says, 'I know you're in love with her.' And he ties part of the chain around his waist. And he says, 'Tell me you're not.' What could I say? I told him I didn't know. Maybe that was true. Maybe I don't need to know like that, like he always did.

"I told him to give me the anchor." I keep my eyes down but still sense Kǎi Míng and his simmering fury. "He spewed some of that crap he always did about you, only this time he spewed it about me. His death would be on my head. I could wake up every morning knowing that and try to look in the mirror. I got closer and put out my hands. I told him, again, to give me the damn anchor.

"He ran at me and swung it like a battle axe.

"I twisted out of the way. It whistled past my ear.

"He raised it over his head.

"I grabbed it, but he forced it down anyway. It turned in the air and clipped his temple. Blood spread over his cheek. And then he ran. I heard the splash."

Méi Lì's tears are wet on my neck.

"I did everything I could. I pulled off my sneakers and dived into the river. The cold water sobered me up right away, but it must have been thirty-five feet deep and murky. My ear drums felt like they could split open from the pressure.

"When I finally found him, he was thrashing so much, I couldn't get close to him. I circled behind him, but he swung an elbow into my temple.

"He made a horrible sound, a kind of gurgling scream, feral, cat-like. It sounded distant, yet close, as if from inside my own head. I'll never forget it.

"Desperate for air, I tried to get under his shoulders and lift him up, but the blade of the anchor was caught on something. I tried to free it. I couldn't. I tried to unfasten the chain, but he caught me with another elbow. My lungs burned. I fought back the panic. I don't know if the pinpricks of light everywhere were from the blow or from lack of oxygen, but I couldn't stay down any longer.

"I pushed off from the spongy floor of the river and shot up, kicking and pulling myself toward the light of the surface. I popped up and drank in the air like it was the first breath of my life.

"I panted hard until the stars went away. Then I dove down again, but I only lasted half as long. The river seemed twice as deep. My arms burned. My head felt like a balloon. When I reached where I thought he'd been, I realized the current had carried me away.

"I swam back to the surface and tried to orient myself based on the piers and the buildings, but my vision was blurry, and everything looked the same." I sense something shifting in front of me but can't tell if recounting the story is weakening or strengthening Kǎi Míng's anger. "I went down a third time and a fourth, but I never found him."

"I know I should have gone to the police. At first, I was terrified they'd say I murdered him. Kǎi Míng wasn't the only one who sensed something between us. I had the oldest motive in the world to want him dead.

"Then, when everyone read the suicide note he posted, there didn't seem to be any reason to tell the cops. I figured I'd missed my chance. Only a guilty man would have waited that long to speak up."

Méi Lì's spine straightens, and I can feel the tension growing in her body. She spins off me. She takes my drink from the coffee table and throws it at him. The glass flies over his shoulder and shatters on the edge of the overpass to the kitchen.

She squares off against him, back hunched, hands fisted, her beautiful face contorted in rage, inches from the bloodied mask that once was his face. "Is that what you wanted? To ruin the two people who cared about you most!" Her voice is a shrill and jagged shriek. "To steal every ounce of joy from our lives because you threw away yours? To send one or both of us to jail?

"In the beginning, I thought you believed in love. You don't. You're nothing but hate! Where does it come from, hate? Where does it go? At least we had some happy memories together. Who else will burn incense for you? Who else will keep alive the memory of who you used to be? Who else will cry for you? Why don't you take all your hatred and use it against someone who never cared?"

I rise, thinking to pull her away from him, but he's already gone. I rest a hand on her shoulder, and she collapses into my embrace, her body shaking, her choked sobs muffled in my T-shirt.

2

In trigonometry, no one ever sits at the desk to my right, the one where Kǎi Míng used to sit. I never look directly at it. Even with a glance in that general direction, visions of the bloated corpse hover in the periphery of my vision.

We've just finished going over the homework when one of the guidance counselors takes me out of class and leaves me alone in the faculty meeting room with the plain-clothes detective. I know she told me her name when she interviewed me the day they found Kǎi Míng's body, but I'd been too nervous to remember it. For days after that, I'd feared constantly that she would show up somewhere and question me further, but she didn't. Over time, I'd pushed those fears aside. The investigation was, as far as anyone knew, closed.

"Do you know why you're here?" She has a disturbing flatness to her tone. Her English is strongly accented but fluent. She probably thinks in the language, rather than thinking in Mandarin first and translating in her mind.

I shake my head, afraid my voice could give something away.

"You were not truthful with me in our first interview. You were with Kǎi Míng on the peer the night he died."

How does she know? Surely Méi Lì wouldn't have run to

them after I brought her home. I wait, but the silence grows more and more oppressive.

Out in the hall, a locker slams.

"You were caught on security video."

Was I, though? I can't recall seeing any cameras along the shoreline. In the States, cops can lie as much as they want in interviews. Can they do the same here in Taiwan?

The fluorescent lights buzz overhead. The ceiling vibrates with the groan of a chair on the second floor.

"We know about the love triangle."

I can feel the moist chill of sweat forming beneath my knit shirt.

"This is your chance. Tell me what really happened." Her voice is stoney, her face emotionless. "Things will go much better for you."

Will they? Should I ask for my dad? Should I ask for a lawyer?

"We got a warrant to bug your apartment. We know *everything*."

I can't string together any words for a response, but my chest is too tight to speak anyway, as if all the oxygen has been sucked from the room.

She places a cell phone on the faux wood table, the controls to an audio app glowing on the screen. She brings one finger to the play button.

I want to grab her wrist. I can't listen. All the endless days trying to convince myself that my feelings for Méi Lì weren't real when she was with Kǎi Míng. All the endless days when she wasn't with him but he couldn't let her go. The wall of guilt and suffering that held us apart after his death, and then, finally, to share a moment together, only to have it stolen.

I want to scream. I want to run. But instead, I collapse into myself and wait.

Her finger taps the screen.

A long silence. Then, the jarring sound of a glass being placed on a coffee table.

I can't relive those moments. I can't.

Then, the sound changes. A shrill cry like a cat, bubbling and gurgling as if underwater. It grows louder and rasps in the tiny speakers of the device.

The detective looks at the phone, startled and confused. She taps the skip button a few times, but the noise is even louder and more distorted. She pauses the recording and looks at the phone from several angles. She lays it on the table, frowning darkly. "No matter. We have other copies. They cannot all have become defective."

I wonder. If one can, then why not all? The energy in the room has changed. I'm no longer lost and defeated. I stand. "I am free to go if I choose, right?"

The detective senses it, too. "Yes, for now."

I thank her and leave the room to head back to trigonometry, closing the door quietly behind me. The teacher is talking about a graph labeled Cosine on the whiteboard. I try not to look at Kăi Míng's empty desk, but the feeling on my right is less of an angry presence and more of a hollow absence.

3

This time, I'm the one who wants to confront our fears.

We make our way past the pushcarts and the savory smell of huāzhī chuàn, marinated squid on a bamboo stick, nearly overpowered by the pungent fermented odor of chòu dòufu, the city's famous stinky tofu.

At the wharf, we find the pier where it all happened. A massive pile of burned spirit money marks the spot, probably from Kǎi Míng's parents. I can only imagine how much they must have burned at the funeral and the gravesite.

The haze has burned off a bit. The sun feels warmer but less suffocating. In the distance, a ferry leaves a gently arcing white trail in its wake.

We rent a pair of kayaks, and I'm surprised at how well Méi Lì keeps up with me—at least until I really dig in hard. I fly over the waves, spindrift spattering my arms, free. When I'm spent, the crosscurrent spins my kayak around, and I paddle back to her. We sit, jostled by the waves, dipping a paddle now and then to keep our bearings.

"I don't want to forget him," she says.

"No. We won't."

"I mean, not just who he was at the end."

"No. All of him."

"We didn't want to hurt him," she says. "It seemed like the harder we tried, the worse we made everything."

A jetliner inches across the sky, making a mournful sound.

"Do you think," she says, "we deserve to be forgiven?"

"I don't know." I think about Kǎi Míng's parents, the

kids at school, and the online trolls. "Some people won't ever forgive us, but he has. Maybe that's all that matters."

Without words, we both paddle back to the wharf, unhurried, the sun at our backs.

END

—

A recovering musician with one gold record on his living room wall and countless unsold ones in his attic, **AVRAM LAVINSKY** has published a dozen short works in esteemed magazines and anthologies. In a starred review, the American Library Association's Booklist called his story, "Playing God," a "particular standout" in *The Mysterious Bookshop Presents The Best Mystery Stories of the Year 2023*. He's also earned starred reviews from the nation's toughest critics, his three teenage sons, although not often.

CHICAGO

J.R. Blanes

"Come on, Lamar, it'll only take a minute," Dominique shouted at her boyfriend's backside.

Focused on the game playing on his console, a pair of bulky headphones wrapped around his skull, Lamar replied, "I walked him all day, and my shift starts at eleven."

Dominique couldn't believe they were fighting over who would take Cassius out for his late night pee. It wasn't like she hadn't just finished a twelve-hour shift driving a CTA bus back and forth from the Southside to the Northside, dealing with stupid motherfuckers who pretended like they'd never heard of a thing called traffic, while he sat around playing an online football tournament—the real reason he didn't want to walk Cassius.

"Baby, my feet hurt and I'm tired. All I want to do is kick my shoes off, collapse on the couch, and fall asleep to *The Chi*. Can't you do me this favor?"

"Aww, poor lady, why don't you take a seat right here?" Lamar reached out, eyes still plastered to the screen, took her hand and led her onto his lap, looping his arm around her waist so he could still click the buttons on the controller.

Whapping his tail against the hardwood floor, their poor pup whined at Dominique like he might explode any second. If they didn't get him out soon, he'd soak the carpet or leave a heap of shit on the rug in their bedroom.

Standing up, Dominique snagged the headphones from Lamar's ears. "Cassius really needs to go."

"Dammit woman." Lamar hit pause. "I'm in the red zone. Fourth and nine. Now I have to waste a timeout."

"Good, while you're in timeout you can take Cassius for a quick pee walk."

"It's third quarter of the league championships."

"So?"

"You have to understand, if I leave now, it'll break my concentration."

"I'm gonna break your *head* if you don't take this dog for a walk—"

"*Baaaby!*" Lamar glanced over her shoulder at Cassius whimpering for one of them to have pity. "Can't he wait like twenty minutes?"

"You gonna clean the mess if he goes on the floor?"

Lamar's expression softened to mimic Cassius' sad puppy dog eyes. "Couldn't you take him? I fixed the water heater like you asked. After I'm done with this, I'll run you a nice, warm bath."

"With bubbles?"

Lamar drew a cross over his heart. "Done."

"If I find any wet spots or doo-doo in this house we're going to have a reckoning."

Lamar pumped his fists in the air in a quick celebratory dance before returning to his game.

Dominique couldn't help but laugh. As much as Lamar irritated her sometimes, he was a good man. *What would she do if she didn't have him around to act the fool?* She kissed him on his head and snapped her fingers for Cassius to follow. He rushed after her.

Dominique slipped the gentle leader around Cassius' muzzle and snapped the latches behind his floppy ears. He thrashed his boxy head, trying to shake the contraption off. Dominique didn't blame him. It's not like she would've enjoyed someone leashing her either. But a 250-pound black woman walking a 100-pound Rott received unwanted attention, even in the South Shore. Didn't matter that neither she nor Cassius were dangerous. It was just how people perceived them.

Soon as she stepped outside, a cloud of nasty cigarette smoke hit Dominique directly in the face. She waved it away, hacking. A raspy clearing of a throat accompanied a loogie splattering on the cement walkway. Through the gate dividing the yards, Dominique spotted Yolanda Jones sucking on a cigarette as though she was furious it hadn't riddled her with cancer yet. But Yolanda was as cancerous as any bad habit. Once on her bad side, she'd find every way from Tuesday to make life a living hell.

Yolanda flashed Dominique a phony smile. "Good evening, Ms. Thomas," she said in her strained smoker's voice.

Dominique replied with the same artificial pleasantries.

Cassius sniffed the air then sneezed as if he'd caught a cold. He lifted his leg, emptying his full bladder beside the gate. Yolanda watched him, irritation sweeping across her face as she huffed smoke in Dominique and the dog's direction. Narrowing her eyes, Yolanda sneered a mouthful of gold caps, her ugly mug chasing the poor pup behind Dominique's legs as soon as he was done.

Though she denied it, Dominique knew Yolanda had called Animal Control on Cassius that one time. Said he tried to bite her when all he'd wanted was to lick her hand. Dominique had to explain to the officer that her dog was a cuddler not a killer and meant no harm. It was only after Cassius snuggled against the officer's leg that he went away.

Yolanda pulled the same passive-aggressive shit with Dominique and Lamar too. Whenever they threw a party, or raised their voices above a whisper after 10 p.m., she'd come banging on the door and shouting at them to keep it down. She claimed to have bad nerves. Then there was the one time she'd pulled a gun on Lamar because he forgot his keys and she thought he was a burglar climbing through the window. Probably would've blasted his damn head off if Dominique hadn't come walking up right then.

"Full moon." Yolanda pointed at the pale face in the sky. "Better stay indoors tonight. Shit's gonna go down. I think I already heard gunshots."

"I didn't hear nothing."

"You just got home."

"You been keeping tabs?"

Yolanda took a drag off her cigarette. "Got new neighbors." She pointed the smoking cherry at a set of condos in the distance. "You know that's never a good sign."

"Why you say that?"

"Look at what happened to Bridgeport. That neighborhood's like Wyoming…if you know what I'm saying."

Dominique couldn't deny the truth there. Cross 71st and it was like you drove to the burbs. They opened a Whole Foods and a Starbucks and a yoga studio. City had started paving over the craters in the road and cleaning up the parks that they'd ignored complaints about before. Pretty soon, Dominique and Lamar wouldn't be able to afford the rent on their bungalow, and they'd have to move so far south, they'd have a foot in Indiana.

"I'm just taking Cassius for a quick walk." Dominique gave a slight tug on his leash. Cassius whimpered in retort.

Yolanda dropped her cigarette and smothered it beneath her heel. "You be careful now. Don't say I didn't warn you."

Something ominous in Yolanda's tone raised the goosebumps on Dominique's arms. But before she could ask what, Yolanda slithered inside her home and shut the door with a decisive click.

They strolled down the tree-lined block of Yates Boulevard. The streetlights clicked on to do battle with the murky glow of twilight, blotting the stars so only darkness stretched overhead. Dominique and Cassius passed historic stone bungalows where folks chatted with each other over drinks on their stoops. Kids played tag and threw a ball around a yard. Over at the Simmons' house, their teens were hanging in the garage with some of their friends, blasting Bone Thugs-N-Harmony. Dominique cracked a joke about them listening to their parents' music. They all laughed, and one of them said, "What's good is good." Dominique couldn't disagree. She bopped her head to the beat as a slight breeze blew through her hair. She bent down and gave Cassius a scratch behind the ear. He stuck out his tongue and wagged his tail. Spring had come to the city, and after a brutal winter of sub-zero degrees, everyone couldn't wait to throw off their coats and enjoy the sunshine. In Chicago, you didn't get many of those days, so you had to make them count.

They hooked a right on 72nd over to Phillips Avenue, and she stopped to let Cassius sniff around a soft patch of lawn. A new condo building shadowed the east corner where the Fish & Chicken used to be. Dominique didn't remember seeing them build the monstrosity, but these days they threw them up faster than a child with a Lego set. A "For Sale" sign creaked in the wind on the spiked front gate, which looked like it had been erected to keep people from getting in…or out.

A different kind of music swelled from somewhere nearby: an ominous, bass heavy rhythm that got louder and faster with her quickening heartbeat. Unwilling to stand in the building's shadow any longer, Dominique begged Cassius to hurry, but the stubborn pup wouldn't poop until he found the perfect spot. Just as he was about to squat, someone screamed a slew of curses, causing them both to leap high enough to catch some serious air.

Fuck!

Now they'd have to start all over again. Cassius always had difficulty relieving himself after being disturbed.

Dominique was about to pull Cassius across the street when a figure came stumbling out from behind the condo building, mumbling. In the light, she could see he definitely wasn't from around the neighborhood. Some Logan Square hipster in a torn overcoat, stained tweed pants, and muddy Chelsea boots. What was he doing on the Southside?

"Hey bro, you lost?" Dominique asked. "6 bus about four blocks east of here on 72nd and Exchange."

The hipster wrenched his head in her direction. The music pulsed from his glowing earbuds. Debris dusted his frontiersman beard and his eyes were as bloodshot as if he'd been on a weekend bender. A hollow pit in her stomach warned Dominique to run. She started to quietly back away, but before she got more than two steps, Cassius growled. The hipster unleashed a long, wailing howl. He flung open the gate. Cassius barked wildly. Dominique sensed danger too. Maybe she should've listened to Yolanda after all.

The hipster started to amble toward them, sliding his right foot behind him. Dominique yanked Cassius back toward 72nd Street, and said to the hipster, with a smile, "You take it easy now." Soon as they hit the corner, they were off and running.

Pulling a hundred-pound Rott backwards while he lunged and growled was like dragging a plow through cement. Dominique tugged Cassius so hard his claws scratched lines in the sidewalk. The gentle leader jerked his head to the side, tightening around his snout as drool spooled from his black lips. Dominique begged Cassius to leave the man alone. Begged him to calm down. Begged him to behave. She'd never seen her beloved pup act like this before, even around Yolanda, but Cassius had sniffed something foul about the hipster, like he'd climbed out from the sewers.

Either way, the motherfucker scared the shit out of Dominique. She'd dealt with her share of crazies working for the CTA, so she knew one when she saw one.

He followed them, making noises more animal than human, not running, but hobbling, tattered boots sliding along the sidewalk. Still, he gained on them, as if she moved in reverse while he moved in fast forward. When he got close, he swiped at Dominique, his dirt smeared fingers snagging one of her braids. Cassius leapt, whipping the leash from Dominique's grip, and hit the lunatic in the chest like a bullet, knocking him clean off his feet while ripping the braid from her scalp in the process. The hipster landed on his back with a "Huh!", jolting the earbuds from his ears.

"No Cassius!"

Dominique pulled her dog off the man's chest. They raced toward home, tears falling down her cheeks as she shouted for help.

The streetlights clicked off in succession, enveloping the block in darkness. Footsteps scurried on every side of her. Figures darted through backyards. The hipster was back on his feet and chasing after her.

Up ahead, someone ran across the road, stopping momentarily in the center. Dominique halted too, afraid to step any closer. Cassius growled and pulled against the leash. The longer Dominique looked the more she thought it might be Mr. Hurley from a few doors down. He sometimes left biscuits for Cassius in a bowl on his stoop. She called out to him. Mr. Hurley looked over his shoulder and took off running down the alley. Three more figures hurried after him. A scream tore through the silence, followed by what sounded like cleats stomping wet mud.

Out of the corner of her eye, Dominique caught a flash of another figure passing behind a neighbor's gate. The hipster's racing footsteps neared. The houses along the block were all dark. Dominique darted to the nearest one and began banging on the door, begging to be let in. Cassius clawed the wood and snarled. No one answered, but the floors creaked, and garbled voices muttered from behind the locked door. Goosebumps pricked Dominique's arms.

She retraced her steps, quietly crossing through their yard to the street.

Dominique tried several houses with lights on. Shadows swept across closed curtains. A tumult of groans, rasps, sobs, and howls greeted her cries for help. At the Ferguson's place, she found the door unlocked. She stepped inside with the dog, slipping in a sticky trail leading from the living room around the wall as if something large had been dragged. Perhaps a leaking garbage bag. Behind the wall, someone gargled as if rinsing their teeth with mouthwash. Cassius whined softly, pacing beside her. Glancing down, Dominique saw Cassius's pawprints on the hardwood floor beside the sticky trail. They were red. Clutching her hand over her mouth to stop from screaming, Dominique and the dog ran from the house.

Nearby, screams echoed down the street. Dominique turned around but couldn't distinguish anything but the outlines of the houses. Cassius sniffed the air and growled.

What the fuck was going on? she fretted as she rushed along the street. Dominique just prayed Lamar was safe at home.

As she drew closer to the Simmons, the eerie piano jangle of Bone Thugs-N-Harmony's "Mo Murder" bumped along. The kids and their friends were no longer hanging out, though the garage door was still open. The folding chairs remained, one tipped over on its side, and the Echo Dot glowed an ominous red. In the garage, Dominique yanked the cord and came away with blood on her hands. She lifted her foot from a puddle of, what she hoped, was motor oil.

Dominique ran to their front door and banged on the

glass. "Mr. and Ms. Simmons, it's Dominique Thomas, please let me in," she cried, looking around but seeing no sign of her stalker. "Please let me in! Marcel? Brayton? Are you home? Somebody? Please!"

From behind the door came munching noises, like a pack of hungry dogs were chowing down on a big bowl of kibble. But the Simmons didn't own dogs.

A hand slapped the window. Dominique's heart jumped into her throat. The glass squeaked as the palm slid down the pane, smearing red. Whimpering, Cassius pulled Dominique from the door and down the driveway.

Dominique stepped out of the Simmons' driveway. The light across the street flickered, shining on the hipster's silhouette scuttling toward her, crouched low and reaching out to grab her. Picking up the pace, she and Cassius raced toward home. She glanced over her shoulder. The streetlight shut off, cloaking her pursuer in darkness, but his footsteps were never far behind.

When they reached their gate, Dominique retrieved the keys from her pocket, but her frantic fingers fumbled with the latch. Out of desperation, she kicked the gate open, drug Cassius across the short walkway, threw open the door, and slammed and bolted the lock behind them. She peered behind the curtain at the sidewalk. There was no sign of the hipster. She prayed he'd deserted his pursuit.

"Babe, you alright?" Lamar turned in his seat in front of the computer, headphones dangling around his neck.

Breathing hard, Dominique responded, "Some crazy guy…chased me home…and the Simmons…something attacked them…in their house…they're…dead…I think."

"What?" Lamar hopped to his feet.

"The Simmons. I think they're dead."

He joined her at the window. "Are you sure?"

"Yes, I'm goddamn sure. How can you ask me something like that? They were attacked by…crazies."

Lamar clasped her shoulder. "I believe you, okay? But right now, I need you to take a couple deep breaths and tell me exactly what happened."

Dominique tried to explain the situation, but the whole thing sounded insane, even to her ears. Maybe she was losing her mind.

"Tell me what the motherfucker looked like?"

"Like a squatter from Logan Square."

Lamar glanced out the window. "Looks like he's gone now."

Dominique pulled her phone from her pocket. Brows raised, Lamar asked what she was doing. "Calling the police?" She answered as though it was obvious.

"You think that's a good idea?"

"Some madman attacked me and chased me home! Yes, I think I want the police to handle this." Dominique dialed 911, sighing in gratitude when the dial tone trilled.

Lamar unleashed Cassius from the gentle leader. Dominique couldn't stop shivering and her heart thundered mad beats. Rubbing her back, Lamar promised he wouldn't allow anything to happen to her or Cassius.

The gate crashed open, and the hipster slammed into the door, rattling the lock in the splintered frame. "What the fuck?" Lamar nearly jumped out of his flesh.

The operator, a woman who spoke as if she had better things to do, picked up the phone and took their information. There was a breath of hesitation when Dominique rattled off their address. She should've expected as much. The Emergency Communication Center probably had an encyclopedia full of crime stats on the South Shore, half of which were elicited by the police themselves. The bored operator inquired about the situation. Dominique held the phone toward the door. "Someone's trying to break into our house," she shouted. She didn't need to say anything else. The operator informed her a unit was on the way.

"How soon can they be here?"

"We have a patrol car en route, ma'am," the operator responded.

After she hung up, the three of them moved back towards the kitchen. Lamar yanked the silverware drawer open. "What are you doing?" Dominique asked. He brandished a butcher's knife. "You are not going to stab anyone."

"I will if that psycho thinks he's going to bust in here." He came around the counter and motioned for Dominique to take Cassius and move near the backdoor. "Now, if he gets inside, I'm going to hold him off while you and Cassius rush out the back and stay with Yolanda until the police arrive."

"Do you think she'll let us in?"

"She will if you tell her someone is trying to break into the place."

A shadow passed by the window, tall and lanky and monstrous. Though Dominique begged him not to, Lamar went to take a look. "I want to see the fucker." He put his eye to the glass. A fist slammed the pane. Lamar fell on his ass and scooted backward, knife held in front of him.

The hipster boxed the window, cracking the glass. Cassius barked, spewing slobber. Dominique threw her arms around his thick, furry neck. She owed him her life.

"Goddamn cops," Lamar lamented. "Never here when you need them, always around when you don't."

The hipster paced back-and-forth in front of the window. "What is he doing?" Lamar asked. The motherfucker slammed his body against the door again. Bang! Bang! Bang! Dominique folded herself, along with Cassius, into Lamar's arms. All three shook with each succeeding blow. Bang! Bang! Bang! The bolt strained under the pressure. The hinges creaked, the frame rattled, but the door held. Still, Dominique didn't know for how long. From the look of it, not much.

"We need to bar the door," Dominique told Lamar.

He placed the blade on the table and helped her carry the sofa across the living room. They tipped it on its feet and wedged the backrest beneath the handle.

Dominique dialed the police again and spoke to another operator while the hipster continued his rampage. She agonized over the yard decorations he destroyed: the ornamental iron wall trellis of hanging ivy, and the customized garden sign with her, Lamar's, and Cassius' names emblazoned on an aluminum plaque. Seethed over her fresh garden of False Indigos being stomped, and their mailbox being smashed to pieces.

Dominique reminded herself they needed to be strong. It was the only way they were going to survive this.

The minutes dawdled, along with the police's arrival, stretching into a hellish loop. Sometimes things would go quiet, and they'd think the hipster was gone, then he'd start over again. Dominique thought the torment would never end.

Lamar promised to put a hurting on this motherfucker if he managed to break inside. Twice she had to block Lamar from confronting the crazy bastard when he'd almost knocked the sofa over.

Cassius hunched low to the ground, ready to pounce. His tail wagged like a honing signal and his floppy ears raised like antennas. He bared his teeth and growled, unleashing the occasional chorus of barks.

Dominique called the emergency hotline three more times, explained the situation to three different operators—each less helpful than the last—and received the same desultory reply. A patrol car was on the way. *Well, if they were on their way, where the fuck were they?*

The sofa crashed to the floor, the lock snapped, and the

door swung open, slamming into the wall. The hipster stepped into the foyer and wailed a high-pitch screech. Blood vessels spider-webbed the whites of his eyes. Snot leaked from his nose, and drool spooled from his lips into his ratty beard. His Chelsea boots smeared a trail of bloody goo.

Cassius charged, jaws snapping, and sprung into the air. The hipster punched Dominique's lovable pup in his snout and knocked him to the floor. Cassius' legs twitched as he whined in pain.

"Baby!"

With a violent battle cry, Lamar charged, drove his shoulder into the intruder's chest, wrapped his arms around his waist, lifted him off his feet, and tackled him onto the walkway, the door slamming shut by an invisible hand behind them.

Dominique rushed over to Cassius. She pulled his body into her arms, weeping into his fur and telling him everything would be fine. He licked the blood dripping from the nostrils of his cold black nose.

From behind the closed door, the hipster munched, slurped, and burped. "Lamar?"

Dominique grabbed a broom leaning in the corner. It wouldn't hurt the motherfucker, but maybe keep him off long enough for her to rescue Lamar. She opened the door wide enough to peer through the crack, and caught a glimpse of the lunatic devouring her man's face. He'd removed the flesh from Lamar's left cheek, the eye missing. But Dominique noticed Lamar's chest still rose slightly.

Dominique raised the broom over her head. Something squished beneath her heel. She lifted her foot. Lamar's flattened eye stared back at her. Dominique leaned into the flower bed and puked most of a six-inch chicken sub and a bag of Cheetos.

The hipster glanced up at her from his meal and smiled, bits of flesh and muscle stuck to his teeth. With all her strength, Dominique swung the broom upward as if driving a ball on the golf range, catching him right under his chin. His jaw clamped shut, severing the tip of his own tongue, and he flipped backwards. Dominique picked up the knife and grabbed Lamar's arm, dragging him back inside, slamming the door and pushing the sofa back in place.

She pulled Lamar to his feet and carried him to the bathroom, where she wrapped a towel around his head, covering the empty socket, while trying to work out an escape plan.

Dominique threw one of Lamar's arms over her shoulder and slipped her fingers through his belt loops for added support. She hauled him through the kitchen to the door leading into the backyard. Cassius hobbled after when she called him. Dominique clutched and turned the handle. Through the kitchen door window, movement, then a claw of sharp shellacked nails scraped the pane with a perfect horror movie "eeek!" A woman with a frazzled blowout, smudged eyeshadow, and a mouth painted red with blood screeched like a drunken college girl hailing a taxi.

The motion lights flashed on. A horde climbed over the fence from the alley into the backyard like rats scavenging for food. The fence collapsed beneath their weight, and they stormed over one another, stomping a few heads into mush. *What the fuck?* Dominique hadn't seen a mob like this since she drove transit for an RV convention at McCormick place.

The swarm surrounded the house. A lawn chair smashed the kitchen window. Shards of glass sprayed the sink. Turning on each other, some of the horde pulled each other's limbs off and shoved their thumbs into each other's eyes. They bashed their heads into the wood sill as they scrambled to climb through the window. A troll in a tailored business suit squeezed his bulky frame through the jagged hole, the serrated edges slicing through his fine threads, blood spilling from the gashes. More of them followed, tumbling over the sink.

Dominique gripped the knife handle tightly. She marched toward the front of the house, dragging Lamar with Cassius in tow. The front door toppled open as more of the creatures collapsed into the foyer like dominoes. They reached their arms toward the duo. Froth spilled from their mouth, soaking their zip-up hoodies and chinos. Bloodshot eyes bulged behind designer sunglasses. Blood dyed their frosted hair. They were everything Dominique hated about the passengers who rode her bus. *Didn't she deal enough with these assholes on the daily?* Now they were breaking into her home and harming her family.

Dominique pushed Lamar toward the stairs and told him

to take Cassius to the second floor. From behind the multitude, the hipster climbed over the threshold. "Die motherfucker!" Dominique shouted. Charging forward, she sunk the blade into his chest. A brume of dust floated from the hole.

Fuck.

Surrounded by this putrid mob of urbanites, Dominique's CTA uniform was shredded to ribbons. They scratched her skin and tore at her hair. She swung the knife, slicing the fetid creatures' flesh while backing up the stairs. Once she forced some distance between them, she hustled upstairs, taking two steps at a time, and joined Lamar on the second floor. Brave Cassius led the way, sniffing to see if the coast was clear of the rotten fuckers. The horde stumbled over each other in pursuit, trampling their tribe and knocking them over the banister. Half-carrying Lamar, Dominique hustled down the hall, and followed Cassius into the bedroom. She locked the door and shoved the dresser in front of it as the mob splintered the jamb.

Dominique ordered Lamar to climb out the window onto the roof. "I'm not leaving you behind," he said.

"I'm right behind you."

She followed Lamar onto the roof, carrying Cassius under her arm.

The rat-tat-tat of an AK ripped through the shrieks of the swarm. Dominique and Lamar splayed flat against the shingles, feeling their bodies for bullet holes. Cassius barked but was thankfully unharmed. They were all still in one piece.

They glanced next door. Yolanda fired rounds from her

deck at the hungry mass in her yard. A Patagonia-clad tech bro climbed up a phone pole in the alley and tried to hurdle onto Yolanda's deck. His head exploded into mush from the slug of a .45. A jet stream of smoke poured from Yolanda's lips. "There's your venture capital, bitch," she said.

"You two got anything to defend yourself?" Yolanda shouted over the roar of her weaponry.

Dominique showed her the knife.

"That'll never do." Yolanda fired off another round. "Haul your buns on over here. I may not have an arsenal, but I got more than a kitchen knife."

"How? They're all inside my house. Lamar and Cassius are injured…"

Growls rumbled from beneath. Cassius growled back. A trashy chick smelling of stale beer snagged the gutter, and began pulling herself up, but Dominique kicked the bitch's hands loose, and she fell screeching to the sidewalk.

"You're gonna have to jump," Yolanda said.

"Have you lost your damn mind?" Dominique asked Yolanda.

"Come on, girl. No time to argue. Either you hop your buns over here or you two are on your own." Yolanda fired at the horde trying to climb up her walls.

Before she could stop him, Cassius sprang from their roof to Yolanda's. All three of them looked at the dog in amazement.

The dresser fell, and the intruders piled in like a crashing wave. Dominique kissed her man on the lips, long and hard, then shouted at him to jump. Lamar leaped from the rooftop to the deck.

The hipster stuck his head out the window; screeched. Dominique drove the blade into his socket and out the back of his head. "Eye for an eye, motherfucker," she said as that lunatic fell backwards into the horde. They began to tear him limb from limb.

Bending her knees slightly, Dominique made the sign of the cross and took a deep breath. *Lord, save me now!* She hurdled through the air, arms flapping, legs jogging, as the masses swiped at her kicking feet. She'd almost cleared the sidewalk when suddenly she plummeted like stones were tied to her ankles. For a moment, she thought she was dead meat.

Yolanda snagged her by the wrists. Hot pain ripped through Dominique's shoulders as she slammed against the brick siding. She thought for sure she'd torn her damn arms off. But she didn't have time to think about it. She scrambled up the wall as Yolanda hauled her over the railing. They fell onto the deck, wheezing, as Cassius licked their faces.

The pair jumped to their feet

Yolanda led Dominique and Lamar to her bedroom, where she opened her closet, slid the panel behind her wardrobe open, and handed him a Glock 9mm and Dominique a .45 along with a bag of extra clips. She loaded the AR-15 and slid a .39 into her boot strap.

"Looks like someone has been preparing for the apocalypse," Dominique said.

"In America, a girl's got a right to protect herself, and I ain't about to let nobody take what's mine. Can you shoot?"

"Gonna have to learn fast."

"It's easy. Aim and pull the trigger. But be careful with the kickback. Baby's got punch. When you empty a clip, reload, and start shooting again. Don't stop shooting 'til we either kill them all or run out of ammo.

Yolanda glanced at Lamar. "How about you?"

"I work security, remember?" He aimed out the window and pecked off a sniveling lawyer in a boxy cardigan who was attempting to make the leap.

Right as they walked back outside, sirens blared down the street. "Of course, now they decide to fucking show up," Lamar said. Going a good sixty miles an hour, a cop cruiser crashed into a streetlight across from Yolanda's house. An officer flew through the windshield and skidded along the asphalt. He got up, face hanging from his skull like carved ham, and joined the party.

Yolanda pulled a cigarette from her pack with her teeth. She asked Dominique if she wanted one. Dominique didn't see why the hell not.

Inhaling the smoke deep in her lungs, Dominique glanced at the full moon. "How did you know some shit was going down tonight?"

Yolanda chortled. "I used to live in Bridgeport. Now keep your eyes peeled. It's going to be a long night."

END

—

J.R. Blanes lives in Chicago with his wife and neurotic dog. His short fiction has been published in several magazines and podcasts such as Tales to Terrify, The No Sleep Podcast, *Thirteen*, and *Creepy*, among others. His first novel, *Portraits of Decay*, was published by Ruadán Books. In between bouts of writing and dog wrestling, he plays bass guitar and records music. Coffee is his nightmare fuel of choice.

Former technologist and world traveler, **R. B. WOOD** is an MFA graduate from Emerson College and the founder/CEO of Ruadán Books. Along with his editing passion, R. B. is a writer of speculative dark thrillers. Mr. Wood has had numerous titles published and is currently working on his next thriller. His shorter, weird stories have appeared in multiple anthologies and online magazines. R.B. and his wife Tina adore animals and are self-professed "crazy cat people." You can find him online via rbwood.com and on most social media platforms.

Photo © 2024 by David A. E. Dixon

Boston-based artist and writer, **ANNA KOON**, has published articles for a variety of periodicals, one poem, two screenplays, and a children's book entitled: *Willamina, Queen of the Worms*. She is the founder and director of an educational series presented to various arts organizations throughout Massachusetts. Additionally, she works as a creative coach and editor. Anna lives at the top of what was once the women's quarters of a Victorian mental institution with her husband and two whippets, Zeta Puppis and Nimble Nimbus. Learn more about her @ www.a2n2.net.

Also from Ruadán Books

Available Now

Winter in the City—Edited by R. B. Wood and Anna Koon

120 Murders: Dark Fiction Inspired by the Alternative Era—Edited by Nick Mamatas

The Black Fire Concerto—by Mike Allen

COMING SOON

Five Funerals—by Jeff Somers

Portraits of Decay—by J.R. Blanes

Darling—by Mercedes M. Yardley

The Ghoulmakers Aria—by Mike Allen

Born of Malice—by Xan van Rooyen

www.RuadanBooks.com

RUADÁN
BOOKS